Dedalus published Oliver Ready's translation of *The Zero Train* to great acclaim in 2001. Here are a few comments:

'*The Zero Train* by Yuri Buida is the most   book I've read this year. It has been h··   , and was shortlisted for the   'ing, brilliant and deeply mc   'hat Stalinism did to individu
   Helen Dunmore in   ..*ur*

'It's a brutally powerful l   ... a landscape of railway track and sidings that coula nave been postulated by Beckett, but shot through with grotesque, surreal lyricism. "All the women he'd ever known had smelt of cabbage. Boiled cabbage. Every single one." Except Fira. He saw her naked once, washing, "her heart and its bird-like beat, the gauzy foam of her lungs and her smoky liver, the silver bell of her bladder and the fragile bluish bones floating in the pink jelly of her flesh." A sensational novel, moving, unforgettable.'
   Brian Case in Time Out

'Oliver Ready's translation conveys with a sure hand the power and grace of Buida's supple prose. His style is at once lyrical and shocking. The norms of Socialist Realism are manipulated with an angry bravado in this violent elegy for Ivan Ardabyev.'
   Rachel Polonsky in The Times Literary Supplement

'A strange, Kafka-like parable.'
   Carrie O'Grady in The Guardian

'Natural affections are in short supply at the ninth siding. Some of those employed there go mad. Others merely lose hope. Ivan clings to the necessity for the Zero Train to pass smoothly through; this gives purpose to his existence. There are women of course, provided by the authorities. While Buida describes the Zero Train as if it was human, possessing personality, the prostitutes are described as if they were machines, made up of moving parts. Then Ivan, to his surprise, falls in love; he has met the ideal woman, the essence of femininity. This leads him to perform a spontaneous action: murder. Spontaneity is alien to the system, which exists to suppress personality; and from this moment the system begins to crack. Does the Zero Train still run, or only in Ivan's mind? Everything falls apart.'

Allan Massie in The Scotsman

'Set during the Soviet era, this remarkable novel was short-listed for the Russian Booker Prize. A remote, police-run settlement called the Ninth Siding exists only for the mysterious Zero Train that halts there. Buida uses the idea as the basis for a haunting, Kafkaesque parable of Russian history.'

Harry Blue in Scotland on Sunday

'This spare, swift 1993 novel explores the professional and emotional burdens borne by Ivan Ardabyev, a "railway forces private" assigned to a train settlement somewhere in rural Russia. The Kafkaesque Zero Train, which arrives and departs with unfailing precision, bearing an undisclosed cargo, is a perfect metaphor for the implacability of total regimentation, and the bitterness and paranoia it breeds in its dulled "workers". Buida captures their deadening experiences brilliantly in the details of Ardabyev's blind thrusts toward a fuller life, and final act of resistance. A rich, provocative allegory (which might be compared with Victor Pelevin's *The Yellow Arrow*)– and a fine introduction to an important contemporary Russian writer.'

Kirkus Reviews

'*The Zero Train* is not really a creaky old allegory. It is a reflection on our desire for allegory; that is to say, it's a calculation of the precise value, and danger, of conceiving life as a secret. Like *Don Quixote*, this is a story about how, by evasion and blindness, anyone can come to find themselves tilting at windmills.'

Thomas Karshan in The Moscow Times

Yuri Buida

The Prussian Bride

Translated by Oliver Ready

Dedalus

Funded by
THE
ARTS
COUNCIL
OF ENGLAND

eastengland|arts

Published in the UK by Dedalus Ltd, Langford Lodge, St Judith's Lane, Sawtry, Cambs, PE28 5XE
email: DedalusLimited@compuserve.com
web site: www.dedalusbooks.com

ISBN 1 903517 06 0

Dedalus is distributed in the United States by SCB Distributors,
15608 South New Century Drive, Gardena, California 90248
email: info@scbdistributors.com
web site: www.scbdistributors.com

Dedalus is distributed in Australia & New Zealand by Peribo Pty Ltd,
58 Beaumont Road, Mount Kuring-gai, N.S.W. 2080
email: peribo@bigpond.com

Dedalus is distributed in Canada by Marginal Distribution,
Unit 102, 277 George Street North, Peterborough, Ontario, KJ9 3G9
email: marginal@marginalbook.com
web site: www.marginalbook.com

Dedalus is distributed in Italy by Apeiron Editoria & Distribuzione,
Località Pantano, 00060 Sant'Oreste (Roma)
email: grt@apeironbookservice.com
web site: www.apeironbookservice.com

First published in Russia in 1998
First English translation in 2002

The Prussian Bride copyright © 1998 by Novoe Literaturnoe Obozrenie,
ul.Kostiakova 10, Moscow, Russia
The Prussian Bride translation copyright © Oliver Ready 2002

The right of Yuri Buida to be identified as the author of this work and the right of Oliver Ready to be identified as the translator of this work has been asserted by them in accordance with the Copyright, Designs and Patents Act, 1988.

Typeset by RefineCatch Limited, Bungay, Suffolk
Printed in Finland by WS Bookwell

THE AUTHOR

Of mixed Russian, Polish, Belorussian and Ukrainian descent, Yuri Buida was born in 1954 in the town of Znamensk in the Kaliningrad Region. Formerly part of East Prussia, this region was incorporated into the Soviet Union after the Second World War. Buida worked there as a journalist until moving to Moscow in 1991, where he quickly established himself as one of the most exciting writers of the post-Soviet avant-garde, publishing prolifically in all the leading literary journals.

The Prussian Bride (1998) is the second of Yuri Buida's books to be translated into English, and, like *The Zero Train*, was short-listed for the Russian Booker Prize. It also won a prestigious Apollon Grigoriev award for Russian fiction in 1999.

THE TRANSLATOR

Oliver Ready was born in 1976 and is currently researching for his D.Phil in modern Russian literature at Wolfson College, Oxford.

He has worked as a journalist in Russia, and has published in a number of newspapers and magazines in Moscow and in the UK.

His translations include *The Zero Train* for Dedalus in 2001.

Translator's Note

Yuri Buida wrote the stories collected here over many years, some before his move to Moscow in 1991, and many subsequently. This volume represents a translation of roughly three-quarters of the collection *Prusskaya nevesta* (The Prussian Bride), published in Moscow in 1998; the selection was made jointly by the author and the translator. Over the last few years further stories in this cycle have appeared in the Russian literary journals.

A number of people have contributed generously to the preparation of this translation. In particular I salute once more my guru via email, Sergei Roy, the editor of *Moscow News* and a translator of great skill and erudition. He has acted as consultant throughout the project, checking every page of the translation against the original and finding improvements and cause for invigorating criticism on each of them. Closer to home, I would like to thank Liubov Osinkina, a fellow graduate at Wolfson, for her unstinting help and expertise; Jennifer Baines and Subhi Sherwell for careful reading and excellent suggestions; Richard Short for an iambic pentameter and other instances of verbal ingenuity; Jim Naughton for inspired solutions to intractable problems over a few pints; Andrew Hobson for the same, and for kindly having me to stay on Naxos during work on the book; Mike Mitchell for his translations of Schiller and Benn, and Jim Reed for his translation of Pushkin's 'I loved you'; finally, thank you to my parents, Nigel and Marisa, for their support in every way.

Contents

The Prussian Bride

Instead of a Preface

Hearing footsteps, Matras and I crouched down and sank into the shadows cast by the boulders of the cemetery wall. Matras' father appeared on the path in the light of the lamps swaying beside the railway crossing. He had a secret trade selling off German tombstones to Lithuanians, and if he caught anyone near the cemetery with a crowbar or a spade, he'd threaten to feed them to the vicious ghosts that he lured with fly agarics.

'Come on,' whispered Matras when his dad vanished into the gloom. 'That way.'

Keeping our heads down, we made our way between crooked, rusty fences deep into the cemetery. We squatted and aimed our torches at a grey, lichen-spotted granite slab. The time before, we'd managed to shift it after a long struggle. But this time, too, another hour's work was needed before the scrawny thirteen-year-olds could squeeze through the newly opened crack. Yet another half-hour was spent with pliers and screwdrivers removing the heavy lid of the coffin, which rested on a tall brick plinth.

'Now for the light,' said Matras.

'One, two, three!' I switched on the torch.

Before us, her arms folded on her chest, lay a young girl. On her upper lip, near the side of her mouth, a mole was visible. She was wearing a white dress, made, it seemed, of gossamer or the stuff out of which butterflies' wings are cut, and white shoes with gold heels. A tiny heart-shaped watch ticked away on her left wrist.

'Like she's alive,' croaked Matras, as if his tongue had turned to paper. 'It's ticking.'

The girl sighed, and at that same instant her airy dress and smooth skin were turned into a cloud of dust, which settled slowly along her knotted spine. We gazed entranced at the yellow skeleton, at the white shoes sticking out absurdly with their gold heels, at the heart-shaped watch, still ticking, at the thick hair in which the dark-yellow egg of her skull was nesting. Out of a black eye socket there suddenly fluttered a tiny butterfly.

Matras swore in terror.

My bladder contracted and I barely had time to pull down my trousers.

Matras hastily removed the watch, a chain with a small cross and a pale little ring from the skeleton. We crawled out and leant on the slab with all our weight. Eventually, it went back into place.

'The torch!' I remembered suddenly. 'We've left the torch in there. In the coffin.'

'Never mind.' Matras slipped me the watch. 'Let's leave it on, it'll be nicer for her.'

Three years later excavators ploughed through the cemetery, leaving deep pits in their tracks for the heating system. Schoolkids made off with skulls and bones to frighten their teachers or the girls in their class. The workers got the boys to fetch them wine. Our idol Sasha Fidel, a seven-foot lad with a curly black beard and a bandit's gap-toothed smile, had the funny habit of making the sign of the cross before tipping the bottle: to make sure the cemetery ghosts didn't inflict hiccups on him. One evening his excavator caught fire and burned up within a few minutes with Sasha asleep inside. It was claimed that when the charred body was extracted from the cabin, the dying lad breathed out a black butterfly, which hovered a while over people's heads before dissolving in the gloom. Sasha was buried in the new cemetery. The old one was abandoned.

I was born in the Kaliningrad Region nine years after the War. From childhood I've been used to streets being cobbled or bricked, and lined with pavements. I'm used to steep, tiled roofs. To canals, sluices, dyked marshes, to perpetual damp and forests planted in rows. To dunes. To a sea whose flat waters shade imperceptibly into a flat shore. And I knew no way of understanding this world other than by inventing it. One day I found out that my little native town used to be called not Znamensk but Wehlau. Germans had lived here. This had been East Prussia. Fragments remained: a Gothic echo, a quirkily shaped door-handle, part of a shop-sign. Unlike a hermit crab unthinkingly occupying another sea dweller's shell, I had to know at least something of the life that came before mine and gave my life its form. Teachers, and adults in general, were of little help. Not that they weren't interested in the past of this land, it's just that they had no time for it, and anyway they'd been told that the past of other people was no concern of theirs. It was enough to know that this had been a 'stronghold of militarism and aggression', that Kant was born and died here. As for the Prussians who inhabited these lands before the Germans, for some reason they were counted as Slavs. Old-timers would tell you that this building had been the town's school and that one the transit prison. Or the other way round. Some could dimly remember the brief period when Russians and Germans had lived here together, before the Germans were taken off who knows where, to Germany most likely. The land became ours. For now and all eternity, so spake the truth, tasteless as a pebble from the river. A handful of books supplied a few pitiful facts: the conquest of the Prussian lands by the Order of the Teutonic Knights, the foundation of Königsberg, the rout of the Teutons on the fields of Tannenberg and Grünwald, Peter the Great in East Prussia, the Russian charge at Gross-Jägersdorf, the French attack in the Battle of Friedland, the Tilsit peace treaty, August 1914, April '45 . . . And life? What kind of a life was it here? Old-timers shrugged their shoulders. They spoke about the Germans' passion for digging secret underground passages. About the Amber Room. Pavements washed with soap. Fishermen who handed over their entire catch to the authorities even when they were collapsing from hunger. Then the Gerermans were deported. A ten-twenty-thirty-year layer of Russian life trembled on a seven-hundred-year foundation about which I knew nothing. So the child began to invent, gathering the fragments of that life and transforming them by the force of his imagination into some kind of a picture . . . It was the creation of a myth. Close by, a stone's throw away, lay an enchanted world. But if a Russian in Pskov or Ryazan could enter an enchanted world which he had inherited by right, what was I here, a man without a key, of a different race, blood, language and faith? At best a treasure-seeker, at worst a grave-digger. With her first sigh the girl Prussia turned to dust. I heard the song of sorrow sung by a few hundred horsemen in white cloaks who had abandoned their dear homeland for Prussia – a country of horrors, a desert where a terrible war was raging (so wrote Peter of Duisburg, chronicler of the crusades). Cannons thundered with ammunition hewn from the moraines of prehistoric glaciers. Hanseatic caravans crawled along in the mist. The devil himself, in the guise of a monstrous fish, raised his back over the expanse of the Frisches Haff. Haws and hips blossomed. The scent of apples. Rain falling in every season of this eternity, quivering in the sea breeze.

Prussian time . . .
I lived in the eternity which I saw in the mirror.
It was life that was a dream at the same time.
Dreams are made of the same stuff as words.

In his preface to *The Marble Faun*, Nathaniel Hawthorne wrote that, 'No author, without a trial, can conceive of the difficulty of writing a romance about a country where there is no shadow, no antiquity, no mystery, no picturesque and gloomy wrong [. . .]'. It seemed to me that that was exactly how things stood in my adored homeland. In the place where I was born. Shadows and secrets belonged to an alien world that had plunged into non-being. But, in a strange way, these shadows and secrets – or perhaps the shadow of a shadow, the hint of a secret – became part of the chemistry of my soul. At one time I felt split in two. As a child I took pride in the victory of the Slavs and Lithuanians at Grünwald, while feeling bitter sympathy for Ulrich von Jungingen, Grand Master of the Order, who fell in a desperate skirmish with the Poles and was buried in the chapel of Balg castle, on the shore of the Frisches Haff. Later, I realized that in the twentieth century the Russian intellectual was faced with the same dilemma regarding the Russian past. That must have been when I understood that dreams have no nationality; words do, but not the Word, which erases every difference between Schiller and Aeschylus, Tolstoy and Hölderlin, and above all between the living and the dead – between the reader and the long-departed writer. The writer, the dreamer, lives not in Znamensk or Wehlau, but in both places at once, in Russia, in Europe, in the world.

My little homeland has a German past, a Russian present, a human future.

Via East Prussia, German history became a part of Russia's; and vice versa. Which is exactly as it should be when we recall what a gigantic crossroads of blood the land between the Vistula and the Niemen has always been.

That girl, whose repose Matras and I disturbed, was a bride: not a stranger, nor yet a wife. The relations of love that exist between the living and the dead are the highest manifestation of memory, like the relations between the ideal groom and the ideal bride. And the kiln where love becomes the lime that binds us is nothing other than the Word. In one of his poems Rilke expressed this emotion with one word, *Ichbinbeidir*, Mewithyou.

In his 'Ode to Joy', Schiller wrote of this divine force:

> Healing spell that binds together
> What convention sets apart;
> Men once more will all be brothers
> When you rule within their hearts.
> O ye millions, I embrace you,
> With one kiss for all the world.

A century and a half later he was answered by another German, Gottfried Benn, with 'The Whole':

> Brighter at first it was, the thing you wanted,
> Forward aiming, came close to belief,
> But when you saw then what you ought to do
> Looking stony-eyed down on the whole,

17

> The thing in which your living gaze was caught,
> No longer fire-bright, now scarcely shone,
> A naked head, all bathed in blood, a monster,
> Upon whose eyelash hung a single tear.*

In the twentieth century people once more became aware of our need to strive for the Whole, and equally of the fact that this road is a tragic one, paved with the disorder which, paradoxical though it sounds, is also the source of this striving. Perhaps, the only source.

That girl, of course, never existed. It's a myth, one of the myths of my childhood. But her watch, that tiny heart-shaped watch, carries on ticking. (The time? Eternity). A mole blooms in the corner of her mouth. A butterfly flutters out of her eye: the black butterfly of dreams.

'We are such stuff as dreams are made on . . .' Shakespeare. An Englishman, I believe, but that's immaterial in the world of eternity, in the House of my bride . . .

* Translations of both poems by Mike Mitchell.

A Stopover on the Way to India

Some maintain that the *Generalissimo* never existed. Not so. The ship existed all right: there was no vessel bigger in the world. Its propellers sent the Volga splashing over its banks and its gross capacity was 88,000 tonnes. It was built for a clearly defined purpose and the crew was set the following task: to reach the shores of India and discover the town of Bhagalpur, situated in the region of Orissa in West Bengal, on the River Ganges and the Calcutta–Delhi railway line. Population: approximately 69,000 (according to the 1921 figures). Exports: rice, maize, wheat, peas, millet, indigo. France was also to be discovered along the way: territory, 550,965.5 sq km; population: 41,834,900, of which 760,000 were Italians and 67,000, Russians; rubber industry index (of the first quarter of 1935 *vis-à-vis* 1913), 760; textile industry, 61.

The crew was made up of experienced sailors, scholars, soldiers, fresh-faced female collective farmers from the Dynamo sports association, and writers ranked Major and higher according to their achievements in the field of national literature. The ship was stacked with provisions, live cattle and fowl, the sturdiest *ZIF* bicycles in the world and the best galoshes in the world from the Red Triangle factory.

On June 1, 1952, the *Generalissimo* set sail from Moscow in the direction of the Baltic Sea. Brass bands played on the decks without pause. Every half-hour a bronze siren with a flat Mongol face and sharp canine tits sang the March of the Enthusiasts from the prow. A foaming wash, scarlet from the blood of fish, reared above the stern. Handsomely barred portholes shone like gold in the sun. Luxuriant garlands of flowers, indistinguishable from real ones, tumbled down the sides. Just such a vessel – not a ship but an overflowing cup – appeared before us one early August morning in 1952.

Many wondered then and later why the captain of the *Generalissimo* chose our town in particular for a brief stop-over. But it's no great mystery when you consider the circumstances: ours is the last town but one before the open sea; on its well-equipped jetty barges load up all summer with excellent sand and top-quality gravel, our reserves of which must be about the largest in the region, if not the world; the town has a bathhouse for sixty people; two canteens, Red and Blue; paper and noodle factories; other light industry; a secondary school in whose clock-faced turret lives a rusty golden cockerel; a boarding-school for the mentally disadvantaged, where many register their offspring long before their birth; the barber's where Longjohn worked before being elected to the post of chairman of the local soviet (for some reason our town was classified on paper as a city-type settlement); idiot Easy Lizzie, employed as yard-sweeper, shit-carrier, messenger and sometimes even policewoman if the district officer had gone on a bender; her daughter from an unknown father, Lizetta, who strutted her stuff come winter or summer in a sack-like dress made from patched-up sheets so as to feel freer than any bird and deprive the townsmen, whose mating calls she willingly returned, of any grounds for complaint; Gramp Mukhanov, who out of sheer malice and bloody-mindedness had raised his wooden WC far above the tiled roof of his house, fixing it in place with poles and rusty pipes tied together with wire (he risked his life twice a day, did Gramp, clambering up the rickety ladder to his starling-house; a minute later the town's sharper-eyed inhabitants could follow the distant flight of his excrement as it fell through a hole in the cabin floor into a basin on the ground); pleasant streets paved with cobblestones and vertically-set bricks; the waterfall on the Lava; the sluices on the Pregolya; reliable telephone and telegraph links to remote and close-lying populated areas; an abundance of fresh milk, dogs, May-bugs and early-ripening apples; a water-spirit who lived in the swamp near the paper mill and whose extraordinary manhood filled women with righteous indignation when they compared it to that of their husbands. In short, giving the town its fair due, there was nothing even remotely strange about the fact that one early August morning, after straightening out the entire course of a narrow little river and emptying it of water, a snow-white giant moored by our pier to the welcoming cries of Longjohn, Easy Lizzie, Lizetta, Gramp Mukhanov and other townsfolk, five thousand and more (excluding the inmates of the local prison).

Removing his boots and socks, Longjohn climbed up the carpeted ramp onto the deck. In his outstretched arms he carried bread and salt on a towel stamped with the hospital's black seal, and his employment certificate opened wide in the name of Katznelson Adolf Ivanovich. Accompanied by the band, the rest of the townsfolk followed him in a triumphant throng.

I remember to this day how the captain – three metres tall, with a bronze chest and a moustache arranged neatly down his shoulders – showed us round the ship and acquainted us with the siren and the other members of the crew. Among them, as I recall, was a man entrusted with the task of conquering the imagination of the French and Bhagalpuri natives. He had a little door in his chest and behind it an artificial glass and metal heart produced by the Chelyabinsk tractor factory; it kept the blood circulating more efficiently than any natural heart and could be ventilated if necessary. I remember the captain lending me his binoculars: I saw the contents of our townsfolk's pockets and even the enormous hairy mole on Lizetta's tummy, just to the left of her belly button. It was an unforgettable sight. No one makes binoculars like those any more. The captain also showed us the part of the ship where eight thousand hand-picked cyclists pedalled away in total darkness on special machines and kept the propellers in motion. In the ward-room we were offered fruit, but, and I say this with regret, we did not dare to try them, although they seemed so similar to the genuine kind.

Our meeting culminated in a football match between our sportsmen and the crew of the *Generalissimo*. It goes without saying, does it not, that our bastards didn't stand a chance in hell? The guests showed real class, scoring more than fifteen times – and that's only counting own goals. Their centre-forward was particularly outstanding. For all his angelic patience, he finally got sick of our goalie's insolent tricks and gave him a boot in the jaw, after which our keeper tried to slink off the pitch. Of course, we weren't about to let the sonofabitch get away and were ready to hand him over to the centre-forward. But this most magnanimous of men let us deal with the lout ourselves, which we did, knocking the cretin's guts through his gullet.

Orchestras played on the ship all day until sunset, interrupted only by the solo performances of a flautist whose name not even the filthiest foul-mouths could repeat. The heavenly sounds of the flute sent the listeners into a trance. Children, swept away by daydreams, refused to go home. No one was forcing them to anyway.

All night long until sunrise we kept dragging supplies over to the boat. We handed over – voluntarily, I can assure you – all that we had and even what was yet to be. The captain thanked us with tears in his eyes, reproaching us from the bottom of his heart for a display of generosity that might be followed by famine. But that prospect didn't frighten us in the least.

In the morning, after hanging and shooting our footballers, who had lost with clearly malicious intent, the crew of the *Generalissimo* cast off. Drowning out the shouts from the shore, the orchestras thundered away on the decks so loudly that the brains of some of the bystanders nearest the water shot out through their noses and ears. The ship departed, leaving a dry river-bed in its wake and banks that had been ironed flat and spattered with minced-up fish. We went home with heavy hearts. And only once we were home did we realize that the children had all been left on the ship. The music must have bewitched them. We were envious of our children and the lucky chance they had gained to see the world.

The only people not caught up in the general euphoria were Longjohn, Easy Lizzie and Gramp Mukhanov. In secret, they set off after the *Generalissimo*. Getting stuck in the stinking silt, they covered a mile with the greatest difficulty and, with daylight fading, found the ship. Its black rusted hull lay athwart the river-bed. Weeds and shrubs had pushed through the gaping holes in the sides; the cabins were occupied by snakes and mice. As for the flat-faced siren with canine tits, all she could do when they tried to help her out of the silt was open her bronze eyes a fraction and mutter an old folksong: 'Off to the fair went the fair merchant. . . .' Those were her last words.

Longjohn squatted and somehow managed to roll himself a fag with trembling fingers. Then he suddenly remembered his children and wife, who'd died in the gas chambers at Auschwitz, and burst into tears.

They found Mukhanov's eldest son in the osier thicket by the stern; he didn't recognize his father and couldn't tell them a thing. As they were pulling him out, Easy Lizzie disappeared. It's thought that she went to look for her children. Longjohn, Gramp Mukhanov and his son returned home, but nobody believed that they had found the ship, still less in such a state. To judge from the reports in the press, it had successfully crossed seas and oceans and was now nearing the first Indian port. Ruined? Black? Rusty? No! No! In our memory it would always remain a huge snow-white beauty with gold lettering on her side and a high foaming wash at her stern, scarlet from the blood of fish . . .

The Seventh Hill

Come this way and I will tell you a story! Come this way, to this hill of sorrow, to the Seventh Hill, raised nearer to heaven than all others by nature herself, where flocks of gentle angels rustle quietly past on thick August nights, gazing at the vale of our world with fiery-bright eyes, at the focus, centre and navel of this world, at the town of towns, sprawled over seven hills between two yellow rivers; at our town-cum-settlement, whose scarlet-tiled roofs bathe in the greasy summer verdure of lime and chestnut trees, or freeze under the iodine-scented winds of winter; at this mangy clutch of houses and barns reeking of mould and boot polish, pigs and kerosene, and oozing the death – fir and thuja – that surrounds the Seventh Hill from all sides, this land fit for sowing but not for reaping . . . Here, between the graves of the idiot Easy Lizzie and the old woman nicknamed Sindbad the Sailor (famed for her tireless quests for empty bottles), here, right next to that quivering nameless tree, you will find the final resting-place of the sewage collector Lavrenty Pavlovich Beria and his sub-ordinate Vitya the Negro, veteran of the African partisan movement. The very same grave that caused the cemetery to be closed.

Come this way and I will tell you a typical Russian story: one with a plot but no purpose.

Lavrenty Pavlovich turned up in our little town soon after the official announcement of his death. He was immediately identified as Beria by Andrei the Photographer, who grabbed the new arrival by the ear and blathered: 'Shave off your beard, twist your nose like that and your ears like that, and you're the spitting image.' Chased by the town dogs, the stranger took to his heels and hid in the Red Canteen. Pouring her new client a moderately watered-down beer, Fenya inquired with an innocent air: 'What's happened to your pince-nez, Lavrenty Pavlovich?' But the locals tore him away from her and hurled him onto the rubbish tip to keep him out of trouble, where he spent the night coming to his senses in the company of Kolka the Camel, the gypsy Seryoga and dozens of wild cats.

In his first few days in our town he tried showing identification papers, made out in a different name, of course. But who's going to check the papers of a man who sets himself up as assistant to Farter, the ferryman? Farter lived in a rickety wooden cabin in the osier thickets by the water, brewed hooch out of sawdust and had women over every evening. Beria obediently stoked the stove, barked at passers-by and manned the ferry while his boss snoozed away. In the mornings the ferryman stood on the sand by the water and released his pent-up wind with such force that gullible carp floated belly-up to the surface. Then he cleared his throat with every expletive in the dictionary, all of them directed at the workers building a wooden bridge near the ferry crossing. The bridge threatened to deprive Farter of the bread and vodka he was guaranteed every time a wedding or funeral procession passed by. He sent Beria over to the bridge several times with a jar of kerosene, but each time the sorties came to nothing: the raw timber simply refused to burn. For this, the ex-minister was mercilessly beaten.

Eventually the bridge was completed, and the ferry was chopped up for firewood. The ferryman took to hard boozing and hell-raising. A week later he was found in the osier thicket with a three-sided metal file wedged in the back of his skull. And although it was Vaska the Cock who ended up in prison (his wife had paid occasional visits to the cabin by the river), we knew the real story: Beria was to blame. Only he could have lodged the file in such a way that it could be neither extracted, cut free or broken off. The ferryman had to be buried face-down.

Whatever went wrong, however big or small, Beria was to blame. Beria and no one else. It was because of him that the calves drowned in the oil leak from the roofing-paper factory which filled the fetid ditches of the sports ground; because of him that the potato harvest failed four times in ten years; that lightning burned down two houses on Seventh Street; that

Mukhanov and his son drowned in their jerry-built boat (the bodies were never found, although there were rumours that some poachers, using TNT to stun their catch, blasted the Mukhanovs out of the Pregolya's silty depths; locked in an embrace, father and son floated downriver, crossed the Baltic Sea, and unpiloted, negotiated the Great and Little Belt, the Øresund, Kattegat and Skaggerak, before heading off to drift in eternity among the ocean's boundless graveyards . . .). It was because of Beria that boys grew up as hooligans yearning for the corrective institution, and girls as shameless virgins yearning for hooligans; that it poured for months and green mould munched right through the houses to the inhabitants; that there were thirty days in June, and thirty-one in July; that we were born and we died. And although some clever dick or other was always trying to say different, we knew: Beria was to blame. And no one else.

He married a woman called Meat. This shapeless elephant was always ending up under a train, on the redundancy list or in bed with a drunk. She gave birth to all sorts of things: cats, mice, and even little green little devils that tended to be witnessed by nearly sober guys. It goes without saying that Beria denied everything: he was no Lavrenty Pavlovich but Nikolai Nikolayevich; he was no Georgian either – his family came from Skotoprigonievsk; and he'd certainly never been a minister, since he could neither read nor write, and anyway his great-grandmother used to sleep around with horse-thieves, Jews or other such rascals. Cobblers. Who'd buy that story?

One day Beria tried to give the town the slip, but he was caught two thousand seven hundred and twenty miles down the road, and was promptly sent back. Once he realized there was no getting away from us, and no conning us either, he withdrew into the role of town sewage collector. Straddling a stinking, leaking barrel, he methodically did the rounds of the courtyards and the four public latrines, and hypocritically refused to engage in any political discussions of the weather or predictions for the potato harvest. He wore hip boots and a service jacket with bone buttons dyed in violet ink. He never lent money to anyone, which was all the proof we needed to assume that Beria was saving up by wrapping his notes in condoms and tucking them up his arse.

And so it continued until the arrival in our little town of Vitya the Negro, a veteran of the African partisan movement who knew seventy-five epithets for the word 'sand' and could quote Stalin's entire collected works from memory.

Fleeing colonial oppression, Vitya had crossed the Kalahari desert on his own, sustaining himself with dry burrs and dew-drops that collected at night on the burnished barrel of his assault rifle. His tracks disappeared in the impassable jungles of equatorial Africa and were discovered again when he emerged from the impassable elder thickets between the bathhouse and the market, guided by the smell of female latrines. Along the way he had lost neither his ideals nor his four-pronged fork, which he kept in the top of his boot. He immediately felt at home in our town. He came to love dried bream and slightly watered-down beer, and the ecstatic, aston-ished howls of the blondes who sometimes wandered over to express solidarity with the warring peoples of far-flung lands. It was they who discovered a strange object that had sunk below the skin of Vitya's heavily scarred chest. It was a little metal figurine of the Generalissimo, hidden from the enemy's sight, and it served Vitya as a kind of amulet. It was even thought that Vitya's virility depended on the figurine's disposition. Indeed, when the Generalissimo was smiling on the Negro, the yells that issued from his cubby-hole brought cats of the female sex scurrying over from all quarters, feverishly miaowing.

Since Vitya had no skills other than shooting at faltering targets, he was given a job as Lavrenty Pavlovich's assistant. From the very first day, Beria felt a savage hatred towards the poor Negro. Firstly, because Vitya was always hounding him with questions about the Leader. 'Shit', Beria would reply. 'Shit and shitty shit is all I give a shit about.' Secondly, because Vitya loved a quarrel. 'Bet you Stalin was Lenin's illegitimate son!' Thirdly, because from dawn to dusk he gave full-throated renditions of the immortal Zulu epic, 'Questions of Leninism. Eleventh edition. State publishers of political literature. 1945. State Censor No. A32018. Printed from the 1941 matrix. Price: 3 roubles, 50 kopeks. First Model Printing-Press of the Poligrafkniga Trust of the State Publishing House under the Council of People's Commissars of the Russian Soviet Federal Socialist Republic. Moscow, 28 Valovaya Str. Order No. 3907.'

'Shit,' Beria would interrupt as he drew up his horse near the Red Canteen. 'Shitty shit.'

'You should be shot as an Enemy of the People,' said Vitya, shaking his head in concern. 'You're a people's enemy.' And both went off for a beer, which they loved.

It was inevitable that the sewage collectors would come to blows one day; the only surprise was that it took until August 5th – payday.

On that fateful day, as luck would have it, the Red Canteen had its delivery of fresh beer. And, as luck would have it, Beria ordered an extra pint to mark the event. 'Bet you can't drink a hundred pints without pissing,' said Vitya, turning red. 'Bet you can't!'

Beria stared with loathing at the Negro, before unexpectedly spluttering back: 'You're on. A hundred roubles.'

Silence descended upon the canteen, and the onlookers exchanged knowing glances: only an Enemy of the People would bet a sum as big as that. Vitya slammed the money on the table and told Fenya to start pouring. He was guffawing like a lunatic, his eyes fixed on Beria.

Beria was choking from all the beer but when, still choking, he saw off the seventy-fifth pint, the Negro could only manage a sour grin. The onlookers kept a close eye on the Enemy of the People's movements, just in case he tried slipping out to the loo. But all Beria did was swell up more and more, and breathe out more and more viciously with each pint. Finishing up the hundredth, he raked in Vitya's money, spat on the ground and, boots squelching, made his way to the door. The crowd, taking a despondent Vitya with it, streamed outside.

With some difficulty, Beria clambered onto the barrel, threw aside the hatch and set about pulling off his boots. A yellow stream gushed out.

For a few moments everyone looked on dumbstruck until Kolka the Camel shouted: 'He pissed where he drank!'

How the men laughed! How they guffawed! And the merrier they became, the more fiercely the eyes of the veteran of the partisan movement blazed with fury. 'He conned me!' he yelled at last. 'The murderer conned me!'

'Least he conned you fairly,' said Camel, trying to make him see reason.

They weren't able to stop Vitya in time. Grabbing the four-pronged fork from his boot, he flew onto the sewage barrel and with a single lunge to the heart took the life of former minister Lavrenty Beria. Losing their balance, the pair of them tumbled into the barrel.

Our attempts to extract the bodies met with no success. We had to bury them just like that, in a barrel full of shit. And although we poured more than a tonne and a half of quick-lime into the grave, the cemetery, I'm sure you'll understand, soon had to be closed.

Since that time the flocks of gentle angels have tended to sweep somewhat quicker over the focus, centre and navel of this world. Sometimes they avoid our town of towns altogether and, stealing past the seven hills, disappear into the thick gloom of August nights, nights that reek of mould, pigs and a barrel full of sewage, repository of death and sorrow . . .

Sly Fly

The real name of this hunched-up little fellow with a skull as flat as a pancake and slanting eyes that tumbled onto a strawberry nose that tumbled onto fat, unevenly cut lips, was Flytrap. Leonty Flytrap. But in the town he was known only by his nickname, Sly Fly. Watchman at the Park of Culture.

'What do you watch out for?' folk quizzed him. 'The broken swing? Or the lassie with the oar?'

Leonty gave a sly smile.

'Secret.'

'What do you mean, secret?'

'I know what I know,' dodged Sly Fly as he tried in vain to tug his cap with its chewed-up peak over both ears at once. 'Myst'ry.'

In the park, the white shells of fairground attractions, tangled up with vines, lay about among rotten lime trees and wild thickets of euonymus. A creaking door led into a pneumatic shooting gallery, where, behind a counter covered in crumpled sheets of aluminium, blue-nosed Vitaly clanked around with his artificial limbs, always ready to welcome his mates with a working-hours half pint of vodka. Towering plaster sculptures were strewn around the park: sportsmen with plaster muscles, fishermen holding monstrous plaster sturgeon and miners in postures that suggested dislocated hip joints. There was no fence here, but there were gates, regularly coated with poison-blue paint. Sly Fly unlocked them every morning with great ceremony and bolted them in the evenings, booming at distant pedestrians: 'Park closed! Closed!'

The windows of his little house looked out onto the path, with the oar girl's monumental bum in the foreground. The sculptures were his pride and joy. All day long he wandered round the park with a bucket of whitewash, painstakingly touching up cracks in plaster elbows and stains on plaster knees. The girl with the oar received special attention, and Fly cared for her plaster curves with genuine affection, muttering strange incantations as he did so.

He lived a solitary, closed-off life. He didn't even use the public bathhouse, which made people suspect some kind of physical defect – a tail, say, or wings. What's more, he didn't drink vodka; he kept an open house and plentiful food for stray cats (sometimes he had as many as three hundred swarming around); and, to cap it all, he carried out breeding experiments with animals and plants. Halfway loopy, that was the local verdict.

Yes, breeding was his passion, uncontrollable and senseless, like every passion. He'd cross everything with anything: currants with gooseberries, turnips with raspberries, cats with goats, sheep with bats ... The results of his experiments bloomed, grew, ran and yelled in the garden and in the park, scaring chance passers-by and blue-nosed Vitaly's mates. One minute a mouse would miaow cheekily at weak-nerved Gramophone, another minute a sheep up a tree would shit on Kolka the Camel. Luckily, most of the creatures simply died without leaving any offspring.

'About time you gave all this up,' Vitaly advised him gloomily. 'What good's it to you?'

'Well,' said Sly Fly, screwing up his eyes. 'S'pose you crossed a cat with a dog, what would you get then?'

'A messed-up arse,' came the instant reply. 'Its gob's always gonna be chasing its tail. You should get married instead.'

Sly Fly nodded pensively.

It was a thought that occurred to him too once every three or four years. Matchmakers would offer him brides and Sly would pay visits and drink tea. He kept his eyes fixed on the table and tried to tug his cap with its chewed-up peak over both ears at once. Then, in the end, he'd refuse.

'Nah,' he'd say, shrugging off Vitaly's reproaches. 'We don't want ones like that. She's deaf.'

'What do you want one that can hear for?' Vitaly would snap, rabidly jangling his prostheses. 'Cross her with a chicken and she'll lay eggs. Useful, eh?'

After much humming and hawing, Sly Fly would finally forced out an answer, as if disclosing a great secret:

'She's ugly . . .'

'What about you? Cross between a Negro and a motor-cycle! Who'd want you?'

'Someone will,' Sly Fly would frown. 'There's gotta be someone.' And he'd walk off.

Vitaly would follow him with his gaze for a good while, and although he carried on swearing at him, inwardly he marvelled at Sly Fly, even if he couldn't say why.

The watchman wrapped the statues up in straw and sacking for the winter, but by spring the tatty plaster would already start cracking and each year he had to use more and more putty and whitewash.

The only other person to be found every day in winter in the snow-covered park was blue-nosed Vitaly, stubbornly sitting out his shift behind the counter, swigging home-made booze and strong tea, and reading *The Brothers Karamazov*.

But one spring, Vitaly flipped. At midday he suddenly jumped out onto the porch of the shooting gallery with an air rifle and, shrieking incoherently, discharged a volley of bullets at the cats, Sly Fly and Battle-Axe, who had called on Fly for some salt. By the time the ambulance turned up, Vitaly had barricaded himself in the gallery and emptied his rifle. Then he shat himself and collapsed under the counter, from where, stinking unbearably and clanking wildly, he was lifted out and shoved in the ambulance. His steel leg got stuck in the door. The medic spat and ordered the driver to go anyway. The van moved off to the sound of Vitaly's desperate cry: 'Freedom to the brothers Karamazov! Hurraah!'

Left alone, Sly Fly began to let things slip. He immersed himself in *The Three Musketeers* and *The Brothers Karamazov*, reading aloud in the shadow of the girl with the oar. Every now and then he'd break off and throw searching glances at the plaster face. When winter set in, he dragged the statue into the house.

That first night, once she'd warmed up, the girl put the oar to one side and, blushing coyly, slipped off her panties and singlet. 'They're tight,' she whispered, gazing shyly at the man drawn up on his elbow, 'and sore.'

Gasping for breath, Sly Fly realized at long last why he was born into this world and welcomed her in his arms.

A few days later, Mitrokha the alcoholic wandered, as he often did, into the park, and without thinking nudged open the watchman's door. He found Sly Fly in an ice-covered bedroom. The oarless girl was sleeping peacefully beside him, and her beautiful hair, speckled with hoarfrost, was strewn over the pillow. Mitrokha left on tiptoe.

At the inspection and autopsy no physical defects were found on Sly Fly. Treasure-hunting volunteers scoured the house, garden and park, but found nothing. We never did discover the source of Fly's cunning, nor of his secret.

The plaster girl was chucked into the thickets of euonymus – cracked right through, with one arm held out in front of her and her sensuous lips slightly parted. Battle-Axe placed two coppers on the girl's eyelids. She was dizzy and felt a tightening in her throat. Slowly lowering herself to the ground, Battle-Axe gulped back tears and massaged her chest: her heart was aching and wouldn't let up.

'Lord,' she whispered. 'Is this our life, or just your dream, o Lord?'

Alles

Ah yes, the way the world is, there's no one happy but the blind. Only they were spared the turmoil that so nearly led to the ruin of our town. Only they could not and did not press themselves to the peephole in the side of the box in the middle of the parlour. It was draped in scarlet plush, that parlour, and the swindler who owned it had hung a handwritten sign at the entrance: *The Parlour of Desires. Price by agreement.* Some said the owner had sneaked into town disguised as a decomposing corpse in a soldered zinc coffin, others recalled some nephew of Scabby Svetka: rumour had it that Svetka used to keep him locked up in the cellar during the daytime, letting him out into the garden at night, where he grew carrots that women were ashamed to handle in public . . .

Whatever the truth of the matter, this chap – three foot tall in his cap, with eyes that had sunk almost to the back of his skull and squeaky orthopaedic boots that could be heard from the other end of town – managed to set up his parlour where the old chemist's used to be: scarlet plush on the walls, a black box on a tripod, price by agreement, no children under sixteen.

What was meant by 'price by agreement' became clear on the very first day and caused real merriment in the town.

'Pay with whatever you want,' said the owner. 'We'll do a deal. Then come and look here, and *alles!*'

'You what?' said Battle-Axe.

'Kaput,' explained Kolka the Camel.

'Con merchant!' raged Fenya, waitress at the Red Canteen. 'Just see if I can't show him up!'

After catching and slaying a sizeable ginger rat with her own hands, Fenya wrapped it up in a serviette, stuck on the label *State Produce* and marched off to the parlour, outside which almost the entire adult population of the town had assembled. Flashing a honey smile, Alles accepted the rat with a steady hand and, gesturing theatrically, invited Fenya to the box.

'You will see yourself,' he purred. 'You will see the fulfilment of your most secret desires, whose existence maybe you don't even suspect yourself. You will peer into your future.'

Ten minutes later a pale Fenya walked out with a face like a dead rat. She staggered blindly onto the pavement. The crowd gave way. She took a few more shaky steps.

'You really saw something?' Gramp Mukhanov stopped her.

'Yeah,' whispered Fenya. 'I really did, Christ almighty I did.'

And she collapsed, mighty breast first, into a puddle.

'Next?' intoned Alles sweetly, casting his sunken eyes over the crowd.

We believed him and poured in.

We paid however we could. Ten eggs, a rouble, a handful of dead flies – Alles took them all without grumbling. On bended knees, the client would walk up to the black box, breathe in the smell of mothballs and, his spine creaking glassily, press his eye to the hole. For the queue waiting outside five minutes passed like five years, but we didn't complain: each of us was striving to understand why the lucky so-and-so's who'd been in the parlour never told anyone anything about it. Not a word. Some walked out giggling or wearing twisted grimaces, others made a beeline for the White Canteen opposite and asked Lyusya for half a pint of vodka straight up, yet others wandered over to the cemetery and sat till dusk on benches by their parents' graves . . . But no one told anyone a thing. Mothers to their daughters, sons to their fathers, workers to their bosses: zip. Gramophone, famed for her verbal incontinence, didn't trust herself and, without using anaesthetic, sewed up her mouth with a fishing line.

After visiting the parlour, Longjohn, the chairman of the local soviet, suddenly refused his daily portion of hooch and chicken droppings, and sent the idiot Easy Lizzie packing (she always came by to fulfil her boss's last desire of the day, and the first of the night).

The director of the music school, surname d'Artagnan, finally made up his mind to offer his hand and heart to the pop-singer Alla Pugacheva; he'd been secretly living in sin with her portrait for eight years now.

The accountant at the timber works, One-Eye Petrovich, shaved meticulously, scented himself and, taking aim in a clouded mirror, slit his throat neatly from ear to ear.

At this time strange disappearances began to be noticed in the town. Like the cobbled road from the prison to Bath Bridge, which vanished no one knew how, when or where. All the black dogs went missing in one go, along with the carp in the Pregolya and the Lava. And the typewriters that lacked the letters *d* , *v* and *l*. The Georgian tea that Gramp Mukhanov rolled his cigarettes with. The slogan above the awning of the headgear shop claiming *The Hats of the Party are the Hats of the People*. The nocturnal rustle of the osier thickets between the market and the bathhouse. The scent of thuja at the old cemetery. Flies.

One day Gramp Mukhanov found that there were no longer any steps going up to the savings bank, where old folk gathered to tell one of their thirty-three favourite stories. The scales fell from his eyes. He saw the corpse of the town without its eternally damp, mould-green fences and flies buzzing over the trash heaps, without shit floating down the Pregolya, without typewriters lacking the letters *d*, *v* and *l*, without the irrepressible womanizer One-Eye Petrovich, whose glass eye radiated energy that burned through women's skirts to their knickers, without the hats of the Party and the hats of the people . . .

He saw it in horror and yelled:

'Alles!'

Men and teenagers under sixteen answered his call and dashed to the Parlour of Desires, but it goes without saying that Alles, whose eyes had sunk to the back of his skull and whose squeaking orthopaedic boots could be heard from the other end of town, was nowhere to be found.

No one heeded Gramp Mukhanov's requests to save the black box for research. They smashed it to smithereens, pounded it in a mortar, drenched it in kerosene and set fire to it. The ashes were entrusted to Arkasha Shitson to be eaten, since everyone knew full well: nothing but shit ever came out of Arkasha.

The initiative was successful. Everything that had disappeared from the town slowly returned, even Fenya's dead rat wrapped in a serviette labelled *State Produce*. The turmoil subsided and only happiness, it seems, left us all never to return. All except the blind, that is. That's the way the world is: there's no one happy but the blind . . .

China

Late one spring evening, Lonesome Katya heard a noise by the front door. Throwing a shawl over her shoulders and arming herself with a poker, she stepped outside. A man was lying on the porch with his face to the wall. Katya squatted and, keeping her distance, prodded him in the shoulder with the poker. He gave a hollow groan and rolled over on his back. His face was black with blood. After hauling the stranger indoors, Katya made sure he didn't smell of vodka. She woke up Yuozapas from the house opposite, and he obediently harnessed his horse and took the man to the hospital. Returning home, Katya discovered a little suitcase on the porch, tied round with string. She chucked it under her bed and lay down to sleep beside her daughter.

Two days later, swaying and clutching at fences, the man wandered back to the hotel over the river, his head looking enormous from bandages. Katya gasped, grabbed him by the hand and dragged him into her room.

'The suitcase,' he croaked. 'Where's my suitcase?'

'It's here, right here,' Katya said. 'Lie down now.'

'Some bread,' the man asked. 'Gimme some black bread.'

She brought him a loaf of fresh bread. Clenching his teeth, the man tore off the bandages and pasted his shaven head all over with soft, warm dough. Katya gave him the bed in the big room, while she and her daughter moved into the tiny storeroom.

For a week the stranger wouldn't accept any food or answer to any of the male names Katya could think of. Hotel chores took up her whole day, and in the evenings she traded harmless insults with the tipsy men who were in town on business at the paper mill and couldn't keep their paws off her. Later on she'd kiss her six-year-old Sonya and collapse on a straw mattress into a deep and joyless sleep. She dreamed of her first husband, who went north to earn money and snuffed it there; her second husband, who gulped down a whole bottle of meths to cure a hangover and died on the spot; her third husband, Sonya's dad, who crashed his lorry through the spring ice on the river. 'I'm unlucky,' she'd tell other women with a guilty smile. 'Must have been born under an evil star.' She was small and skinny, and thin veins throbbed on her scrawny neck.

When the stranger finally showed some life and had his first bite to eat, Katya took him over to see Doctor Sheberstov.

'He pasted it with bread, you said?' The doctor quickly ran his hands over the patient's head. 'Better than shit, I suppose. Dizzy? Painful? Hands shaking? Show us.'

Instead of stretching out his hands in front of him, the man took out a flick-knife and pressed the tip of the blade to a fat pad of writing paper lying on the table.

'How many?'

'What?

'How many d'you want me to cut through?'

'Erm . . . nine,' said Sheberstov.

'Count them.' The knife disappeared back into the man's pocket. 'Nine.'

After counting off nine sheets that had been slashed with the knife, Sheberstov stared at the tenth: not the slightest mark had remained.

'They're not shaking,' said the man. 'Thanks.'

'Well well,' said Sheberstov. 'I wouldn't whip out knives like that too often around here if I was you.'

On the way back the man bought vodka, sausage, chocolate and a gold watch. For Katya.

'For me?' gasped Katya. 'Listen . . . at least tell me what your name is?'

'Call me Pyotr.' He shrugged his shoulders. 'It's all the same.'

Before going to bed, she tried out the gold watch on Sonya's arm. It slipped down to her elbow. Katya kissed the sleepy girl, who was smiling and smellled of chocolates, dabbed her armpits with *Red Moscow* perfume (a gift from the trade union on Women's Day) and adjusted the straps of her night-shirt on her skinny shoulders. Then she suddenly remembered about clipping her toenails, which were hard and gnarled from wearing poorly-fitting shoes.

'What are you up to in there?' Pyotr called. 'Are you sleeping or what?'

With toenails half-clipped, smelling of sweat and perfume, Katya sidled gawkishly into the room, lay down on the bed, stuck her chest out to make it look bigger, and started a new life once more.

Pyotr fished out a rocking-chair from the attic and managed to repair it with some wire and nails. He sat on it for whole days at a time, staring at the wall in front of him where he'd hung a small map of China. Katya never asked him about anything. Some days he might not even say a word: breakfast, lunch, supper, all in silence. He'd just sit in the chair in front of the map, smoking roll-ups.

Busying herself around the hotel, Katya didn't even notice when and where the suitcase under the bed disappeared. 'I put it away,' was all Pyotr would say. At the end of the month she found a wad of banknotes on the little table under the mirror. She counted them, and gasped for breath.

'If people see me with those they'll laugh me out of the shop,' she whispered that night into Pyotr's shoulder. 'Or arrest me. Is it all from the suitcase?'

'Spend a little at a time,' said Pyotr. 'Life's over.'

Katya laughed softly: she was happy.

She put on weight, started to forget how to purse her lips so tightly and no longer lowered her eyes when she walked past other women's men.

In the evenings Sonya would climb up on to Pyotr's knees, and, rocking quietly on the chair, he would tell her about China. It was a country of yellow earth, sluggish rivers and sweet-tasting goldfish. Yangtse, Huang . . .

'Where's that? What is it?' Sonya asked.

'Here it is. A river. Like that one.' He nodded towards the window, beyond which the Pregolya silently flowed. 'Huang.'

'This Huang is called the Pregolya,' Sonya said. 'Does that mean that our China is called Russia?'

'That's right. And their Russia is China.'

The people who lived by the rivers there had wings for shoulder blades. Sensing the approach of death, they would bid their nearest and dearest farewell and fly off to Lake Tsiling-tso where they saw out the remainder of their eternity; the living were banned from going there. The Chinese never travelled or fought wars, having realized long ago that space and time are one and the same thing. They didn't love anyone, but they didn't hate anyone either. When they visited one another, they flew on the backs of gorgeous pheasants. They lived on apples and tea, which grew like grass in their gardens. Just for their children, they bred tiny animals – wolves, elephants and tigers that grew no bigger than a kitten.

'I wanna mini-elephant ...' the girl would murmur sleepily.

'Tianjin,' Pyotr would whisper. 'Jinan ... Nanjing ... Shanghai ... Ningbo. ... Canton ...'

When the girl fell asleep, he would carry her to the bed in the storeroom, where the gold watch hung on a nail driven into the wall: Katya was too embarrassed to wear it.

'These are fairy tales you're telling her,' she said. 'They're not really true, are they?

'What does it matter?' he replied after a while. 'How do we know there's a country like that anyway? There isn't.'

'What do you mean?' Katya flapped. 'Everyone knows about China ... Just look at the map.'

'Everyone knows about hell, too,' Pyotr sniggered. 'Everyone knows about it but no one's been there. There are pictures of that too. And books. I read one once ... some blokes travelling around hell.' He sank into the armchair and added: 'Twenty years I've been carrying this map around with me. All I have to do is pin it on a wall and I'm home. In China. Changping, Chengdu ... Blows your mind!'

After conversations like that Katya would dream of dead husbands and wake up panting in their arms.

Pyotr found work for the winter as the hotel boilerman and locksmith. He fetched coal from the cellar, looked after the boiler and replaced the washers in the leaky taps. When the hotel's few residents tried to strike up an acquaintance with him on boring winter evenings, they met an impenetrable wall of silence. After hearing them out, Pyotr would turn his back and lose himself in contemplation of the map of China.

In spring, Sonya fell through the ice on the river. After a shot of vodka, men waded in and prodded around for a long time with boathooks under the ice, but they didn't find her. Returning home, Katya went into the storeroom, looked at the gold watch hanging on the nail, and fainted.

Pyotr didn't comfort her. They would lie for hours in bed without talking. It was quiet enough to scream. Katya snuggled up to Pyotr's big body but she couldn't get warm. Once she asked in a groan:

'Sweetie, why do you never smell of anything? Not sweat, not feet . . . At least use some aftershave or something . . .'

'It's no use,' he answered, but that evening he slapped on the strongest kind. In the morning he went to see Longjohn at the local soviet and they had a lengthy talk about something. He called on the joiners at the timber works. Then off to Half Pint, leader of the band that blared away at weddings and funerals.

On Thursday the sounds of the brass band dragged young and old out onto the street. In the black-lacquered funeral lorry rested a child-sized coffin decorated with paper flowers and thuja, with drowsy Katya sitting alongside. Pyotr strode behind wearing a black suit and a hat pushed low over his eyebrows. The band followed at a respectable distance. A dumbstruck crowd brought up the rear, and more folk gathered at the cemetery than had been seen since the burial of Stalin's statue (instead of melting it down, they'd buried it on the Seventh Hill according to all the rules and rituals).

'But the grave's empty,' whispered Battle-Axe, breathing garlic into Longjohn's ear. 'Ain't that a sin? There's no person there.'

'You don't bury a person,' the chairman of the local soviet answered calmly. 'You bury the dead.'

One Sunday in May, Pyotr suddenly stopped his rocking-chair and, without shifting his gaze from the map, quietly announced:

'That's it, Katya.'

In the evening Katya found him on the porch. He was dead, bullet in the face. The suitcase was sprawled alongside, ripped in two. Katya took Yuozapas' horse and brought the body to the hospital.

The policeman Lyosha Leontyev arrived an hour later.

'Done the operation?' he asked Doctor Sheberstov.

Sheberstov's eyebrows leapt up his forehead.

'This is called an exhumation.' He crooked his finger. 'Come over here. Never seen anything like it.'

They went down to the cellar, past the kitchen along a narrow and damp brick-walled corridor, and into a long room in the corner of which lay blocks of grey ice. Sheberstov switched on the lamp under the ceiling and lifted the sheet. Leontyev slowly raised his hand to his mouth.

'How long's he been like this? When did it happen?'

'He died about a year ago,' said Sheberstov as he drew the sheet back over the fetid body, which spread like blancmange over the granite slab. 'The bullet added nothing, take it from me.'

When they returned to the doctor's office, Lyosha gulped down a glass of sour compote, caught his breath and said:

'What am I going to tell the authorities? What a mess!'

'It's a mess for the living,' said Sheberstov.

Katya sank into the armchair and stared at the map of China, an irregular stain yellowing on a grey wall in the twilight. She didn't even notice herself dropping off. When she woke, she tried, without knowing why, to find Tianjin on the map. Swallowing the lump in her throat, she whispered:

'Tianjin.' Turned her gaze. 'Huang . . .'

Huang on the map, Pregolya outside the window. A river

and a river. Here Pregolya, there Huang. Here and here. There and there.

'Huang!' she moaned out loud, and began to cry.

She had suddenly realized that from now on she was doomed to contemplate this map, to live in this China, in this hell . . .

Name of Lev

The sun rises in the east, the Public Prosecutor doesn't drink, Sundays are for football.

That's the law.

The first out onto the pitch would be lanky Yashka the Basher, foppishly dragging his feet and wearing a black sweater with patched-up elbows and the number 1 on the back. Katso, a rubbery Georgian, came bouncing onto the lawn after him: he had a round shaven head and black shaggy eyebrows over half his forehead, from the middle of which an enormous nose floated out like an icebreaking stem, propped up by the thick brush of a black moustache. Then came Young Boot-Licker, son of Old Boot-Licker, with a charmed crust of bread hidden in his underpants to shield off any cunning strikes; Sergei Try-Hard, smiling through two rows of steel teeth, meticulously sharpened before the game with a metal file; Kolka the Camel, who had a red band on his right leg to show he was forbidden from taking penalties with it lest he endanger the life of the goalie; Cuddly Klein, whose lips were the colour of scarlet jam and who carried his own teeth, from the milk ones to the punched-out molars, in a purse on his chest; Black Beard, whose hide seemed about to crack any minute under the strain of muscular flesh; Sergeant, with his heavily bloodshot eyes and a black thread wrapped around his bullish neck – for luck; Tolik, a loud-mouth joker with a bulging Adam's apple who once contrived, on a bet, to tie his member into a knot; Aliment, who notched up an 'alimentary' goal every game thanks to a secret nail in the sole of his boot; and lastly, Ivan Studentsov, who had nothing noteworthy about him except his height . . .

To the rasping whistles of the kids lolling on the grass behind the goals, Name of Lev would come trotting out onto the pitch. But no, this wasn't the fat barber who was famous all over town, boasted that he could shave any client with his nail and wore a grimy overall split at his drooping belly. The guy who ran out into the middle of the field – in a black shirt with a snow-white turn-down collar, black shorts and socks, a ball under his armpit and an immutable flat whistle bobbing on a fatty chest – was the presiding god of the football spectacle, greeted by the brass band (just trumpets and drums) and the kids' ecstatic refrain: 'Off with the ref! Off with the ref!' After hands had been shaken and ends chosen, Name of Lev would give the first peep of his whistle and, as ritual ordained, bring the ball into play with a light touch of his boot before ceasing to exist, like a god who, after setting the ancient machine of life in motion, interferes only by necessity, and not by request.

At half time the fans lounged on the grass by the fence, spreading newspapers and laying out fresh cucumbers and tomatoes, bread and pork fat that reeked of garlic: it would be warmish and already melting, but there was still nothing better after a brimful of vodka.

Kids wielding coppers would besiege the enormous van where Fenya from the Red Canteen, wearing as always her oilskin apron, sold fruit-drops, biscuits and lemonade that went squeak in your nose.

The musicians, fortified by a quick drink, would play *On the Hills of Manchuria* and *The Waves of the Amur*. The band was led by the totally bald trumpeter, roly-poly Half Pint; his son Quarter Pint, glumly rocking over his loathsome drum, kept a lonely distance.

After the final whistle, the team would sit with its back to the changing-room, and Andrei the Photographer snapped a painstakingly composed victory tableau: in the centre stood the coach, the referee and the boss of the factory that financed the team and the stadium; in front of them squatted the captain Black Beard, holding a cup or a pennant; to the sides sat the players, in sweat-drenched scarlet shirts. Afterwards, a capacious trophy would be taken from the prize cabinet and filled to the brim with vodka. The cup passed from the players to the factory boss to Gramp Mukhanov, who had a cigarette stuffed with Georgian tea instead of tobacco lodged permanently in his lower lip, and onto Longjohn, the chairman of the local soviet who'd once worked with Lev at the barbershop. Even old Sindbad the Sailor had a swig, keeping a hawkish eye on the kids in case they made off from the changing-room with her lawful prey – empty bottles.

In the event of a defeat the drinking bout naturally turned into a fistfight, culminating in a thorough beating for hapless Quarter Pint.

But neither victory nor defeat prevented the players and spectators from rendering tribute to the fairest, firmest and most impartial referee of all peoples and times; for just such a referee, without exaggeration or reservation, was Name of Lev. And if the law stated that the sun rises in the east, the Prosecutor doesn't drink and Sundays are for football, then we could add with a clear conscience: Name of Lev never makes a mistake. His qualities were so well known that the federation sometimes allowed him to referee important fixtures involving our town's team. Once, in recognition of his merits, the players and spectators mucked in to buy up all the laurel in the local shop and presented Lev with a wreath the size of a car wheel. It was a bit ragged, but they meant it with all their hearts.

Then everything fell apart.

In the League Cup final, Name of Lev stopped the game and declared a penalty against our team: Cuddly Klein had handballed in the box.

Afterwards, many maintained that yet another toothache had caused Klein to behave as he did, but, whatever the truth of the matter, the player said quietly (for the whole stadium to hear):

'I didn't touch it. There was no handball, Lev.'

Even Vasya Voilukov, deaf from birth, could hear the fly that had settled on his bald patch scratch its armpits.

Name of Lev was stunned. No one had ever argued with him. No one. Ever. He was always just. The law made flesh. Everyone knew that. No one doubted it. Not even Lev.

Klein reeled back and his teeth chattered.

'There was no handball,' he repeated, and dropped in a dead faint.

The referee turned his gaze from Klein to the public. Nothing like this had ever happened. Could ever happen.

'Penalty' Lev heard someone say, only realizing a second later that the voice was his own. 'Penalty!'

He blew the whistle.

'Off with the ref!' yelled a tubby little kid from the stands, aghast at his own audacity. 'Off with the ref!'

An ear-popping cacophony of shouts, whistles and thousand-tongued wails fell upon Lev. 'Off! Off!' The few voices trying to stick up for the referee were smothered in a hurricane of sound, which was amplified by the brass band's roar.

Name of Lev blew the whistle.

A striker ran up and shot.

Yashka the Basher dived.

The ball rocketed into the net and slithered lazily to the ground.

Name of Lev pictured to himself for a second what was about to happen in the stadium and what would happen in the changing-room after the game, and he cursed the fact that the town's population was greater than one person and that it would have been better for that one person never to have been born.

He was rescued by the policeman, Lyosha Leontyev. At the final whistle Lyosha hared out onto the pitch on his motor-bike, bundled Lev into the sidecar and tore off at full pelt under a hail of rocks towards the stadium gates, which no one had thought of locking.

Coming to his senses outside his home, Name of Lev frowned plaintively.

'What'd I do wrong, Lyosha?'

The policeman gingerly massaged the bruise under his eye and muttered:

'You did nothing wrong, Lev. You were right, but you shouldn't have done that. Got it?'

'Nope.'

Lyosha sighed.

'You've got truth, they've got justice. Grin and bear it:

truth's a lonely business. And a proud one. But no one likes the proud. Out you jump.'

That evening the players summoned Lev to the White Canteen, where they moved the chairs around and sat the barber-ref in the middle. The thirteenth person was Lyosha Leontyev, invited by the footballers in case their nerves didn't hold out.

After a vodka, the players accused Lev of injustice. Betrayal. Lack of patriotism. Derision of football, the town and the world. Sacrilege against the laws of men and the laws of God. Pride.

Name of Lev also had some vodka but refused to acknowledge his guilt.

Cuddly Klein stood up to break the silence.

'I swear,' he said, 'that there was no handball. And if there was, then let my hand wither away.'

The way he looked at his right hand, everyone knew: it wouldn't wither away even once his body had become a handful of dust.

A few days later Klein lost control on a slippery road and his car smashed into a tree. The driver was almost unharmed, save for a fairly hefty blow to the right side of his body against the dashboard. But it was just this blow that proved fateful. It wasn't long before his hand began to shrivel. When it had withered away completely and hung down like a twisted rag, Klein decided to cash in his chips. A purse full of teeth was placed in his grave, from the milk ones to the punched-out molars.

'Happy now?' Kolka the Camel asked Lev. 'Got what you wanted?'

'Me?!' Name of Lev was dumbfounded. 'What are you on about, Camel?'

'Who else?!' asked Camel in amazement. 'Wasn't me, was it?'

Cuddly Klein's funeral briefly reconciled the town dwellers, divided between those who thought Klein had committed a foul (a paltry minority), and those who blamed it all on Lev.

But after the funeral even those who sympathized with the barber-ref no longer dared say hello to him.

When, the next morning, Name of Lev discovered the first dead cat outside his front door and realized that the last one would be slipped his way on the day of his funeral, he straightened up to his full height (by sticking out his belly) and hollered at the sky:

'I'm not guilty!'

'Guilty!' came the echo.

The sun rises in the east, the Prosecutor doesn't drink, Sundays are for football. The sun may rise in the west, the Prosecutor may drink himself blind, but Sundays will always be for football.

Then the law collapsed.

Kolka the Camel hit the bottle.

The black thread on Sergeant's bullish neck tore in two and could no longer be tied back together.

Lev's daughter married Black Beard and the only living creature that Name of Lev could talk to at home without yelling was his reflection in the mirror.

At the shop, he was given cobblestones wrapped in paper instead of bread. His regular clients preferred nicking themselves badly with blunt razors to going to the barber's. Kids no longer played at being the ref strutting out onto the pitch with a whistle on his fatty chest. People walked past Lev like he wasn't there. No one seemed to notice his lengthening stubble, the mad glare in his eyes or his faltering gait.

'Name of Lev? Eighth grave on the left, Seventh Hill,' they'd tell anyone who asked, convinced that they were telling the truth and nothing but.

One day, just for a laugh, Lev went to the cemetery and found that the tombstone adorning the eighth grave on the left on Seventh Hill really was inscribed with the words: *Name of Lev. Barber.* No date of birth, no year of death, as if a fleshless spirit was lying under the ground. A fleshless name. The name of justice.

'Justice that no one needs,' whispered Lev.

At first he carried on arguing with the men who wandered

into the barber's, but he soon realized that it was pointless. One stranger cut short his outpourings with an impatient gesture and said:

'I know the rest: he died and was buried hugging a football. People don't bear grudges. Short back and sides, please. No cologne.'

When, just for a laugh, he stole an apple at the market and nobody noticed – although everyone, including the seller, had seen – Lev realized that he really had died.

He boarded up his front door, closed the shutters and grew a beard. He got a job at the barber's under a different name and ceased paying attention to the ever more complicated history of the fateful football match whose outcome was decided by a penalty: 'unfair' deemed some, 'fair' said others. As the years passed, more and more people took the side of the referee. The bearded barber would nod his head and agree with everyone, but he kept well out of any arguments: 'I don't understand a thing about football. When was it anyway? Five, six years ago? Straight at the temples or slanted?' 'Might even be ten,' old men nodded pensively.

On Sundays he headed off to the cemetery and sat for a long while on the bench by the grave, gazing at the hazy photograph of a cheerful referee with a flat whistle on a fatty chest. Sometimes he brought along a can of paint, or a hammer and some nails. The grave was well tended. His daughter came once a year from a neighbouring town and never failed to visit the cemetery with her husband and children. She'd thank the kind man who looked after her dad's grave, and slipped him a rouble or two. Black Beard would pour out a glass of vodka. 'Let's drink to Lev, a good man. Refs like him come along once in a lifetime. And that penalty – did you hear? – he was right, you know.' They drank to the memory of Lev.

From the cemetery, Lev would walk to the stadium. The fence had long since been pulled down, the posts had rotted and collapsed, the changing-room had been filched brick by brick. Cows and geese wandered about on the lawn.

In the evenings he sat till late in the barber's in front of the bottomless mirror, occasionally topping up a measuring-glass from a little bottle of pure alcohol which he hid from the cleaner in a drawer with his equipment. He drank until the greenish depths of the mirror yielded up the faces of the footballers, the wide-open mouths of the spectators and the happy eyes of the kids, greeting the ref with their ecstatic refrain: 'Off! Off!'

He suffered a heart attack. At the hospital he revealed his real name to Doctor Sheberstov.

'Doctor, I died before death,' he said. 'I'm lonely.'

He spoke about his daily fare: soup in which a bay leaf floated around, torn from the massive wreath once presented to him by the players and fans.

'We all die before death,' Sheberstov moralized. 'What's a name? Just a sound.'

'But the name's all that's left on the tombstone,' Lev objected, dutifully swallowing a pill.

Leaving the hospital, he met Kolka the Camel in the White Canteen. Camel was arm in arm with the green drink-devil who'd been keeping him company for several years now. It was a Saturday and Camel was fuming uncontrollably against whoever had broken the universal law by cancelling football on Sundays.

'It's all Klein's fault,' Kolka concluded. 'If he hadn't been so pig-headed, if there hadn't been a penalty . . .'

'Not true,' Lev declared. 'Klein wasn't to blame.'

'Then it's the ref,' Kolka insisted, egged on by the green devil. 'Must be someone's fault, there's no football any more.'

'It's not the ref's fault either,' said Lev, standing his ground.

Totally confused, Camel let rip with every insult in the book. And that's when Name of Lev summoned him to a duel.

The next day, the little town was stirred by the raucous clamour of the brass band, and thousands hurried off to the stadium. The livestock was chased off the pitch and new goalposts were fixed. Name of Lev took up position between them, wearing a black shirt with a snow-white turn-down collar, black shorts and socks. The players clustered in the penalty box: pot-bellied Yashka the Basher; rubbery Katso and his four sons; the eternally masticating and far from young Young Boot-Licker, son of Old Boot-Licker; rusty-toothed Sergei Try-Hard; Kolka the Camel, arm-in-arm with his devil friend, who was throwing dark looks at Black Beard and Sergeant; Tolik, who was entertaining the public with a new trick: touching his ear lobes with the tip of his tongue; Aliment and Ivan Studentsov . . . Yes, they had accepted Lev's condition: if even one player scored a single goal, the barber-ref would confess his guilt to all, and the charge of cheating would be lifted from Cuddly Klein.

Yashka the Basher was the first to try. His crafty shot was spinning low into the left corner, but Lev just lazily stuck out a leg. No goal. Katso fired a cannonball at the goalie's chest, but Lev caught it in his palms and sent it back to the spot for Young Boot-Licker. But neither Boot-Licker nor Black Beard nor Sergeant nor Sergei Try-Hard nor Tolik nor Aliment (wearing his precious boot with a secret nail in the sole) nor Ivan Studentsov could pierce the goalie's defences. Name of Lev agreed that anyone who wanted to could have a go for Cuddly Klein. There were plenty of volunteers. Gramp Mukhanov stepped up to shoot, as did Sindbad the Sailor, still clutching her string bag full of empties; Longjohn had a whack, and so did Battle-Axe, flying at the ball like a cock at a hen, and the policeman Lyosha Leontyev, and the Prosecutor, and Doctor Sheberstov, and the green devil, trying hard to make Lev look the other way. They even let me have a pop, but to no avail. No one could score, and Lev didn't even break sweat; he just got paler and paler. So then Kolka the Camel took the red band off his right leg and shot. The ball froze in Lev's hands.

Lev suddenly sank to the ground, toppled over on his side and lay there with a smile on his lips.

He was dead.

'So who won?' Katso asked in a whisper.

'We did,' croaked Camel. 'And him.'

He was buried with a ball in his hands, wearing his ref's uniform and a whistle on his fatty chest. Half Pint and Quarter Pint had never played *On the Hills of Manchuria* and *The Waves of the Amur* as harmoniously and as movingly as they did then. The entire town accompanied the deceased to the cemetery. His grave was the eighth on the left at the very top of Seventh Hill. His tombstone was inscribed: *Name of Lev. Lev Isaakovich Regelson. Barber.* No date of birth, no year of death, as if a fleshless spirit was lying under the ground, kin to a fleshless law: the sun rises in the east, the Prosecutor doesn't drink, Sundays are for football . . .

My Brothers the Larks

Quarter Pint dreamed of solitude all his life. Among people he felt embarrassed, lost. He'd tuck himself away in a corner or behind someone's back, just so long as he wasn't noticed and teased for his ridiculous appearance, all tufts and clumps. It was as if his head had been moulded out of plasticine by a ham-fisted, fidgety child who'd dropped his work halfway through, leaving a bumpy lump with fingerprints all over it. The hairs on his head sprouted in bunches, bushes and taper-ing strands, refusing to come together in a pleasing form. It all started when young Quarter Pint dreamed of a beard and an abundant moustache; all he got was birch twigs and a tail – and even that was straggly and tatty.

After his mother died, the person who scared Quarter Pint the most was his father, for whom the five-year-old layabout, forever hiding in a corner to dream or read, was a mere nuisance. His dad led a group of vodka-sodden musicians who performed at weddings, funerals and at half time at soccer matches. To give his son something to do, Half Pint dragged home a large drum and sat Quarter Pint down for a lesson: 'Hit the thing!' This lesson was more than the neighbours could stand, so dad got in the habit of sending his boy out into the garden every day, under the old apple tree, where a petrified Quarter Pint, screwing his face up in terror and comically shaking his shaggy mop, whacked the taut belly of the drum with his wooden mallet until he could no longer think straight. He hit it and hit it, just to calm his father down: for the minute Half Pint could no longer hear the blows from the garden, he was out like a shot to pummel his son. Eventually the neighbours also got used to the drum-beats, like to the thudding of their hearts. But the noise distracted Quarter Pint from his dreams.

Endless drumming sessions led to aches in his back and joints. His dad wasn't against the odd break: 'But ten minutes and no more!' So Quarter Pint would collapse onto the turf, bend over and thrash around epileptically, hoping that acrobatics would lessen the pain. He plaited his legs, folded his arms behind his back and stuck his nose under his armpit. Flipping over onto his front, he touched his ears with his heels. Lying on his side, he threw one leg over his neck. Then, for several minutes, he'd lie stock-still, experiencing the bliss of repose.

When Half Pint saw him one day, lying motionless in an unnatural posture, he panicked. Quarter Pint himself was so scared he lost the ability to speak, and screwed up his eyes so tightly in anticipation of a blow that his eyelids convulsed. But his dad didn't touch him. Instead, he crept out of the garden on tiptoe and made for the hospital. 'Catatonic,' said Doctor Sheberstov. 'Call it life, my friend.' Which did nothing to soothe tipsy Half Pint.

As for Quarter Pint, he rejoiced at discovering his father's fear of unnatural postures and from that day, if he suddenly felt like being on his own for a while, he was ready to twist himself into shapes that could appear only in a mad geometer's delirium. Lengthy training sessions taught him to turn his joints inside out, and his postures acquired an entirely natural appearance. He only had to freeze in a figure of eight and he'd immediately be left in peace to relish his solitude and to dream unconstrained. He understood now: freedom is unnaturalness.

He dreamed of winning the lottery. Heart thumping, he listened to stories about lucky so-and-so's who'd been given a lottery ticket as change at the bakery and had wound up – 'Who'd have thought it?' – as owners of a car, a woollen blanket or a fountain pen. Yesterday a man like any other, today chosen by chance to outfox the Law. The lottery became a symbol of freedom for Quarter Pint, cutting man loose from the Law's rusty chains. Who'd have thought it, and suddenly. Oh, that 'suddenly'! No, Quarter Pint wouldn't have taken a car, a blanket or even a fountain pen. He'd have taken his prize in cash and bought something totally useless: that's what freedom was for. A crystal vase. A handkerchief. A songbird. Although to buy a bird for money would mean doing a deal with the Law. No, he wouldn't buy a bird.

Birds made him envious and excited, as did everything which stepped even an inch outside the frame into which his dad was intent on pummelling him. The boy was jealous of anyone who allowed themselves to wear their shirts open-necked, comb their hair with their fingers, go to bed after ten, hurl stones at windows or peek at women in the bathhouse on Fridays. But people, large animals and objects were all subject to the laws set down by his father, he who could punish a dog or shatter a pesky chair. Birds were different: they could fly. Small, unclean, brainless, a bunch of fragile little bones, a handful of feathers, a thimbleful of blood. Perhaps, Quarter Pint mused, other animals had also flown in antiquity, maybe even people: it's no accident that sometimes they dream of doing so.

Everyone knows that the ability to speak resides in the tongue: cut it out and you'll only be able to make animal noises like Aphinogen, Quarter Pint's neighbour, whose tongue had been ripped out by shrapnel at the front and had been sewn back on, only the wrong way round. The old geezer couldn't speak. Birds too, then, must have an organ enabling them to fly. But Quarter Pint was unable to discover it, however many of them he dissected into ribbons and threads with the aid of a razor. He found bones, a blue-grey filmy substance, and intestines; that was all.

When Quarter Pint first saw an X-ray of his own thorax, the revelation shook him to the core: man is empty. And although Madame Citrinyak, the radiologist who resembled a wrinkled monkey, explained to him that this was not so, Quarter Pint stuck to his guns. Man is empty. He consists of airy cavities filled by bluish-white mist in which the half-transparent heart and liver float freely alongside the ribs and the grey wadding of the lungs. Quarter Pint set about gathering his X-rays and quickly acquired an entire collection. Doctor Citrinyak would occasionally yield to his insistent requests and take an extra image of his bumpy head or of one of his hands. X-rays hung on threads all around

Quarter Pint's room – on the lampshade and windows, the walls and the door of his wardrobe – swaying in the draughty air and attesting to the fact that the ability to fly had been given to man from the earliest times; now it had merely dissolved through his organism.

When the lad grew older and stronger, his dad brought him into the band. Quarter Pint beat his drum at funerals and at half time, tossing his bumpy head and gazing sorrowfully at the celebrations of life and death. Like his dad, he started boozing, but he got drunk quickly and clumsily, and his fellow drinkers felt an irresistible urge to clobber his face in. Not for any particular reason. Just because.

Like his father, he got into the habit of calling on the famous town whore, Zoika the butcher, whose terrifying female strength came from a diet of raw beef. Zoika was a slaughter-woman at the meat factory and liked to finish off the punier pigs by holding them by their hind legs and slamming them against the ground. Her appetite for vodka and men was insatiable, and her uncontrollable and evil tongue struck fear into all. Quarter Pint was the only man she left alone, perhaps because there was nothing to be said about him. He demanded nothing from women, and could sit in a corner of her room all evening without saying a word, staring ahead at a fixed point. Here people didn't pester him with questions, didn't ask why he sat in silence, or what he was going to do tomorrow. Zoika cooked, did the laundry, washed her hair or got drunk on her own, forgetting all about Quarter Pint.

But sometimes he broke the silence with a question:

'What do you dream about, Zoika?'

Zoika would tear her eyes away from her little finger, which according to her level of intoxication would double or turn into a monstrous member with a crooked nail (this particularly amused her), and give a detailed answer:

'No one's ever said to me: I love you, Zoika. Understand?' She lifted her hand to silence him. 'So here's me thinking: if some guy like that did turn up and said, "Zoika, I love you" – oh!' Her lips curled sensuously. 'I'd gob all over his face! And again! Then I'd give him one right there.' She showed him where. 'And again! Just like that! Then I'd throw him head-first into the shit and rub him in it.'

Quarter Pint would nod pensively.

He kept a bird in a cage at her place. She was amazed when she first saw it.

'What d'you want that for?'

'I just want it.' Quarter Pint carefully picked up the tiny bird made of feathers, iron and wire. 'I've been making it for three years now. It's done my eyes in. Like it's alive.'

'But what for?' Zoika persisted, studying the toy curiously.

'I want it to be like a real one. I want it to fly.'

'And if it does fly? It won't have any nestlings. It'll fly a bit and rust over, the pigeons will crap on it, it'll fall in the gutter and end of story. God makes thousands of them every day without asking you first, and they fly all right, they have nestlings.'

Quarter Pint nodded gloomily.

'Got to dream about something.'

'And there's you saying you hate your dad! You're his spitting image. Anyway, where'll you find a soul for it? Without a soul it's just a corpse, better if it didn't exist at all. Some Einstein you are!'

But there was no deterring Quarter Pint, even though he couldn't explain to himself why he was making a bird.

He dreamed of birds and talked to them. The first problem he came across was how to address them. 'Lads', 'blokes' 'mates', 'chicks' – none of these names were any good. 'Brothers?' Better, but not all birds answered to that, not all of them liked it. 'Brother ravens' – doesn't work, does it? Who'd say that? 'Brother ravens' is OK, but that's about it. 'Brother sparrows' – iffy. But 'my brothers the larks' didn't sound bad at all. Almost had a ring to it.

His dreams of birds were joyous ones. He flew and talked to them with words that he would be ashamed of using in everyday life. Like 'love', for example. Waking up was loathsome, bitter. The weight of his own body humiliated him.

'You're unhappy,' said Zoika after hearing out his rambling thoughts. 'Or else you're just normal: here's no place for happy people . . .'

'What, you mean no one's happy?'

'I mean no one should be,' insisted Zoika. 'Find one happy person and the world will fall to bits.'

Quarter Pint got older, played the drum, drank clumsily, bought lottery tickets. He was forty when he finally finished his bird-toy. He chatted to it, sang, shouted, pleaded with it, spent hours breathing into its gaping beak. It was no use: it didn't fly. Nor, he realized, would it ever. Placing the box on the shelf next to the plush hare and the cat-shaped glazed moneybox, he went on a drinking spree. A few days later he won a fridge in the lottery, but this didn't cheer him up at all. He sold it and organized a booze-up with the money. His dad had a few too many and laid into Zoika. In a sudden fit of cockiness, Quarter Pint weighed in for the worthless tart. Livid, Half Pint beat up the pair of them. Zoika came to her senses first. Hearing Quarter Pint's drunken whines from the far corner, she flew into a rage and hurled herself on him. She pounded him until he started choking blood. Then she collapsed onto her bed and sank into a sleep so heavy it was no longer hers. Quarter Pint grabbed the box with the bird and, groaning and swaying, made for home. In his room, he set the box on the window-sill, lay down, cast his gaze around his dingy surroundings, where his innards hung on threads, and died, having managed to take up such a fantastically unnatural pose that even after death he wouldn't be touched, even then he'd be left alone. And when these eyes too were closed and there was no one left to see, the bird found its way out of the cage, whistled, flapped its wings and flew away.

At his burial, Battle-Axe announced out of the blue:

'If there is a God, then there must also be a Quarter Pint.'

Afterwards these words were all that people remembered. Quarter Pint was forgotten.

Porcelain Feet

The shoe shop was located on the town's central and only square, which was paved with blue-grey cobblestones and crossed on rare sunny days by the shadow of the spireless Protestant church, moving as slowly as the hour hand on a clock-face. Before falling on the flat roof of the stall that sold beer, moist cigarettes and sandwiches filled with dry, curled-up slices of sausage resembling rotten autumn leaves, the shadow floated majestically into the shoe-shop window, which was graced by two female porcelain feet in high heels. Another dozen such feet – white, yellow and pink – were displayed inside the shop, which was thick with the smell of leather, polish and *Amphora* tobacco from the pipe of the shopkeeper, Captain Lyosha. His face, covered in a white felt beard, could only ever be seen by the customers through a veil of blueish aromatic smoke. When people asked how he'd come by those legs, he'd reply: 'Found 'em knocking about in the storeroom . . .'

Even though it was the only shoe shop in town, the women didn't much like looking in there. All because of those white porcelain shoes in the corner, on the plywood stand covered in crimson plush. There'd been plenty of customers willing to try the shoes on, but in thirty years they'd never fitted anyone quite right, and the women, naturally enough, felt somewhat piqued. After failing at the first attempt, the renowned beauty Nina Logunova soaked her feet for three days in boiling water mixed with vodka and glycerine, then kept them in boiling Vaseline for another three, until they became so soft they could pass painlessly through a keyhole. But in the end even she was only just able to squeeze into the porcelain shoes; as for taking a step or two, that was out of the question.

'So what kind of feet do you need, then?' Nina asked in a tizz. 'Shapely ones? Bent ones? Fat ones? Thin ones?'

'Beautiful ones,' Captain Lyosha answered with sadness. 'But don't ask me what that means.'

Gazing enraptured at some beauty or other sailing down Seventh Street on her way to the disco, men would smack their lips and say: 'Like she's wearing porcelain shoes!' Captain Lyosha would merely grunt: 'Right, as if . . .'

Women disliked him. Word went round that the ageing loner, pretending to clean his shop in the evenings, didn't just wipe the porcelain shoes with a cloth, but stroked, caressed and almost – ugh! – kissed them.

A bachelor, he lived in a small flat on Linden Street above the vegetable shop. The shop assistant Figura (who owed her nickname to her perfectly cubic figure, her cubic chest and cubic legs, and to the fact that she wasted the shop's vegetables – spuds and carrots – by chiselling funny figurines out of them, then displaying them in the window) occasionally shared Captain Lyosha's lonely evenings. Lyosha had once been a sailor on a trawler, but an accident had left him lame and he was sent ashore. He shunned other people's company but could occasionally be seen drinking on his own. Figura said he kept a picture of his former wife at home: an indescribable beauty. The local connoisseurs of the soul were all set to weave a tear-jerking tale of love and betrayal when Kolka the Camel, called over by Lyosha to help with repairs, recognized Marilyn Monroe in the photo and the rumour died at birth.

That day, eighteen-year-old Liza Stoletova ended up in the shoe shop quite by chance: a stormy summer shower had driven her into Captain Lyosha's emporium. The Captain puffed on his pipe, glanced sleepily at the plain girl in an old print dress, and lowered his eyelids again, sinking back into sleep or memories (one and the same thing). Perhaps that was why the meaning of Liza's question took a while to get through to him. He blinked, coughed his lungs out and, waving the smoke away with his hand, lurched towards her so abruptly that his fragile little stool cracked beneath him.

'You mean, you want . . .'

'So others can but not me?'

Captain Lyosha's gaze shifted from her face, where a smile

had lost out to fear, to her feet in their one-rouble sandals, where her toes poked out with grimy nails that had been artlessly nibbled at with tailor's scissors. It was just those toes which for whatever reason provoked a fit of hilarity in Captain Lyosha.

'Blaze away,' he said through his laughter. 'You only live once!'

'Or never!' laughed Liza.

Captain Lyosha barely had time to raise his hand to his face to wipe away a tear brought on by mirth before Liza was standing before him in the porcelain shoes.

'Try walking round a bit,' Lyosha whispered. Then he burst into a full-throated yell: 'Walk, I'm telling you!'

Liza took a step, turned around and, after executing several swift and agile dance moves, stopped in front of Captain Lyosha, smiling expectantly.

'Again,' he asked in a hoarse whisper. 'Again . . . please . . .'

In less than an hour an enormous crowd had gathered on the square outside the shop. Ignoring the rain, the astonished onlookers gazed in silence at the Cinderwench in her high-heeled porcelain shoes. No one could understand: what was it about this plain-looking girl? Why did the shoes fit her of all people? Feet like any others, a figure like any other, a face you'd never remember unless you saw it at least three times . . .

So what had taken place? What had happened? Something important, of that there could be no doubt in anyone's mind.

'What sort of feet has she got then?' asked Nina Logunova to break the silence. She was as perplexed as she was annoyed. 'Suppose you think they're beautiful?'

'They're porcelain feet,' Captain Lyosha announced after a little consideration.

Taking great care, he helped Liza back into her shoes and said:

'I'll give them to you on your wedding day.'

'Agreed,' nodded Liza.

No one so much as thought of making a sneering comment about the prospect of yesterday's Cinderwench getting married.

'Ah, if only I was eighteen again!' sighed Gramophone. 'I'd also . . .'

But what that 'also' was she didn't say.

'If granny had a dick, she'd be granddad,' Gramp Mukhanov uttered profoundly, turning his back on Gramophone. 'Just think: porcelain feet . . .'

Half a year later Liza got married to a decent chap. Captain Lyosha kept his word: on the day of the wedding he solemnly presented Liza with the promised gift. Radiant Liza, yet more shapely and beautiful in her porcelain shoes, gave the first waltz by unanimous request to lame Captain Lyosha.

Seven years later, Captain Lyosha died. He was found in the shoe shop with a burnt-out pipe clenched between his teeth and surrounded by beautiful porcelain feet, white, yellow and pink . . .

By then Liza was a mother of two. She'd done her accountancy training and got a job at the margarine factory where her husband Ivan had worked his way up to be the boss of the electrical section. Her legs had become chubby, gelatinous and rippled with fat veins like washing lines. But each year on her wedding anniversary, she'd slip the same porcelain shoes on her yellow, now hopelessly calloused size six feet. Heaven knows how she managed, but once a year she did, and every time her husband would remember how Captain Lyosha had called them porcelain feet, although no one knew what porcelain feet were, just as no one knows what beauty is, or love, or death . . .

Theme of the Bull,
Theme of the Lion

The rain was nipping at his heels and whenever the man stopped it hung behind him like a rustling silver curtain, washing the bloodstains off the road. After pausing for breath, the man continued on his way, slowly, staggering, eyes fixed straight ahead. He was spotted near the Garage; on the last bridge; opposite the White Canteen. He was seen resting for a while, leaning against the wall of the barber's – Name of Lev switched off the clipper, lowered a moist palm onto his client's half-cropped crown and, with infinite sadness in his mind, said: 'With all this rain, I've already forgotten when I last ate ripe tomatoes' – but no one, of course, took any notice of the man who made for the square with faltering steps. In the middle of the square he fell on his back, arms flung wide. Returning from fishing, Gramp Mukhanov stopped dead in his tracks and, shielding his eyes, gazed at the gaping wound in the stranger's chest. Who knows how long he'd have stood there like that had it not been for the lady chemist, whose scream caused a commotion among those sitting on the benches under the chestnut trees. Two lads from Irus' gang tore off to get Lyosha Leontyev. But no sooner had they dived into the elder thickets – the start of the quickest route via the stadium to Seventh Street – than rain lashed down on the square. People stood in silence around the dead man and watched as the streaming rain wiped the bloody wound off his chest, then the hairs off his head, and a little later his eyes and lips. By the time the policeman came hurtling up on his motorbike, the rain had abated and was just drumming cheerfully on the shiny-clean flat stones where a corpse had been lying only ten minutes before.

After hearing out Irus' muddled explanations, Lyosha fastened his eyes on Gramp Mukhanov.

'Was it you who thought up all this crap?'

Gramp threw back his head and his eyes suddenly took on a sentient expression. With a great effort he suppressed his sense of hurt and anger, puffed vigorously on his venomous cigarette stuffed with top-quality Georgian tea, and, smiling strangely, pointed to somewhere behind Leontyev's back:

'So what kind of crap is that, then?'

An enormous white bull with gold horns was approaching the square from the direction of the river, and on it was mounted the most beautiful woman in the world. Strutting alongside the bull was a red lion, which the woman was leading on a leash.

Thus did the Goddess enter the little town.

She took her lodgings in the hotel on the other side of the river, in a tiny room with a round little window looking out onto the lake. Her sudden appearance in this labyrinth of dark corridors reeking of mothballs, fried onion, paraffin and boiled potatoes scared the wits out of Zoika. Hearing footsteps, she'd come out of the kitchen wiping her hands on her oilskin apron, and stood rooted to the spot on seeing the most beautiful woman in the world with a lion on a leash. But the Goddess, paying no attention whatsoever to Zoika's crazed howls, skipped up the stairs to the first floor and disappeared into her room.

The guest in the next room woke up and clasped both his hands to his chest, trying to keep his heart from bursting out of his body. Jumping out of bed, he opened the window and saw a white bull with gold horns grazing peacefully down below. The man lit a cigarette. His wandering gaze lingered on the picture that covered almost the entire wall above the bed: a buxom girl in a white cap was clipping roses that resembled cabbage heads with a huge pair of scissors; a young man, leaning his elbows gracefully on a fence, was standing nearby with a wicker-basket full of bright red apples. But now neither girl nor boy was left on the canvas: just some legs sticking out of the bushes, jerking rhythmically. Unable to understand what was happening to him, the man sank with a groan to the cool floor. He suddenly raised his head: the naked buxom girl was beckoning to him, and two rose petals clung to her left

86

breast. As he was losing consciousness, the guest thought: 'Drinking cologne can seriously damage your health.'

Exposing his back to the long-awaited sun, Sweet-Wrapper rested his head on his arms and closed his eyes in bliss. Suddenly some kind of force lifted him about twenty centimetres above the ground. Sweet-Wrapper looked around in bewilderment, and there and then the most beautiful woman in the world emerged from the osier thickets with her dress over her shoulder – there was nothing else on her. She walked ceremoniously past the frozen Sweet-Wrapper and vanished behind the sheds. Her footprints, clearly marked on the sandy path, exuded an exciting aroma.

With a howl, Sweet-Wrapper tore after her across the rubbish dump, which was littered with shards of broken bottles and scraps of barbed wire. He bounded up to the first floor, leaving a trail of blood in his wake, and stopped in front of a door inscribed with an obscenity. He knocked and the door opened. The red lion gave a restrained roar. But Sweet-Wrapper, squealing faintly, just shifted from foot to foot on the threshold, never taking his eyes off the golden drop on the Goddess's stomach, which on other women is called the belly button. Only when the lion rose with a growl and shattered the massive ashtray on the window-sill with his tail, did Sweet-Wrapper rush to the door opposite and lock himself in the toilet.

Zoika had taken to her bed in a fit of unquenched fury; even her teeth had started aching. But the second she heard a strange noise from the first floor, she was up in a flash. The noise was coming from the toilet, but no matter how closely Zoika listened, she just couldn't work out what was going on in there. Tossing all notions of etiquette aside, she smashed in the door with a mighty kick and stood on the threshold, hands on hips. The hotel toilet was a miracle of design and construction: exceptionally narrow and long, the room had a high ceiling and a teeny little lavatory pan by the far wall, seated on which a person felt his insignificance with particular acuteness. Here a man felt no less comfortable than in a prison cell. The effect was crowned by the deafening roar of the water as it was released any old how down into the toilet, where it twisted about in a howling maelstrom, spitting water and excrement to all sides, before streaming down the pipes with a hollow, mournful rumble. Guests left the toilet with the firm intention never to write poetry and with no illusions whatsoever as to their place in the real world. In the dim light of a weak little bulb, Zoika made out a person on all fours by the far wall. She shrieked, leapt out into the corridor and only just had time to press on the door with all her weight before it shook from a heavy blow. Another quickly followed. Taking advantage of the pause, Zoika took her keys from her pocket and locked the toilet.

Trying not to make any noise, she slipped out of the hotel and didn't catch her breath until she was on the new bridge. In the midday heat of July, the red-brick hotel building, shaded by ginkgo branches, seemed gloomier than ever.

'They've all gone bonkers,' Zoika moaned. 'And this is only the start of it!'

Men gathered in the Red and White canteens, drank beer and talked of nothing but the Goddess. Even the old fogies sitting on the steps to the savings bank entered into spirited debate of the stranger's merits. The idiot Vita Pea-Head sped along the streets on his moped and shouted something so incomprehensible that many fancied they were hearing a hymn to the Goddess.

Cats howled without pause. Dogs hungrily rubbed their noses in the tracks left by the Goddess on the asphalt and stones, and chased tiny Phiz, who, yelping pitifully, tried to scamper away from the befuddled mutts. She hid under Battle-Axe's porch, where Grandpa was living out his days. He was the oldest dog in town and he'd kept himself going for the last thirty years on sour milk and ground radish; Battle-Axe put eggs under him and chicks hatched right on time in the middle of winter. Anyway, it was Grandpa who, driving Phiz into a state of indescribable astonishment, got what the other dogs had been pestering her for so assiduously.

A brown horned beast, which turned out to be a bull,

caught sight of a heifer running past and sprang out from the butcher's shop-sign. But it could only offer the red-haired virgin a Platonic relationship: in accordance with the strict instructions of the trading authorities, the artist had depicted the bull without its organs of reproduction.

Arkasha and Natasha, two dusty plaster mannequins from the dressmaker's above the barber's, suddenly leapt from their positions and started dancing to the music of Tchaikovsky on the radio. After a spin around the cramped shop, they danced out onto the street and then across the square towards the hotel. Plaster busts rushed out after them from *Clothes*, and plaster legs from *Shoes*.

Word suddenly got round that Andrei the Photographer had managed to take a picture of the Goddess. Knocking over tables, chairs, beer mugs and fences, the men raced over to *The Three Palm Trees*, the photo studio with a colourful sign showing three exotic plants on the shore of a violet sea. Without batting an eyelid, Andrei demanded twenty-five roubles per photo, but that didn't stop anyone; in less than an hour the first lucky customers had become the owners of soggy pieces of cardboard depicting the most beautiful woman in the world mounted on a white bull. Meanwhile the crowd outside *The Three Palm Trees* was growing and buzzing menacingly, and the first battered brawlers were being led off into the shade, smearing blood all over their faces.

The air thickened and dark clouds closed out the sky, yet the storm was slow in coming. Dancing broke out instead.

After being empty all summer, the hall on the ground floor of the hotel was opened specially for the occasion. The dust was swept off the windows and chandeliers, which hung in clusters from the ceiling beams, and three thousand one hundred and seventy-three records were lugged into the hall.

'What's all this?' exclaimed Evdokia when she saw the mountain of black records next to the gramophone on the stage. 'Dancing till the second coming, are you?'

It wasn't yet dark outside when the hall burst alight and hordes of people, dressed up to the nines, charged towards the little table at which Evdokia was sitting. She sold all the tickets in the twinkling of an eye and, unable to bear the stuffiness in the hall any longer, just chucked it all in, leaving the ticketless on an equal footing with the owners of blue scraps of paper marked with the black stamp – *Dances*.

The hall couldn't hold everyone so people crowded outside, sipping cheap wine as they waited for the Goddess and smoking to stop themselves shaking. No one doubted that she'd come to the dance.

Raphael the Pigeon-Fancier was being pressed against the iron rails of the porch. He looked up at the sky, where thousands of his pigeons were calling to one another, took a deep breath and suddenly shot forwards and up. A second later, without a clue how he'd managed it, he found himself in the hotel corridor. The noise outside subsided.

His heart pounding, Raphael stepped onto the staircase, soundlessly repeating a line of verse that had suddenly come to mind:

'There dwells the sweet-tongued nymph with sunlight hair . . .'

Lightning blazed in the distance, but people didn't hear the thunder: Raphael the Pigeon-Fancier had appeared on the porch, arm in arm with the most beautiful woman in the world. They passed through the parted crowd and entered the hall.

'What is it she smells of?' Andrei the Photographer muttered pensively. 'Something really . . .' He clicked his fingers and smacked his lips.

'Shit!' Evdokia snarled. 'Pig shit! Mark my words . . .'

But at this point the music thundered into life.

The Goddess gave the first dance to Raphael the Pigeon-Fancier, who suddenly realized that he would never see or speak again. Nor did he come to his senses when the music stopped and he was shoved away from his partner and out of the hall. Infinitely lonely and happy, he wandered down deserted streets, and his pigeons rustled their wings above him. Muttering, 'There dwells the sweet-tongued nymph with sunlight hair . . .', he climbed up a pigeon-fouled staircase, which spiralled like a corkscrew into the hollow gloom and brought him out onto the roof of the water-tower. For days on end he used to observe pigeons in flight from here and compose poetry, but he was in no mood for that now. One look at the scaly ripples of the tiled roofs, at the cobbled roads, at the tarred roofs of the sheds at the foot of the tower, where pigs romped around and grunted, at the little town unexpectedly wrested from the dark by a flash of lightning, and the Pigeon-Fancier's eyes filled with tears. Sensing that his heart was about to burst any second from his chest, he took a deep breath and, with a smile of utter exhaustion on his face, stepped out into the pigshit-smelling void.

With the disappearance of Raphael the Pigeon-Fancier, there was an unexpected change in the mood of the men, even though none of them noticed it: many lost all self-control and whispered in their partners' ears indecencies intended for the most beautiful woman in the world. Lads from Irus' crew sauntered around the hall, 'accidentally' shoving the dancers. For the moment, though, no one was rising to their bait.

A cloud of tobacco smoke hung overhead. Marinochka asked Garlic to open the window. He clambered onto the window-sill and tried to pull out the rusty latch, but he wasn't able to, so he kicked out the window and its frame in fury, sending them crashing down on the idlers assembled outside. The other windows flew out noisily – that was Irus' lads finishing off Garlic's work.

Noticing that the most beautiful woman in the world had made for the toilet, Shurka pulled on her white cotton gloves and dashed over. Dulya and She-Bear hurried after her. As soon as the Goddess emerged from the toilet, Shurka grabbed her by the hair – then, her gaze clouding over, she fell on Dulya, toppling her into a puddle of urine sprinkled with bleaching powder. The Goddess had vanished.

'Bitch!' Dulya hissed. 'You're always making a mess!'

Clenching her teeth, she thumped Shurka full in the stomach. Her friend writhed about on the floor, but no sooner did Dulya try getting up than Shurka dealt her a hefty kick in the kidneys. Dulya tumbled onto her back, her hair fanned out over the stinking puddle and Shurka, snarling viciously, trampled all over it. She-Bear suddenly leapt out of the cubicle where the Goddess had been and sent Shurka flying over to the sink with a kick on the bum. Then, waving her massive arms towards the ceiling, she shouted ecstatically:

'Look, Shurka! She pisses perfume!'

Irus' lads were already brawling behind the stage, while he, tossing the dyed locks with which he tried to cover his premature bald patch, was breathlessly telling Villiput and Garlic yet again about his dance with the most beautiful woman in the world: he'd got an electric shock when she placed her hand on his shoulder.

Flying past him in the dance, Irus' wife playfully rapped him on his balding crown with her fan. He reacted instantly, but his blow fell on Arkasha. Shoving Natasha aside, the mannequin grabbed a knife from under his shoddily tacked together waistcoat and threw himself at the offender. Irus leapt back and a knife flashed in his hand, too. But it wasn't the pocket-knife he usually carried around: this was heavier, with a long, broad forged blade and a fanciful bone handle in the shape of a dragon with red stones for eyes. Irus had no time to register his surprise: Arkasha was on him in a blind frenzy. In the incredible crush, the dancers had nowhere to go and, eyes tightly shut, they flew between the brawlers, miraculously eluding the deadly steel. The music was blaring so loudly that dust and bird droppings showered down from the beams. Fights broke out all over the place. Yelling wildly and brandishing knives that had appeared heaven knows how, everyone tore around in a circle to the music . . . Unable to restrain himself, Kolya-Mikolai ripped off Dulya's dress, which reeked of urine and bleaching powder, and threw the hysterically guffawing girl to the floor. A minute later, there was no telling who was Kolya-Mikolai and who Dulya: the dancers laughed as they trampled a bloody pancake in the middle of which flickered four eyes, two green and two

black. She-Bear was being raped on stage, and with every upward thrust record fragments flew out from under her monumental bum into the hall. Crushed on all sides and with a knife in his stomach, Garlic was trying in vain to force his way out of the crowd. The Goddess was flying in the arms of a skeleton whispering gallant obscenities in her ear. Another skeleton, wearing a broad-rimmed hat and a scarlet coat, sneaked a hand under Shurka's skirt during the whirl, winking at Marinochka as he did so. A black giant with twisted horns on his head suddenly grabbed Marinochka by the legs and, swinging her around like a club, did the squatting dance. Karen sank his teeth into one of the Goddess's legs and the Goddess had her work cut out freeing herself from the insane muscle man. Karen was left holding a shoe and wolfed it down straightaway. V P cut off his member with an enormous curved knife, and shouting 'Beauty will save the world!' hurled it at the Goddess's feet. Bob and Frolik got down on all fours and scurried among the dancers, grunting. Their example was followed by another ninety-seven men, and two women who'd secretly shaved their legs. In the unbearable heat, sweaty women with their hair let down were spinning to the music, embracing blood-drenched men, squealing pigs, mannequins and skeletons. Only one-hundred-year-old Merry Gertrude jumped up and down on the spot by the stage, monotonously yelling: '*Seid umschlungen, Millionen!*'*
Thousands of pigeons swirled in the thick smoke overhead, blocking out the light and shedding feathers and droppings on the dancers. Suddenly a white bull with gold horns appeared in the middle of the hall. He bellowed loudly and streams of icy water mixed with excrement gushed down from the ceiling: that was Sweet-Wrapper, who'd decided to get out of the toilet come what may and had broken through the floor, sending the lavatory pan crashing down and releasing the water.

The ice shower sobered everyone up in a flash. Women hurried to cover their nakedness, men inspected their

---

* Be embraced, ye millions. (Schiller, *Ode to Joy*)

bloodied knives in perplexity. Pigs pressed themselves shyly against the walls.

'It's all her doing, the bitch!' Shurka suddenly howled, crying from shame and pain. 'It's her! Her!'

Looking around in confusion, the Goddess stepped back towards the stage. There wasn't a single stain or scratch on her body.

'It's her!' shouted the women. 'Her!'

The men surrounded the most beautiful woman in the world, now curled up into a ball.

At this point the bull bellowed a second time, the red lion appeared on the threshold, and Vita Pea-Head flew in on his roaring moped through the knocked-out window. The crowd gave way in terror. Vita grabbed the Goddess and, stepping on the gas, hurtled out of the hall, hitting the lion's ear and vodka-glazed Evdokia with his front wheel.

The bull bellowed for a third time. Lightning flashed, the lion leapt into the crowd, and all was plunged into darkness – growling, howling, wailing, squealing, clanging, crackling, grunting darkness.

Clinging to the walls, Evdokia struggled out of the hall, shut the doors, hung a heavy padlock on them and shakily set off home, picking up a little piglet on the way and tucking it under her arm: she'd found it grunting plaintively in the elder thickets.

Early the next morning the town was woken by Evdokia's wild and drunken howling. Mixing swearwords with prophecies of the end of the world, she was demanding the return of her piglet, which, to spite its owner, had turned into a human being.

Armed with shotguns, men dashed to the hotel. In the dancehall they discovered a mountain of dead pigeons out of which poked the dead lion's snout and a menacing paw; in the toilet on the first floor they found a debilitated Sweet-Wrapper hanging in mid-air from a door-handle; in the room next to the Goddess's, the guest was asleep, clutching to his chest a scrap of canvas torn from the picture over his bed. The most beautiful woman in the world had vanished.

Only towards evening did they find the gold-horned white bull on the sandbank below the waterfall, pasted with bloodied bird feathers; and under the new bridge, Vita Pea-Head, with a smile of utter exhaustion on his face and a gaping wound in his chest . . .

The Miracle of Battle-Axe

A poem

Fir and thuja wafted through the town, fir and thuja – Battle-Axe was dead!

Water spurted out of Capitolina's kettle and turned into blood, and the old woman realized: Battle-Axe was dead.

Decrepit Aphinogen suddenly felt the emptiness in his mouth fill with living flesh – his tongue, ripped out by shrapnel forty years before, had grown back – and his first thought was 'Battle-Axe is dead', and his first word:

'Swines!'

But this referred to his son-in-law and his mates, who were finishing off the last bottle of *Lilac* perfume in the garden. Mitrokha knocked back the phial and nearly choked: fragrant lilac blossoms had poured down his throat.

News of Battle-Axe's death spread from mouth to mouth, shop to shop, bus to bus, from the paper mill to the noodle factory, from the margarine factory to the meat plant, from the timber plant to the oil workers' district, and the last to hear it was the Public Prosecutor.

He threw his dogs one last scrap of meat, wiped his hands on the towel that hung on the back of a chair whose legs seemed to have grown into the ground (since the death of the Prosecutor's wife the chair never got taken inside come winter or summer; in early spring the Prosecutor would strip a thick layer of rust off its iron frame and smear the whole stool in sweeping strokes of light-blue paint, which more or less clung to the wooden slats of the seat and back, but by midsummer began to peel off the bars of the frame, as if they were made of some special type of metal possessing an indomitable ability to shed paint) and, turning his long horsy face to his companion, exclaimed:

'At times like this you're sorry we haven't got a single church bell.'

He lowered himself into the chair and, with his legs wide apart and hands resting on his knees, spoke again in his impassive, inexpressive voice, a voice that could just as easily belong to some inanimate object – like say, his well-worn but meticulously polished boots:

'News like that should be announced to the sound of mourning bells. Just think: Battle-Axe is dead.'

Leaning right back, he placed his right foot on the seat and wrapped his hands round his thin ankle. He would remain in this uncomfortable position all morning, gazing straight ahead with his tiny grey eyes, but noticing neither the greetings of the passers-by, nor the dogs who warmed themselves in the sun or burrowed under the fence – dogs on which, rumour had it, he spent a large part of his pension. Without even checking his watch, he'd go in to eat at exactly twelve o'clock. Returning to his usual spot afterwards and now hoisting his left leg onto the chair, he dozed away until some inner clock-work mechanism informed him it was time to drink tea. He spent the evenings on that same chair, with a book in his hands. Sometimes it was poetry but more often it would be an old volume of *History of the Russian State*, wrapped neatly in white paper. In wet weather he wore a rubber raincoat over his linen suit. As for visitors (they hadn't stopped coming even after he retired), he received them here too, in the yard, sitting on his chair under the kitchen window, and only heavy rain would induce him to invite a guest into his house: into a cold dusky room with a portrait of his wife on the wall, a table covered with an oilcloth and adorned by a bronze inkwell, and bookcases of all sizes bulging with tattered volumes.

He suddenly stirred.

'She didn't die at home, did she?'

For the first time his voice betrayed the sound of something very distantly reminiscent of sadness or perplexity.

'No,' Sashka said. 'At the market.'

Which wasn't far from the truth.

Barely able to stand the pain that had been racking her for two years now, she had somehow made it to the market, unnoticed by everyone (which of itself may be considered a miracle). It was there that the policeman, Lyosha Leontyev, had found her. Bare-headed, flabby, old, sick, the woman was sitting on the ground, slumped against the wall of what was once the paraffin stall. She didn't respond to Lyosha's questions and just shook her head, gazing with wide-open eyes at the ruin and neglect that had befallen the market ever since it had been deprived of her attentions: the paraffin stall had long since been turned into a furniture dump; her 'residence' had become a refuge for spiders and mice, as had the buffet, where red-faced men in unbuttoned sheepskins received a brimful of vodka and a sweet from the ever-sniffling Zinaida; the chilly stone cell where the household goods store had once been was now a vodka shop, while hardware was sold in the glass box recently built next to the public bathhouse; empty wine and vodka cases were piled up high under the awnings, where the smells of cheap tobacco, smoked meats, boot polish, onion and fried sunflower seeds still seemed to linger. The Corner, formed by two brick walls, had also disappeared: this was where horses used to be tied, where traders swarmed selling junk, ancient shoes and home-made pocket-knives, and where Vaska the Cock and the gypsy Seryoga used to dance drunkenly to Battle-Axe's harmonica: two half-naked men, wet from sweat and scarlet from the vodka, excitement and cold, who locked arms every Sunday without ever settling their argument as to which of them was the fierier dancer. The Corner was pulled down when the glass box was built.

Gently supporting her by the arms, Lyosha somehow lowered the woman into the side-car. All through the journey he couldn't cough up a lump that had got stuck in his throat. Battle-Axe sat with her eyes closed. This time, dozens of people saw her: they stopped and stared as the motorbike swayed precariously over the potholes and crawled down the cobbled road.

At the hospital, Lyosha helped her climb out of the side-car; it was then that her strength deserted her once and for all and she sank heavily onto the road. The instantly assembled crowd was so astonished by what had happened that no one so much as thought of trying to help the dying woman, or even to cry.

Sashka pulled down his cap and added proudly:

'They'll lay her out in the club so everyone can say their goodbyes.'

When Sashka left, the Prosecutor felt with a sharp and sudden pain that something had loosened from the stone that he usually called his soul, and had dropped irretrievably into an abyss.

What could it have been?' he muttered, running the end of his tongue over his parched lips. 'What's ended?'

'Friday,' Katerina answered sadly, hanging the last wet doormat on the fence.

Doctor Sheberstov had no time for the timid objections of his wife, children and grandchildren. With a contemptuous snort, he put in his false teeth, picked up his heavy stick with a handle shaped like a snakehead, and strode off to the hospital: a cross between a behemoth and a port crane, as Battle-Axe used to put it. On the corner of Seventh Street he suddenly stopped. A simple and sorrowful thought had left him gasping for breath: from now on he'd be a different person. And this was nothing to rejoice about, for there was only one metamorphosis which he considered more or less seemly at his age – death.

Flashing his stick at his wife, who had unwisely poked her head round the corner of the nearest house, Doctor Sheberstov completed the hundred metres to the hospital with ease. The crowd parted and he strode importantly past the silent people up to the top, to the very top, to the tiny room under the roof where Battle-Axe's body lay on a zinc-coated table under a snow-white sheet.

The head physician – a young chap with a flaxen beard and the arms of a blacksmith's striker – lost his composure on seeing the huge old man on the threshold, with his round bald head and his long twirly moustache. Doddering old Citrinyak, who'd dragged herself over from the bluish twilight of her X-ray room, screwed up her watering red eyes and frantically nodded her wrinkled monkey's muzzle:

'Come on in, Ivan Matveevich, my light one . . .'

'Sit, Claudia!'

102

Putting his stick in his left hand, Sheberstov drew back the sheet with his right.

'Dead!' No one could understand what this cry contained more of: dismay or indignation. 'Battle-Axe!' He swung round towards the medics. 'What a woman she was! Her walk! Her breast! What a sleeper, what an eater!'

Ancient Citrinyak – a mummy in a white coat – clasped her monkey's paws.

'Once a ladies' man, always a ladies' man, Ivan Matveevich!'

Sheberstov waved her away and walked out, shuffling the soles of his monstrous shoes.

He paused on the porch, cast his furious gaze over the hushed crowd and, striking his stick hard on the marble step, exclaimed indignantly:

'She's dead, damn it! Dead!'

When the other doctors and nurses had left the room, the head physician asked in a muted voice:

'That there . . . What is it, Claudia Leibovna?'

She looked at the body under the sheet and suddenly smiled. There was pride in her voice.

'The only woman who never responded to Doctor Sheberstov's pestering.'

The head physician thought he saw a streak of red break through the radiologist's usually sallow complexion.

'Forgive me . . .' He caught himself speaking more drily than he would have liked. 'What's she got on her back . . . and on her stomach?'

'Stars,' the monkey immediately replied. 'To remember the Minsk Gestapo by, my light one. There are seven of them, just like she had seven kids. Not her kids.'

The young man recalled those five men and one woman (the second woman, her sister, he knew of only by hearsay): six perfect copies of Battle-Axe, seven including the sister.

'You're trying to say . . .' He stumbled. 'So these six, I mean seven . . .'

'That's right, my light one.' The monkey nodded her teeny

head. 'They're all the same age, you see. They say she brought them into the town in a bag like kittens, but that's not true. She didn't have to get on any train for them: the children's home was next to the old sawmill then.'

She shook a fag out of a crumpled packet and lit it, clamping the cardboard mouthpiece firmly between her small black teeth.

When it got dark in the room, she suddenly came to her senses and realized bitterly that she'd been left alone once again, and once again she couldn't remember what she'd been thinking about all that time. Clinging to the wall, she began her slow trudge down the stairs, leaving in her wake the smell of strong tobacco and the boot polish that she used every day to clean her wrinkled-up shoes. She stopped on the first floor, struck by an unexpected thought: 'Who on earth's going to bury her? And anyway, can this really be happening?'

The little window in the post office was obscured by someone's massive back, which was covered in faded tarpaulin. From the other side of the plywood partition came Sweetie-Pie's plangent voice:

'Operator, dearie, be a sweetie, has that call gone through yet to Mozyr! Mozyr!'

Her sister, Fish-Pie, was sitting on a hard chair in the corner with her dog, Phiz, in her lap. She was angrily examining the specimen forms and letters that had been stuck on the wall opposite her.

'Is anyone ever going to bring this town to heel?' she snapped without looking at Lyosha Leontyev, behind whom the main door had just slammed shut. 'Some people seem to think nutters can wander around wherever their fancy takes them!'

'He's not doing anyone any harm.' Lyosha tapped on the tarpaulin back with a crooked finger. 'Excuse me . . .'

The back moved to the side, and in the gap Lyosha saw Sweetie-Pie with earphones round her neck.

'Has Hatchet sent any telegrams at all?' Lyosha asked. 'To his kids, maybe.'

'Hatchet?' Sweetie-Pie sighed deeply. 'Battle-Axe's fella couldn't even tell you where the post office is. Mercy on our souls!' She grabbed the receiver and shouted desperately: 'Well, dearie, what about Mozyr then? What else, Lyosha?'

Leontyev poked a folded piece of paper through the gap and a crumpled ten-rouble note.

'Send telegrams about Battle-Axe to these addresses . . . Urgently', he specified after a second's thought, handing over another five roubles.

'I'll write a complaint!' Fish-Pie said with menace in her voice. 'You're obliged to reply to citizens' complaints!'

Phiz woke up and growled at the policeman. He sighed.

'Then you're better off addressing it directly to me. And don't bother signing.'

He saw Vita Pea-Head from a distance: the madman was standing by the railings and gazing intently into the darkness. His moped lay in the middle of the bridge. Lyosha slowed up and killed the engine. Vita Pea-Head started waving his arms about manically.

'It jumped over there!' He stared again into the gloom, which had swallowed up the market and the osier and elder thickets that surrounded it.

'Right.' Lyosha nodded. 'What's this "it"?'

'A monkey's head, horse's neck and paws, a blind dog's body . . .'

'Blind dog's body,' Lyosha repeated pensively. 'What did you squabble with Fish-Pie for?'

Tilting his head to the side, Vita looked attentively at the policeman.

'I'm asking you about Fish-Pie . . .'

'Trollop!' said Vita through clenched teeth. 'Pollort. Troll-roll. Rollolop!'

Yet again Lyosha found himself thinking: 'He's no loony. Just playing the fool. A bit more than everyone else.'

'Stop squabbling. And don't go out in the dark.'

But he knew full well: Vita wouldn't venture out in the dark. All night long he rode his little moped around town, but only along well-lit streets – darkness filled him with panicky terror. He slept by day in a room without blinds, curtains or even so much as a scrap of tulle over the windows. When night fell, he wheeled his bruised and battered moped out of a tumbledown shack ('Wonder who fixes it for him,' Lyosha thought. 'Can't be Kalabakha, he'd fleece his own mother. Maybe Blinker?') and started his rounds of the sleeping town: a real hulk of a man with a small head on a long neck, astride a tinkling moped that came his way God knows how. He was a patroller, ready at any given moment to warn the town about a sudden invasion of giant ants, extra-terrestrials, drunkards or children. People got used to him, just as they got used to Jaundice, who also sometimes rode about town at night on her bicycle, if she wasn't jumping over her skipping-rope, or lifting dumb-bells, or guzzling carrots, her love for which had flared up with quite amazing force when she turned seventy (carrots were all she grew in her vegetable patch and she ate at least a kilo of them every day); just as they also got used to Fish-Pie, to her little whims, her hump and tiny Phiz, and to her battered old hawker's stand right next to the Ladies at the bus station, where, pursing her brightly made-up lips and holding the entire human race in contempt, she sold flat pies filled with cabbage, jam or fish . . .

Only after turning into Seventh Street did Lyosha realize what had been troubling him ever since Doctor Sheberstov had announced Battle-Axe's death: it was the ever-intensifying smell of fir and thuja, the smell of death, sadness, the transfiguration to come, and memory. The tiled roofs, the running dogs, the fences turned green from never-ending rain, the street-lamps' dull light, the walls of the houses, the smoke from the chimneys (to ward off damp, many kept their stoves going even at the height of summer): all of it exuded the smell of fir and thuja, a smell that was thick like syrup, like dark-green resinous wine, and sent heads spinning . . .

In Hatchet's house (three other families lived there too, but the house was known as Hatchet's), it was dark and quiet. Lyosha knocked and the hollow sound reverberated through the empty flat, or rather, through the emptied flat, for she who could amply fill any space with her work, her bustle, her voice and her mere flesh, even spaces that could not be enclosed by four walls and covered with a roof, well, she was lying over there now, on the second floor of the hospital, under the most ordinary of sheets, which more than covered the lump of flesh that out of mere inertia was still called Battle-Axe. Just another mortal and dead woman, for all that she had raced through life like a tornado, a whirlwind, a hurricane . . . And now the space unoccupied by her was humming to the echo of her voice, her tread, her life. An absent life was echoing: it was absent in the entrance corridor that reeked of mould, absent in the kitchen, absent in the children's room, where some tailless creature scampered away soundlessly on the bare floor, absent in the living-room, absent in the bedroom . . . It seemed to Leontyev (in fact, he was willing to swear on oath that it was so) that the objects, books and furniture abandoned by their owner were crumbling, collapsing, decaying and dissolving into this gloom with mind-bending speed, as if all he had to do was leave the flat and the objects, books and furniture would turn to dust in a matter of seconds. In the living-room only the trunk and the cupboard with the cracked mirror were in their usual places. The rest of the furniture had vanished somewhere, along with the painting that took up the whole of the blind wall: a copy of Vasnetsov's *Three Heroes*, painted by some nameless artist who'd given each hero a bushy green beard. This was the trunk that everyone used to talk about so much. There were only two like it in the town, but the first, belonging to Tanya-Vanya, had disclosed no secrets at all. Lyosha knew that for a fact: he'd been present at the ceremonial opening of the old woman's trunk, in which, to the astonishment and inexpressible chagrin of her numerous relatives, who'd pinned their hopes on an enormous inheritance, all they'd found was a rusty contraption for distilling hooch (scared by Leontyev's admonitions, Tanya-Vanya had stowed it in the chest long before and had never found the time to hand it over to the police or chuck it out). Lyosha grabbed the lock of Battle-Axe's trunk and it disintegrated into dust. The heavy lid opened without a creak, but Leontyev didn't even have time to rest it against the wall before a soft, crumbling ball flew out of the trunk into his face and immediately dispersed throughout the room. The lid banged shut again. The room, weakly lit by a streetlamp, filled with dancing snowflakes: thousands of large, shaggy flakes.

'Wretched moths!' Grandma Coz turned on the light in the corridor, and now Lyosha, too, saw the moths in their thousands: shaking off the dust from their wings, they collided senselessly in the doorway.

The policeman slammed the door shut and passed his palm over his face.

'Why are you here, Androsovna?

'Coz I was asked to get a book. It's in the bedroom, Hatchet says, on the shelf.'

'And where's he?'

'In the shed.'

He went outside. Someone growled from the gloom, 'He's not going anywhere,' but however hard the policeman stared, he couldn't make anything out except for the old horse Bird, who was chewing something and slouching against the wall of the house. A smell of sewage wafted over from behind the shed, which meant that the barrel was over there somewhere, less a barrel though than a wooden box on wheels with a poorly-fitted square hatch on top and a plug at the back that was forever dripping. Atop this box, pulled along by the sleeping nag, Hatchet would methodically do the rounds of the courtyards, leaving a very particular scent in his wake and sending the children into raptures. As soon as they caught sight of the aromatic equipage, the kids would start shouting in chorus: 'Wakey wakey dung fly! We can smell a poo pie!'

Lyosha tugged at the bolt on the door; from behind it came the screech of a badly set saw. Then he called Hatchet, but there was no reply. It was dark in the shed.

'Maybe you'd like the light on?' Lyosha asked hopefully.

'Not bothered,' Hatchet said, so clearly it was as if there was no wall between them. 'Lyosha, you seen?'

'Of course,' Lyosha replied instantly, only realizing afterwards what Hatchet had meant. 'I expect they've moved her over to the club by now.'

'Then what?'

'What d'you mean, then what?'

'I see.' Hatchet paused. 'So you're gonna be burying her, right, diggin' up the ground an' all . . .'

'And what's your idea?' Lyosha asked huffily.

Hatchet started laughing.

'You'll see. You'll all see.'

'He's flipped,' Lyosha thought. 'Although all of us . . . No one believes she's really died. How's anyone going to believe she'll be buried?' Yes, she was no more, she who all the old-timers, and many of the younger folk too, thought was as inseparable a part of the town, as characteristic a feature, as the ancient church on the square, the red-brick water-tower by the railway crossing near the old cemetery, the waterfall on the Lava, the tiled roofs showing scarlet in a deluge of lime leaves, the Gypsy quarter, the hump-back bridges, the Pregolya bridges, the cobbled roads, the elder thickets and lines of thuja trees, and a great deal besides, without which it is impossible even to imagine this little town cut in three by two rivers whose murky waters flow unhurriedly between low loamy shores sunk in thickets of osier and hawthorn. For as long as he could remember, she had always been here, near at hand, in many places at once, it seemed, not just near Lyosha Leontyev but near every townsperson, even when the town was still called the Settlement. She was here and everywhere, now and always. She was ubiquitous and immortal. In summer wearing a not-so-clean smock, with only two buttons done up and slippers on her bare feet; in winter wearing a black coarse coat with the hide of an unknown beast on the collar ('She caught and strangled it with her own hands,' Hatchet used to say after a vodka or three in a lowered voice tinged with ecstasy and holy terror, and for some reason no one could find the words to call him a fibber). For days on end she charged around the streets and shops, butting into every conversation, and turning it into a heated argument; she punished and pardoned, picked up fledglings fallen from their nests, sick cats and stray dogs;

she shamed drunkards, grabbed squabblers by their hair and ruled supreme at the market; to some, especially children, it seemed as if she even wielded power over clouds and dreams. She did it all with equal and unflagging ardour, and you could only wonder in amazement how she found the time and strength for housekeeping, rearing seven children and working, first as a packer at the noodle factory for twenty years on the trot, then as a – how d'you call it? – supervisor at the market, and as a ticket-seller on summer evenings at the open-air cinemas . . . It seemed as if the energy generated by this woman would live on after her death, and anyway, how can you lay energy to rest, how can you bury a whirlwind, a tornado, a hurricane?

Trembling all over and gasping for breath, Vaska the Cock wriggled out from under the heavy, sodden net of sleep and prised open his puffy eyelids. For several minutes he gazed without thinking at the ceiling, listening to the fading clatter of hooves. His head was aching, his body felt swollen, and with every movement his heart turned into a ball of little insects, like a bad attack of pins and needles. Something squelched in the dark and Vaska realized that if he didn't have a drink immediately, even if it was only water, he would never get rid of this sensation of having gorged himself on burning ash. Overcoming his dizziness and a pain in his chest, he got out of bed, flung his arms wide and made for the door. Only in the kitchen did he stop to wonder: who had that been squelching in the bedroom? Or had he only imagined a fat-lipped snout covered in frog slime? Vaska fumbled for the light switch, got a faint electric shock and remembered: about time he fixed the wiring. Grabbing a grimy glass off the table, he virtually fell into the sink; the sudden movement sent his blood rushing to his head, his heart started thumping frantically, and scorching sweat covered his body from top to toe. A stream of vodka gushed from the tap. 'Right,' Vaska thought. 'Something's happened to Battle-Axe or I'm for the madhouse. But first, a drink. Saints rest in peace.' Pinching his nostrils and screwing up his eyes, he downed the contents of the glass and only afterwards heard the creaking of the floorboards and a sound like an enormous piece of wet tarpaulin being dragged through the doorway. He opened his eyes and froze: with a glass in his right hand, fingers pinching his nose and lips stretched out like a pipe, ready to breathe out, and his last thought was 'God, what must its tail be like then?'

Eighty-five of the very sturdiest men, each of whom had no less than two children, carried Battle-Axe reverentially out of the hospital and loaded the body, which exuded the smell of newly-blossomed peonies, into a thirty-hundredweight lorry. It was the only such lorry in the town, and its miraculous preservation was probably due to the fact that from time immemorial it had only ever been used as a hearse. At the wheel of the black-lacquered vehicle sat Nikita Petrovich Moskvich, his yellow beard drooping to his waist and covering the medals for frontline service which he'd worn specially for the occasion. They lowered the body carefully into a boat (for no suitable coffin had as yet been found). Nikita Petrovich adjusted the photo of the Generalissimo on the windscreen and, jamming the horn, drove off to the club.

Eighty-five of the very sturdiest men, each of whom had no less than three children, reverentially removed the boat from the lorry, carried it solemnly into the hall with the parquet floor – where old women in white shawls, black skirts and jackets were already seated along the walls like peas in a pod – and hoisted the boat onto a pedestal covered in scarlet plush.

The first to start crying was Capitolina, followed by Evdokia, who had six fingers and two toes missing, then Valka, then Genovepha together with Dangolya, then Merry Gertrude, the one-hundred-year-old madwoman who never missed a funeral and from whom nothing had ever been heard except '*Seid umschlungen, Millionen*'*, and after them the rest of the women: those who were in the hall, and those who were in the park behind the club, and on the dyke on the Pregolya, and in the hayfields over the river, and in the bathhouse

* Be embraced, ye millions. (Schiller, *Ode to Joy*)

(Friday was women's day there), the marital bed and the maternity home . . .

When the menfolk, coughing politely and jostling in the wide exit, finally left the old women alone with the deceased, a man wrapped in a ragged cloak strode into the parqueted hall. Water was streaming off him, as if he'd just climbed out of the river. Without addressing anyone in particular, he enquired as to which of the relatives of the deceased would deign to accept thirty thalers from him, a debt which, the stranger said, had been weighing on him for almost two hundred and forty years now. They tried explaining to him that Battle-Axe had died at sixty-five, but the stranger just sniggered bitterly and asked how, in that case, he might get to the nearest coaching inn. Naturally, he was sent over to Zoika from the meat factory. The stranger departed, leaving an enormous puddle of water on the floor, which twelve women spent an hour and a half mopping up and carrying out in pails borrowed from Kalyukaikha, the Sungortsevs and Slavka.

Only then did Grandma Coz finally appear with Battle-Axe's favourite book. The sobbing subsided and the peonies exuded a sharper fragrance when Capitolina opened the shabby volume, cast her austere gaze over the women and declaimed in a sonorous and solemn voice: 'How ravishing, how luxurious is a summer's day in Little Russia!'★

Early that morning the librarian Frost Frostovich had discovered that all the roses in his front garden had turned into peonies overnight and were exuding the aroma of fir and thuja. After swallowing a raw egg and a glass of slightly salted water, he set out for the club, where a group had already gathered in the former buffet: the Prosecutor, Capitolina, Lyosha Leontyev and Merry Gertrude, who was slouched against the round iron stove and embarrassing everyone who walked in with her withering, wide-eyed gaze. As soon as Frost Frostovich rested his crutch carefully against the wall

★ The opening line of Nikolai Gogol's story *The Fair at Sorochintsy*, from the collection *Evenings on a Farm near Dikanka*.

and sat down, Doctor Sheberstov asked Leontyev, as though continuing a conversation (although they all had been silent until the librarian's arrival):

'So it's us who'll be burying her then?'

His question was nothing like a question, save for a faint hint towards a particular type of intonation. Moreover, the librarian even fancied that he had caught something resembling satisfaction in the doctor's voice.

Lyosha shrugged his shoulders.

'I've sent telegrams to the children.'

'They don't count!' Doctor Sheberstov just couldn't stay seated. He jumped up and, waving his stick around, paced the room heavily from corner to corner. 'To the table!' He brandished his stick, forcing everyone to take a step back. 'So?'

The Prosecutor took a tiny notebook in a home-made cover out of his pocket and, without opening it, started talking in his dry, colourless voice, which might just as easily have belonged to those figurines he sometimes cut out of paper. He'd prepared a register of the duties for the departed's nearest and dearest: they had to think about getting a coffin, an outfit for the deceased, a hearse, a burial pit, a tombstone, food and drink for the wake, and so on and so forth.

Listening to this bony old fogey, who even on a day like this wouldn't change his clerical manner of speaking, whether he was talking about love, the division of property in court or Melville's metaphysics, Frost Frostovich recalled how Battle-Axe had once said of the Prosecutor that he kept breathing out of pure pigheadedness, and also, perhaps, to spite her. Then he, Frost Frostovich, with his characteristic penchant for bombast, had said something like this: if a clutch of doomed defenders of an all but vanquished stronghold were to require a flag as a symbol of fortitude or at least of stubbornness, then the Prosecutor would fit this role ideally – his scraggy body could easily pass for a staff, and his far too baggy linen suit for a flag; and even if the fortress fell, but the man–flag, man–symbol were by chance to survive, then, in the face of all the evidence, he would retain his conviction that the stronghold had resisted, that the game wasn't up, and no one would manage to persuade him otherwise, thus leaving only one available option: to annihilate him physically, plough over the ground in which he'd be buried, and forbid people from even coming close to that place so as not to be accidentally infected by pigheadedness. Doctor Sheberstov had agreed: yes, few could be compared with the Prosecutor when it came to pigheadedness. The Streltsy, perhaps. Or the Urazovs. Or, indeed, Battle-Axe herself. Trust her – out of sheer pigheadedness – to get married, or rather to take to husband a man like Hatchet, who, at the end of the day, was only good for cleaning out cesspools on a more or less regular basis, something which you could even train an ancient nag like Bird to do if you tried hard enough . . . 'You're only saying this,' Battle-Axe had shouted, 'because I didn't want to marry you, you damned skirt-chaser!' She'd flung the book on the counter and walked out, pulverizing the rotten library staircase with her heels. 'Maybe she's right,' Doctor Sheberstov had said, wiping his veiny neck with his huge chequered handkerchief. 'But the real issue here is that she's pigheaded. Right?' He'd stared at the librarian with his bulging eyes. 'She gave her word and married the man she'd given her word to. Her word!' 'At the end of the day, she refused everyone,' Frost Frostovich had remarked. 'You and the Prosecutor.' 'The Prosecutor!' the doctor yelled. 'I can picture that! No bended knees there. Would you care to register our matrimony?' 'He read her poetry!' Frost had objected. 'Pushkin, I think. But not Blok, that's for sure.' 'Poetry?' Sheberstov was dumbstruck. 'How d'you know?' 'It happened right here, where you're standing,' Frost had said, pointing at the feet of the doctor, who hurriedly stepped aside in surprise. 'She was standing here. Him, here. And she refused him.' 'I'll say!' the doctor had shouted. 'She turned down every self-respecting man there was in order to boss this oyster about!'

'So all that's left is to dig the pit and make *kissel*!'* said Doctor Sheberstov, concluding the Prosecutor's inevitably

---

* A jelly-like dessert made from stewed fruit and traditionally served at the end of the wake.

dull speech, and Frost Frostovich realized that he'd missed just about everything these people had got together for and, so as not to be left out, enquired:

'What about the band?'

'That's the Prosecutor's job!' Doctor Sheberstov waved his stick about imperiously. 'You, Lyosha, deal with the relatives! And you . . .' He turned about sharply towards Capitolina. 'You sort out the food. There's plenty of women.'

'*You* could never get enough of them,' Capitolina reminded him poisonously.

'And you were good enough for two!' cried the doctor, slapping the dumbstruck old woman on her shoulder. 'Right then!'

Banging his stick on the wooden floorboards, he walked out of the club.

The Prosecutor helped the librarian down the steep staircase. On the street, looking straight ahead, as if into nowhere, he said:

'I have a strange premonition . . .'

'Today's a day of premonitions,' Frost Frostovich replied chirpily. 'And memories.'

'It seems to me as if all of this was thought up from beginning to end by Battle-Axe herself. And that once she disappears, all this will disappear too. Don't you think?'

They fell silent.

'You know,' the librarian's voice sounded as gentle as ever, 'any change is the disappearance of something. And the appearance of something else.'

'We'll all just die off,' the Prosecutor said drily. 'And she'll remain.'

He didn't finish. Narrowly avoiding the roofs of the houses, a low-flying IL-2 attack aircraft flopped down on the grass in front of the club, and out leapt a pilot in a bloodied flying suit. Dragging his left leg, he entered the parqueted hall, tore off his helmet and fell prostrate before the plush pedestal.

'*Chirimeh . . . sheni chirimeh . . .*'* He brushed something

* A Georgian endearment used in the sense of 'darling' and literally meaning 'let all your ills pass on to me'.

off his eyelashes and turned to the old women. 'How did this happen?'

They told him about Battle-Axe's passing, and he nodded his head and moved his lips sadly. He was led away for bandaging and then laid down in the billiards room.

People gathered around the aeroplane, standing there in silence. No one dared go up to the machine, whose hard body had still not cooled from the fury of war.

'Smells like death,' blind Dmitry suddenly said. He walked up to the airplane, pressed his cheek against its armour plating and began to cry. 'My angel . . .'

That moment marked the beginning of the pilgrimage to Battle-Axe's coffin. First up, accompanied by five delightful children, was a corpulent beauty who possessed the type of self-control that is akin to haughtiness. People recalled a certain highly capricious seventeen-year-old, who had contemptuously rejected the advances of a travelling artiste – a conjurer, ventriloquist and hypnotist. Spurning tours in Paris, Yurbarkas and Rio de Janeiro, the artiste had stayed on in our little town, wilting from a sense of hopelessness. In the morning he could be seen in the barber's, where Name of Lev would strive in vain to erect at least some likeness of a haircut on his client's bald pate; he took lunch at Fenya's, in the Red Canteen, while in the evenings he strolled along Seventh Street dressed all in black, carefully sidestepping the cowpats and trying to burn a hole with his gaze through the windows of the inaccessible beauty's bedroom. To attract her attention, he gave free performances right there on the street: he produced live rabbits smelling of mothballs from his silk top hat and flocks of pigeons from his sleeves, read thoughts, predicted the future, swallowed swords and, when they ran out, kitchen knives and safety razors. Even the kids soon got bored with him, yet the cruel beauty never rewarded him with so much as a flicker of her attention. So then he announced a farewell show in the club, which was attended by virtually every solvent townsperson. After demonstrating a cascade of breathtaking tricks, he moved on to hypnosis. Many were willing to submit to the influence of his bewitching gaze, but not her, the one and only. So he used his magic to bring her out of the audience and get her marching on stage. She marched, limping for some reason on her left leg and screeching an idiotic song that began with the words 'Soldier Maria'. She obediently carried out the artiste's commands, while he stood at the very back of the stage with his arms folded on his chest, darkly whispering: 'Waterloo . . . Waterloo . . .'. Suddenly, among the guffawing, groaning, weeping audience, Battle-Axe stood up. Raising her hand, she secured a deathly quiet, climbed up onto the stage, and said something under her breath to the artiste. Forgetting all about his cloak, top hat and tripod, he flew out of the club, threw himself into a waiting black car that immediately turned into a horse, black as a rotten tooth, and leapt behind a stationary cloud. When the girl tried to hang herself, Battle-Axe cut the rope and took her home with her. A month later, having received the blessing of her paralysed granny and the necessary funds from Battle-Axe, she left on the Leningrad train. Now, fifteen years on, she had appeared by the coffin of the woman thanks to whom no one ever dared call her Soldier Maria to her face.

Next came Gash, the same guy who once left the town mounted behind Hatchet on the sewage barrel. No, Battle-Axe couldn't claim the credit for unmasking this smart operator, who used to do a secret trade in cockerel-shaped fruit-drops, home-made sweets, second-hand furniture, worn-out clothes and shoes, and hooch: all of it through middlemen of course, old folk who only got a pittance and often didn't even know who they were working for. No, it wasn't Battle-Axe who unmasked him, but eight-year-old Alyosha Ryazantsev and the sorry drunkard Sergeyushka. After using the sugar allotted to him by Gash for hooch, Sergeyushka tried to get out of his fix by filling the moulds for the sweets with water. He coloured them and put them out on the porch overnight – it was winter. What was he counting on? Clearly, on the fact that adults don't usually taste the cockerels they buy for their kids. That was why he got so scared when Alyosha unexpectedly came up to his stand and that was why he made a run for it, hounded by a kid clutching a five-kopek piece in his little fist. The boy got his pink cockerel in the end, which was when he discovered that his fruit-drop was really an ice-drop. But it was Battle-Axe who, after subjecting Sergeyushka to a merciless interrogation, discovered who the alky was working for. It was she who, in the presence of one hundred and seventy-six dumbstruck witnesses, uttered the immortal phrase: 'That's not the way we do things here.' And it was she who ordered that good-for-nothing Gash to be thrown out of town atop the stinking barrel, a command carried out under the vigilant supervision of Misha the Meat-Chopper, Vaska the Cock, and Avvakum Mukhanov.

Gramophone came to bid farewell, grateful to Battle-Axe for having once saved her daughter from the devil, who'd had designs on the honour of her silly girl and her silly son-in-law. Everyone knew this story in which Battle-Axe assumed the heroic role of exorcist: wielding a shotgun, she'd walked out fearlessly at night into the garden where, according to certain accounts, the devil had arranged an ill-fated tryst, and with mighty and pitiless blows of the butt she'd chased the Prince of Darkness from his hiding place behind the currant bush into the Rotten Ditch, where the roofing-paper factory dumped its oil waste.

Thousands upon thousands of people flocked down Seventh Street to the club and crowded in the parqueted hall, where the old women took turns to read in singsong voices from the favourite book of Whirlwind-Woman, Market-Tsarina, Sovereign of Clouds and Dreams. They bade farewell to the Immaculate Virgin, Guardian of the Weak and the Destitute, Lady-Hero; to the Pimp and Thief, as she was called by Nosikha, whose newly-minted son-in-law had been lured from his 'honest marital bed' by Battle-Axe's daughter; they bade farewell to the woman on whose appearance in the town the iron cock, that rusty golden cock, leapt out of its little house on the school clock and froze for all time with its beak wide open, its neck outstretched, wings flung wide and a 'Cock-a-doodle-do' caught in its throat; they bid farewell to the Witch and the Snake: many, many women, whose husbands had once vied with one another like madmen for her favours, knew for a fact that the Witch carried the dried hearts of her numerous lovers in the pocket of her night-shirt and had seen with their own eyes how she flew by night in her mortar (on her broomstick, on a red bull, on a white lion, a black crow, a sewage barrel, on Hatchet, on Touch-Me-Not, on complex sentences with subordinate modifiers of manner, measure and degree) and how, leaving her false flesh in her bed, she'd crawled through the sleeping town in the form of a beautiful snake, sucking milk from cows and causing minors to see sexual hallucinations; they bade farewell to Battle-Axe . . .

. . . Once more, as he had an hour before, he thought: 'Nothing I'm doing was my idea.' He paused on the bridge, ran his unseeing gaze over the sparkling water, and loudly announced:

'Plain fatigue, that's what it is.'

Fatigue, of course. This woman was capable even after her death of exhausting whomever she wanted and forcing people to do whatever she'd thought up for them. Not for nothing had they once thought her a sorceress, the Prosecutor remembered with a smirk. And it was far from impossible that all this had been conceived and thought through by her from beginning to end, in every detail. Oh, she'd made sure of everything: that she'd die exactly where she had, and exactly how she had; that she'd stir up the whole town with her death and disturb even those who knew almost nothing of her past; that she'd be laid in a boat instead of a coffin until someone – but not her family, of course – went to the trouble of finding a more or less fitting receptacle for her dead flesh; that all the flowers in all the little front gardens would turn into her beloved peonies overnight; that every conversation – whoever and whatever the topic – would inevitably end up being a conversation about her; that she'd be placed in the parqueted hall, to which people would be inexorably drawn, some because they truly wished to bid her farewell, others to immerse themselves in memories of events of which

Battle-Axe was an invariable attribute (for no event of note ever took place in the town without her participation) . . . an attribute like the Solingen razors, so thin they'd become transparent, like women's rubber overshoes and felt cloaks, like the paraffin stoves, like the faded dogrose petals and the butterfly wings that had turned to dust between the pages of the fifth (Barykova–Bessalko) and fifty-ninth (Phrantsoz–Hohusai) volumes of the Schmidt Encyclopedia. Yet others came out of pure curiosity. She'd also taken care of what Sheberstov would say and what the Prosecutor would reply, how Dangolya would swear and how much petrol Vita Pea-Head would burn . . . She'd thought it all up, just as she'd thought up the events, names and people who'd yielded almost without grumbling to the furious force of her market-square magic. No, she hadn't simply nicknamed people, she'd entitled them: the telephonist Anastasya as Sweetie-Pie, hump-backed Maria as Fish-Pie, Ivan Andreyevich, with his cotton-wool hair and cotton-wool beard, as Frost Frostovich, and silly, nattering old Gramatko as Gramophone, and from that moment it never occurred to anyone that these people could have different names, and that events could be explained differently from how they were explained by Battle-Axe. This was a world which she had created, or rather which she had recreated according to her will and under-standing, and it was just this world (only faintly different, perhaps, from the one which managed to exist even without her, but different nevertheless) that must vanish and plunge into non-being. Battle-Axe's water-tower. Battle-Axe's roads. Battle-Axe's pigeons. Battle-Axe's waterfall. Battle-Axe's sluices. Battle-Axe's clouds. Battle-Axe's dreams. Battle-Axe's rain. Battle-Axe's sun, moon and stars. Battle-Axe's space. Battle-Axe's time. Lastly, Battle-Axe's Red Canteen, added the Prosecutor, rounding off the register with a touch of irony. He'd never felt as old, feeble and useless as he did now. Ducking his head under the low arch of the entrance, where it was cooler and smelled of sour beer, he suddenly thought: 'But it hurts. It hurts.'

*

In his dealings with the musicians, the Prosecutor received unexpected help from the stranger in black. Water was streaming off him as before, so Fenya had sat him at a little table near the drainage hole in the floor and had expressly forbidden him from moving. When Grisha, thundering against 'all those jumped-up smart alecs', declared that he and the other musicians weren't prepared to play at this funeral for the usual fee, the stranger suddenly broke off from his noodles and beer and butted in:

'Then we'll get by without you.'

The stranger's attempt to stand up – for greater effect, most likely – was immediately intercepted by Fenya's menacing stare. Fenya was dozing as usual under the complaints' book with a picture of a pop star on the cover, yet she still managed to keep a watchful eye on every customer. Sighing and lighting up a cigarette, the stranger threw the match into his beer mug: it flared up with a quivering blue flame.

'And how are you going to do that?' Grisha asked acidly.

At that same instant the instruments heaped up in the corner flew out of their shabby cases and, suspended in the air, struck up Chopin's Funeral March in perfect harmony. Coming to their senses, the musicians threw themselves at their trumpets and cymbals, but the instruments rose up beyond their reach towards the ceiling.

'So?' the stranger in black asked pensively.

'Your price?' groaned Grisha.

The Prosecutor laid the money out on the table.

Stepan Mukhanov – who'd lived the life of a wanderer for twenty years, sending his dad an occasional letter with the return address *Siberia, Poste Restante* – had come back to the town in order to make his name as the builder of the most crooked coffins and least reliable boats in the world. He flatly refused to accept any money for Battle-Axe's coffin ('Don't get me wrong, I've nothing against money. But by evening the whole town will know I took payment for the coffin. And I've got to live here. Understand?') and suggested that the Prosecutor choose any model he fancied.

'Take that one there.' He nodded at some construction distantly reminiscent of a long boat in the corner of the shed. 'Just try fitting a mare like her in an ordinary box!'

The Prosecutor talked to Andrei the Photographer about the epitaph that should grace the tombstone. The Photographer, who usually informed his clients quite coldly that he took five roubles for a line of prose on a tombstone and ten for a line of verse, turned down the proffered fee.

'The result will be the reward,' he explained. 'For the moment it's beyond me how I might enshrine our idea of her life in a few lines: orphan, partisan, workhorse, Penelope, witch-doctor (here the Prosecutor could barely resist a smile), disturber and maker of peace, whirlwind, tornado, hurricane – in short, a woman who tried to exhaust every possible version of existence . . . By the way, who's paying for the tombstone? Not you, is it? Or Doctor Sheberstov?'

The Prosecutor pursed his lips and turned to leave.

'Don't be offended,' said the Photographer. 'Maybe I shouldn't take this on. After all, everything we can say about her is contained in a single word: "Battle-Axe". What's there to add?'

Vita Pea-Head promised to dig the grave by evening; he had considerable experience in that line. The only thing was to remember to pay him in one-rouble notes: Vita would take offence if he was given just one ten-rouble note, thinking he'd been paid too little.

Back home, the Prosecutor shut himself up in his study. For several hours he sat there without stirring or noticing the light gradually fade outside. A cart clattered down the street over the potholes. On that evening, too, a cart had clattered down the street, and the sound was still lingering when there was a knock on the door and in walked Hatchet. No, the Prosecutor (an investigator then) hadn't called for him. What's more, he didn't even much want to meet let alone talk to this person, whose arrival had caused such a hoo-ha in the town: who was this jewel that everyone had been waiting for? And for whose sake exactly had Battle-Axe been turning everyone down? Ah, for a guy like this, a real weed of a man, no height or belly to speak of, with sleepy eyes gazing out in anguish from a blank face. Oh well, a good missus finds work for every utensil. So here he was, greeting the Prosecutor in his tired, indifferent voice and, without even taking off his grubby cap or looking where to sit, lowering himself into the chair by the door and beginning to speak.

'No,' the Prosecutor (still an investigator then) had said. 'This is some kind of mistake: there's no reason at all why I need to know this. This is your private matter.'

'Right you are,' Hatchet had agreed indifferently. 'So, I'm saying, when the Germans got 'ere, I weren't even seventeen . . .'

'This is your private matter,' the Prosecutor said once more. 'Goodbye.'

Without stirring, Hatchet had continued his story:

'Uncle took care of us when dad died. It's Germany or the Polizei for us, he said. Me, I had three sisses and mum to look after. Nothing for it. So they gave me a rifle and made me a guard coz I was still only a little squirt. Grain, hay, horses. I was like a black sheep in the Polizei. Anisim Romanov called me a pisser. Or'nary folk thought I was a rat an' all . . . This Anisim got himself hung by the partisans pretty quickly. I went and saw his tongue. Blue, it was, nearly down to 'is belt. So I started thinking: wait till them partisans catch me. What are they gonna care if I'm a guard? They'll hang me jus' like that with all them Judases, they will. Once I was guarding the hay and the partisans showed up. I helped 'em load up. One of 'em – he weren't local – charged at me and wanted me shot. His prick's not grown but he's already a rat, he says. So their CO sticks up for me: he's not a rat yet, just thick. Uncle flogged me with a cleaning rod for the hay. Helpin' the partisans, he says, scared of the Sovs, are yer? Time they get here, we'll have all the partisans and then we'll skin yer, sonofabitch. That got me. Who's we, I says? Germans, who else, he says. But I ain't signed up to be no German. So they hit me some more with the rod. When the front got close, the Germans and coppers were like animals, they had special missions to burn people in the villages . . . One day they nabbed all our women who had fellas in the partisans or the Reds. Stuck 'em in the stable in the old estate. You guard these heifers, uncle says. Amrosy's gonna watch and check yer behaving. Amrosy, he was a stableman when we had collective farms. A sorcerer, too: he had spells for kids' hiccups and cured the animals. A whisp'rer. When the Germans came, he joined 'em straightaway. Interrogatin' was what he was good at. Best of all, he liked torturing women and girls. Happy as Larry he was when he saw me. It's boring boozin' on yer own, he says. So we go into the shed. It smelled funny, only I didn't notice at the start. We had a glass. Want me to get a woman out for yer, he says? Don't worry, he says. Randy as hell, they are, before they die. Yeah, I says. Then the smell hit me: petrol. Petrol, I says. Him, Amrosy, he's larfing. We'll fry the angels in the morning, he says. And the kids? Just drink, he says. So we drink. Mostly I can't take booze, me, but it was like water then. Not water – petrol. All stinking of petrol. We had some more. Amrosy hit the sack and told me to keep a lookout. I went out. I'm walking about, listening: no partisans, fat chance. Suddenly someone's calling me. I go over – it's her. The door's on a chain and there's a big gap. Let us out, she says. I tell her I ain't got the key. Let us out, she says, least the children, then have what yer want: me if yer want. Wait, I says, but I can hardly speak: all the lads, real lads, chased after her, and here she is – with me . . . What, yer don't believe me, she says? I give yer my word, let us out. Hang on, says Amrosy suddenly behind me, I'll let 'er out. What, he says, want this one do yer, pisser? Don't worry, he says, Amrosy won't grass. Then she says: kill 'im, she says, kill 'im. My flesh was crawling. What's this? Amrosy says. He makes towards me but he slips, so I run the bayonet through him. Hard as I can. He chokes and falls. He's got the key, she says, take it. I throw myself at him but he's still alive, kickin' in the mud and sputterin'. So I bayonet him twice more, then I fall on him, trying to get the key. As good as dead, he was, but he still wouldn't give up, lashin' at me and sputterin' all the time. I kept missin' with me hands, got meself covered in his guts and blood looking for the key. Opened the door. She took me hand. Why are yer wet? Amrosy, I says. How many? Forty with the kids, she says. The women were yelling and trying to kiss me on the hands. I shouted at 'em and they backed off. We started running. We only got to Travkina ditch when I could 'ear motorbikes. Well, I tell the women, run and God help yer. They scarpered and I hid in the ditch. Dark already. There's a bike on the hill and it starts blazin' at the women and kids. I fired three times – the bike shut up. I looked back: the women were almost in the forest. The bikes were blazin' again – machine-guns. I took the first one out, so they turned to me, mad now. Fair enough, I think, so I fired at 'em some more. Then there was a shot from behind. I looked: couldn't see the women anywhere, but now there was people running from the forest. I fired one at them too – yer never know. Then there was a noise near the forest: the partisans havin' a pop at the Germans from mortars. The same fella who wanted me shot when they came for the hay jumps down to me in the ditch. What yer doing, he says, blazin' at yer own men? Let me kiss yer, yer shit . . . We didn't stay in the partisans for long. First she was hurt then the Gestapo got her. When our lot came, they sent me where they had to, I'm not grumbling. I'd done a year and a half when she wrote me the letter. I'm waiting, she writes, don't mind what yer like, just get back alive. An' I did.'

'I see,' the Prosecutor had said. 'Only I don't understand . . .'

'I didn't make her,' said Hatchet. 'I wrote her so from the camps: don't wait if yer don't want, have yer promise back.'

'But what I don't understand,' said the Prosecutor, 'is why you've told me all this?'

'For yer to know.' Hatchet got up. 'Yer want to know about 'er, don't yer? And about me too . . .'

He left, but the Prosecutor (still only an investigator at the Prosecutor's office then) had sat in the study for a good while more. The next morning he proposed to the woman who became his wife. When Doctor Sheberstov asked him mockingly how come this 'venerable jurist had forgotten the lady of his heart so hastily to acquire a lady of the stomach', the Prosecutor had replied in a level voice:

'If you permit yourself one more disrespectful criticism of my wife, I'll smash your face in, Doctor Sheberstov.'

The Prosecutor pulled out the desk drawer, felt for an envelope, shook out a scrap of paper that had been folded in four, and only then thought of switching on the light. The piece of paper had been given to him when he was the assistant to the then Prosecutor, an asthmatic old man who even in summer wore a thick greatcoat-like affair.

'This make any sense to you?' the then Prosecutor had asked him angrily, noticing a smile on the face of his assistant as he ran his eyes over the petition. 'Haven't the foggiest what I'm supposed to do about it.'

'I'll take it if that's all right with you.'

'And what are you thinking of doing with it?'

'No idea. Nothing, probably.'

Back home, he'd read the petition over again: seventeen women were demanding that a stop be put to Battle-Axe's outrageous behaviour. She'd put the evil eye on the men, who were unable to think about anything or anyone except her, the snake.

Bumping into Nadya Sergeyeva, whose signature was first on the petition, he asked straight out:

'You don't really believe in all this nonsense, do you?'

It seemed he'd underestimated the force of female hatred. Looking him up and down with eyes burning with indignation, Nadya had hissed:

'That's neither here nor there, us believing or not. If you couldn't give a toss, we'll deal with it ourselves.'

That same evening the petition signatories had stormed into Lyubishkin's smithy, where Battle-Axe was waiting for a handle to be soldered onto her saucepan, and asked her for conclusive proof that she didn't dabble in magic. With a scornful smile and a steady hand, Battle-Axe picked out a white-hot nut from the forge and clenched it in her fist. When the women recovered from their fainting fits, she unclenched her palm and threw the nut back into the forge –

her hand wasn't even red. Later, when she'd become famous as a witch-doctor who could cure toothache, insomnia, hiccups and colon cancer with the laying on of hands, she called those who saw her actions as miracles 'superstitious idiots'.

He looked at his watch, tucked the envelope into his pocket, turned off the light, and put on his hat.

The dogs stirred in the yard, but the Prosecutor didn't take them with him.

'You might have turned the light on.' Lyosha ran his hand along the wall, groping for the switch. 'Where's it gone? . . .'

'Don't bother, Uncle Lyosha,' a voice stopped him. 'It's all the same now.'

'Up to your tricks as usual.' Leontyev shook his head disapprovingly. 'What will people say?'

'Suppose the rest have turned out normal, have they?'

'They went to bed ages ago.'

'And thank God. Stop looking for the switch!' cried the young man, irritated now. 'You'll have plenty of time to admire me. Or have you . . .' He laughed softly. 'Or have you also come to take a peek at the trunk?'

The policeman felt his face flush crimson.

'Have you seen your mother at least?' Lyosha asked sternly.

Lyosha's eyes had got used to the dark, and now he could clearly discern the thin figure of the man sitting on the trunk.

'Mother. Yeah, Mother, who else? That's what the orphanage directress said then, too: this is your Mother, she said. Not your mum: Mother. But that hardly seemed important then. We were just scared stiff of this woman who charged into the dorm and ordered us to get our things together. Not that *she* was trying anything on: she didn't call herself Mother, just told us to get ready. You'll come and live at my place, she said, ignoring the directress, who was wittering on, saying it wasn't that simple, it all had to be registered officially, there was an established procedure for all this . . . So you establish the procedure, she said, and I'll take these. How many are there here? Seven? Seven it is.'

'How can you remember?' Lyosha broke in. 'You were the youngest. You must have been what – four? Five?'

The young man laughed again.

'Forgotten, have you? Battle-Axe's kids are all the same age.'

'But you were always the youngest,' Lyosha objected.

'So it seemed.' He fell silent. 'It still amazes me: why didn't she give us different names? Well, why did she let us keep our orphanage ones? Not like her.' He lit up, chucked the match on the floor. 'Five boys and two girls suddenly became brothers and sisters. But we weren't brothers and sisters . . .'

'What's the difference,' Lyosha muttered.

'Nothing at first, of course, but later . . .'

'Don't beat around the bush.' Lyosha gave a heavy sigh. 'I know what you're driving at. They've dug the grave next to her.'

'Too right! Mother and daughter, side by side.'

The young man began talking: chaotically, incoherently, in a desperate attempt to return once more to that distant morning, furiously snatching minute after minute from the past, hour after hour, day after day, choking with pain, hatred and terror, as if ten years (or more?) hadn't passed since that day, as if it had happened yesterday, no, not even yesterday, not even an hour ago, as if it were happening now, this very minute, here and now, again and again. Lyosha, roused at dawn by Jaundice, was running again to the market, running through the rain-drenched stadium, through the ruins overgrown with elder; he'd forgotten all about his motorbike, hadn't even had time to get dressed properly; running, panting and thinking about one thing only, not thinking but passionately hoping that all this was just the imagination of that damned Jaundice, who'd been cycling around town all night as usual and had happened to look in at the market just before dawn. Her imagination. Of course, that's what she'd said: I fancied I saw someone running out of there, and he saw me and rushed off behind the bathhouse, towards the river. Of course, she'd imagined the rest of it too, the rest which didn't yet have a name but which was charging forward to a head-on collision, mindless of the road, blind and unstoppable. He'd come out on the road (his imagination!) and seen people crowding by the gates (his imagination!) Someone had put a hand on his shoulder and said in a whisper: 'Not that way. Left.' In the corner, where the horses used to be harnessed, where Vaska the Cock and the gypsy Seryoga danced furiously on Sundays, there, on a pile of rubbish near a bulldozer, lay this girl, (his imagination!) face-down, her left hand tucked under her, her right one clenching the torn top of a boot poking out of the trash. 'She was warm when I found her,' Jaundice squeaked behind his back. Lyosha looked helplessly around: boarded-up shop windows; awnings beneath which lay piles of empty wine cases, ploughed-up earth; a bulldozer; blue-grey osier thickets surrounding the market on three sides ... So that night, probably just before dawn, she'd slipped out of the house, ignoring her mother's orders and her brother's desperate pleas, and run down here along deserted streets, shivering from the night chill and also, perhaps, from terror: she must have sensed something, had some forebodings, knowing as she did the man who'd made her leave her bed to come rushing down to the market, eyes darting about in fear. 'Blinker,' Lyosha had called without turning round, 'take some guys with you and check the hotel ...' 'We've already been,' Blinker immediately replied. 'He's not there. Zoika says he left during the night, she didn't hear when.' 'Capitolina!' Frowning, Lyosha sought her out in the crowd. 'Capa, go to her ... But not on your own, take Gramophone or someone, Dusya or Dangolya ...' But *she* was already elbowing her way through the crowd to the policeman – actually, no, she didn't even see him – and climbed onto the rubbish while Lyosha stood there like a numbskull, gazing stupidly at her fat varicose-veined legs sheathed in worn-down, laceless men's boots. He gaped at her until she yelled, 'Well, give us a hand!' then he obediently climbed up and grabbed hold of the icy legs. 'No, we can't,' he croaked. 'It's the law.' 'Sod off,' she snapped. 'Why the hell did he have to shave her? Help me, you bastard!' Blinker brought some tarpaulin and they wrapped her up in it – carefully, so that the head, held on by a thin ribbon of skin, wouldn't break off. They also threw in a bundle which had been found nearby: Battle-Axe took one look at it, and placed it next to her daughter without a word . . . So this young lad hadn't seen any of this, hadn't seen her, his 'sister', until they brought the coffin into the house and placed it in the largest room, this very one, where the trunk was now. But then he'd only glanced at her, turned away and within an hour he was already out of town. So he hadn't even gone to the funeral. 'I know,' Battle-Axe had said. 'I'm not her mother. It's only now I've become her mother. I'm to blame for it all. (But there was no remorse in her voice.) It's me who told her she shouldn't even see this scoundrel, this killer, this . . . He's got to be found, Lyosha. ('They're looking for him,' Lyosha had said.) Yeah, I could see what sort he was straightaway: a rolling stone, a thief, a tramp, a killer, never had a father, never mind a mother, born rotten, clear as daylight. And the only reason he turned up here was to trick her and kill her. And everything he did here was to pull the wool over our eyes. So he stayed at the hotel. Found work. Looked for orphans. Kept low – until the time came for him to kill that other person, that guy . . . ('There's no proof,' objected Lyosha.) That's your job: to find proof. Mine's to say: it's him who did it, everyone knows, though no one saw. So what? As if you've got to see to know. It's him who lured that guy to the Dump, killed him and robbed him, then buried him in piles of used paper, hoping he might just get stuffed in the grinder, be turned into cardboard, end of story . . . ('No one knows,' Lyosha objected again. 'No one knows anything even now.') Sod it then. Fine.' Even when she heard that the killer had been caught, she wasn't interested in knowing who it really was. She just asked, 'Where'd he stick her clothes?' and that was it. What was there to say anyway when everything had already been said and done? In one night she'd lost both a daughter and a son: a son who wasn't the brother of this girl, who loved her, a son whom she'd ordered firmly to get this stupid love out of his head. That girl was meant to be his sister, simple as that. And anyway, the girl had made her own choice in favour of the stranger with a crooked fringe and a wispy thread of a moustache on his fat upper lip; in favour of a person for whom no one – no one – felt anything except disgust, as if he'd been striving for that effect himself; in favour of this half-cripple with grey eyes pencilled on a grey face . . .

'All right, Lyosha.' The young man lit another cigarette, flicked his long hair off his forehead. 'It's clear enough. She couldn't have cared less about me, and it beats me why this story still bothers me. In the end she chose her own fate, although, of course, that was stupid: to spite Mother – that's how it looked and maybe that's how it was – she got involved with a man who filled her with terror. I'm sure of that: she was terrified of him, though she can't have understood why. She said to me then: he'll take me away from here. But in fact he hadn't promised her a thing. So she left home. Because if she'd stayed with me, she'd never have got away from here, even if afterwards we'd gone off somewhere. See? She wanted to leave, to find another world. It was Mother who . . . no, I don't blame her! But it's Mother who taught her to dream of another world. Mother and auntie. Mother started it. It's Mother who called her not Vera, but Veronica, it's Mother who told her about a life of paradise, about the warm sea in the south, where she'd never even been herself, Mother who showed her the dress . . .'

He jumped up from the trunk and threw open the lid.

'Turn on the light! To your left!'

When the light came on, the young man took out from the trunk (where Lyosha recognized the bundle found near the dead girl) a moth-eaten, crumpled, faded velvet dress with a lace collar. Yes, the scarlet velvet, riddled with little holes, had become all dull and dusty, but the dress was staggeringly beautiful as before, and its every fold breathed that life where there were no vulgar Veras, only sumptuous Veronicas, where music was always playing, where warm water splashed and palm trees rustled, and whatever else had been thought up by that woman who had only ever read two books in her life – *The Three Musketeers* and *Evenings on a Farm near Dikanka* – and who had never seen this world close-up, except maybe in *The*

Indian Tomb or *Under the Roofs of Paris*. A dress that had been worn only in this room, in front of this cloudy mirror, just a few times a year, in secret from everyone, even from the family, and those few days were celebrations of a dream for the mother and the daughter. It was no longer a dress, then, but a symbol of another life, the life which the mother could not live – maybe because she'd given her word to that man, her husband, maybe just because she lacked the courage, who knows. Anyway, her daughter hadn't given her word to the person considered her brother: not because he was meant to be her brother, but because he was a part of *this* world, the one she had to flee, and she'd found the courage, she'd flung herself at the secret, at all that beauty which had been so long in coming, she'd rushed headfirst and it was hardly her fault that the path led straight into the rubbish heap at the market . . .

He slipped the dress carefully onto a hanger and hung it on the door of the cupboard.

'That's all,' he said, more calmly now. 'I mean that's all there was in the trunk. No money, no jewels, no savings book, no dragon; a dream. Such as it was. Dirty, dusty, crumpled, moth-ravaged, vulgar, fatal.'

Before dawn, on a sandy island below the waterfall, the poachers who for several nights running had been lying in wait for whatever it was that had been tearing their fishing nets, bludgeoned a monster with their oars. It had a monkey's head on a long neck, horse's feet and a blind dog's body. In the monster's stomach they found three torn drag-nets, a rusty sewing machine and a cheap glass smelling sharply of vodka. The dogs refused to eat the meat.

At midday the funeral procession moved off down Seventh Street. Screeching unbearably, sparks spraying from under their wheels, three trains came to a halt: two carrying freight and one carrying passengers from Vilnius. Over the roofs of the town, over the lime trees and rivers, over the surrounding fields and forests there floated the thick voice of the Trumpet: the mighty whistle of the paper mill. To it were joined the whistles of the noodle, margarine, meat and knitted-goods factories, and those of the flour mill and of the bread baking plant . . . The diesel locomotives started hooting, and so did Charlie Chaplin, the steam-engine seeing out its days on the sidings, not even fit to be used for shunting any more. Cars and buses, motorbikes and mopeds all honked away. From the Pregolya came the whistles of the barges on their way to the quarry for sand and gravel. The birds in the sky, the beasts in the woods and the fish in the rivers all froze in mournful silence.

Capitolina walked at the head of the procession, holding a little cushion on which a medal glimmered dully: *To a Partisan of the Great War, First Degree*. Behind her Genovepha and Dangolya carried a picture of Battle-Axe: they'd discovered at the last moment that no one had kept a single photograph of her, so they'd had to cut out a picture from a twenty-year-old local newspaper, in which the outline of a person holding a box of vermicelli showed through a fog of print. Then came two hundred people carrying funeral wreaths and another twenty with the coffin-lid. The black-lacquered lorry crawled along at a speed befitting the occasion. Its loadspace, open on all sides and decked with branches of fir and thuja, carried the boat bearing Battle-Axe's body (at night they'd tried transferring the deceased to Mukhanov's coffin, but the coffin had fallen to pieces). Battle-Axe was clasping to her breast a piece of paper that the Prosecutor had slipped under her dead, crossed arms at the very last minute.

In the first row behind the lorry, their eyes fastened on the swaying stern, walked Valentina, Grigory, Mikhail, Big Pyotr and Redhead Pyotr (the same Redhead whom a livid Battle-Axe had caught one night in the garden waiting for his lusty, stupid sweetheart and had driven out with the butt of a shotgun), Ivan and Vera-Veronica (they hadn't managed to drag Hatchet out of the shed where he was frenziedly making something), and also Soldier Maria with her cherubic children. Behind them strode Lyosha Leontyev in full uniform, Doctor Sheberstov wearing all his decorations on his immense chest, the Prosecutor, Frost Frostovich, Merry

Gertrude, the attack aircraft pilot who'd already acquired the nickname Chirimeh, and the stranger in black, streaming water as before. Vita Pea-Head was riding his motorbike alongside, having switched off the engine and pushing himself along with his feet. Behind them walked Gramophone and her daughter, an ageing beauty; Andrei the Photographer in his wide-brimmed hat with a long scarf round his neck; the placid craftsman Stepan Mukhanov and his father Avvakum Mukhanov, a cigarette lodged for all time in his lip and stuffed with Georgian tea of the highest quality; the Conjurer, wearing polished black boots and reeking of mothballs and rabbit's pee; Sweetie-Pie and her sister, Fish-Pie, with Phiz in her arms; Nadya Sergeyeva and her sixteen girlfriends; the lonely blacksmith Lyubishkin; Valka and Jaundice; decrepit Aphinogen with a brand-new tongue in his mouth; blind Dmitry; Zoika from the meat factory, the famous whore who fed herself on raw meat; the permanently sniffling barmaid, Zinaida; Fenya from the Red Canteen; the gypsy Seryoga; Mishka Cher Sen with his five Chersenikins; monkeyish Citrinyak; Grandma Coz with an alarm clock ticking away loudly in her handbag; Misha the Meat-Chopper; Dusya-Evdokia, with six fingers and two toes missing (a memento of the Leningrad Blockade); Gash and Sergeyushka, with iced cockerels in his mouth; Alyosha Ryazantsev arm in arm with Alexei Sergeyevich Ryazantsev; the Streltsy; the Urazovs; Irus and his gang; Blinker, smelling as always of engine oil; Genka and Vovka Razvodov, tipsy as ever; the musicians, tied with ropes to their instruments; Tanya-Vanya astride a trunk with a hooch-distilling contraption in her hands; the Prosecutor's dogs; Kalabakha; the head physician with a flaxen beard and the arms of a blacksmith's striker; Virtue, Love, Compassion, Sympathy and Hope in their frivolous apparel; the editor of the local newspaper, Yuri Vasilyevich Buida, with his wife Yelena Vasilyevna and children Nikita and Mashenka; the little paper figures which the Prosecutor liked cutting out in his spare time; the moth-ravaged velvet dress; the Fifty Fattest Women, the most outstanding of whom in all respects was state goods distributor Lidochka, who weighed exactly twenty-five stone (without her boots); Arkasha Shitson, who once ate a bucket of boiled potatoes in a single sitting; old woman Three Cats; Bun; Seryoga and Mitrokha; Millionaire, who'd become the butt of everyone's jokes after his wife gave away to a passing gypsy the ancient sheepskin coat where this scrooge had been hiding his money for ten years; the green-bearded *Three Heroes* and *The Three Musketeers*; the Prosecutor's chair; the beekeeper Rudy Panko★; the Prince of Darkness from the Rotten Ditch, stinking of oil waste; the red bull; the white lion; tear-stained complex sentences with subordinate modifiers of manner, measure and degree; Barykova–Bessalko; Phrantsoz–Hohusai; semi-transparent Solingen razors; paraffin stoves; poachers; Battle-Axe's water-tower; Battle-Axe's roads; Battle-Axe's pigeons; Battle-Axe's waterfall; Battle-Axe's sluices; Battle-Axe's dreams; Battle-Axe's clouds; Battle-Axe's sun, moon and stars; Battle-Axe's space; Battle-Axe's time . . .

Ever since waking up, Doctor Sheberstov just hadn't been able to get shot of the burdensome feeling that all this funeral business would end badly. 'Mark my words!' he shouted at his wife. 'This is no ordinary funeral! No ordinary female!' All journey long he was expecting some dirty trick or other, so he wasn't surprised when Gramophone whispered in his ear that Battle-Axe seemed to have stirred in the boat, and he just ordered her to be covered in a blanket from head to toe. Nor was he surprised when, after passing the last bridge, the lorry's engine cut out. No one else was surprised, either: it had been cutting out at the same spot for almost forty years now. But this time they couldn't get it started again. With a loud snort, Doctor Sheberstov ordered the coffin to be carried, and one hundred and fifty of the very strongest men immediately took the boat down from the vehicle. The procession moved on.

'We've seen nothing yet,' Doctor Sheberstov whispered loudly to the Prosecutor. 'Just you wait!'

★ The narrator of *Evenings on a Farm near Dikanka* by Nikolai Gogol.

'It seems to me,' muttered Frost Frostovich, 'that this will be the story of how we failed to bury a certain woman.'

Accompanied by the band, lamentations and tears, the many-coloured snake of the funeral procession turned into the avenue of lime trees near the former children's home and climbed to the summit of the cemetery hill, where a boat-shaped pit already yawned open in yellow sand. They lowered the coffin gently to the ground.

Here the roar of bronze trumpets and eleven thousand seven hundred and fifteen women suddenly ceased. The silence was broken by a joyful whoop:

'Look, it's Hatchet! Hatchet!'

The crowd surged forward to the fence and froze.

Over the hummocky field, bucking and flapping its lowered sides as if they were wings, rushed the black-lacquered lorry. Gripping the steering-wheel with one hand, Nikita Petrovich Moskvich was just managing to stay on the footboard. His sole concern was for the tow-rope not to snap: to it was tied an enormous kite whose two wings were fixed to the sewage barrel. With his legs splayed wide over the barrel's hatch and his face purple from the strain, Hatchet was mercilessly urging Bird onwards: the ancient nag just couldn't understand whether it was him galloping or some miraculous force carrying him forwards, and he raced on, shutting his eyes in terror, gulping air into his wide-open mouth and farting thunderously.

'Hatchet!' yelled Doctor Sheberstov. 'Hatchet!' He fell silent, trying to find the right words, then suddenly burst into ear-popping laughter. 'C'mon, you sonofabitch! C'mon! C'mo-o-on!'

And thousands of people, all appearing to lose their minds at once, yelled at the tops of their voices:

'Go on! Go on!'

They howled crazily, waved their arms about, stamped their feet, cried, whacked one another on the back, guffawed, and in a blind, rabid, oblivious frenzy, demanded a miracle:

'Come on, Hatchet! C'mon! Don't let us down!'

Bird's legs suddenly thrashed about desperately in mid-air,

the sewage barrel leapt up on a tussock and sailed off, smoothly fluttering its gigantic wings, which had been sewn together from patched-up night-shirts, darned socks, knickers, bras, buttonless smocks and a coat with the hide of an unknown beast on its collar – higher and higher, over the field, over the woods, over the roofs of the town that was saturated in the smell of fir and thuja. Then the people suddenly turned round all at once and saw a white dove dart out from under the sheet covering Battle-Axe ('See,' said Doctor Sheberstov. 'Warned you') and shoot up into the sky after the sewage barrel. After the first dove, out came a second, a third, a tenth, a hundredth, and now thousands and thousands of thousands of doves, loudly flapping their wings, were heading for the heavens in a gigantic swirling column of white smoke, to the House where this fate too will be measured according to the measure of man, that is, the measure of an angel . . .

In the ensuing hush everyone could hear the rusty Golden Cockerel with unusual clarity: creaking out his wings, shaking his rust onto the roof of the school, he tried to force out a sound that got trapped in his throat, gurgled there and finally flew out over the little town:

'Cock-a-doodle-doo! Cock-a-doodle-doo! . . .'

Eva Eva

Evdokia Evgenievna Nebisikhina aroused in all the anticipation and foretaste of generous love and inexhaustible happiness when she arrived in Wehlau in one of the first special trains bringing Russians to East Prussia after the war. In fear and puzzlement the settlers absorbed the strange-sounding names of the ancient cities – Königsberg, Tilsit, Insterburg – and peered at this alien land: its cramped fields and well-tended forests, narrow asphalt roads and stone houses with tiled roofs sheltering the parents of those who had burned the settlers' villages near Pskov, Smolensk and Orlov. In fear and puzzlement they trod along the platform's dark-blue stones and pressed closer to the soldiers and officers of their army, which had already made itself at home here in all these towns ending in *au* and *burg*. And only Evdokia Evgenievna looked around her and smiled as naturally and lightly as if she were the lawful heiress to this seven-hundred-year-old fiefdom whose cramped fields, dyked marshes and white dunes plunged straight into the cold waters of the Baltic. The soldiers and officers cast avid glances at the golden-eyed beauty holding herself aloof with a little suitcase in her hand. 'A magnetic woman,' barked a sergeant with a black moustache, but she just let her eyes glaze over him in faint mockery and strode off in the direction of the children's home. By the next morning everyone knew that there was a new nurse at the children's home. Evdokia Evgenievna: Eva Eva.

The black-moustached sergeant was right: Eva Eva really did turn out to be a magnetic woman. Men fell in love with her at first sight, children rushed to her the minute she called, and even women immediately forgave her for her beauty.

This devastated, burnt-up town that had twice changed hands and was populated by homesick Russian soldiers and silent Germans, who reeling from hunger, washed the pavements with ash instead of soap and exchanged their daughters' virginity for a lump of soldier's bread – this cowering, charred little town, all worn out by suffering, revived with the appearance of Eva Eva. The apple and chestnut trees suddenly bloomed; the birds that had waited out the war in lands where no newspapers are printed suddenly returned; the black bulls and their East-Friesian brides, flaccid from inertia, suddenly felt the urging of desire . . . And even bony Martha, whose sons had died in Africa and on the Volga, saluted the cars bearing guffawing soldiers over the railway crossing.

There wasn't a man in town who didn't try to win Eva's hand: generals and soldiers, officers and quartermasters from every arm of the forces. The mere mention of her name was enough to set off arguments that were settled with the crunching of teeth. Two young pilots, after quarrelling over the golden-eyed beauty, took to their fighter-planes to resolve their duel with a head-on collision. But she just laughed and the only gifts she accepted were flowers, even though she had at her disposal the reparation stores of all East Prussia.

Just imagine our amazement and indignation when we discovered that Eva Eva was living with the mute, Hans. Heavens, with Hans. With this lanky half-wit who got laughed at even by the Germans. At the children's home he acted as watchman, boilerman, gardener and herdsman. He was disciplined and docile; even when he was being scolded, he just nodded his assent, trying to stretch his lips into a smile. This never worked, though: shrapnel from a high-explosive shell had torn through both his cheeks, shattering half his teeth and ripping out his entire tongue. Then one morning we saw him leaving her room. How and when they came together, how and when they realized that they were meant for each other, and how they did so without speaking is known only to the god who watches over the mute and the beautiful. When Major Reprintsev, the head of the children's home, asked her about all this, she answered with a disarming smile: 'I love him. I feel sorry for him.' That was all she could say – a woman, one look at whom was enough to make every creature of the male sex lose its mind, from generals to sparrows.

With laughter, too, she paralysed our feeble attempt to

ostracize her, and flashed a nickel-plated Browning at the guys who pestered her the most. It had an inscription on the handle: a gift from Marshal Zhukov.

At night the men living in the streets nearby tossed and turned in their beds, chewing cigarette-stubs and listening to her happy groans and the provocative senseless lowing of her beloved. Men came to look at him from as far away as the air squadron four miles outside town. But no one dared touch him, partly because they didn't want to quarrel with Eva, partly, let's be honest, out of respect for his physical strength: Hans could unscrew a rusted nut from the hub of a car wheel with only his finger and thumb. And when the commandant, Colonel Milovanov, found a plausible pretext to throw him in the lock-up, Eva Eva just came along, just grabbed the keys off the table in the commandant's office and simply let the mute out, while everyone present, including the guards and Colonel Milovanov, could only follow her with rapt gaze. Hans carried her home in his arms. '*Ich liebe dich,*' she kept telling him, unembarrassed by the onlookers. 'I want a baby. I want a big belly.' And, swallowing the first consonant, she called his name in such a voice that even the phallic tank barrels turned towards her: 'Ans . . . Ans . . .'

Time passed, but Eva didn't get pregnant.

With Major Reprintsev's permission, she adopted a one-armed, ten-year-old boy, nicknamed Susik (Jesus) by the other kids. He was a quiet type and had only one hobby: shooting his catapult at the local Germans, who feared him like the plague. For ammo he used steel ball-bearings which tank crews had given to the children's home as toys. He reacted to his new circumstances with total indifference. He didn't let Eva dress him, went to the bathhouse with the soldiers, ate with them and came home only to sleep. Eva Eva meekly bore his insults ('German tart! Nazi slut!' Susik would mutter icily through his crooked slit mouth) and meekly waited for him to return, so that, once she was sure he had fallen asleep, she could kiss his closed eyelids.

The kids at the children's home took a dislike to him and showed him no mercy in their games. When they played at war, he usually ended up with the role of prisoner under interrogation. They beat him with a whip made from doubled-up telephone wire, burned his stomach with a cigarette and poked needles under his nails. Susik would grit his teeth and say nothing, which drove his 'enemies' to fury. 'Nothing good will come of this,' the head of the children's home warned Eva.

He was right. Playing at war one day, the kids strung Susik up from a pine tree and held a stone-throwing competition to see who could hit his tightly clamped lips. When someone struck the target, Susik's lips suddenly opened, and out tumbled an absurdly long violet tongue.

Hans carried Eva unconscious to the hospital. Doctor Sheberstov unbuttoned Eva's whites and whistled when he saw a hideous scar stretching like a winding cluster from her left breast to her golden pubis.

'How did you get this?' he asked when Eva had came round and he had carried out a full examination.

'Near Warsaw. I was a paramedic in the infantry.'

Doctor Sheberstov swallowed hard.

'Evdokia Evgenievna, I have to tell you that you . . . that it's unlikely you'll ever be able to have a child . . .'

For a long time she said nothing, lying on the couch with her eyes shut. Then she sat up and looked at the doctor, who had hidden his hands behind his back.

'So what's all this for?' she asked quietly, touching her breast with her hand. 'And this . . . and this . . . What for? Turns out the only thing I'm good for is being a whore, right?'

'It's the war,' said the doctor, looking away.

'God, but why?' she said, rapidly buttoning up. 'Why me?'

'War's war,' muttered Sheberstov. 'It's no one's fault.'

She didn't leave her room for several days. She lay face-down on her bed, dropping off then waking to the dull noise of her blood.

There was a knock at the door. She didn't answer.

'Eva,' called Nastya, the laundrywoman. 'Evushka, don't take it so hard. Let's go. Who knows, we might still catch them at the station.'

Evdokia lifted her head with difficulty from the pillow.

'Who?'

'Who?! The Germans, of course.'

'Which Germans?'

Nastya leant over her.

'What's up with you, my love? Are you sick?'

'No.' She sat up on the bed. 'What's happened?'

'They're being deported. All the Germans, kids and all. Twenty kilos of junk a head, and *auf Wiedersehen*! My landlady's twisted off a brass door-handle. A souvenir.'

'Why are they being deported?' Eva was already on her feet, quickly buttoning up her shirt and touching up her hair. 'I don't understand.' She looked out the window: two soldiers holding rifles were forcing old Martha into the middle of the cobbled street. 'What for? Where to?'

'To Germany. Order from Moscow. Don't rush off, I'll ask a friend to take us by car, we'll be there in a jiffy.'

The sergeant with the black moustache helped the women out of the car and shouted to the guard:

'They're with me!'

They were let through. From far ahead came the sound of the locomotive's slow, panting breaths. The soldiers clanked shut the freight wagons, paying no attention to the Germans standing stock-still in the doorways. Officers fixed lead seals on the doors.

'Hans!' Eva screamed at the nearest wagon. 'Ans, my darling!'

A young officer in Ministry of State Security uniform turned away and, breaking one match after another, finally lit up.

She rushed down the train in the slanting beams of the searchlights. Chubby Nastya ran after her.

'Ans! Where are you? Where are you? I won't let them!' Eva shouted, fighting off Nastya. 'I won't let . . .'

Soldiers sprinted up out of the dark and wrestled her to the ground, pressing her against the platform cobbles.

The train clanked and moved off.

'Ans!'

Eva tore herself free and stumbling as she ran, stormed into the waiting room.

'Telegram!' she screamed fearsomely through the glass at the telegraphist girl. 'To Stalin! Express!'

The State Security man came up to her from behind and gently took her by the elbow. She shoved him away without looking at him.

'Telegram!'

The telegraphist turned away.

'Please,' said the man in a loud whisper, although there was no one else in the room. 'Let's go. It's an order. Understand? An order.'

She stared at him for a few seconds as though she were blind.

He took her arm and led her away. Nastya, puffing and panting, grabbed her by the door.

'Let's go, darling . . . Thank you, young chap . . . Let's go . . .'

In the car the sergeant with the black moustache slowly lit up before suddenly saying as he gazed into the dark:

'Colonel Milovanov has shot himself.' He puffed out smoke. 'Because of his Elsa. That's deportation for you, girls.'

He released the clutch.

The next day Eva Eva quit her job and bought a ticket to Moscow. Wearing a fashionable, tight-fitting outfit, high heels and perfume, she arrived at the station a minute before the express was due to depart.

We never saw her again. We just found out later that she had stood for a long time on the platform at the end of the carriage, smoking and ignoring the conductor's questions. As for the conductor, well, he suspected something was up when he checked the platform once more after they had passed Vilnius and saw the door flung open and a slim handbag

146

dangling on the handrail. A mangled body was found in the bramble by the track: a bullet through the temple, a nickel-plated pistol clenched in a shattered hand, legs all covered in blood and creosote. Dead, of course she was dead. But this was no longer Eva Eva. No, no, this wasn't her, golden-eyed Eva Eva, who aroused in everyone's leaping hearts the anticipation and foretaste of generous love and inexhaustible happiness . . .

Rita Schmidt Whoever

'Dunno.' The bony old man in a crumpled linen suit leaned back. The curved runners of the rocking chair creaked as they rolled over the uneven floorboards, from which rose a heady smell of oil paint mixed with pine resin. 'I don't know and no one knows why she decided to leave her daughter here. Or why she chose those women in particular. Maybe she was afraid the girl wouldn't last the journey. Who could tell where they'd be taken?' He lit up. A lonesome bony old man in a badly washed and unironed linen suit with yellowed lapels and cuffs, wearing a narrow-brimmed straw hat pulled low over his eyebrows with a crooked silk ribbon of indeterminate colour wrapped round its crown, and cracked black boots out of which poked skinny, hairy ankles. Alone in a room with a tiled stove in the corner and a home-made bookcase laden with volumes in disintegrating cardboard covers and dusty tea glasses in whose dusty cobwebs chewed-up fag-ends hung aslant, quivering whenever a lorry clattered past the house down the cobbled road. 'We didn't even know the Germans were being deported. Sure, maybe some people guessed. Guessed without really believing it. There were thousands of them living here in their own houses. We were the newcomers, the flotsam and jetsam, all from different places, coming and going. But they'd been living and burying their dead here, in this East Prussia of theirs, for seven hundred years already.' He tipped his ash onto the floor. 'So she just turned up at these women's house. Out of the blue. With her daughter, wrapped in a yellow cloth blanket with a scorch mark from an iron. These two old nags, Martha and Maria, who I lived with too. A little Jewboy, a ginger Yidlet picked up by two witches.' He coughed drily. The young man winced. 'To Martha and Maria then. With her girl. Those two weren't surprised. She's giving her away. So what? We've got a Yidlet, let's have a Krautikin too. Never a calf without a piglet. They didn't do it for free. On top of the girl they got six silver soup spoons and a teeny shell-shaped silver watch with a mother-of-pearl cover. Fair and square. Stick her somewhere, the table will do. Damn you Nazi scrooges – six spoons and a tiny watch. What's that in her hand? Rita was clutching a wisp of oat straw, which she drew to her mouth the second she found herself on the table. Animal, just look at you Germans, the Lord will be your judge, you're just not like normal people. And that was it. In the evening the Germans were convoyed down to the station, put in freight wagons and sent off. Only Rita was left. And Merry Gertrude, the mad old woman, a German was she or a Lithuanian, dancing barefoot on the dusty road and always belting out one and the same song: "*Seid umschlungen, Millionen, Diesen Kuss der ganzen Welt!*"★ No one else, not one German male. Like there never had been. Houses under tiled roofs, Protestant churches, cobbled streets and asphalt roads thickly planted with limes, narrow canals and sluggish sluices, the wan German sky over the flat Baltic – yes, all this remained, but in a flash everything had become ours. Scarily ours. And, of course, the bits and pieces which they couldn't take with them (they were allowed twenty kilos of stuff each, so they only took food and the brass door-handles with lions' heads which they'd twisted off their front doors for souvenirs): china and faïence, books and furniture, coffee-pots and paintings . . . So the six silver spoons soon found their place among others. Plus the silver shell-shaped watch with a mother-of-pearl cover. That was it. A void. And in this void: a girl with a wisp of oat straw in her mouth and a mad old woman dancing barefoot in the dust by the station: *Seid umschlungen, Millionen*! And these two women built like horses, sisters with square faces bordered by dark shawls, with identical drooping warts as birthmarks on their veiny necks, dressed in oilskin aprons and men's boots with yellow string laces that grubby hands had turned black at the ends. All that was known about their previous life was that punishment squads had burnt their parents in their hut and

★ 'O ye millions I embrace you, / With one kiss for all the world.' (Schiller, *Ode to Joy* translated by Mike Mitchell.)

that their fiancé had died at the front. Their fiancé, get it? One for the two of them. That was what you understood from their accounts, for when they did choose to open their mouths, they spoke about one and the same guy: a brawny peasant, steel-capped boots, service cap with a glossy peak, an accordion, blue eyes. ("Grey," Maria would argue. "Blue," hissed Martha. "As you like," Maria would immediately give in. "Still grey though.") He fell in the storming of Königsberg. To kill him, the enemy had to wheel out an enormous cannon and fire a shell point blank at his heart. No, they took him prisoner and tortured him for days. Cut him up alive. Dug out his eyes with an awl. Ripped his nails off with the flesh still stuck to them. Desecrated his corpse. Whose fiancé was he? And was he really? Yes. Mine. "No," Maria would meekly object. "Mine. We kissed." "I don't care if you fucked," Maria would hiss. "He promised he'd marry me. If it hadn't been for those bastards . . . those Germans . . ." "If it hadn't been for them," echoed Maria, "those antichrists." And both would look with hatred at Rita as she crawled along the floor. "So why did you take her in?" Battle-Axe asked one day. "For those spoons, was it, or the shitty watch?" The sisters exchanged silent glances. "The Lord knows," Martha replied with a strange smile. "He sees and knows everything." Both crossed themselves fervently, searing each other with hate-filled eyes. Longjohn asked them the same question when they finally showed up at the local soviet to register the girl. Gotta be done, hasn't it? Right. What's her name then? Rita. Margarita. Father? Hitler. Adolf Hitler. "Cut it out!" the chairman of the soviet frowned. "These aren't kids' games we're playing." Hitler. Adolf. Get it? Longjohn turned red. "Adolf Schmadolf, idiots!" he shouted. "I'm Adolf too, so what? There's plenty of Adolfs running around. But that guy's no ordinary Adolf, he's Adolf Hitler. Feel the difference?" Adolf. Only his surname's Schmidt. But maybe that's just to fool people. See, no one's seen this Schmidt guy. Maybe he never existed. I mean, maybe he was a soldier, or someone else. The real Adolf. "Shut it," Longjohn flared. "There are no more Schmidts around here and never will be. We'll have her down as Kuznetsova. Kuznetsova Rita Adolfovna, dammit! Write it, I'm telling you. And stop dragging the antichrist into it!" Martha stared at the chairman, smiling. "The antichrist," Maria whispered. "Did you hear, Martha?" "I heard," the other replied, frightening Longjohn – how, he couldn't have told you himself. But the girl got her document: a certificate attesting the birth of Kuznetsova Margarita Adolfovna, Russian. Everyone who's not German or Jewish is Russian. Just how it should be, tip-top.'

Digging his heels into the floor, the old man turned round in his rocking-chair, his back to the window. Dropped his burnt-out fag in a glass. While his nephew was making tea and sandwiches in the grimy kitchen – soot-covered ceiling and walls, a sink rusted round the edges, a bucket beneath – the old man sat without stirring, eyes closed. He seemed to have fallen asleep. But the moment the young man appeared in the doorway, he flung his bony arms out wide and cried in a silly voice:

'So they started living together! Happily ever after!'

The nephew dragged a wobbly little table into the room and set down the teapot, a plate of sandwiches and a bottle of vodka. He threw a glance at the dusty glasses.

'Use the cups!' the old man ordered. 'A full one for me.' He drank it in one, with a jerk of his enormous Adam's apple. Sniffed the bread and exhaled, groaning weakly. His face reddened. 'You don't look like me, though.' He raised his hand. 'Be quiet. Don't look like my sister, either. Amazing.' Shaking his head, he reached in his pocket for a crumpled pack of cheap fags. 'You found me in the end. After so many years.'

'And all those years we've been looking,' said the nephew. 'Ever since the war. Mum always believed we'd find you.'

'Yes,' he said, nodding quickly. He lit up, inhaling with obvious pleasure. 'Don't be shy, eat. Yes . . . The war. How is it again in our lingo?'

'Holocaust,' the nephew replied. 'Catastrophe.'

All these phrases – 'our lingo', 'tip-top' – irked him. He didn't like the fact that his uncle didn't even seem to accept himself as a Jew at all. A dirty old man, he suddenly swore to himself, and blushed to the point of tears when he caught himself doing so. You couldn't even call him an old man: he wasn't yet sixty. In '42, when brother and sister lost each other, he'd been six . . . or was it eight?

'Holocaust,' the old man repeated with relish. 'Sounds better than catastrophe. There have been lots of catastrophes, but only one Holocaust.' He looked at his nephew guiltily. 'Forgive me, I'll never get used to it. I've always known I was Jewish, but I've never known what that is. That's just the way it went. Holocaust, my boy.' He choked on the smoke, coughed violently, and waved the smoke from his face. 'I have only one life, and that's there . . . then . . .' He poured himself half a cup of vodka and drank without hurrying. 'One little life.'

'Sorry,' muttered the nephew, 'but I still haven't understood what the women needed this girl for . . . this Rita?'

'Dunno.' He pulled his hat down over his forehead again. 'To hate. To love.' He paused. 'For her to live. What God gives isn't ours to take away. Yes . . . In the evenings Martha got her on her knees in front of the icon and said: "You're the daughter of the antichrist. You're German. You should be praying even when you sleep. You should suffer. You should atone." What was this taciturn, dark-eyed girl supposed to atone for, a girl who didn't know a word of German and who said "collidor" until she was fifteen? Whose guilt was she meant to be redeeming? The Germans'? Or whose? She was quiet, never spoke unless she was spoken to. She looked after the cow and the pigs, worked from morning till evening in the vegetable patch with the witches, washed her own and other people's rags, and all this from the age of five, like a clockwork doll, never a word of complaint. That's how it should be, yes, she should suffer, yes, she should atone. What does that mean? Don't know. Whatever God says it does. He'll say. He'll say one day: come here, Rita, little German bitch, now I'm going to punish you, punish you without even judging you, just because you were born in the wrong place at the wrong time, because German blood flows in your veins, because your countrymen perpetrated the Holocaust, because I am the God of the Jews and the Russians, and you're a German . . .' He suddenly broke off. 'I get out of breath. Yes. Me, I kept out of it. A lame ginger Jew, taken on as an apprentice to the barber with the odd moniker Name of Lev. He greeted anyone who walked in with the words: "Good-day, boss." To which the correct reply was: "Good-day, guv." Or: "Seen better". That was the custom. I lived at the top of the witches' house, in a cubby-hole with one window and a low ceiling. I could never fully straighten up. Sometimes she came up to me. Sat quietly in the corner. Moved her lips. What is it, Rita? She'd look for a bit, shake her head: nuffin', and go away. Or she'd carry on squatting there, her bare knees poking out from under a short dress that was all washed-out and patched over time and again. She smelled of household soap. Nothing else. What are you thinking about? God. And what do you think about him? What he's like. And what's he like? A judge. Yeah, of course, but what kind? No kind. Then all of a sudden she goes: does God have a soul? And it's my turn: dunno. Ask Martha. She says nothing. Course she won't ask. It's always the same: she gets back from school, rushes through her homework (she studied like everyone else: badly), and off on her chores. To suffer. Atone. In summer, Maria's heels would chap – she went barefoot from May to October. Tiny little worms got in the cracks. In the evenings, Rita carefully plucked them out with a match. Ticklish and painful. Maria lay on her bed, and Rita would get down on her haunches with the match and start plucking the woman's heels. Maria breathed deeply, squealing, "It tickles, you stupid girl!", or croaking, "Careful down there!" Rita would purse her lips and with tears welling in her eyes, carried on poking around with the match. Maria kept breathing deeper and deeper, flinching, groaning, then she'd suddenly jump off the bed, rake Rita up in her arms, clasp her against her stomach, tightly tightly tightly, press her, squeeze her and then release her just as suddenly with a drawn-out groan, and push her away. "My little birdie," she'd sing in a thin, feeble voice. "My birdie." She'd lie prone for a long time, staring senselessly at the ceiling. Rita would crawl off to her corner and try not to look at Maria. She didn't understand any of it. She was terrified. These women aroused nothing but horror in her. Not every minute, of course, but most of the time. They beat her for the smallest thing. Martha did it. What's that nasty look for? Eh, little bitch? Come on then. The girl would obediently pull off her dress. And? Removed her stockings. Hurry up, no one's going to steal your pearls here. Took off the faded washed-out bra covering her barely marked breast. Then her knickers, from which all colour had drained: the elastic had left a chewed-up trace on her chubby kid's tummy. Come over here. She went over. Well! Got down on all fours. Martha would trap her between her knees and whack her on her pink child's bottom as hard as she could with a doubled-up clothes line. Red marks immediately flared up. More. More. More! Martha would be breathing deeply and jerkily, her eyes glassing over, her face hardened in a smile. The girl shuddered with every crack of the clothes line. Scream! The girl screamed. Scream again! She screamed louder. Howled. Martha threw back her head; she'd be hitting her with the palm of her hand now, with both hands, she'd be tearing into the thing quivering and writhing beneath her with her fingers . . . Understand?' The old man abruptly leant forward towards his nephew; the floor creaked loudly beneath the rocking chair. His nephew nodded. 'I said: if I see or hear this happening one more time, I'll kill you. And you. They glanced at one another. "Aren't you a softie?" said Martha. "She's a German. She loves us. Don't you, Rita?" Yeah, of course. That's nothing to do with me, I said. I'm a Jew myself. But if I see, hear or find about you getting up to things like this with her again . . . is that clear? And why aren't you saying anything? She raised her eyes towards me. Yasha, I love Martha. And Maria. Don't talk rubbish. Yasha, I love . . . When I got back from the barber's the next day, the door was locked from inside and there was a rolled-up cloth blanket on the porch with a scorch mark from an iron, and a little bundle with my stuff in it. Fair enough. I kicked the door and shouted at the top of my voice: "Don't care: if I see or hear or get to know about it, I'll kill you. All right?" Name of Lev invited me to live at his but I refused: he had a big family squeezed into one room. So he managed to sort me out with some digs above the barber's, where the dressmaker's opened up later on. She went on living with the women. What else was she supposed to do if she had no one except these witches? School cattle-shed garden. Garden cattle-shed school. A dark-eyed taciturn girl, scared of music . . .'

'Music?'

'Music,' the old man repeated. 'Bog-standard music. The hags had a gramophone and a pile of trite old records. Pre-war bon ton. They used to travel to church once a month, some sixty miles away, in Lithuania. They'd get back late, both a bit tight, drink wine and listen to the gramophone. For company they had the watchmaker nicknamed Achtung, a man who always held himself bolt upright. He had an extremely high, clear forehead and a prominent brow under which, deep in the gloom, black eyes were hidden. Maybe they weren't even black – there was no way of telling. His lips always shone as if they'd been smeared with fat. Handsome lips. A tall wiry fellow who accompanied the women to church in Kibartai but never looked in himself. While they were doing their kneeling and crossing, he wandered around the shops or sat on a bench. A tall wiry fellow in a black suit, with a newspaper and a cigarette, his lips slightly twisted in a permanent smirk, meticulous to a fault, a bachelor who looked after himself, a real man. Never said much, polite. He worked as a watch-maker, hunched over behind a glass partition in his booth next to the shoe shop, with an eyeglass that he rarely pushed up his forehead. I don't know – though it's not hard to guess – why as a child I was scared of the word *Achtung*. It amused the watchmaker. He'd suddenly shout "Achtung!" for no reason and guffaw as he watched the little Jewboy scampering off to hide in a dark corner. Martha and Maria would gently tell him off. The watchmaker brought records with him. One day he put on Mozart. Yeah, Mozart. I don't remember what exactly, I just remember the letters on the record. "Sodding screechers," the hags grunted. Little Rita listened with eyes widened in bewilderment, then in terror, and crawled slowly down off the stool, grabbed Maria, buried her head in Maria's lap, and fell to the floor on her side. Commotion followed. They brought the girl round. Maybe the salad was off? No way. Only later did they realize: the music. Achtung started the gramophone and it all happened again. They didn't play Mozart any more. Smirking, Achtung would wag his finger at Rita: "Try being naughty and I'll put the music on." The music. All the rest wasn't music. Even when she'd grown up, the sound of the violins turned her all feverish and shivery, though she never fainted again. She'd take herself off to the garden or the cowshed, or further away. Strange.'

'Strange,' the nephew agreed. 'Look, the sun . . .' He cut himself short (God, what am I talking about!). 'Strange.'

'Strange, yes.' The old man nodded. 'This watchmaker . . .' He splashed a little more vodka into his cup. 'Rita became pretty once she'd grown a bit. Really pretty. I met her every day after school, walked her to the bridge: further was out of bounds, mummies would have seen. That's what she called them: mummies. How else? Mummy and mummy. We'd just walk along, chatting or not saying anything. A poorly-clothed girl and a poorly-clothed, lame and skinny barber. I'll take your satchel for you. Don't, they'll see. All right, I won't. Why are you so scared of them anyway? Cretins. Don't, Yasha. But they beat you. Not any more they don't. Any more! Any less? Yasha, I'm theirs. How's that? I haven't got a mother, they're like a mother to me, why can't you see? I'm theirs. They're mine. (I knew this meek girl would get into a fight if anyone insulted Martha or Maria in front of her, and I could never understand it.) So? They were a bit like mums for me, too: they saved me, a little Jewish kid, when I was running any which way from the SS. See, you do understand. And they don't have anyone, except us. It's just they can't say it. We were coming up to the bridge. See you. See you. Rita, I . . . Don't Yasha, don't touch . . . I wasn't thinking of touching her anyway. There were others. I only found out about them later, from her own lips. Give me those . . . Over there, in the oven . . .'

The nephew groped about in the cold oven and found several packets of cigarettes.

'One's enough,' the old man grunted. 'Throw the rest over there. Or over there.' He kneaded the tobacco for a good while in his bony fingers. The house was quiet. Over the river, trains rumbled through the station, carrying oil. It was getting dark. 'The kids caught her at the river.' He winced then lit up, loudly smacking his lips. Shook his head. 'Hardly boys, though . . . teenagers, fifteen- or sixteen-year-olds. You know, just the age. She used to bathe well away from anyone, choosing out-of-the-way spots, glades in the osier thickets. Stripped off and jumped in. Swam for a bit, threw her clothes on her wet skin and pegged it back home. But this time they caught her. Grabbed her. There must have been six or seven of them.' He paused. 'What are you always so secret for, all hush-hush? There's a whole bunch of us here, have a dip with us, go on, what's stopping you? One got hold of her shoulders, another took her legs, they chucked her in, stood and laughed. She circled in the water, grabbed a willow branch, wouldn't get out, waiting, looking without saying anything, on her guard, scared. What are you looking at? Out you get. Come on, don't be scared, we'll get you anyway. Someone stretched out a hand and they helped her onto the shore. Irus, ginger Irus, king of Seventh Street, with all his crew. She's not bad, eh? Yeah, she's all right. How about a game? Mums-and-daughters? What d'you say? We're all for it, unanimously, ha-ha. How about spin-the-bottle, no cheating, eh? They span an empty bottle. He's yours. Nothing to be so scared about, he won't bite! I have to go home. We all have to go home. You'll live. I've got to go home, let me go. Please.' The old man groaned as he turned in his chair. The floorboards creaked. 'That stupid idiotic "please". Gives her away immediately. Pretty pretty please. Aren't we the precious one? Don't touch me. Look here, what's this she's got? Not tits are they? And what's this? Look, little hairs! And there was us idiots thinking she was still a little girl! But she's already got hairs on her little cunt. Let me go! Let me go! Careful, one more sound out of you and you'll wash up at the lock, end of story. They'll investigate, but what are they gonna find? She tried to struggle free, slipped and fell. Thrashed her legs about, trying to protect herself. They hit her, again and again. She screamed, but shut up straightaway. Please, oh, please. As if she didn't understand that with this one word she was robbing herself of her defence: their fear. Someone, hurrying nervously, caught the elastic of her knickers with a pocket-knife and scratched her skin, drawing blood. They got scared, she screamed. "Please" again. Fascist whore! German tart! Scared dumb, she tried to crawl away to the water, ignoring the blood and her shredded knickers. The wounded animal wanted to save its skin in the water, and they realized that . . . Irus unbuttoned his trousers. He was older than the rest of them so he had enough self-control. The others just wouldn't have been able to do it . . . She stared straight at his hands, as they loosened one button after another. What, interested, are you, you animal, think we'll have you like normal people? Like a woman? Take this! She froze. The kids laughed excitedly. Irus, legs splayed open, drenched her in yellow urine, drenched her stomach, and the urine ran down to her hips . . . Piss on her! In her mouth! Stop right there!'

The nephew started.

'That was Achtung,' his uncle explained with a weak smile. 'A right old merry-go-round. Just Achtung, the watchmaker. Out of the ground. Or down from the sky. But if we're mis-using metaphors, then out of the ground, of course. Stop right there. They split and scarpered. They hadn't expected this. She was lying on the chilly clay, looking up at him, little, tiny, wretched, helpless, yearning for a miracle – and there it was! Achtung! A god. See, it was only later that it became clear he'd been hiding in the bushes from the very beginning, even before the kids showed up. Peeping at her, was he? For sure. Just couldn't stand it once they'd got their hands on her. She saw him as a god and deliverer, she was all his, from top to toe, bare naked, with a scratch low on her stomach, an offering, take me. His for the asking, half-girl, half-woman. What did he see then in her eyes? And anyway, is there anything to be seen in the eyes of a hounded animal? All right, gratitude:

161

have me. But not in that sense, of course. She can hardly even have been aware of it . . . she still didn't understand, see . . . she wasn't a woman yet. I mean even if she'd say "I'm yours", it wasn't in the sense of "your woman". Just: yours. Your thing. Your beast. Your cigarette case. Your boots. Whatever you want. Yes, something like that happened, she'd tell me about it later, when the time came. But what was he thinking then? What was he thinking as he gazed down at her, at her stomach drenched in yellow urine? Why didn't he touch her then? You see, then – at that moment, only then! – she'd have welcomed him as a god, a father, a brother, as I don't know what, but not as a rapist, and I even think she'd have been grateful to him for being satisfied just with that . . . Merely with her body. Her little body. The wretched gift of an offering spared by a god. Not her soul, see. All she'd have yielded was her body . . . I don't understand it. I'm scared of understanding. He just said: "All right, up you get, no use freezing like that, let's go." Then: "I won't tell anyone, don't worry." Why didn't he touch her? Maybe because any human is still less animal than human? Even if only a tiny bit less, a droplet, a spark, but that spark alone is enough to say to yourself before you die – at least to yourself, if you've decided there's no God – that I too was a human being? But maybe that's just romanticism . . . Well, I don't know. He didn't touch her. Didn't take advantage. Although . . . although maybe he was scared of those hags. He had his fun with both of them, and they clutched at him like the last thread in their lives: thought he'd drag them back from the next world . . . He wasn't fussy. Not that he got any stick for it in the town. Life's full of surprises. Some like it one way, others another. He didn't run stark naked down the street, didn't kill, didn't steal. So he liked bedding a couple of over-the-hill women, or maybe one at a time – big deal! Their business: Martha's, Maria's, Achtung's. Lots of tongues wagged, of course, and fingers too, but that's nothing: life's not life if you can't smear your neighbour with shit. Others were even jealous: look at him sitting pretty, sucking two mums and not giving either of them his pay-packet. Life of Riley. Martha was ready to scratch Maria's eyes out, that's for sure. She tried more than once. They vied with one another to lead him on. If old flesh and bones didn't do the trick, they'd lure him with hooch. Martha was the first to realize that apart from hooch, they had other bait in the house. That dumb Kraut Rita. She'd grown up a bit, become curvy, downy. It was time. No, all right, those can't have been Martha's exact thoughts. Even in her head she can't have said to herself: "It's time." That's going too far. I expect something just stirred in the place where other people's souls shiver. Stirred, tugged, pushed, rose like a lump in the throat: he doesn't swallow my bait anymore. But let him come anyway. Just come. At least to gape at *her*. Coz that's what he does. No shame at all. She bends over, he looks. She sits, he looks. Some- times all secret-like (ha-ha), from the corner of his eye, like he's not meaning to, other times he doesn't bother trying to hide it. Just looks at her. And why not? Young, fresh, tasty meat. Not like Maria or what have you. He can look, he won't eat her. It's not her he's here for, not yet. It's me. And some- times Maria. The bitch. She does it on purpose, moaning so loudly when he's on her, the cow. Ancient cow (she was two years younger than Martha). Croaks and squelches, like an old galosh in a puddle. What's it to him? Men are men. Vodka then a woman. Any will do. This one or that one. He's his own master. Come here. Rita went over. Let's go, then. The girl was scared: she always got scared when Martha started talking in a voice as if she was trying to swallow something but couldn't. She always talked like that when she ordered Rita to take her clothes off for a beating. But there hadn't been a beating for a while. Martha opened her trunk and had a good rummage among the mothballed rags. Have that. The stockings were nearly new, smooth, not ribbed ones, real ones, like grown-ups have. And this too. And that. Goodness, lace. Bit big, though. Never mind, you'll wear it in. Grab a needle and make it fit. Thank you. Take this, too. Stop wearing your vest, you're not a kid. Here, try this. She looked, narrowing her eyes, as if she was taking aim. That'll do. Good enough for marrying in. Thank you. What's with all these thank you's? Go and put your hair up. In the evening, Rita sat at the laid table, scared of even moving and feeling horribly uncomfortable in her new underwear, which rustled under her new dress and seamed stockings, smelling of *Carmen* perfume, turned deaf by all the new sensations and gawping blindly at Achtung, who was excited by her changed appearance. That night, he embraced *Carmen*-scented Martha so feverishly and with such strength that by morning she was ready to forgive Rita even for her German birth and antichristian origins. The next time, though, Achtung got drunk too quickly and cleared off home, disappointing both Martha and Maria. The sisters beat Rita mercilessly. Stripped her naked, stripped themselves naked, and beat her up. Tortured her till morning. Any way you can think of. Witches. Shits. And she made a run for it. It was some kind of animal impulse, obscure, instinctive: she slipped out the door and ran wherever her legs carried her. To the osier thickets by the river. Where else? She sat there until the early hours, shaking from the cold, then decided just as unexpectedly to return home. She chose a roundabout route: past the roofing-paper factory, through the vegetable patches. She treaded cautiously, her heart in her mouth, frightened by every shadow, every rustle. Ducking and holding her breath, she crossed the railway track (the gravel scattered under her feet, Lord have mercy). Clutching wiry chicory stems, she climbed down towards the pit where the roofing-paper factory had been discarding oil waste and resin for years. Her cloth shoes were immediately soaked through, and she heard a squelching noise beneath her feet. She froze, but the squelching was coming closer and she didn't have time to turn round before someone's hands grabbed her and pulled her sideways, and a body pressed against her. She squirmed, squatted sharply, kicked the dark, crawled off with a squeal towards the pit, lashing out at the darkness steeped in the hot smell of garlic and aftershave, hit something soft – croak: shit! – and again, then she swung round and, to her own surprise, threw herself at the smell of garlic and cologne, hit out with her knee, her fist, sank her teeth in, and suddenly the soft thing she was hitting and biting yielded and soundlessly slipped down the moist grass into the pit, gurgled there, and that was it . . . She jumped up and, without looking back, ran off towards the vegetable patches, leapt over the fence, collapsed on the grass, stopped dead, and lay there for an hour, maybe two, just lay there, cooling off and absorbing the shivery chill of the night, cold moisture and despair, until she told herself: that's it, I've killed him. I've killed a human being. Now Your punishment has come to pass, O Lord. You've caught me. She struggled up and, barely lifting her feet, dragged herself out into the meadow through an unlocked gate. A thick fog was swirling over the oil pit. Rita yanked a post out of the fence and began poking around with it in the stinking oily depths, occasionally bumping against soft objects. The sun broke through the fog. Rita cried. Eventually, she tossed the post away and trudged off home. Dead, already executed, a shadow of her own shadow, reeking of oil waste and wet from the night dew. Neither Martha nor Maria dared even ask where she'd been all night: they just met her on the threshold with a lantern, staggered back and silently let the girl into the house. She climbed the stairs, leaving dark stains on the steps. The water in the wash-basin smelled of oil waste. The *Carmen* cologne smelled of oil waste. And even the thought, "You can't cheat fate", smacked of oil waste, as of blood.

'Achtung stopped visiting the sisters. Stopped without any explanation. In the end Martha couldn't stand it any more and went off to see him. The watchmaker offered her weak tea in a whitewashed kitchen that reeked of paraffin. His face was covered in bits of plaster, the joined semicircles of the bites – tooth on tooth – were smeared with iodine. The potent aroma of oil waste seeped through the smells of medicine and paraffin. "Fine." Martha stood up heavily. "Make your mind up and come." "You know how it is," Achtung answered gloomily as he closed the door, which was covered in faded russet oilcloth.

'Back home, Martha didn't say anything to her sister. What was there to say? She knew how things stood. They'd given the snake a roof. Brought her up. Put shoes on her, clothes on her, nursed her, fed her. Sprayed her with cologne. Bitch.

Bitchuvabitch. Open up. Who am I speaking to? Just you wait . . . you'll be sorry . . . God sees everything. Knows everything. Remembers everything. He won't have any of it, He won't forgive you, Nazi scum.

'From that night on, Rita locked her door with a key and an iron bolt.

'Time to talk about Fuffy. Or have I talked about him already?'

'No. Maybe we should turn the light on?' suggested the nephew.

'It won't get any lighter.'

The old man fumbled for his cup and bottle in the dark, poured, swallowed, loudly exhaled. Lit a cigarette. It was stuffy in the room. The young man wiped his brow and dried his hand on a handkerchief.

'Fuffy.' The uncle sighed. 'Don't remember what his real name was. They nicknamed him Fuffy. Mockingly, with a hint of contempt. Mercilessly, when you think what this man went through in his life. He was badly wounded in the last days of the war, spent several years going from one hospital to another, eventually managed to find this little town where his wife, the only person close to him, had been recruited to work. That Fuffy – he was a ball of spite . . . He seemed to exude spite unceasingly, day and night, for no reason at all. It was simply the energy that sustained him, and at the same time, the form of his existence. Spite consumed him, ate away at him, gnawed, guzzled, burned him from inside. A bony fellow with skin charred by the scorching heat beneath. An entirely hairless skull, slightly pointed at the crown and streaked with a lumpy bright red scar. The flakes of his lashes had smouldered to whitish ash. The pupils of his round eyes had burned to grey, and under them hung flabby bags of grey skin, forever quivering from a nervous tic. He had little lobeless ears pinned to the skull, hard as though they'd been chiselled out of dead bone. Colourless lips. It was as if he permanently radiated tension, and people just got tired of looking at him. So this twisted man with a wooden leg and a crutch clenched in his sweaty hand appears before his wife. A man who's long since cooled from the pride of victory but still hasn't forgotten that he's a soldier of truth, a soldier of justice, a soldier of freedom and whatever else Josif Vissarionovich thought up for them . . . Well, as for his wife . . . A frisky, plump, run-of-the-mill young thing who'd shacked up ages ago with a healthier, younger husband, recognizes in terror that the spite-consumed cripple before her is her legal husband, the same guy she'd buried, wept for and forgotten years before when she received the notice of his death. Straight out of a novel . . .'

'Right,' the nephew grunted. 'Romanticism.'

The rocking chair and the floorboards crackled and creaked. The old man broke into peals of quiet laughter.

'And what were you thinking, that I'd tell you the truth and nothing but? There's no such truth. No court can thrash that out of a person. Anyway, the facts die, only the legend lasts. The lie, if you like. Now there's something you can't argue with. Only an idiot would think of finding out whether that guy from La Mancha really tilted at windmills. Only cretins bother their heads about whether the carpenter's son really existed and whether he really was crucified on that little hill . . .'

'Golgotha,' croaked the nephew, swallowing the vowels. 'Uncle Yakov, but you're . . .'

'Me!' yelled the old man. 'And that's why I'm telling the story, and I'm not asking you to believe me . . . or not believe me . . . I couldn't care less,' he said without expression. 'Every man is free to decide for himself what to believe in and what to cry for.' And, without pausing for breath: 'So, Fuffy. His wife got some stick, of course, but not for long: life went on. You can't expect the impossible. They felt sorry for him – yeah, sure, he was a cripple – but why let himself go? He beat the woman so savagely he broke his crutch on her. Someone ran over to the factory, thank God, and her new husband, a lanky seven-footer, hared over on his bike, swept Fuffy up and carried him out. He didn't throw him out, he carried him in his arms, clasping him to his chest like a baby, and Fuffy just quivered feebly, swaddled in the fine fellow's powerful muscles. Then he stopped twitching, too, and just lay there with his eyes closed. The fine fellow carried him across the whole town to the old brick gateway and set him down carefully on a stump in the shade of a chestnut tree. Put him down and left. Fuffy just carried on sitting there in exactly the same position on the stump in the shade of the chestnut tree. Sat with his eyes closed, monotonously rocking forwards and back, softly howling, until the shadow of the chestnut tree covered the whole town and turned into night. He howled away on a single note: till dawn, I think. But when old Urazova looked out of her window in the morning, he was no longer there. At first they thought he'd just hobbled away. But he'd had a different idea. He'd moved into the loft of the old stable, where they set up the sawmill later. The sawmill below, Fuffy in the loft. Filled with spite, scorning all offers of help, all words of compassion, all charitable gestures. Proud. Fuffy, in a word. He lay stretched out on a trestle-bed for days at a time, a half-dead reproach to all those bastards. Just lay there staring at the ceiling. He wouldn't even turn round when old Urazova brought him some grub. Sure, he crawled outside sometimes, went down to the yard and even occasionally helped the sawers, for which he'd get some *Hunter's* fags, six kopeks a pack, or a glass of vodka. He didn't ask for any of it, they gave of their own accord. But what's stuck in the memory is a guy lying dead still on his trestle-bed in the corner of the loft, withered up good and proper, blackened by the spite searing him from inside. To hell with the lot of you. Every now and again, someone would move in with him. Mukhanov junior lived in the opposite corner of the loft for a whole year on a bundle of straw and sawdust; he'd had a row with his father and eventually quit the town for good. They lived for twelve months together, side by side, and never exchanged a word. Not one word. One winter he was joined by Leg Over, that bedraggled young alky, always smiling through gapped teeth, a red-faced, wheezy-voiced foulmouth who laughed back at anyone who ribbed her about her room-mate: "Idiots! A fella like 'im's one in a million. When he sticks 'is rasp in, he saws away till mornin', I'm tellin' you!" Fuffy threw her out in the spring. An outcast . . . He'd cast himself out. Now that's pride for you. If his old wife had been a bit less thick of skin and brain, she'd have wound up in the loony-bin for sure. Her new husband went to see Fuffy a number of times, offering money: just leave. No. So he left himself, taking his wife with him. Fuffy ended up alone. To hell with the lot of you. People started to forget why he'd settled in the loft in the first place. They got used to him and stopped mentioning him so often. Let him be. One man lives in a palace, another in a hovel, Fuffy in the loft. Not as if there weren't enough weirdos in this town, where folk gathered from the four ends of the earth. Like Wench, who crapped under any wall she found herself by and then drew the sun on it with her own shit. Like Avvakum Mukhanov, who stuffed his cigarettes with top-quality Georgian tea and guzzled raw carp when he was out fishing. That's why he kept salt in his pocket: he'd catch a bream, dip its head in his pocket, and pop it straight in his mouth. Like Jaundice, who ate a kilo of carrot a day and tore around the town at night on her bike. Like Vita Pea-Head, who carried a heavy padlock in his pocket to whack people on the head with if they paid him for chopping firewood with a ten-rouble note instead of ten crumpled one-rouble notes. And Fuffy, lying prone in the loft over the sawmill and pro-cessing his accumulated spite into urine. Maria got into the habit of visiting him. No one knows what went on between them but Martha and Rita found her often enough in the loft, dead drunk, and had to drag her home. "Some Romeo you've found," Martha would wheeze. "Moron!" But Achtung never came, and Maria would head off once more to the sawmill, cleaning her teeth beforehand with a rag dampened in liquid ammonia and taking along a bottle of hooch. Her sister's reproaches had no effect on her and the next morning the younger sister would be sitting on a stool in the kitchen with a vacant gaze and drinking small gulps of diluted iodine. "You'll croak," Martha usually prophesied as she rolled out the dough. "Or else he'll kill you, the nutter." He didn't. She took her own life. While Martha and Rita freed the rope and dragged the body to the hatch, Fuffy didn't bat an eyelid. He lay on his trestle-bed, stared at the ceiling and smoked a roll-up that stank of burnt bone. "Look at you," Martha said, shaking her head. "A person kills herself in front of you, and you . . ." Then he propped himself up on his elbow, looked at Martha and Rita through spite-scorched eyes, and drawled: "I'd have helped her, but I've only one leg, see." Fuffy . . . Shit. Stinking shit. But there was no getting by without him. That night, after drinking herself into a stupor, Martha lay in wait for Rita as she ran barefoot from the toilet up to her room, and threw her off the stairs. Rita came round just before dawn on the floor, her head all bloodied. The iron bolt had been ripped roughly off her door and lay in the middle of the room, bristling with bent screws. There was a mop in the corner. Rita lay down under her blanket clasping the stick. She'd barely closed her eyes when the stairs creaked under Martha's weight. "Now your hour has come," muttered the drunken witch. "Here it is, your hour, your bridegroom striding towards you, you whore . . . Now you'll see . . . You'll lie in one hole with Maria, my one and only . . . You've lived a bit, time to say your goodbyes, Nazi scum . . ." She tossed her hair back off her wide manly forehead and saw Rita. "The Lord chose you," she said, shaking her finger at the girl. "But he chose me too . . . Your job's to suffer, mine to punish you . . . Now I'll scrape the meat out of your shell . . ." Rita hit her without warning: a blow to the forehead with the stick. Martha grabbed hold of the shaky banisters. Rita hit her a second time. The witch fell like a sack on the steps. All over. Her dark hair, streaked with grey, became wet. That was blood. That was the end. From now on she couldn't live in this house. But where then? There wasn't a single normal person who'd take her in. She was just no use to anyone. She was sixteen. Even if a normal person did offer her shelter, Martha wouldn't back off, she'd claw at her, scrape her out, trample and suffocate her. She wouldn't stop for anyone. She was in her senses, she was normal all right. Rita was also normal. So Martha would get her. She'd leave her alone in one scenario and no other. That scenario was called Achtung. But Rita wouldn't go to him. So she went to Fuffy.'

The old man stopped to catch his breath.

'Shall I open the window?' the young man suggested.

'Eh?' asked the old man.

'The window . . .'

'Go on, do . . . it's stuffy!' He threw his hat on the floor and leant back in his chair. 'Really stuffy. You see, she didn't want to stitch me up. She thought I was too normal for her to come to me. She couldn't permit herself that. For me to stain myself by saving a little bitch. For people to point their fingers at me: here's the guy who took in the Nazi scum. Took her away from Martha, who'd been a second mother to her. Instead of that mother who flung her at the mercy of fate. Martha saved her. Think of Martha what you will, but she saved her. And look how this ungrateful little bitch paid her back. And how that Yiddish scum helped her. No, Rita decided, filth to filth. Shit to shit. Then there'll be no confusion, no questions. That's what we thought anyway. What was there to be surprised about? Blood talks in the end. The bitch left like a bitch, the ungrateful animal crawled off into the dirt she was used to, the shit she loved best, the shit she could never get enough of. To Fuffy, what could be shittier? Everyone's happy. Martha's left on the stage in the role of abused virtue, nobility and selflessness. Too right, it wasn't her who hung herself. Rita slinks off vermin-like to her vermin lair. The rest are ringside angels. Including me.'

The nephew breathed in the night cool, smelling of silt from the sandbanks and rotten leaves.

'Did you feel hurt?' he asked.

'Hurt?' the uncle burst. 'Yes . . . Suppose we can call it that. I was hurt. Annoyed. Disheartened. Insulted! Destroyed! Well, all right, she'd made her own mind up. But it wasn't as if I was a stranger! She could at least have said . . .'

'She could,' the nephew echoed.

'She decided everything herself. And rightly for herself. Like she was taught. With all she'd absorbed: you should atone. Suffer. Become the lowest of the low, slave of slaves. And she did.'

Loudly smacking his lips, the uncle lit up yet another cigarette. The smoke trailed towards the window.

'So that's what she became. Fuffy wasn't surprised. At least I doubt he was. He was probably pleased. Ah, that's what I thought. They're all the same. This one too. Pure on the outside. Well well. Clear enough: just another person smelling of household soap. No different from shit. Wash as much as you like but you won't get cleaner. Pigs are no dirtier. He had a sty made from off-cuts and roofing paper, built onto the sawmill in the corner of the yard. He had a vegetable patch, too: potatoes, cucumbers, parsley, onion. Didn't need anything else. Swill for the piglet, weeding. That was all that had to be done. He spoke through clenched teeth, without even looking at her. Not as if he really needed her. But now you've come you can stay. Piglet and garden: that's the lot. The paraffin stove's in the box, careful with the flame. And don't go blabbing about it to anyone. There's a mattress. Main thing's the piglet and the garden. And don't natter too much. Better if you don't natter at all. But I can see you won't want to anyway. Right? Good. In the evening he lay with a roll-up stinking of burnt bone between his teeth and read a scrap of newspaper in the light of a 45-watt bulb hanging on a twisted cord above his trestle-bed. She lay on her mattress, wrapped in an overcoat. His overcoat. Without turning his head or taking his fag out of his mouth, he asked: "Happy?" Of course she was happy, happy as Larry. Come here. Take yer clothes off. Well. Get yer gear off. All of it. Well. Don't want to? Then scram. Button up and scram fast as you can. Well? Good. Come here. And don't yell, I don't like it. No, not like that, turn over. On yer stomach, I'm telling you. I can do it like that with anyone. With you I can do it this way too. Good! He raped her and when, biting her lips, she crawled off the bed, he prodded her painfully in the side with the crutch. Good girl. You'll survive. You'll do. You'll do for a woman in the meantime. Get to sleep. And no whining over there.'

Something fell onto the floor and started rolling. The

young man squatted and caught the sound with his palm. It was a button. A small button, the kind used for shirts.

Swallowing loudly, the old man drank from the kettle.

At the station a diesel locomotive gave a short whistle, iron clanked.

'But . . .' The uncle cleared his throat. 'But I wasn't the only one snivelling. Achtung couldn't stand it either. He held out as long as he could, but he still gave in. Thought it would turn out his way, but it turned out hers. Thought patience was the key, but she didn't have enough of it. Or else she used it wrong. When he saw her in the yard of the sawmill, he just froze with his jaw hanging out. Stands there with his gob wide open, not breathing. But he understood everything straight-away. Look at her in her dirty smock, shuffling over to Fuffy's shed with a mucky pail in her hands. So that's how it is then. Crystal clear. He came round again. She was standing legs spread wide over the vegetable patch. She turned round to see who was walking by, then back to her business. There was always folk walking by here. She didn't even squat. She just stood there, still wearing the little frock she'd long grown out of, bum in the air. Watch away, I don't care, I'm like a husband's missus now, nothing for me to be ashamed of, I've got a master, I'm his thing, his slut, stinking slut. Two days later Achtung made up his mind to go to see Fuffy. He found him on his trestle-bed, reading a newspaper. Rita was cleaning a bowl in the corner, head bowed: *shik-shik* with the rag, *shik-shik*. At first she couldn't catch what they were talking about over there. Blah blah blah. You're crazy, Fuffy suddenly says. Five hundred, Achtung says. Now that's money. That's money, says Fuffy, but what good's it to me? Achtung again: it's money. Up to you, of course, you're the master, the lord. The lord, Fuffy drawled. Hey, get over here. Rita went up to him. Achtung hums and haws, keeps glancing at her and then looking away. Fuffy's eyes dart from her to him. He sniggers. C'mon then, out of yer gear, no not here, in yer corner. She undressed without a word. Achtung covered his eyes and went pale. Terrible how quickly and obediently she did all that, like she was a robot not a human. Fuffy whistled, like he was calling a dog. She got down on all fours and crawled over to the trestle-bed. See, he says. Yeah, whispered Achtung, five hundred, straight up. Sure, Fuffy nodded, but you can have her for nothing. Interested? Right now, take her, do what you want with her, she won't even squeak, free of charge. Five hundred, Achtung whispers, and for good. You're a real bastard, Fuffy. A shit. Me? Maybe I am, but at least I get it for free. I didn't buy her, she came herself. I can throw her out, else she can leave herself if she wants. I'm not holding her back. She holds herself back, without a penny. But you want her for money. What if she doesn't want to, eh? He prodded her in the stomach with his crutch. He wants to buy you. For five hundred. That's good money, girl. I didn't buy you. Don't even know how much you're worth. Maybe more, maybe even nothing. How should I know. Your money, girl, think about it. Take them. Five hundred, big money. You can leave some place. With money like that you can go to the ends of the earth, or even to that Naziland of yours. She looks from one to the other. Money? Five hundred? Doesn't make any sense. Money for what? What, to buy her? Are they really talking about her? About you, you. She shakes her head, swallowing her tears. No, not like this, no, no, no. Nothing to be done about it then, Fuffy says. You wouldn't believe how chuffed he was. She doesn't want to, he says, she's not for sale. Least there's something which can't be sold. For money, anyway. Rita's standing starkers in front of him, looking so tired it's as if she's not there, as if she's just a thing and nothing more, a living thing with bruises on her back and her sides, with bitten little tits, with hands red from cold water. Get to yer corner, Fuffy ordered her, what's with all this prancing around starkers in front of strangers? He laughed. Maybe he was pleased by Rita's loyalty, maybe such strange loyalty touched him, maybe for the first time in his life . . . how can you tell? Maybe that was the final straw for Achtung. And, of course, the fact that Rita just turned round and shuffled off to her mattress – she was walking away from him! – and that Fuffy seemed to have taken a final decision, and that none of this could be recovered or replayed, that all of it was happening half-jokingly, like it was nothing serious, like in a dream, as if a person was passing through you, you try to grab him, hold him back, but he's like light and goes right through you. Like water. A squirting noise: Rita turned round but she understood nothing at first. Fuffy was lying prone just the same as before. Achtung was leaning over him, moving his lips, but she couldn't hear anything. What were they whispering about over there, she thought in fright as she sat down on her mattress. Christ, Achtung said, that wasn't meant to happen. He sank down by the trestle-bed. Fuffy didn't stir, just lay there, covering his face with the newspaper. Achtung broke the silence: why aren't you saying anything, eh? What are we going to do next? She looked at him without speaking, still not understanding, wearily pulling on her clothes. You know all this is because of you, Achtung went on. Do you understand that or not, eh? Standing with her back to him, she got into her knickers. Christ, Achtung whispered, look at her flashing her bum around. Are you going to say anything or not, you Egyptian mummy? What, she grunted, what d'you want? He was silent and his silence was such that she turned round and looked at him closely, screwing her eyes up till they ached and tears appeared. Her heart started thumping. Achtung watched silently as she tottered up to the trestle-bed, her eyes fixed on the darkening newspaper, from the corner of which a heavy drop trickled and fell onto the wooden floor. Because of you, he repeated in an expressionless voice. She gingerly lifted the part of the newspaper which had slipped onto Fuffy's chest, then lowered it immediately. Just don't start yelling, he said quickly. We've got to think what to do. What's there to do, she asked vacantly, I don't know what to do, we should tell the police. We've got to get out, Achtung said, and quick. Drench the place in kerosene and light a match. Simple. They'll think he did it. From the paraffin stove. In his sleep. Or drunk. Nothing will be left by the morning. They won't be able to tell the bones from the burnt logs. Where's the paraffin then? There, she said, but what for? He calmly repeated it all. And again. In the end she raised her head and looked him square in the face. No, she said, maybe not even understanding what she was saying. No, we can't. We can't. Idiot, he said quietly, all this is because of you, understand? Because – he swallowed and could barely finish the sentence – because I love you. That's the way it is. She shook her head. I'm not going with you. She laughed. He lifted the newspaper slightly and wrenched the razor out of Fuffy's neck. Incredible, he sighed, it went right through to the neck. Who'd have thought it . . . I'm not going with you, she repeated with a smile. And although he still hadn't understood why she'd suddenly started smiling, or what this smile meant, he sniggered in reply: "Up to you. But you'll come, you know. No kidding. You'll come running." Then, without pausing: "In '43 we had to shoot a deserter. Like you're supposed to. We led him out and he dug himself a pit. Some entertainers had come by the regiment then. Ditties, tap-dancing, a singer . . . Well, we stuck this guy in the pit he'd dug himself, and the lads went off to the show. It was right nearby: this was the frontline. They left me on guard by the pit in case he tried to make a run for it." She listened with interest, her head to one side and her mouth slightly open. "The jokers were joking, singing ditties. The soldiers were splitting their sides. This guy in the pit laughed his heart out as well: he could hear it all, you see. I went over to the pit and he was at the bottom, laughing and clapping. Everyone clapped, and he clapped along with them. Laughed. It was a good show. When the entertainers left, we shot him, of course, and filled in the pit. Like you're supposed to." She nodded. All right, he said, folding the razor. You can smile for the moment. Clap your hands. But you'll come anyway. I'm going now, understand? He kept his voice down and spoke clearly, so as not to frighten her and drive home to her everything he needed to. So I'm going now. You'll stay here. People will turn up, the police will come. A dead man's lying here. You're here, right next to him. Who killed him? You'll say I did it. Ridiculous. I was home. Sleeping. First I hear about it. You've got bruises on your body, he beat you, treated you like dirt . . . He tortured you. Everyone knows what Fuffy's like. So you got your own back. Like you did on Martha. Same on Fuffy. There's no

176

one but you. No one will believe you. No one. Think about it. You're already thinking, right? Good. Think. Quickly, mind. She shook her head. No. He smiled weakly. You won't just come over, you'll come running. Who'll hide you except me? Only me. Now I'm leaving and you'll drench the whole place in paraffin and light a match. Then you'll come over to me. I'll wait. You'll ask to be let in. I'll hide you in the basement. Feed you. Won't tell anyone where you are. You burnt up along with Fuffy, end of story. You'll live in the basement for the time being, then we'll make a run for it. We'll leave. For good. And we'll forget all this – for good. So I'll be waiting, OK? She shook her head again. "Got any matches?" he inquired with concern. "Here are some nice new ones, a full box. No one's going to mourn for him. They'll gasp and sigh a bit, then forget. He was alive and now he's gone. People don't rip their hair out for a person like that. And you've got your whole life in front of you." I'm not a German, she suddenly said. He nodded. As you wish, fine by me: you're not a German. What kind of German are you anyway? You can't even speak their lingo. Expect all you know is *Hände hoch* and *guten Tag*. Well, *auf Wiedersehen*. He paused by the hatch. Don't think too long, or else, who knows who might show up? He dived down the hatch. Stumbled on something below. The door creaked. Silence. And that was when Rita realized: that was it, her life was over. Her previous life, at least. Not much was left now: just to live another life.'

'She came to you?' asked the nephew.

'Not immediately,' said the old man. 'First she poured paraffin all over the floor. Sat for a bit and had a think. Started drying the floor with a rag. Realized she was going mad. Chucked the rag away and ran. Breakneck. Luckily I was only a stone's throw away. She knocked, came in and sat here by the window reeking of paraffin, shaking, crying . . . Yes. I've got to admit I'd been expecting something like that. Not that exactly but similar. Not that I'd really believed it would happen, or knew . . . But I'd been expecting it. It was some kind of hopeless expectation of a miracle. And it happened. How was I supposed to know that genuine miracles are mixed with

177

blood? Anyway, it happened. I didn't realize straightaway then that nothing's more dangerous than miracles. For behind them – or worse, in them – is fate. Destiny. What else? Death? And death. A signal. At last she told me everything she wanted to. From the very beginning: what I knew, and what I could never have known. She needed to pour everything out, to fulfil every person's dream: at least for once say everything you want to say. As a rule, few manage it. Perhaps almost no one. And maybe that's for the best, I don't know . . . But we all strive for the Garden of Gethsemane.'

'The Garden of Gethsemane?' the nephew repeated.

'That's just the name I have for it. Because he didn't just grieve there. He spoke his most secret thoughts, his greatest anguish, and it didn't matter whether it was to himself or his father. He said his all; I mean, he finally became himself. After that a man's capable of anything. An act of heroism, or of unheard-of baseness. Maybe Judas was Judas because he wasn't able to say his all. But that's by the by. She did say her all. Morning came. I laid her on her bed, locked the door and went to work. The minute I got to the barber's, I realized what was up. It was a Saturday, the place was full of oldies. Good-day, boss. Good-day, guv. Seen better. They've found Fuffy. Really? Really. In that loft of his. Lying on his trestle-bed under a newspaper. They lifted the paper. Head to the side. Razor what did it. Sliced right through the neck to the bone. Here to here. Huh. Who found him? Achtung. Who? You know, the watchmaker, Achtung. What the hell was he there for? Not what but who, get it? S'pose he was after that German girl, that pup, Rita. Now there's a slut. So? So he turns up and there's Fuffy sliced open. Dead? Course he was dead. Stick his conk on a dish if you want. Lopped off by a razor. Razor? Or something. What then? Something else. What? How'd I know? Achtung goes to the coppers, to Lyosha Leontyev, I mean. What does Lyosha do? What d'you think? Goes over, has a butcher's, turns his conk around. Whose conk? Not Fuffy's, stupid, his own. Where's the lassie, he asks, who's seen her? Huh. There you go. What a slut. A Nazi's a Nazi: one race. Fuffy's no saint either. True enough, but why do that? He's a human bein', ain't he? Living. Not now he's not. Not now, clear enough. Where's the girl then? God knows. Ran scared. How old's she? Fifteen? Sixteen? Obvious, ain't it, pissed herself and hid somewhere. So what, she'll come crawling out, they'll get her. Where's she gonna hide here? They'll find her. Maybe it's not her. Maybe. But who else? Martha says it's her too. And Martha's like a mum to her. Mums don't grass on their kids just like that, do they? No. So Martha's yellin' away, rolling about on the floor, screaming: it's her. Her. Truth's thicker than blood. Are they gonna stick her inside or what? For doing someone in? They could hang her for that. But she's just a kid. Maybe they won't hang her then. Just bang her up, for life an' all. I'd deal with her sort meself. We didn't scare enough of 'em in the war. One race. That bloody race. What race, you idiot? What's she got to do with it? What's she not got to do with it? Nothing. But she killed 'im. Yeah, true . . . And so on.

'At lunch Lev let me leave the barber's and I ran over to the policeman, Lyosha Leontyev. Martha was already with him, the witch. Sitting up straight, wooden-faced. It was her, couldn't have been anyone else. All right, Lyosha says, thank you. It was her, Martha starts up again, without looking at me. She did it, Lyosha, that scumbag. Her hour has come, Lyosha, as it was decreed. By who? By Our Lord. Your Lord decreed forgiveness, too. She made as if she hadn't heard. The Lord brought her mother to my house. It was Him who put that bitch in my care. He let her become who she did. Let her open up, so we could see: so that's what she's like. And she opened up. And we saw. I'd like to see her, Lyosha says. Now the hour has struck. Lyosha said nothing. Nor did I. So what do we do now? What we usually do, Lyosha says. Find out what and how. It's her. Maybe it's her, maybe it's not. Right, so that's how you see it, Martha says. Fine. I see. So you'll find out. Not clear enough for you yet. I'm not that Lord of yours, Lyosha says. I see, Martha says, getting up, then it'll have to be me. What d'you mean, you? I'll find this animal. And? Martha pursed her lips and was off. So, Lyosha frowns, what have you come for? I told him everything. Everything. What she told me, I told him, from the very beginning, day by day, year by year, not skipping a thing. As I was telling him, I was praying he wouldn't interrupt: she'd be finished if he did and I'd be wasting my breath. He didn't butt in once. He chain-smoked and listened. He heard me out, paused for a while and said: "So you want me to believe her. You and her, I mean. That's clear enough. Achtung . . . Might well be. But might not be. Eh? Why did she run off? S'pose she went soft from the fright? Never mind. What next, then? I go up to this Achtung and say: hi, you're suspected of murder, come on, confess it. And he'll just come out with it all? Funny, eh? Whip the razor out, will he? It was chucked in the shit ages ago, in a loo somewhere or in the river. Clean out all the bogs, will we? Comb the river? Right. Even if she shows up now and tells it all like it was, so what? Achtung was sleeping. End of story. The girl's lying because it was her who did it and now she's trying to dump it on someone else. Achtung found him in the morning, the blood was already dry, he ran to the police straightaway like an honest citizen . . ." So I asked him: "Do you believe me or not, Lyosha?" He studied me closely, sighed. "D'you believe me or not?" I yelled. "What, are you saying you don't know Rita? Are you telling me you don't understand what's going on? Stick me in then! Bastard! You're the Nazis around here! Can't you see this is murder? She won't hand herself over to anyone just like that. She's got one way out now, understand? One. Is this what you want? Is it? She didn't kill him, Lyosha!" "Quiet, you ginger idiot," the policeman said. "I'm not deaf." He puffed on his cigarette. "Some crossword you've set me, lads. Down, across, it's all the same." Then, out of the blue: "Doctor Sheberstov's autopsied him already. Didn't find anything much. Hmm . . ." He says nothing, I say nothing. I'm gulping back tears. "A piece of razor got caught in the spinal cord in his neck," Leontyev carries on. "Imagine how hard he must have stuck it in? The razor got caught in the backbone. When he yanked it out, the blade chipped and a piece stuck in the backbone. Like this." He shows with his fingers: a tiny little thing. I'm looking at him, but I don't understand anything. To hell with this bit of razor. What are we going to do? Lyosha sighed: "Go, Yasha, we'll sort this out somehow. That's my job. That's life, see? God, all the way through to the backbone!" "So what are we going to do?" "Just look at you, Yasha," Leontyev says. "You look terrible. Drop by at the hospital, ask for some pills. To calm you down. Sheberstov will give you some. He understands these things. Stop twitching. Go to the doctor, Yasha. And we'll do what we think's right and what the law tells us to." "Which law?" I wailed. "What are you saying?!" "How else, Yasha? The law's the law." He hustled me out. I sat down on the porch, completely dazed. So it had all been in vain, for nothing? So I, the only person she'd trusted, hadn't helped her? That couldn't be how it was. Shouldn't be. It was enough to drive you nuts. Mad. Then it was as if someone had thrown a bucket of cold water over me. Mad. The doctor. Of course, the doctor! I raced off to the hospital.

'I wasn't sure if I had the strength for all this, but I understood that I had no choice. She was lying there in my room, maybe she'd already woken up and was gazing at the ceiling, listening, thinking . . . Awful: thinking.

'I flew up the stairs to the first floor, knocked and walked in. Sheberstov took one look at me and roared: "Yasha, you look like you've just shat out a hedgehog!" "Doctor, it wasn't her who did it. It was Achtung. Understand? Not her." Then he stared at me like I was a lunatic. I sank to my knees and repeated: "It wasn't her." "Right," said Sheberstov. "You get up, or else I'll have to lock the door. Well?" I didn't get up. "Up to you." He shrugged his shoulders. "Matter of taste, I suppose. Some people like being on their knees, others on chairs." He locked the door with a key and sat down. "Well?" I told him everything. Right from the beginning. Talked for a long while. A very long while. But there was no other solution. Repeating stories is always harder, because you're tempted to tweak what you said in the first place. But that was something I couldn't do. I spoke. Waited. My mouth ran dry and my throat tickled as if I'd gorged myself on burning sand. "Hmm," says Sheberstov. "Let's suppose that's true. Then what?" I said nothing. He poured me some water from a jug.

"Let's suppose," he says again. "There's the key. It's easy enough." Then he shook his head. "Yasha, I've never done anything like this before, understand? No, you don't." "I understand." "Hmm." He sighed. "And it's all the same to you? Well well. Know what this is called? It's called bluffing . . . You don't play cards? Ha. It's when you haven't got a trump in your hand but you say you do. The rules allow it, a risk's a risk. But that's cards. While this . . ." He put the key down on the glass sheet covering his table. "And then what? The fragment's not the important thing. It's the razor you need. Or else he won't admit it." I opened the safe. "Next to the folder." I took the little paper parcel. "Close it. Give me the key." I hovered by the door. "Scram," he said. "What I'd do to see his face . . ."

'I was shaking all over, and I ran as if in a dream, and everything I did was as if in a dream.

'I stopped on the bridge. No, I thought, I can't go back to the barber's. It's almost funny: for five minutes I tried to invent some story to fob Lev off with. I suddenly laughed: God, what was I on about! I had to calm down. Trembling hands wouldn't get me anywhere. I deliberately started walking slower, although mentally I was already in my room, next to Rita. I climbed the staircase and counted the steps. One. Stop, breathe in breathe out. Two. Stop, breathe in breathe out. Three . . . I knocked. What on earth for? Opened the door (I had the only key). She was sitting on her bed, resting against the wall. She'd hung rags of some sort over the window, over the newspapers which I'd put up the same day I moved in here. The room was half-dark. Breathe in breathe out. So how are you? All right? Slept a bit? Yes. Hungry? No, thanks. Come on, you must be, we'll think up something, throw something together. At least some eggs, eh? Up to you. Rita! I said it's up to you, Yasha. All right, that's fine. What's fine? Maybe you'll have some vodka, eh? Wine? I've got both. I quickly fried some eggs in butter, put a clean towel on the stool, dumped the frying pan in the middle, a bottle of red dessert wine, two glasses. Well, to it all working out! What's all this for, Yasha? What d'you mean, what's it for? It's how it should be. Down in one! I was having an attack of verbal diarrhoea. Eat, please. It's nothing special, I know, but you've got to keep your strength up, come on, pile in . . . She poked her fork around in the yolk, smiled wretchedly. Things are bad, eh, Yasha? I faked astonishment (it's always easier to fake something exaggerated, unnatural). What do you mean, bad? Bad's when you die, but you and me, we're not there yet! We're not, Yasha? Come on, Rita! Rita! Snap out of it! I'm all right. Don't look at me, eat. We're not done for, we'll live. Things will turn out all right, God willing. God. Yasha, why are you talking about God? Rita, what are you on about? Nothing. What are people saying? I cautiously told her bits and pieces of what I'd heard. What about Martha? Martha? Yes, what's she saying? What d'you expect her to say . . . it's always the hour has come and so on . . . The hour has come. Rita! She turned away to the window. Rita, everything will be OK. We'll prove it wasn't you. We'll prove it was Achtung. She said nothing. C'mon, girl, everything will be fine, everything will be OK . . . then we'll leave . . . "Yashka!" the cry came from the staircase. It was Martha. "Yashka! Open up!" Rita flopped onto the bed, like a rag doll. Silently, face-down, clutching her head. "Yashka!" The voice was getting closer. "I know you can hear me! Open up, I'm telling you!" She hammered on the door. "I know she's with you! Rita! I can smell you, little bitch! I can smell your stink! You've got nowhere to hide from me, you wretched animal! Yashka!" We said nothing. Martha was panting on the other side of the door. "She's crying," Rita suddenly whispered. "She's crying, I know it!" I shook my head. "Rita, my little girl," Martha said from behind the door in an infinitely tired voice. "I've been like a mum to you . . . Rita . . . you know I never had any children of my own . . . and never will . . . you're the only one, only you . . . You're mine, Rita . . . Why are you hiding from me? My little one . . ." Rita shook her head. "Yashka, you bastard!" Martha shouted. "Damned Yid! Stop leading her on! When God asks, what'll we answer? Eh? We shouldn't be afraid of people, but what about God? God! Rita! Out here now!" I grabbed Rita's shoulder. She shuddered, then she was still. Martha was shouting her lungs out. For ten minutes she raged. Then the staircase creaked. I counted the steps. One, two, three . . . Breathe in breathe out. Breathe in breathe out. Silence. I approached the window on tiptoe, turned up the corner of a rag: Martha was moving off down the street. She turned the corner and was out of sight. That's it. "That's it," I whispered. "She's gone." Rita looked at me. "She's gone away, Rita, why are you crying? Don't, please!" She lifted herself up with difficulty and sat slumped against the wall. Yes, she's gone. It's her who's gone. It's me who can't. She's understood it all. She said it right: the hour has struck, yes. God won't let her, the German bitch, out of his strong arms. He's followed her, followed her all her life, like Martha, he's deliberately let her live till now, so that she could see for herself. God hasn't got a soul. Only flawed creatures – like humans – have got souls. Maybe that's exactly their flaw, having a soul . . .'

'Was that her talking?' the young man asked sceptically.

'No, of course not. She thought that. She tried to say that, but with different words. That's me talking. Yes. Man and soul. Man is not soul. He has a soul. But God is soul, therefore he doesn't have a soul. Therefore he's not man and not woman, not child nor old man, not German, not Russian, not Jew. He's Nobody. He's Whoever You Want. Therefore he's everywhere and everything. If there is no God, then it means there is and he manifests himself in anything and everything, in that whose name is Whoever. I mean No One. I mean in the person prepared to renounce his name and himself and become Whoever. Like His Son, the greatest Whoever. She seemed to be raving. Rita! No, Yashenka, I understand everything now. I can't leave. I've always tried to live like everyone else, but it's never worked. Can you call it life? Can you call what I was and how I lived a life? It's not life. It's so far from life you think: maybe the only reason it was given to you was so you'd become no one? I mean, you were turned into a nobody: not a Russian, not a German, almost a thing, a little animal, and if you were given a tiny bit of beauty, then only for you to understand better that you're no one, that the only thing left for you in life is to take the last step. Rita! No, Yashenka, I'll say this, I must. There's always something between people that stops them loving each other. Always something unforgiven. The past, the present . . . something unsaid or not fully said . . . Or take the war. Blood, which doesn't have to be shed. Something unfinished. Something that hasn't been overcome. People want to overcome it but it doesn't work out. Martha, Maria, Achtung, Fuffy, all of them, they all need someone who can come between them and say: forgive. Who'll say: look, here is somewhere you can dump all your resentment, all your sins, in this vessel of sin. I'll lead you there, but to do it you'll have to step over me, over my blood, even if it's not shed. Here I am, a nobody, take me, fill this emptiness with yourself, and this will be your world . . . But who would agree to live in a world like that? I could barely stop myself from screaming. But everyone will agree, she said, because that's exactly what everyone dreams about, they're just scared of saying it. It's like music. And people live in such a world. A world like that. Maybe the only reason they live is because this Whoever exists. And she began again, saying what she'd already said. Like she was delirious. I panicked. Time was slipping away. I had to act. I'd never have forgiven myself for doing nothing. Although I had a vague suspicion, an inkling: doing nothing is sometimes exactly the thing that saves. I don't know how to put it . . . But I did what I did. To this day I'm in agony . . . See, there was nothing in my actions that I couldn't have forgiven myself for. But those are the same actions I can't forgive. Not one. Ever. I got up. Just don't go away, I asked her. D'you hear, Rita? Just don't go anywhere, please, wait for me, I'm begging you. I locked the door. Took a handful of Solingen razors from the drawer in the kitchen. Chose one which was neither very new nor old, with a yellow handle. Broke off a fragment with some pliers. Dropped it in the little bag. Pushed the drawer back under the table. Stuffed the bag and folded razor in my pocket. Flew down the stairs and tore off to the square.

'It was half an hour before closing when I walked into the workshop and said hello. Achtung lifted his head, pushed his eyeglass up his forehead, and gave a friendly reply. No nervousness, no curiosity even. I heard the rumble of a motorbike outside; then it went silent. Right. Slowly – breathe in breathe out – I took the razor out of my pocket and opened it up. The workshop was well-lit, and he could see the blade clearly. I passed him the razor. He took it mechanically, pushed his eyeglass down, mechanically adjusted the tin hood of the lamp which hung low over the table. "It's ruined," I said. "Chipped." "Chipped," he repeated without raising his head. "And?" "A fragment. Yeah. What a way to hit someone. The razor got stuck in the backbone of the neck. The blade was yanked out and thrown away, but a fragment was left in the bone. In Sheberstov's safe. Material proof. Evidence, I mean." "What evidence?" He lifted his pale face, forgetting to push up his eyeglass. "Where did you find this razor?" "Where it was thrown." "You couldn't . . . " He swallowed. "You couldn't have found it there!" I was so overjoyed that I didn't notice him getting up. He suddenly leapt towards me, collared me and flourished the razor at me. But I didn't even have time to be scared: Leontyev caught his arm from behind my back. "Look at you," he said quietly. "It's never that easy. First that one, now this one . . . eh?" He struggled, but Lyosha was holding him tight. He tried again, and suddenly howled. God, how he howled! It was only then I got scared. I started shaking, then collapsed into the chair in the corner. "We don't need you here for the time being," Lyosha said. "Off you go." Policemen entered the workshop, stamping their coarse-cloth boots, and shoved me aside. I forced my way out and sat down exhausted on the step. Someone slapped me on the back. "Alive?" "Yeah." "Some business." He tried to force a smile but wasn't able to. "But I thought something like this might happen. Though I didn't believe it." Lyosha Leontyev came out. He pulled his cap down on his forehead, adjusted the peak. "I'll give you a lift," he said. "You're not up to walking, I can see that." "Too right," I answered with a stupid, feeble laugh. "Not a hope in hell." Doctor Sheberstov slapped me on the back again. "Sure you haven't forgotten anything?" Still laughing hysterically, I gave him the little bag. Leontyev grunted. Released the clutch. He stopped outside the White Canteen. "Let's go in. For a quick double." I didn't object. Lyusya poured out the vodka and threw a couple of sweets on the scales. Leontyev took a third from her box and gallantly handed it to Lyusya. She smiled wearily. "So what are we drinking to?" "Don't know. To everything. To the way it all is . . ." "Come on. Things will turn out all right, God willing." I drank. "Lyosha . . . What's going to happen to her?" He stared at me in confusion. "Lyosha . . . sorry, I think I'll go . . ."

'I raced to the bridge, ran into the yard, and shouted at the top of my voice: "Rita! Rita!" The window was wide open. I understood everything, but I rushed up and ran into the room to make sure it was empty. The kitchen, too. I ran back down. Lyosha's motorbike stood by the gate. "Lyosha!" He stuck his head out of the wooden toilet in the corner of the yard. "What are you yelling about? Fire?" I explained. The policeman whistled. "Right. Where could she have gone?" But I knew where. I ran off. "Yashka! Wait, dammit." He tried to get his motorbike going but the engine wouldn't start. The policeman tore after me, leaving the bike by the house. I got a stitch in my side and had to walk; Lyosha caught up with me. "Well, where? Not to her, surely? Idiot! Wait, dammit . . . Don't get so worked up, Yasha." I'd suddenly realized that my life was over. All the rest would be and had already become my death . . . How can I put it? No idea. But what I used to call my life was over then. Understand?'

The nephew nodded.

'No you don't. That was it. A lived-out, finished life. Once and for all. I mean you can live as long you'll last, however much the body will take, but life − Life − is over, finished, lived-out. That's why I won't leave this place for anywhere, Ilya,' he concluded abruptly. 'Not for anywhere.'

The young man wiped the sweat off his forehead. He still hadn't decided what to tell his mother, and what was more, how to tell her all this.

'For thirty years I've been living that life and that life only, and I have no other, and she is here. While I'm alive, she exists, and that's the only reason I'm alive.'

'She?'

'Yes. Rita. Rita Schmidt. All I can do is remember. My life is half-life, half-memory. And it's more and more memory than life, until memory will be all that's left. That's what I am. But only here. Nowhere else. And never again, and that's the hardest thing. I'm not confusing fate with habit. No. It's just there's nothing I can do about myself now. I don't want to, either. An ageing, no, an aged Jew who doesn't know a word of his own language, a real Whoever, and the girl, a German who can't speak a word of German – here, in this shitty promised land, without which there's no life or memory . . . Where would I go? Understand? No?'

'It'll be hard for mum to understand this truth . . .'

'But there's no other. Actually, there's none at all. Can you call this the truth? What's true is that we went to Martha's, arrived at that cold house, the front door flung open, and the next, walked into a gloomy room, yes, of course Martha was there, and Rita was there, and Martha was sitting on the bed, her fat cow's leg tucked under her, gazing sleepily into the face of the girl stilled forever on her knees and lying stretched out on the bed, an arm hanging down to the floor, a wisp of oat straw clenched in her hand . . . is that the truth? The truth?!' he suddenly screamed, choking on tears. 'But what kind of language is needed then to tell this truth and not die? What kind? Heavenly? Earthly? Living? Dead? Beautiful, like music? Or just as terrifying as music? . . .'

Sindbad the Sailor

Before dying, Katerina Ivanovna Momotova sent for Doctor Sheberstov, who'd treated her all her life and had been pensioned off a long time ago. She handed him the key to her little house and a scrap of paper folded in four, asking him to burn it together with the rest of them.

'They're at home,' she explained in embarrassment. 'But please don't tell anyone. I'd have done it myself, only you see how it's all turned out . . .'

Sheberstov raised his eyebrows but the old woman just smiled guiltily in reply. She was in a very bad way: dying from a sarcoma. The doctor looking after her at the hospital said she was unlikely to get through the night.

The policeman Lyosha Leontyev was having a smoke on the bench by the hospital entrance. Next to the hulking Sheberstov, he looked like a teenager in a police uniform. His cap with its faded band was lying in the sidecar of his motorbike.

'Fancy a walk?' asked the doctor, gazing over Leontyev's head at the midges circling a pale streetlamp atop a wooden post turned green by the damp. 'To Katya Ivanovna's.'

'To Sindbad the Sailor, you mean? She hasn't died, has she?'

'No.' Sheberstov showed the policeman the key. 'She asked me to look in. I'm only a stranger, at least you're law and order.'

Lyosha dropped his fag-end in a wide stone vase filled with water and got up with a sigh.

'Wish it were winter already. . . .'

They set off at a leisurely pace down the slabbed pavement towards the mill, next to which lived Katerina Ivanovna, famous throughout the town for her exemplarily unsuccessful life.

She'd arrived in East Prussia with the first settlers. Her husband had worked at the paper mill, while she'd worked in the hospital as a washerwoman. They'd had four children:

two of their own and two they'd taken from the children's home. The small withered woman had a big household to look after: a vegetable patch, a cow, a piglet, two dozen sheep, chickens and ducks, her ailing husband Fyodor Fyodorovich (who'd been wounded three times at the front) and the kids. In '57 she lost half a leg after getting run over by a train as she was bringing the heifer back from pasture. She'd had to leave the wash-house. Got a job as a guard at the nursery school. That same year her eldest son Vasya drowned in the Pregolya. Three years later Fyodor Fyodorovich died, too: he didn't pull through an operation on his heart, which had been pierced by shrapnel. The girls grew up and left town. The youngest, Vera, got married to a drunken, thieving down-and-out. After dumping their son on Vera's mother, they left for Siberia, hoping to make some money, and vanished. For the sake of the kid, Katerina Ivanovna knitted to order (while her fingers weren't yet riddled with arthritis), sheared sheep and worked all summer long as a shepherd. It wasn't easy for her chasing after the cattle on her wooden peg leg, but the pay wasn't bad and she'd even get fed sometimes out in the field, so she didn't grumble. The boy grew up, did his stint in the army, got married and only rarely – for New Year or May Day – sent his grandma a card wishing her success in her work and happiness in her private life. Katerina Ivanovna's pension was piddling. By and by, she found herself collecting empties in vacant yards, quiet streets and shops, and getting into squabbles with her rivals, boys who on seeing her yelled 'How much for a pound of old hag!' and swiped her booty. Katerina Ivanovna got angry and swore, but her rage would only last so long. Eventually she found a solution. She'd head out of town with a sack on her shoulders bright and early in the morning and hunt for empties in the ditches and woods by the road. Despite the pain from her leg she traipsed many miles every day, returning home with her rich pickings late in the evening, her eyes sunken and hot sweat streaming off her. She crumbled bread into a deep bowl, poured vodka over it and slurped it up with a spoon. Once in a while she'd start singing something afterwards in a quiet, tinkling voice. 'Others in her shoes would have croaked a long time ago,' Battle-Axe, the well-known town Tsarina, would say. 'But she hasn't even really gone bonkers yet.' It was thanks to her bottle hikes that Katerina Ivanovna received the nickname Sindbad the Sailor.

Glancing furtively to both sides, Doctor Sheberstov opened the front door and motioned Lyosha to go ahead. Lyosha turned on the lights in the hall and kitchen.

'What did she want anyway?' he shouted from the other room. 'What is it we're after?'

Sheberstov didn't reply. He unfolded the piece of paper that Katerina Ivanovna had given him along with the key, and his face turned purple and puffy. Flinging the scrap onto the kitchen table, he bent down to avoid hitting his head on a beam and, wheezing noisily, walked over to behind where Leontyev was standing. The policeman was pensively inspecting the old woman's second room. A dim, unshaded bulb shone on a mountain of paper that took up virtually all the available space.

'What's she been doing, writing novels?' Lyosha muttered. 'Look here . . .' He picked up a scrap of paper from the floor. 'I loved you. Even now, perhaps, love's embers . . .' He threw the doctor a puzzled look. 'What's it all about, eh?'

Sheberstov put his stick in his other hand and shoved Lyosha firmly to one side. Puffing and panting, he squeezed through a narrow gap to a bent-backed chair and sat down. He grabbed a handful of scraps from the pile and started reading.

'So what's all this?' Lyosha repeated, gazing in bewilderment at one of the scraps covered with an old woman's scrawl. 'She can't have . . .'

Sheberstov angrily looked him up and down.

'So who do you think invented the soul, the devil?'

All night long they sorted through the papers that Sindbad the Sailor had asked to be destroyed and which she'd hidden from sight for almost fifty years. Every day, starting on

November 11, 1945, she'd written out one and the same poem by Pushkin: 'I loved you'.* Eighteen thousand, two hundred and fifty-two pieces of paper of various sizes had been preserved, and those eight immortal lines were on every one of them, their beauty undimmed despite the lack of punctuation: not once had the old woman used any of the thirteen symbols. She must have written from memory and had made many spelling mistakes; as for the word 'God', she wrote it with a capital 'G', despite the Soviet orthography of the time. She'd put the date at the bottom of every scrap and, very rarely, added a few words: March 5, 1953, 'Stalin's dead'; April 19, 1960, 'Fyodor Fyodorovich died'; April 12, 1961, 'Gagarin flew to the moon'; August 29, 1970, 'Petinka (that was her grandson) had a girl Ksenia' . . . Several sheets were burnt at the corners, others were ripped, and you could only guess at the emotional state she must have been in that day, when she wrote yet again, 'I loved you . . .' Eighteen thousand, two hundred and fifty-two times she'd reproduced those eight lines on paper. Why? Why those eight lines exactly? And what were her thoughts when she wrote the end of the poem, 'As God grant you may yet be loved again', adding neatly, 'Stalin's dead', or 'Fyodor Fyodorovich died'?

Just before dawn, Sheberstov and Lyosha lit the stove and started burning the paper. The stove took only half an hour to warm up, and the room got stifling hot. Both were feeling uneasy, but when Lyosha said, 'What's the difference, burning a person or burning this . . .', the doctor just snorted angrily.

---

* I loved you. Even now, perhaps, love's embers
  Within my heart are not extinguished quite.
  But let me not disturb you with remembrance
  Or cause you any sadness, any fright.
  I loved you hopelessly, could not speak clearly,
  Shyness and jealousy were ceaseless pain,
  Loved you as tenderly and as sincerely
  As God grant you may yet be loved again.
  (Alexander Pushkin, 1829; translated by Jim Reed.)

There was one scrap – the one Katerina Ivanovna had given him – which Sheberstov decided to keep, even if he didn't know why. Perhaps just because, for the very first time, the old woman hadn't written the date at the bottom, as though she'd understood that time is powerless not only over the eternity of poetry, but even over the eternity of our wretched life . . .

The Two Redheads

It was widely believed that Pyotr and Liza Iyevlev were not husband and wife, even though they registered their marriage soon after they met and lived in the same house together for more than forty years, and died on the same day. Only the death and funeral of Battle-Axe brought more folk together than the demise and interment of Pyotr and Liza.

Both were red-haired, young and hot-blooded, not to say outright wild. Pyotr stood out from the crowd whether he was dancing or brawling. Once, for a bet, he danced non-stop for twenty-six hours until his insides were all stirred up like vegetables in boiling soup and his soles were worn down to the heel. Liza was in the factory choir and sometimes, also on a bet, she'd hold top A for a whole hour.

They were too much like each other to form a harmonious couple, yet their evening strolls together and timid kisses eventually reached the point where they had to talk things through. No witnesses were present, of course, but that same evening Liza woke Doctor Sheberstov from his bed and all but dragged him over to Pyotr. A few days later blood-curdling rumours were being spread around town.

Here I'm obliged to make a small digression. Not long before her first acquaintance and friendship with Pyotr, Liza was still trying to get over a painful break-up with the gorgeous stableman, Arvidas. Women spoiled Arvidas, and he loved playing the scamp. One day, out of the blue, he ordered Liza to jump off Bath Bridge into the Lava, and she did so without a moment's hesitation and with all her clothes on, leading many to conclude that a girl would do anything for Arvidas. What those two got up to is anyone's guess, but there were rumours – ah, those wicked tongues – that there was nothing they didn't get up to. Soon afterwards Arvidas just dumped her, easy as you like. The little town was witness to Liza's humiliation: she chased after her faithless man for weeks to come and even fell at his feet, but he, clearly having got what he was after, merely laughed at her entreaties . . .

It was later, years later, that a version of the crucial talk in Pyotr's garden was patched together from slips of the tongue, half-confessions and conjecture. The key to this version was Liza's comment, 'All you blokes want the same thing', a hint, presumably, at her relationship with Arvidas. Pyotr probably started angrily protesting. Perhaps he still hadn't had the chance to ask Liza to marry him. Who knows, perhaps they'd got carried away with their kisses as they lay in the fragrant tall grass at the end of the garden. Liza was a girl in bloom and many men dreamed of her shoulders and neck after seeing her by the river. As for Pyotr, he was a passionate lad, a real hot-head . . . So it's easy to imagine Liza coming to her senses, pushing Pyotr away and saying in a breathless voice: 'All you blokes want the same thing!' This must have been followed by a stormy slanging-match between two excited young people. Pyotr had a curved pruning-knife in his pocket and it was with precisely that knife – we know this for a fact – that he did to himself what all men are terrified even to contemplate. Having exhausted every argument, he resorted to the final step, to a proof of his love such as probably not even God is entitled to ask of a man.

Doctor Sheberstov did what he could, but he's only a doctor after all. When Pyotr finally fell asleep, Sheberstov gathered the bloody rags and trying not to look at Liza, muttered: 'Now you're free. Go to bed.' To this, Liza apparently replied: 'Now I'm his slave and I'll never leave him.' The words may have been different but I can vouch for the gist.

They got married two months later, and nobody in the town reproached the young couple for their quiet wedding, which passed without the customary drunkenness and reckless punch-ups. Naturally, though, a fair number of barbed jokes got around about a castrated stallion and a vigorous mare.

The young couple received a little house off the railway line at the end of Seventh Street, a stone's throw from the club, and every day they could be seen trudging down the track together. A savage fate, if anyone's in any doubt. Russia is a country of railways and not for nothing is our main hero a pointsman.* Man or woman, it's the same deal: a padded jacket, coarse-cloth boots, a pickaxe and a sledge-hammer to keep the track in good nick, endless slogging come winter or summer. The wages were low so everyone kept livestock, but at least you didn't have to worry about grazing land: the strip by the track was all yours.

It can't be said that grief brought the couple closer, but can grief like that ever bring people closer? After a vodka or two, Liza would become livid and yell at Pyotr: 'I'm leaving you! Leaving! Least I can still shag. You don't even have anything to wave around.' But her husband wouldn't let himself get drawn into rows and slipped quietly out to the cattle barn, where he waited for Liza's fury to abate. It never took long. At first, other men sniffed around her hoping for a treat, but somehow no one ever struck lucky. All she had to do was remember her husband's words – 'I won't hold it against you' – and her admirers were sent packing. It was on this topic that Battle-Axe once said: 'Russian women live to spite themselves.'

In the fifth or sixth year of their life together, the Iyevlevs took in a girl from the children's home, sick to the marrow. They nursed her, brought her up and, it seems, came to love her. Nothing much changed in the family with the appearance of Anechka, except that Liza's fury surfaced a little less often. On Sundays the three of them made a point of walking by the Pregolya, behind the Tower, and strolling for hours along the road by the hayfields. They'd find a spot somewhere opposite the Children's Home lakes for a snack, and while Liza and Anechka hunted for crickets in the grass, Pyotr pensively watched the clouds fill with milky blood and groaned a wordless song. As a rule he tried to keep his mouth shut when there were people around, but Liza noticed, sensed, that words

* A reference to the Russian idiom 'to find the pointsman': to find the last in a line of guilty parties to some disaster, who carries out orders from above.

of some sort, or just mere sounds, were stirring inside him, and that he didn't know what to do with them. In the evening all three would have dinner on their little veranda. The soft yellow light of the lamp, dimmed to save paraffin, snatched hands flattened by hard work out of the gloom, and delicate child's fingers pushing back a greasy lock of hair, and peaceful faces softened by tiredness and smiles . . .

As before, Liza did her best to attend the factory choir rehearsals on Wednesdays and Saturdays. Not a day would pass without her friends suggesting she bring her husband along, too, so desperate were they to hear his new voice. Liza brushed the idea aside: the thought of inviting Pyotr to the rehearsals seemed somehow shameful to her, like a hint at that terrifying evening in the garden . . . Yet it sometimes occurred to her that perhaps it would make things easier for Pyotr if he could bring himself to release that word, that sound, which was worrying and gnawing his soul from within. Although, of course, there was no way of telling whether it really would help him to join a choir that sang *Over Valleys and Knolls* and Russian folksongs after solemn sessions at the club to mark state holidays.

In summer the rehearsals took place on the big wooden veranda facing the old park. Anechka would come running to hear the choir and sometimes she'd even stand up boldly in the front row and sing *The Motherland Hears*, melting the hearts of the grown-ups and even of the choir leader Magnia Mikhailovna, a dry, towering old woman who kept her white hair in a bun and wore a shawl that was threadbare like a fishing net. Anxious about his daughter, Pyotr would creep through the park towards the veranda, hide behind a tree and watch. When they spotted him once and hailed him, he ran off. The next time Pyotr wasn't so lucky because he was called by Anechka, whom he could never refuse. She dragged her dad out of the dark and led him to the veranda. Magnia Mikhailovna shouted at red-faced Pyotr and told him to stand with the tenors. Then she flapped her oar-like arms and stared menacingly at the new recruit. Hiding behind his neighbours' backs, he mouthed along to the tune. Magnia Mikhailovna became angry but however much she tried, she just couldn't get him to sing.

Pyotr hung around sheepishly after the rehearsal to help Liza and Magnia Mikhailovna clear the benches and chairs.

Anechka ran up and down the veranda, laughing and singing – very cheerfully, boisterously even – *Those Evening Bells.**

'Anya!' Liza shouted with a laugh. 'Is that how I taught you? Why are you being so naughty?'

'I know how, I do!' Anechka clambered onto a stool, pulled a solemn face and struck up: 'Those evening bells! Those evening bells!'

'How many a tale their music tells', Liza joined in vigorously, showing her daughter how it should really be sung.

'Of youth and home and that sweet time', Pyotr suddenly chimed in sadly and softly, gazing over Liza's head with a distant air.

And as for the next line –

'When I last heard their soothing chime!'
this was sung by three silver voices: the fragile voice of Anya, the strong and resonant voice of Liza, and the pure, heavenly pure voice of Pyotr.

Old Magnia Mikhailovna stood before them with her chair clasped to her chest, and feared only one thing: that she might fall, because her legs had seized up.

Pyotr was no longer afraid of singing at rehearsals and at concerts, as the mood took him and as he felt able to. He and his wife slogged away on the track as before, spending all their spare moments on the garden, the vegetables and the cattle. But, with rare exceptions, on Wednesdays and Saturdays they both went along to the rehearsals led by the irascible Magnia Mikhailovna. At concerts the choir would be greeted by stormy ovations: few had televisions then, and whole families walked over to the factory club, however great the distance

---

* Thomas Moore's poem, translated into Russian in the nineteenth century, became a very popular folksong.

and whatever the weather. The choir entertained them with the traditional *Over Valleys and Knolls* and *Communist Brigades* but the highlight of the concert, awaited each time with increasing impatience in the hall, was the performance of the Iyevlev trio. When they were announced, many in the audience would leap to their feet, and their caps would fall off as they started clapping, egging on their neighbours: 'Don't just sit there, it's the Iyevlevs! Come on!' The whole hall would join in, thirsting for a miracle.

The Iyevlevs would perform a famous folksong and the champagne bottles popped their own corks in the buffet on the first floor.

After rehearsals on summer evenings, the choristers were in no particular hurry to get home: some dragged chairs around, some slouched over a broom in the hall, others smoked philosophically . . . Liza and Pyotr paid no attention to these crass ploys and, if they weren't in the mood, just headed off home. Most of the time, though, Pyotr couldn't bring himself to leave just like that, as if something unsaid was weighing him down, something important which he had to get out that same day, right that minute. He'd wander around the veranda with Anechka, and mutter something inaudibly, now singing under his breath, now breaking off in annoyance: the song was all wrong and it was all a waste of time anyway. Sometimes Liza would try to help, prompting him cautiously with a word or two, or with a simple little tune. Gradually their roaming on the veranda would slow down, as if the Iyevlevs had spotted their prey and were already approaching it, wary of frightening it off. Then someone, maybe even Anechka, would release a sound . . . No, it wasn't a song (although, of course, most of the time that's exactly what it was), it wasn't something definite: Liza weaved her melody, Anechka hers, while Pyotr seemed to wander between them, leaning one way then the other, as though measuring where he should dive or jump from, up or down, it didn't matter, the crucial thing was to find the spot, and then he'd suddenly dive, jump . . . Three voices blended into one and the Iyevlevs would come together and stand facing one another, hardly likely to notice anyone else now, and the melody, entwining as one, would shoot up into the darkness over the park before immediately falling, then soared once more, and so on again and again until the stream of silver sound began steadily climbing up and up of its own accord, then disappeared, dissolving into the night, into the air, and now the night itself was ringing with the fragile voice of Anechka, the strong and resonant voice of Liza, and the pure, heavenly pure voice of Pyotr ... The sound was so high and there was so much of it, it was as if it was no longer there. The full-grown tree of the silver melody rounded out, swelled up and bubbled with its invisible crown, returning the sound to the Iyevlevs, while they merely breathed it in and out, quite detached now, returning the sound to the night. Their voices – but these were no longer quite their voices – rang out over the Pregolya drenched in moonlight, over the hayfields on the other side of the river, and suddenly tired Gramp Mukhanov would chuck away the pitchfork with which he was turning hay and listen in astonishment, gazing at the starry sky: God in heaven, what is this? What's happening? The voices would fly over the streets, bringing together people who went down to the club and clustered in silence near the veranda, enchanted by the completely incomprehensible force of the sound. And now the whole world, shining with stars and the glory of God, was ringing, and the ancient thousand-eyed ogre of the night fell quiet in his lairs and crazy heights, and a sonorous silence set in, such as there must have been when God and the devil had yet to begin their feuding over the soul of man ...

Sometimes this bewitchment would last only a few minutes, sometimes it dragged out for hours, and people would tell of various miracles to do with healing or flying wide-awake. Then the very same people would have a laugh as they reminded one another about that other night and the pruning-knife with which the miracle had begun. Yet on returning home and finding themselves alone, they'd think: 'But if such a thing can happen in life, then it means life's worth living after all? Of course, the knife's not the important thing here. But what is, then? And why does he have this gift, and what is it anyway?' Some little boy would stick his head in his pillow so that his parents couldn't hear him cry, and whisper something so exaltedly nonsensical that you could even die for the sake of this nonsense – right now, this very second, joyfully and even without witnesses . . .

Anechka grew up, married Kolya Suzdaltsev, a metalworker from the flour mill, and had twins. Pyotr and Liza grew old and their voices – all that toiling in the frost and wind – weren't getting any better. As soon as Pyotr was pensioned off, the years of hard labour began to take their toll. He was never out of hospital. Doctor Sheberstov warned Liza that it might be cancer, and that's how it turned out. Within a few months Pyotr's insides had rotted beyond repair and he could no longer move. He was placed in a separate ward but because he smelled so much that not even the old nurses could stand it, he was looked after by Liza and Anechka. They sometimes sang softly to him, but he'd just gape at them stupidly with his tear-filled eyes. Sensing that death was on its way, though, he mustered his strength and sent for Liza. Anechka ran up to her mother when she was darning one of her grandchildren's mittens, wearing little spectacles on her flabby nose. Hearing that Pyotr had called for her, she stuck the needle in the ball, wound the thread around it and left, telling Anechka to stay at home.

As she entered the ward, she knew immediately that Pyotr was soon to die. He tried to say something to her, but only a soft wheezing sound broke from his throat. Liza moved two chairs near to the bed, lay down next to her husband, rested his head on her shoulder, and closed her eyes. In the morning they were found dead.

And that's the whole story of red-headed Liza and red-headed Pyotr. Although I don't think that's the whole story, in fact I even think that something has remained outside this story – life is it, or God, or love, or a sound which comes before words as love comes before life. Something must have been left out, it must, or else what are we living for, Lord?

Villiput from Villiputia

Him. Just him. Alone. There's no one he needs. He's never asked anyone for anything, complained to anyone, expected anything from anyone. He'll do this on his own, too. He'll find him and say: 'This is all you've got to do, brother. Say sorry. It won't bring the girl back to life, sure, but you still have to say you're sorry. For fairness's sake, simple as that. It's all that's required.' All that's required for the world to stay standing and not die with the death of every human being.

Squatting beneath the half-open window, Villiput was listening to the occasional sounds of the awakening town (the Kharkov train had passed through about thirty minutes ago, the one to Riga wouldn't be along for another hour or so) and crushing a dahlia stem in his hands. All of a sudden he got to his feet and looked down the street. The fog, thicker than ever at this time, hung like an immobile and seemingly impenetrable mass from which emerged the murky-blue, almost violet tops of the lime trees, a wooden post with a broken lamp and the tiled roof of the storehouse on the other side of the street. The shed doors creaked in the yard, a pail clattered to the ground. He wiped his hands on his trousers, grabbed hold of the window-frame and, digging his foot into the wall, jumped straight onto the sill. Listened in: quiet. He pulled back the heavy curtain, moist from the dew, and leapt softly into the room. The watery morning light barely scattered the gloom. The photographs on the walls shimmered weakly, as did the bronze chandelier and the doors of the wardrobe towards which he moved. Then he stopped, listened hard and took another step. Drew the wardrobe door towards him. It yielded without creaking and he immediately found the uniform jacket and beneath it the holster. Now he was moving quickly: he grabbed the pistol, shut the doors of the wardrobe and, holding the weapon in his outstretched arm, leapt back to the window. His body was so tense that its every vein responded before his hearing to the slightest rustle in the house. Still facing the door, he caught the edge of the curtain with his free hand and drew it aside. Light trickled in through the gap and he saw her eyes, wide-open and shining as if they were made of polished metal – and there was him thinking that she was sleeping, this woman, who'd been lying in this twilit room for so many years now, motionless and white. She was covered up to her chin in a blanket, and her meticulously combed hair was spread in long, broad wings over the pillow. Labelled medicine bottles, a tall glass and a tablespoon glimmered on a low bedside table. So she'd seen it all from the start, Villiput realized. Never mind, she wouldn't tell her husband. The paralytic, that's how she was known in the town. Lyosha's paralytic. The boy pulled the curtain aside, grabbed hold of the window-frame and jumped out into the front garden. He reached the gate in a few bounds and tore off down the pavement, sensing a chilly lightness in his body.

The half-demolished buildings of the old transit prison towered up at the end of the street. Square granite blocks, strewn with broken brick, led from the pavement to the first building, where a black inscription followed the curve of a semi-circular arch. Next to the Latin inscription, thrusting her torso out from the brick wall, a statue of the Goddess of Justice loomed over passers-by with scales in her only hand (the other hand had been knocked off long ago) and a stone blindfold over her eyes. The walls and surviving fragments of ceiling were submerged in a scree of shattered plaster and tile, and overgrown with birch and elder trees. The basement could be reached by sliding down the few visible steps; down below, some twisted cell bars and rusted bolts had survived.

The boy unlocked a cell door and yanked it open. A dog poked out its friendly muzzle from under boards placed on bricks. Recognizing her master, she crawled out into the middle of the cell with a joyful yelp. The boy stroked her wet coat and threw her a bit of sausage. He checked the cartridge clip, shoved the pistol under his trouser-belt and, sitting down on the damp boards, lit a cigarette. Time to go. What was he waiting for? What signs? Tomorrow they'd bury her. Time was short. Irus was hiding from him. Fool. There was nothing shameful in what Villiput wanted to ask him. The girl wouldn't come back from the dead, but Iris should still say sorry. And so should he, Villiput. After all, it was him who'd handed Galakha over to Irus. He didn't have to, but he did. Of course, he hadn't imagined that things would turn out so horribly, that Galakha would end up pregnant and die from loss of blood as she was giving birth. 'These things happen,' Doctor Sheberstov had said. 'Don't cry, son.' 'I never cry,' Villiput had answered. Yes, that's how he'd replied. These things happen. So it wouldn't be so hard for Irus to come to the cemetery and say 'Sorry'. They could even get by without witnesses. They could get by with just one witness. Villiput, his blood-brother. 'You've gone soft in the head,' Irus had laughed when Villiput first told him why he was pestering him. 'Think I'm so shit scared I need to say sorry? What for?' Villiput explained. Irus laughed out loud again. 'Give me a break! Sure, it's a shame. She died, didn't she? But she was half-crazy, a moron, maybe she's better off like that . . .' Clenching his teeth, Villiput threw himself at him. Irus hit him. Blood streamed from Villiput's nose. 'Shut it!' Irus shouted. 'Soft in the head, you are. Got it from her. I know your little games. Lay off, OK? Or I'll forget you're my brother.' Villiput threw himself at Irus again and was thrown straight back after taking a blow to the forehead which left his head ringing. He caught his breath and croaked: 'You know me, brother. I won't lay off. I'll have to kill you. No shit.' Irus spat in contempt. 'You kill me? Crap. Who handed her over to me? You did. Who shagged her? Me. Who got knocked up? She did. Who died? She died, end of story.' Anticipating little Villiput's next charge, he kicked him full in the stomach. Fly. Tiresome fly. Trust him to go running after the king of Seventh Street, whining: say sorry, say sorry . . . That's what he'd done. Just chased after him and whined away. He got what he asked for, of course: face black and blue, lips beaten to a pulp, his left eyebrow all cut up. Plain hysterical. 'And you want to kill me, cry-baby?' Irus mocked. 'Like this? Fine. More? Take that!' He hit him as only he could: slashing right through him. A guy like that's no pushover. You'll only get him with a machine-gun. Or a pistol. It would have to be a pistol, then.

He checked once more that the gun was firmly in place under his belt, and pushing his bike, hidden until then under the boards, he scrambled up through piles of broken brick. On the pavement he wiped drops of moisture off the handlebar.

The fog was slowly clearing, but it was still quite thick: it was impossible to make anything out a hundred feet down the road. After passing the railway crossing, Villiput stood up on the pedals, climbed up alongside the wall of the old German cemetery towards the church and turned into the yard of a massive white house, which rose like a slab of grimy ice over the lime trees, the wet tarred roofs of the sheds, and the fences, green from the perpetual damp.

A cock crowed behind the house, the well winch screeched. The boy nudged open the door into an entrance-way smelling of cats and rotten vegetables from the cellar, and knocked on a door covered in dusty leatherette. From deep inside the flat came the sound of someone coughing and a long shuffling noise, as if a sack of potatoes was being dragged over the floor. At long last, its hinges screeching, the door inched open. A yellowish, flabby face looked out at Villiput from a gloomy corridor. Kristina.

'What d'you want?' she wheezed. 'Come on, get in.'

The kitchen smelled of the previous day's food. Potato cubes and bits of meat lay congealed in white fat in a frying-pan. To cover a patch of damp, an almost entirely faded Muslim Magomaev* gazed out over the sink from the wall, with a calendar pinned to his forehead.

'Where's Irus?' asked Villiput.

'How did you scare him so badly he's hiding from you?' the woman said with a smirk.

Villiput grinned as well.

'I didn't scare him,' he said. 'He got sick of me. Where is he?'

---

* A singer of Azerbaijani origin hugely popular in the Soviet Union in the sixties and seventies.

He might well not be there. And this woman, his wife, might well not know where her good-for-nothing husband had disappeared to. Or maybe she did know. Not for nothing had she asked why Irus was hiding from him. Crap. Irus wasn't afraid of him. He was just sick and tired of him. If Irus really was hiding, it was from himself. Could be. But then Villiput would have to kill him.

'So where is he?' he asked again.

'Sod off!' she hissed. 'Just look at him interrogating me! I don't know a thing and don't want to know, either. We've had our chat, now get out!'

She grabbed him by the arm and tried to shove him out into the corridor. Villiput broke free and pressed himself against the wall. Screwing his eyes up at the woman, he took the pistol out from under his belt and released the safety catch.

'Listen, bitch,' he said calmly. 'You better tell me where to find him, or I'll kill you. I don't have any time to waste.'

She sniggered before answering, but after peering at his face, which had become unexpectedly pinched, she frowned pathetically and stepped back towards the door. He didn't stir, didn't move, just stood by the wall with his pistol aimed at her face and repeated hollowly:

'I'll kill you.'

She suddenly realized: he'd kill her.

Lyosha Leontyev scratched the pig and the animal stretched out in the mud with a contented grunt. Pouring the rest of the potatoes into the trough, he closed the door of the pen. Looked in at the heifer. She was weak and the bulls were pestering her, so they didn't drive her out into the street and fed her in the cowshed. Everyone was full. Time for his breakfast, too.

After drinking his tea, he went over to his wife. As always, she lay covered up to her chin in a blanket, speechless and, it seemed, fleshless from so many years' immobility. Between life and non-life. He hadn't seen her move for so long that he'd ceased even thinking about her flesh, which had once possessed taste, weight, smell. He didn't think about it, yet this flesh continued to exist, to live according to its own laws, the laws of sin, memory, fate, and he cared for her dutifully, washed and combed her, and nothing ever changed, but today . . . Looking at her closely, he suddenly realized that there was something different about her. As if, under the influence of an unknown inner force, her body had suddenly acquired weight, taste and smell. He'd have called this condition anxiety, if anxiety was something you could weigh or taste. It was as if she wanted to communicate something to him: that was the feeling he had gazing at this motionless face, at her slightly widened pupils, at her barely twitching nostrils, at this apparent movement bursting from within, from the depths of her being, yet incapable of realizing itself in a gesture or a word. It must be something important. Something very important, Lyosha realized.

He ran his hand through her hair. Right, time for him to go. He opened the cupboard and discovered straightaway that the holster under his jacket was empty. Turned to his wife. Was this what she'd been trying to tell him about? Without rushing, he put on the jacket, checked that all the buttons were done up with his palm, gave his shoulders a shrug. Right. Squatting and panting slightly from the effort, he passed his palm over the floor and immediately felt sand on his skin. Sand should never be able to get in: Leontyev washed the floor in this room every day, crawling on all fours and manically scrubbing the boards. Kicking off his felt slippers, he walked alongside the wall to the window and drew the curtain. Right. He went back to the cupboard and lay on his stomach. On the clean floor he could see footprints so faint they were almost invisible, yet he instantly recognized them. Leontyev himself had given those shoes to Villiput on his birthday. The only present which this stubborn kid had accepted from him, or from anyone else. What did he want with a pistol?

Villiput's grandmother, who was hard of hearing, didn't know a thing about it. As you'd expect.

He wheeled his motorbike out of the garage and lit his first cigarette. His head was spinning. He opened the throttle and released the clutch. The bike hurtled towards the gates, a jet of sand spurting from under the rear wheel.

He rode slowly along the streets, returning the greetings of his acquaintances (everyone he met) and thinking about the pistol that was out wandering God knows where while he was riding around here. The motorbike skipped lightly up the slope, its wheels rustling softly over the small granite cubes that gave the road its likeness to the scaly side of a fish. The red alarm lights were still shining in the shop windows. Beyond the ruins overgrown with elder lay the Gypsy Quarter: that was what the townsfolk called this clutch of houses around a spacious yard, where several gypsy families lived. In the yard, laundry was boiling in large vats on camp-fires. Swarthy women were shouting to each other from the doorways and windows. He braked by the newspaper stand on the square. The little town had been built over seven hundred years, first by Germans, then by Poles and Lithuanians, then by Germans again. It crawled out of the marshy land down below, clambered onto artificial dykes, and finally, in an unbroken ring of tightly packed houses, encircled a low hill with an unevenly lopped-off peak where the main square had been built (it was here that the first Russian tanks suddenly appeared in 1945 and dog-tired, smoke-blackened crews poured out, led by a strapping blond captain who, contrary to regulations, wore a strap only on his right shoulder; the other strap had been ripped off by a bullet near Vilnius: 'On V-Day I'll sew on the left one!' He'd had to walk round about ten little gingerbread houses before unearthing an old man with some matches, who lit the captain's cigarette with a rock-steady hand, for he was blind and totally deaf). In the gaps between the buildings, narrow and crooked cobbled alleys could be seen dropping down to the river, while the pyramidal church tower, soared over the mass of steep tiled roofs; during the day – if of course, the day was a sunny one (a great rarity) – the shadow of the tower, like an hour-hand over a clock-face, would slowly go round the square in a circle, while in the evening it would fall on the squat buildings of the police station, the law-court and the little stall selling beer, fried fish and moist flat cigarettes.

Lyosha bought a paper. As he reached in his pocket for his cigarettes, a boy flew past on a bicycle. Leontyev rolled a fag between his fingers and struck a match before realizing the boy was Villiput. He leapt into his seat, kick-started the motor, and hurled his bike forward. He saw the boy braking before the descent down a canal-like alley, and accelerated. The motorbike thundered over the square at full tilt and bounced over the cobbled road, but Lyosha didn't slow up. Aware he was being chased, the boy quickened his pace and turned into the only gateway in the whole town. Lyosha knew that by flying under the echoing arch he'd be taking the shortest route to the river, if he risked riding between the sheds – otherwise he hadn't a hope in hell of catching the cyclist. Then he remembered that two days before old Matras had got drunk and set his shed alight, after which the neighbours had sent him away to sleep it off and had put out the fire. So there was no shed there now; maybe he could risk it? Hurtling under the rumbling stone arch, he aimed for a heap of charred debris and, with barely the time to think 'Just so long as I don't hit a fork or a scythe', he slammed into the still smoking debris with a deafening roar and literally leapt out onto the embankment. The motorbike span on the smooth stone slabs, threatening to slide down into the river. Lyosha closed the throttle sharply and hurled the bike on its side, managing to jump off at the last moment. The engine cut out. The front wheel continued to spin over the water and the spokes sparkled in the first sunrays to have pierced the fog. The terrified boy gazed entranced at the shimmer of the spokes on the surface of the greenish-yellow water. His bicycle lay on the ground next to Lyosha's motorbike.

'A bit more,' said the boy, 'and you'd have been done for, Uncle Lyosha. What were you up to, eh?'

Lyosha took off his cap and smoothed down his hair.

'Morning drill.'

He picked up the motorbike, kicked the starter and the engine rumbled smoothly into action. With a wink to the boy, who raised his thumb in delight, he sped off and was back on the square within a minute. Why on earth had he thought that that boy was Villiput? The same khaki-coloured jacket, all washed out and patched up at the elbows, just as tall – three foot in his cap – and just as skinny . . . So what? Nerves. He stopped outside the funeral parlour. In the window, placed between two vases of calla, was a sumptuous dusty wreath, a source of delight for the town's children and simpletons. One of the latter, Vita Pea-Head, would stand for hours in front of this window, mumbling away in a monotone and shaking the tiny head that crowned his hulking torso. Galakha also liked doing that, Lyosha suddenly remembered. His mouth filled with saliva. She liked it. But Villiput didn't let her hang about here until she dropped. Galakha. Funeral. Villiput. Pistol. Irus. Lyosha cast a helpless gaze over the square. God, what sort of a halfwit was he? Tomorrow was Galakha's funeral. Irus had refused to carry out Villiput's idiotic demand – the whole town knew. That's why he needed the pistol. Why hadn't the penny dropped straightaway? Bleeding obvious. He opened the throttle. Bleeding obvious. Released the clutch.

Leontyev stood the motorbike by the fence, drank his fill of water from the bucket placed on the lid of the well, and only then walked up onto the porch and knocked on the dusty leatherette-covered door. No one answered. He pushed open the door and entered the hallway that reeked of paraffin and the previous day's food, a long corridor with bare floorboards and doors on each side painted dark brown, with brass knobs that had dulled over the years. Clothes smelling of mould hung on hooks nailed into the wall. Galoshes had been dumped in the middle of the corridor. A loud clink came from the other side of a door. Lyosha knocked, threw an angry glance at the galoshes and slammed shoulder-first into the door. The lock snapped and Leontyev found himself in a room pierced by a narrow and watery stream of light, which entered through a crack in the curtains. Kristina was sitting at a round, polished table. She didn't stir when Lyosha broke the lock and charged into the room. Tousle-haired, wearing a crumpled and soiled dressing-gown, she was sitting up straight in her chair, too straight, as if she'd been sitting like that for an hour, a day, or more. A half-empty bottle of hooch, a glass and a plate of mushrooms lay on the table. Lyosha took a chair and sat opposite. Without even glancing at him, Kristina grabbed her glass, drowned what was left of the hooch and wiped her lips with her sleeve.

'I knew you'd come,' she said at last. 'If one of them comes, I thought, you can expect the other. Suppose it was you he nicked the pistol off. A pistol, for God's sake.' She poured some hooch into the glass and pushed it towards him. 'To my health, and to hell with the lot of you. Drink, Lyosha, or I'm not saying a thing.'

Lyosha took a gulp and speared a mushroom with his fork.

'Why did he call me a bitch?!' she suddenly yelled, almost bursting her lungs. 'I'm not a bitch! You know I'm not a bitch! And he knows! Why?'

Leontyev said nothing. Stupid him. Kristina shook a finger at him. Stupid of him not to say anything. Stupid of him to think she felt sorry for her shitty husband who this Villiput was chasing after. Maybe the kid was right. But a person who's right doesn't have the right to call her a bitch, does he? What was she, a tramp? She was seventeen when she married Irus. She had tits like fists and a teeny little bum. And now? Just look at her teeth! She opened her mouth wide, baring two rows of steel. That was Irus, too.

'Letch,' she said, drunkenly tossing her tousled hair. 'Hasn't been able to get it up for ages. Throws himself on little girls. Like this Galakha. How old's she? Fifteen? Bloody letch. Now he's run off to Ilonka, the forester's girl. Think he's run away from Villiput, do you? It's Ilonka he's after. Least the forester might beat some sense into him . . .'

'Hang on,' Lyosha said gently. 'Kristina, try to understand. Villi will kill him. Understand?'

She stared at him goggle-eyed.

'Has he really gone to Ilonka?'

She said nothing.

'Do you understand what I'm saying, Kristina? He'll . . .'

'Ah!' she burst. 'Christ! . . .'

'He'll kill him,' Lyosha repeated in dismay. 'Kristina, are you listening?'

'Ah!' she wheezed again. 'And me?'

'What d'you mean, you?' he asked. 'He'll kill him . . .'

'And me?' She struggled to her feet and pressed her hands down on the table. 'And me? What about me, am I going to be left on my own?' She shook a finger at Lyosha. 'If this kid kills him, means I'll be a widow. If he kills the kid, they'll bang him up and I'm on my own again. All my bloody life I'm on my own!' she cried. 'Christ! Is anyone going to think about me? Anyone, ever? About me?!'

'Right now,' said Lyosha, 'you've got a chance to think about yourself. Maybe for the first time. And maybe for the last. That's the kind of chance you've got.'

She was silent for a good while, swaying from side to side. Then she lifted her head and stared straight at Lyosha.

'Why are you forcing me to choose?' she said, with anguish in her voice. 'Who are you anyway? What right have you got?'

'None,' said Lyosha.

'Then go.' She sank back slowly into the chair. 'Then go, Lyosha. The Eleventh Post's a good way away.'

It was a long climb up a road planted with lime and birch trees. Villiput's bike creaked drily, monotonously, and the boy had to stand up on the pedals to get any nearer to the top of the hill, where the road became narrower and seemed to come to an end, stained by the pale-blue shadows of the trees, their crowns entwining over the asphalt. A winding stream glimmered to the right beyond a sickly line of roadside trees. The heavy expanse of the oak grove rolled in waves down to the shore. The furthest trees hung over a precipice, while below, on the sand by the water, grey-blue stones lay in heaps and pile stumps poked out of the ground. It was starting to get hot and he didn't have a flask or even a bottle to fill with water. He turned down a cart track. From behind the trees emerged the tiled roofs of the First Barracks: that was what the trackman's farmstead was called in the town.

No one at home. A fat piglet wandered around the yard, sticking its snout into the empty wooden troughs meant for the chickens and ducks or into the tall weeds that bordered the barns. New red-brick buildings surrounded the rectangular yard on foundations of unhewn stone. Behind lay an orchard enclosed by a fence made from old sleepers that were all tangled up in hop and vine. Villiput hadn't been to the Streltsy's place for ages, although Ivan Ivanych passed on Marusia's and Olenka's regards whenever they met, and invited him over. In the kitchen Villiput picked up an aluminium flask that had been blown out with a car compressor, filled it, and grabbed a knife made from a bayonet (even though he had on him his blood-brother's knife with the inscription *Irus* on the blade). He'd give them back later. He looked in at the uninhabited part of the house, where hay, saddles, a cracked boat and a 'spider' with which no fish had been caught for aeons were kept, and where strings of dried smelt, mushrooms and thickly cobwebbed bunches of herbs hung down. No one home. Fine, he'd give it all back. Ivan Ivanych wouldn't even ask what he'd needed it all for. That was the law by which Ivan Ivanych and the other Streltsy lived. A law's a law. Every man has his own. Villiput had his too: don't get in anyone's way. But despite himself, sometimes he just couldn't help getting in the way. He'd got in the way of his mum, whom he hadn't known and didn't remember and who was found one day frozen to death at the station with her kid, blue from the cold, wrapped up in a bundle next to her. Nosikha had picked him up and pretty much forgot about him on the very first day. She'd stick something in his mouth, in this bloodless slit on a narrow colourless little face, and be off on her business. Small, skinny, helpless. Lilliput-Villiput. Fine, the main thing was that he was no one's problem. He was alive – so let him live. Let him throw those suspicious glances of his. He won't ask for anything, won't complain about anything, and bully for him. If the kid doesn't cry, the mum's none the wiser. Not that he had a mum anyway. Just a little mound at the cemetery. A piece of plywood for a tombstone. No name, no date. Not a single word or they'd have had to write 'frozen alky'. He had no one, except Nosikha, who gave him a roof and a bit of grub. He'd pay it all back to her. Not for nothing had he been working on the side since he was twelve, loading hay on a state farm. He'd pay her back for everything, to the very last kopek: for the bread, for soup and herring dipped in weak tea, for the suit he'd never worn, the cheapest in the region, still awaiting its hour in its sackcloth bag. He'd wear that suit for Galakha's funeral; the event was worthy of it. He'd also give everything back to Lyosha Leontyev, who, as he'd suddenly discovered, had been washing his clobber for fifteen years and cooking his meals. He wasn't his father. Villiput hadn't asked him to do this. Why on earth should he? And why on earth should a policeman get it into his head to take care in secret of an orphan? He hadn't asked him to. He'd pay him back for all of it, too, to the very last kopek: for the scrubbing and ironing, the lunches and suppers. He'd pay Nosikha and Leontyev back, they knew that, he'd told them. 'Keep your bloody money,' Nosikha had told him impatiently. 'You're alive, so that's that.' But when he went to work at the farm that very first summer, he brought her his whole pay-packet: forty-two roubles nineteen kopeks. 'Well well,' was all Nosikha could say. 'Well well.' That's how he'd pay Leontyev back, too. He was stubborn, didn't ask anyone for anything. Didn't have anyone to ask anyway. He was no one's. No one was his. Except, maybe, Irus and Galakha. But Galakha was lying dead on the table, and Irus still had to be found. His brother. Blood-brother. Almost his very own. 'I like the way you fall, kid,' Irus had shouted as six-year-old Villiput struggled to his feet after his twentieth or thirtieth tumble on the icy slope, which he was trying to get down on rusty skates that he'd found at a rubbish dump. 'You fall well. No snivelling. Good lad. Get over here and I'll tie your boots up.' Villiput hadn't asked him to. 'I can do it myself.' 'A real hero!' Irus tied them up. Taught him how to skate down. No sissying around. Strong, brave, ginger. The strongest, the bravest, the gingerest. King of Seventh Street. 'Anyone who touches this kid has me to deal with. That clear?' That's how it was. Mate. Bro. 'He's my little blood-brother, got it? If any-one even thinks of touching him ... OK?' They even swapped knives like blood-brothers should: Irus kept Vil-liput's, Villiput kept Irus's. They etched their names on the blades: *Villiput* on Irus's, *Irus* on Villiput's. Way it should be. Brothers. Senior and junior. Junior would go through fire and water for the other. Just say the word, brother. And senior didn't skimp on teaching Villiput: 'Try thinking less, brother. So what if this guy's stronger than you. Don't think about it, punch him in the teeth, then we'll sort the rest out.' Now that's education. That's school. Not like the one Nosikha and Leontyev made him go to. In eight years he'd only ever asked Miss one question: 'If I learn that a right angle is ninety degrees, will that make me better? Or worse?' She was speech-less. Came out in spots. Then she jabbered on for half an hour about knowledge is power and learning is light. Sure. No more questions then. No need to have asked that one either. Sure. Knowledge is Power, Learning is Light. Right. No more questions. Ever.

About half an hour must have passed before ruins showed behind the trees. He carried his bike over a ditch. The wall of the nearest house was cracked right through, the first floor had been demolished, and the stone was covered in patches of scrofulous moss. Below, in the surviving part of the house, twilight reigned. A good place to leave the bike. From here on he'd be on his own two feet. Irus would have nowhere to run to. Villiput would get there. Villiput would say to Irus: 'This is all you've got to do, brother. Say sorry. It won't bring the girl back to life, sure, but you still have to say you're sorry. For fairness's sake, simple as that. It's all that's required.' For the world to stay standing. For everything to remain the same. Day and night. Winter and summer. Two brothers: Villiput and Irus. The law. Which no one had the right to break with impunity. That was the only reason Villiput had set out on this path. Not to demand something for himself or bring someone back from the dead, no way. You could only do what was possible, no whinging or whining. Of course, he could choose not to move a finger. When you think about it, the dead person was a total outsider. And a moron into the bargain. He wasn't guilty. Or if he was, only a little bit. See, he'd acted according to the law: his brother had wanted Galakha – no problem. But his brother had knocked her up and she'd died giving birth. So he had to lend his brother a hand, that was the law. His brother shouldn't break the law. If something happened, he had to be helped out. Even if he didn't want to be.

A magpie cried loudly on the other side of the wall and broke into a chatter. Time to move on. Tying the flask to his belt, he set off towards the forest. The smell of mushroom mould and marshy damp wafted towards him.

He entered deep into the hazel thicket, taking a short-cut along the stream to the Station. Here and there were trees knocked down by the wind. Clouds appeared in the sky: small, half-transparent, they raced along in separate groups, visibly thickening to the whiteness of sour cream. When he came out at the edge of the forest, light swift clouds were being chased by curly ones, row after row of them. He climbed down through a sparse patch of aspen to the shallow stream and continued along the shore. Failing to notice a mud pit, he plunged waist-high into water. Clutching a hazel branch, he got out onto dry land, took off his clothes and wrung his trousers until they looked like a thick rope. A hero with no trousers. Not funny. Time was slipping away. He'd got stuck in time as it was, like an insect in jam. He struggled into his wet trousers. He had to get a move on, but without straying from his aim. What was it Irus had said? 'You write your own laws in that Villiputia of yours. They don't touch me here.' Here was where? Gigantia? Normaldia? Oh well, it was Villiputia for him. At the double!

Once out in the open, he checked his step. Station. Crumbling buildings, an embankment overgrown with wormwood and spurge. There was a time when all East Prussia had been a thick tangle of narrow-gauge railways like this one. Now all that was left of them were the embankments and occasionally the station buildings somewhere in a forest or in the middle of a bog. Right. It was then that he saw a man suddenly stand up on the embankment and stride off to the forest. He was walking calmly, swinging his arms in time with his step, and he even seemed to be whistling something. He didn't turn round once. Small wonder. He was the king. Citizen of Gigantia.

'Halt!' Villiput yelled at the top of his voice. 'Halt! . . .'

At high speed the heat was barely noticeable, so Lyosha kept going faster and faster. When he arrived in the yard of the First Barracks, the piglet squealed and ran off behind the well. Lyosha's head was aching a little and he was thirsty. Was it the hooch? What had she made it with, chicken droppings? He drank from the bucket. Ivan Ivanych walked out onto the porch. Leontyev poured the rest of the water over his head and gave a satisfied snort.

'It's boiling,' Ivan Ivanych said. 'Come in, have a smoke.'

'No time. Has Villiput been by?'

'No.' Ivan Ivanych thought for a moment. 'Someone's taken the flask from the house. Must be one of our lot.'

Naturally, he didn't stop to explain why he'd decided it was one of his lot. That's just how it was.

Lyosha checked the petrol level in the tank, wiped the rod on his trousers and put it away under the seat.

'I need a gun,' he said. 'And some five cartridges or so.'

Ivan Ivanych brought out a double-barrelled shotgun.

'What about the carbine?'

'Not for you,' Ivan Ivanych grinned. 'With that one you stick the cartridges in the fore-stock and when you shoot the centre of gravity's always shifting. You have to get used to it. Here you are.'

'What's the quickest way to the Eleventh Post? Through the Station?'

'Could do. But then you'll have to dump the motorbike somewhere. You can only walk it that way.'

Slinging the gun over his shoulder, Leontyev got on the bike.

'There'll be rain by evening,' said Ivan Ivanych.

Leontyev released the brake, and with its engine still off,

the motorbike rolled smoothly down to the cart track. Station. Why not?

He didn't spare his machine and reached the ruins quite quickly. He hid the bike in a hazel-grove behind the half-collapsed house with walls covered in scrofulous patches of moss, and threw a good few branches over the petrol tank. He adjusted the gun and set off towards the forest.

It was quiet on the edge of the forest. The sun scorched his skin. A quivering haze hung over the buildings of the Station and over the tall embankment thickly covered in spurge. Leontyev clambered up and looked around. Not a soul. Broken tiles and chunks of red brick crunched underfoot. Lyosha climbed up to the first floor of the station building. He had a good view from there of the glade, split in two by the embankment. In the direction of the Eleventh Post the forest was thinner, brighter. He had the impression that people were shouting in there. He listened hard. No, he'd imagined it. But the birds were silent and that put him on his guard. Taking his gun in hand, he ran down and set off briskly towards the forest. Once again, he fancied he could hear the sounds of a chase: the crackling of branches, rapid breathing . . . Nerves. He came out on a narrow path, trampled by mushroom-pickers and hunters. Here he heard a shot. He could have sworn it had come from a Makarov pistol and he tore after the sound, ignoring the thorns, crashing through the trees, slipping on mushrooms: forward and onwards, whatever it cost him, forward!

He shot and missed. Thank God. He hadn't wanted to shoot, but the fright had been too great when the back covered in a faded jacket started moving off rapidly and was about to vanish any second behind a double-trunk pine: that was when he pulled the trigger, luckily without having had time to aim. A piece of bark had flown off the pine-tree. While the shot was still echoing, he was already sprinting after the jacket, mindless of the path. He charged into the bushes, scratched himself badly in the dogrose thickets and ran out into the glade. The bushes crackled to the right, and he made for the double-trunk pine. The black jacket flitted between the firs. Irus was running with his head down, but the tops of the young trees gave him away. Villiput raced along the line of trees. One–two–three, one–two–three . . . . He was losing his rhythm and feared that his breathing would let him down. He had to be strong. There was no one to ask help from. Not even his brother. His brother wasn't interested. Irus unexpectedly ran out into the glade. Villiput stopped in surprise and raised his pistol, but Irus darted into the bushes and disappeared. Christ. Had he lost his mind? What was he waving his pistol around for? You can kill people like that. Last thing he wanted. He jumped over the ditch and ran after Irus, whom he could only glimpse in the undergrowth.

Rushing had thrown his breathing. He had a stitch in his left side. A few seconds later, when he was forced to jump again over a fallen tree, the pain intensified sharply and now he could feel something dull and hard thumping furiously under his ribs to the beat of his heart. He felt dizzy and now and then a pinkish mist clouded his vision. For a while he ran with his eyes closed and he was amazed to catch himself doing this. Smashing into a tree or tumbling down a hole was all he needed now. Far ahead of him Irus was running just as steadily and heavily, and it seemed that he could carry on running like that for another ten miles, or even a thousand. The forest suddenly parted, and both ran out into a narrow glade. Irus turned round and Villiput saw his wide-open eyes and bared teeth. Villiput put on a spurt. He was catching up. They were running along the edge of a ravine. There was a chill in the air.

The weather might change any minute, as it often did in these parts, where in summer rainstorms seemed to come out of nowhere, only to be replaced just as suddenly by scorching heat. The ravine stretched right down to the marsh, to the Eleventh Post. So, we'll run that far and what next, Villiput thought? Irus won't go any further. So why run away from him? To wear Villiput out until he was half-dead? Then beat him up to within an inch of his life? But punch-ups had never helped anyone prove anything to Villiput. Irus knew that as well as anyone. He must have panicked. He just hadn't expected that the kid Villiput wouldn't back off. Not for anything.

Thunder. The first raindrops poured down the shafts of light between the trees. Villiput slipped on a smooth root and fell. He jumped to his feet and nearly yelled in anger: Irus had vanished. A glade lay ahead, and the ravine to the right, clearly visible from up there. Irus was nowhere. Hiding, was he? Holding the pistol in an outstretched arm, the boy walked forward slowly, scouring every bush, every tree, every tuft of grass. Irus was sly, strong and pitiless. The slyest, the strongest and the most pitiless brother in the world. Keep your eyes peeled. The rain, which had never really got going, suddenly let up. Villiput paused, and that was when he saw Lyosha Leontyev on the other side of the ravine with a shotgun in his hands. Villiput ducked and scampered off on all fours towards a hazel bush. Panting and keeping his eyes on Lyosha, he crawled further and further away, until he suddenly stopped and fell on his stomach, catching sight of someone's cheap shoes at the last instant . . .

Aiming above Irus' head, Lyosha emptied both barrels. Irus dashed to the side and vanished behind the trees. Leontyev jumped down the slope but he lost his footing and slid right down on his bum. Clutching a blackberry bush, he clambered up quickly and sprinted to the edge of the forest. His instinct hadn't let him down: Irus was running in an arc, trying to skirt a glade as quickly as possible. So Villiput must be there somewhere, too. Rain poured down again, harder this time. In the space of a minute, everything in the sparse forest was damp and slippery.

There were many chopped-down trees and pits. Sanitary felling was carried out here in winter: all the good wood was taken off to the sawmill, the rest was left there. Rotten logs and thick branches lay in heaps. The ground squelched underfoot. Footprints were immediately washed over by muddy black water. Lyosha slowed to a walk. Where on earth was Villiput? At one point he glimpsed Irus' back and thought the boy would also appear any second. But he didn't. He saw Irus again, running up a hillock thick with pines. Villiput should definitely have come into view then. Maybe he'd lost the trail? Lyosha hurried. His feet slipped on the wet grass. Rain streamed down his face and under his collar, but he was oblivious to everything now. He had no right to leave the forest without finding Villiput. He had to do this. Come what may. He fell and whacked his knee painfully against a bough. He thought he'd caught sight of a shadow to the left, and he threw himself after it. He slipped on a rotten log concealed in the grass, and plummeted into a pit, crashing backwards into boggy, sticky mud ... Boughs and logs rained down and buried him at the bottom. Done for. He was sunk up to his chest in mud at the bottom of a deep crater: aerial bombing had left lots of these in the woods. His legs were pinned down by logs. His gun stuck barrels-up out of the mud, submerged from the lock down. He tried to free his legs but nothing came of it. Heavy pieces of rotten wood held him firmly in this trap and he failed at first attempt even to reach the nearest log. Breathing heavily, he leant back. His body was smeared with icy slush. Rain streamed through the ferns on the crater's edge. Lyosha screwed up his eyes and his whole body convulsed. A sharp pain shot through his legs and echoed in his stomach. Serious. Really serious. Looked like both legs were broken below the knees.

When Villiput opened his eyes, the black sky seemed to be crumbling into fragments, and only when he heard peals of thunder did he realize: it was already night, and the white cracks in the sky were flashes of lightning. It was pouring. His head ached terribly. The blow had been struck to the back of it, slightly to the side, and it was there that all the pain was concentrated. Villiput sat up. His head swam and he suddenly threw up. He struggled to his feet, clasping some branches. Keeping his balance was difficult, as if he had no knees. Took a step. Success. Another. Not too bad. The pistol? Irus wasn't a fool: he wouldn't leave him a weapon. And without the pistol Villiput was nothing. Go home, little kid. His knife? Child's play. Mere hands or knives wouldn't get you anywhere with

Irus. Only a pistol. So toddle home, little boy, back to that Villiputia of yours and live there according to your own laws, as you like. Get out from under the feet of kings. Stay out of Gigantia. Off with you. So he walked off, towards the edge of the forest. Yes, he'd walk. But not home, anywhere but home. He didn't have a home. He didn't have anything or anyone. No home, no mother, no father, no brother, no Galakha. And no one had him. No mother, no father, no brother. Maybe only Galakha, because she was dead. Small, skinny, stubborn as hell, a king's shadow, a devoted henchman, a brother. A mouth like a bloodless slit on a narrow colourless little face. Motionless eyes. A pointed chin. Chicken-chested. And measureless pride: me. Just me. Alone. Me. Never bowed to anyone. Never cried. Never moaned. Never asked anyone for anything. He'd pay back his debts to everyone. To the last kopek. To Nosikha. To Leontyev. Just so long as they didn't get in his way. That's all. Not much to ask, was it? Irus himself had told him: 'The laws can't be broken.' Villiput hadn't even begrudged him Galakha: he'd handed her over. What do you expect? They were brothers, after all. For her, though, Villiput counted as brother, father, mother and whoever else a backward girl with a cleft palate, enormous stupid eyes and an idiot's speech was supposed to have. Galakha's mother was probably glad to be rid of the burden. Now there was no one to keep her from knocking back hooch, no one would judge her, not even Leontyev. There'd be a wake soon, to last a year. Her and Nosikha. Villiput used to comb Galakha's hair, feed her ('Here's a bit of bread, Galakha'), protect her ('Don't be scared of geese, Galakha'). She followed him like a little dog: 'Ittya, Ittya (she was trying to say his name – Vitya), wheh we goin'?' 'Over there.' In summer he'd take her on overnight fishing trips, and they slept next to each other by the fire, cuddling up under Nosikha's old padded jacket. He felt frightened and short of breath when she cuddled up too close to him. He'd cover her, walk off to the river and shiver until dawn – from the cold, probably. He couldn't do that. That is, he could, but he couldn't. Simple as that: you can, but you can't. Those were the kind of idiotic laws he had in that Villiputia of his. Others had their own thing, he had the law. Irus had a different law. The three of them were lying in the hayloft. He said to him: 'Run home a minute, kid, eh? I'm out of smokes, get me a cigarette.' He knew what was going to happen in the hayloft. But he went. His brother had asked. Order from the king. When he got back, it was all over. Galakha was purring on Irus' shoulder. He was chuckling away. 'Look at her: stupid, but she still knows what's what. A woman like any other!' And she got a belly like any other. 'Who did that?' was all Lonesome Katya could ask (that was what they called this drunken mother, who used to yell with or without reason: 'I'm the lonesome mum. And who are you? No one, that's who you are!'). Lonesome Katya was having kids at that age, and she was OK. Galakha would survive too. She didn't. Swaying heavily, she timorously carried her enormous belly and looked at Vitya with her stupid eyes: 'Ittya, Ittya . . .' He frowned, agonized, ran away from her. He'd hide at home, screw up his eyes and whack a bread-knife against his palm, whispering: 'A, b, c, d . . .' All the way to the end. His grandma had taught him. It calmed him down. In the morning he prised open his palm: the cut would be healing over, burning slightly, reminding him of one and the same thing. Why had he done it then? To forget himself? And not forget?

The quicker he walked, the less pain he felt in the back of his head. So he started running, but after just a few strides he slipped, fell into some brambles and badly scratched his fore-head. From then on he walked like a robot. In less than half an hour he realized he was tired to death. He wanted to sleep. After all, sometimes a person's just got to sleep. He rubbed his face as he walked. Didn't help. He picked up a pine cone and started gnawing it savagely, biting chunks off its thick scales and spitting them out. His tongue went numb from the sharpness of the juice. He tried doing exercises on the way. But he just felt more and more sleepy. The ground began to squelch beneath him. There was a marsh nearby. He sat down on a stump, crashed out immediately, and fell off. Groaning, he crawled under a wide fir bough, which hung almost down to the ground, pressed his stomach against a bed of needles, and collapsed into a deep sleep.

The rain was relentless, and Lyosha had long since ceased paying it any mind. After lengthy, torturous efforts, he succeeded in yanking the gun out of the mud and somehow standing it against the slope of the crater, fastening it in place with a stick that he drove into the clay. He'd abandoned any hope of finding a support for his elbows in the liquid mud, on which he was lying as on a pillow. He tried several times to reach for the log closest to him, but each attempt proved fruitless: his body had simply been thrown too far back and his bum had sunk too deep. Realizing how much a person depended on his bum, he laughed out loud with all his heart. All right then. All right. He'd definitely claw his way out: he couldn't not do so. For Villiput. For himself. For the woman who'd been lying helpless in her room for all these years. Neither dead nor alive. Now that was someone he couldn't help. And nor could anyone else. 'It's nerves,' Doctor Sheberstov had said. 'This disease is called fate. Heard of it?' Sure he had. His fate, how could he not have heard of it? His and hers. They'd married not long before the war. She gave birth when he was freezing in the Volkhov marshes. With a baby in her arms she'd had to flee the punishment squads with the other villagers and make for the partisans in the forest. It was then, in the crazed flight, that she'd lost her son. Just like that: lost him. Don't take it so hard, women comforted her, your boy will turn up, he won't vanish, good folk won't let him die. A young grey woman met him at the burnt-out site of their home. Give me a baby, Lyosha. I'm cold, Lyosha. Where's my son, Lyosha? They lived in a dugout, like everyone else. Every day she walked down the road along which she'd run to the forest in the winter of '42. 'Vi-i-i-tya-a-a! Vi-i-i-tya-a-a!' she yelled, sang, wailed. He caught her up in a field or in the forest, hoisted her over his shoulder, carried her back home. I'm cold, she'd groan, and he felt this cold and realized: they wouldn't have another child. In spring she fell sick and didn't get up for two months. During her illness her grey hair turned black again, and for some reason this frightened the villagers: it was a bad sign. The local medic said: 'She'll never get better here. Living in a dugout, eating pine bark – what d'you expect?' But that was how they all lived. So he had to try something different. He loaded their meagre belongings on a cart, laid his wife on straw and set out for new lands, hoping to get settled in East Prussia. That's all there was to it. The one and only event in his life, not counting the war. Get yourself a girl, he was told. 'You're in the prime of life,' Battle-Axe would say to him. 'Get someone pregnant and live a new life. You don't have to dump the other one, either.' Sure. She was probably right. He had to live. But he was a duffer. He carried on living with his paralysed wife and no children. He did only that which he couldn't not do. Hardly enough for a normal life. And what he did, he sometimes did in secret. He washed Villiput's shirts in secret, while Nosikha was boozing with Lonesome Katya, or sleeping off a hangover. He cooked the kid's meals in secret. Now that was something he couldn't not do. For a long time Villiput didn't suspect a thing. And when he did find out (Nosikha blurted it out after a few), he went up to Lyosha and said that he'd pay back all his debts. For sure. 'And if you hadn't known?' Lyosha had asked. Villiput was thrown. Perhaps he really did understand that people are not capable of paying every debt back to one another, and that that is why they can still be called human beings. But he wasn't like everyone else. 'It's your business, of course.' 'Mine,' nodded Villiput, small, skinny, with an angry narrow little face on which his mouth resembled a bloodless slit. 'I didn't ask you for anything. So you can be sure: I'll pay it back. To the last kopek.' 'Goes without saying.' Lyosha said. 'Deal.' No hope of explaining to the boy that not every debt is a debt.

He breathed in a lungful of air, tensed himself and jerked his body up as hard as he could, but his fingers just slipped on the wet surface of the log. Failure didn't dishearten him. He tried to find support for his heels. Looked like all his twitching had made one of the logs fall to the bottom; now Lyosha was able to lean on it. He'd sunk almost shoulder-deep into the mud. The pain from his legs was coursing through his stomach and making his heart beat hard and fast. But he had no choice: somehow or other he had to budge this heap of logs and branches. A long rotten chunk of wood struck him in the shoulder, but he ignored the pain. He dragged the chunk close, placed it alongside and sank again up to his throat in mud. He pushed up and almost passed out from the pain. Feeling raindrops merge with sweat on his brow, he rested for a short while without moving. Then he renewed his attempts. No choice. Time was short. In about an hour, he'd already moved about four short logs close to him. At last he had something on which to lean his elbows. His body was emerging slowly and painfully from the sticky, squelching slurry. He paused a few times to take a breather and lay there gazing through the fretted ferns at the dark sky. The rain was letting up. Lyosha tried once more to haul himself out of the mud. He counted the attempts: sixty. The sixty-first wasn't needed. He rested his head against the slope. His legs felt cold. He drew his knees up cautiously to his chest. His boots had stuck in the dirt. Goodbye boots. Shame: in fifteen years he'd only had to have them repaired once. When deaf Nikita was still alive. He turned onto his stomach and crawled up, clutching at roots. He could still put weight on his knees, but not on his feet – no way. Struggling somehow out of the pit and dragging out his gun, he lay on the grass and immediately fell asleep. His dreams were red. He woke up less than an hour later. He tried standing up but after taking a step, collapsed on the grass. As if he had no legs. Then he started crawling. He couldn't care less how he moved. So what if he had to crawl like a worm. He'd do it. At least he'd do what he couldn't not do. At least. As always.

Villiput crawled out from under the fir bough and looked around him. Day was breaking quickly in the forest. The fog had remained thick only over the marsh. The top of a tall pine had turned scarlet. A blackbird suddenly twittered loudly. Villiput stretched. Great! His body felt rested, his head wasn't aching, only his skin felt burning-hot. A house showed through the fog. The Eleventh Post. A stone's throw away. So he'd crashed out under a tree only two hundred metres away. Huh. He brushed off the pine needles clinging to his jacket, shook his trouser-legs and did a few knee-bends with his hands held out in front of him. His body obeyed him. Knocking off thistle heads on his way, he made for the house, separated from him only by some sparse osier thickets. When he parted the dewy branches with his hands (looked like a hot day, he noted mechanically) and stepped out onto the path, he saw Irus right in front of him.

Lyosha snapped awake to the loud cry of a wagtail and lifted his head. The bird circled low over the grass and perched on a hummock, casting a searching glass-eyed gaze at the man. Lyosha turned over on his back and sat up. His legs were swollen, a hot fog filled his head. He drew his gun near, wiped the butt with his sleeve and tried to get up. Pain shot through his stomach; he thought he heard his knees crack. But he stayed on his feet. He could walk. He had to. Come what may. With every step he swore through his teeth: it was easier that way. Opening his eyes, he set himself another target – a prominent pine or a gnarled hornbeam – and headed right for it. Then he'd choose another landmark and start walking again, leaning on his gun and biting his lips till they bled. Just so long as he didn't tumble into a pit. Then he'd never get out. He fell once more and couldn't get up. He crawled. Forward. Whatever it cost him. What. Ever. He dug his elbows into the ground and dragged his body along, threw his elbows forward and dragged his body along again, and so on until his elbows sank into something soft. The marsh stretched ahead, blotched with poison-green duckweed. The buildings of the Eleventh Post were visible to the left. Breathing hoarsely, he rapidly crawled to the house by the shortest route: through the thickets. He saw Irus just as unexpectedly as had Villiput, and just like Villiput, the surprise rooted him to the spot.

Irus was asleep, rolled up in a ball on a bundle of straw. He was wearing cheap blue braces on a washed-out shirt; the sun shone off the clips. His trousers were tied with a piece of rope. His unhealthily white hairy legs were stuffed in heavy riveted boots. He was breathing heavily and a gurgling sound came from his nose. A cobweb clung to his unshaven cheek.

'Well well,' said Lyosha. He pulled himself up on his elbows, turned on his back, and sat up. 'Just look what we've got here.'

Irus opened his eyes. Leapt to his feet.

'Not so fast,' Lyosha frowned. 'Where's the pistol?' He took the pistol, sprang the clip and counted the cartridges. 'Well well.'

'Morning, friends,' came a voice from behind their backs. A young but already greying man in a padded jacket and hip boots surveyed the threesome with interest. 'Just in time for tea. Morning, Lyosha.'

'Morning,' Lyosha croaked back. 'You got a shed with a decent lock?'

The forester shifted his gaze from Irus to Villiput.

'Sure,' he said. 'For this one? Or for him?'

'For me as well,' said Villiput.

'Two sheds then,' said Lyosha.

'A shed each,' the forester agreed. 'Luxury for all.'

He'd done everything that he couldn't not do. Maybe even a bit more. But this was nothing to boast about. That life had long since become memory, that love also. So that life and that love had acquired the finality of an epitaph, the finality of death, and could be put into words. 'And why not,' said Doctor Sheberstov. 'So you locked them both in the shed.' Lyosha looked at the immobile woman, silent witness to this life and this conversation, and said: 'It wasn't me. Seryoga locked them in. The forester. You know, Mitrofan's son.' Sheberstov nodded: of course.

The shed was all in one piece, but divided in two. A sturdy kind of shed. The partition was sturdy, too. Of course, he should have checked himself that there were no holes or cracks, but his legs had given up on him, a red-hot fog filled his head and he just nodded when the forester said: 'Don't worry, Lyosha, it's all taken care of.' It didn't even occur to anyone then that Villiput would use the crack under the ceiling, so narrow only a cat could squeeze through. Judging by the marks on the walls, he'd tried climbing up a few times, but kept slipping. He'd finally had the sense to drag over the milk container, stood on it, jumped up and hung by his hands. Who'd have thought it? It was a real effort squeezing into the crack, and he lost the buttons on his jacket and ripped his clothes badly. Irus didn't stop him. He might even have been sleeping. The long run through the forest had worn him out. He had nothing and no one to fear. He hadn't stolen his pistol, hadn't fired it. All he'd done was run away from a raving kid. That wasn't punishable. So the worst was over; Leontyev could deal with things now. After all, the policeman had the weapon and without the pistol only flies would be scared of Villiput. So Villiput squeezed through. Threw himself at Irus, who shoved him away of course. Still singing the same tune? Still 'say sorry'? Take that then. Not enough? Take that too. As much as you want. I'm not stingy. You're better off not trying. I'd have killed you ages ago, but there's no point. You're not worth it. Perhaps they had a conversation like that. Or similar. And Villiput . . . Well, what could he say to him? What? 'This is all you've got to do. Say sorry. It won't bring the girl back to life, sure, but you still have to say you're sorry. For fairness's sake, simple as that. It's all that's required.' For the world to stay standing and not crumble. That was the law. Irus had said so too: the law can't be broken. What could Irus reply? 'Go back to that Villiputia of yours and live there according to your own laws. And stop getting under my feet.' Chances are Villiput tried to convince Irus a few more times. Talked. Threw himself at him. Got it in the teeth: face all bruised, lip all bloodied. Chances are he squatted for a long time by the wall, summoning all his strength so as not to start howling. Slashed his palm with his knife, whispering: 'A-b-c-d . . .' Perhaps it calmed him down. He realized he couldn't do any-thing to Irus. That guy was stronger. Quicker. Wilier. The strongest, the quickest, the wiliest. And once he'd understood this, he probably fell on his knees. 'Brother, do this, please.' It's clear what the king answered. The kid had exhausted every option. Except the last . . .

'Of course,' Doctor Sheberstov muttered. 'The knife.'

The knife. The kind of knife which blood-brothers are meant to swap. Way it should be. Irus' knife with *Irus* inscribed on the blade, kept by Villiput. Villiput's knife with *Villiput* inscribed on the blade, kept by Irus. Who knows if he thought of this before? Unlikely. But this was his last chance. And it's unlikely he said anything to Irus. Just did it. Irus heard a muffled groan. At first he ignored it: let him groan. But the sound of it . . . So Irus got up from the log and walked over to Villiput, who was scrunched up in the far corner. 'Hey, what's this?' Kicked him. 'What's up with you?' The groan faded. Irus suddenly felt shivery. 'What have you done, you creep?!' he yelled. 'I know what you're like, you bastard. Let's see!' He grabbed Villiput by the shoulder and tugged him close. Stepped back. Hurled himself at the door, pounded on it, screamed: 'Hey! Hey you! Quick! Over here! Open up! Hey!' He went back to Villiput. Still breathing. 'Wait, brother,' Irus whispered, feeling the boy with his quivering hands. 'Wait . . . What have you done . . . Idiot . . . Hey!' He lifted his hands to his face. They were covered in blood. 'What have you done?' Irus croaked, his eyes fixed on the knife handle sticking out between Villiput's fingers, which lay entwined on his stomach. 'Vilipu-u-u-t! Vilipu-u-u-t!' It was probably then that this tough, hardened lad realized: whose knife? Knife – whose? Whom could he convince that the knife with *Irus* on the blade didn't belong to Irus? After all that had happened, whom could he convince that the knife belonged to this puny kid, who'd used his last chance? 'The shit!' Irus yelled as he tried to break out of the forester's arms. 'He's framed me, can't you see? What for? What for??' The forester pinned the lad against the wall. Still crawling, Lyosha made his way over, nudged aside the forester's leg with his elbow, forced his way through to the corner, buried his head in the kid's arms, lay there. There was no one he'd needed. He'd acted as he always had. Him. Just him. Alone. As always, no one else had counted.

Revenge

It was evening, right before sunset. Me and Mum were sitting inside, doing something, and he was out in the yard chopping wood. Then Mum went into the kitchen, and I stayed where I was. He just kept hacking away with his axe, though Mum yelled at him twice to come in to eat.

He's not my real dad, this Stasis, he's my second. The first one, the real one, copped it in the war some place. Stasis was in with a group of old Polizei mates, then he sneaked off and shacked up with my Mum.

The sun was almost in now. Mum calls him again, she's angry. He's muttering something in the dark, but you can't tell what. Then I suddenly see him running with his axe across the yard, and that lot are by the gates and they've started shooting. He falls, crawls a bit and that's it – just lies there.

Mum's shouting in the kitchen, then she goes out. I'm scared stiff, gawping out of the window and keeping dead still. If that lot saw me, they'd laugh for sure. But they haven't got time for that, and scram.

After about five minutes I go out. Mum's crying on the porch, scared of going down the steps into the yard. The neighbours all come round. The policeman turns up. Starts trying to calm Mum down. Like a man knows how to comfort anyone. Mum listens and listens, then she spits on his boots, swears and walks off.

Stasis got buried and we went on living. Mum was really stroppy now, always rowing with the neighbours. No way I wanted to catch one of her moods, so I stopped spending the night at home and moved over to the hayloft.

Late one night she climbed up to me there.

'Come on,' she says, 'get down, you're coming with me.'

'Where, Mum?' I ask.

'You'll see,' she says. 'Come on, move it.'

I can see she's getting mad. Well, I think, nothing for it. I climb down. She grabs the shotgun (left over from my first dad), and nods at me: let's go. I've made up my mind to run away from her if anything happens, but I'm saying nothing yet. Off we go. Down through the park to the railway line, then over to the little hills, then on to the woods . . . Some time for a walk.

It's dark already, frightening: see I was only a kid. But she just walks on. There's dew on the grass and we get soaked right through. I start whimpering: where are we traipsing off to in the middle of the night? I'm tired. She says nothing. I shut up, too: so what if I'm tired, tough.

We walked for ages through the wood, until we came out to the house where the one-legged forester lived then. The house was quiet, the windows were dark, and there was a light, weak as anything, coming from behind the house, like from a little bonfire. I was dead scared.

'Mum, let's get out of here, eh?'

'Quiet, son' she says. 'Keep it really quiet.'

She's scared too. But she makes for the light and I follow her. There's a worn-out awning behind the house, and under it a man's sitting at a wooden table, doing something. The paraffin stove's on at half-flame. First he doesn't notice us. Mum makes a noise.

'Evening,' she says.

He jumps up. Mum raises the gun at him.

'Watch it, bastard,' she says.

The man sits down, looks at us.

'It weren't me. I was just standing by the gates. What d'you want?'

He's scared, blinking his eyes.

'I've come to even up,' Mum says.

'What do you need the kid for? Clear off, kid.'

'He can stay . . . So you're saying it wasn't you?' she asks, calm as anything.

'Not me. What do I want with him, that Stasis of yours? It's Yuozapas and them two, his mates, not me. Leave, eh? I got a wound, see, my hand's broke.'

He shows her his bandaged-up hand.

'Get over here, you bastard,' Mum says, furious.

242

He might have stayed where he was, but she's got a gun.

'Don't do that,' he says quietly, coming towards us. 'I got three kids, three treasures.'

'Pray,' Mum says.

'I'm sick of believing in God,' he says. 'Don't.'

He starts yelling madly.

Mum shoots him twice in the face, throws the gun in the grass and runs for it. We run and run till we come out on the railway line. Then she lies down on the ground, flat on her belly, and cries a while.

When we got back home, she lay down in her room. Like always I went to bed in the hayloft. Sleeping there was great, like in heaven: it smelled of apples, hay and just a bit of cow.

All next day, Mum was out. Near evening she comes in with a bottle of hooch, sits in the kitchen and drinks. She can't take it and she's coughing, but she drinks all the same. She'd bought it off Grandpa Kolka, that mean old neighbour of ours.

'What kind of mother am I?' she suddenly shouts at me. 'I'm trash, son, trash.'

Tears again.

We go on sitting there in the kitchen, the three of us: me, her and the cat. I drop off without noticing. Then she's shaking me and saying all sober-like:

'Get to bed now, off you go.'

'And you?' I ask.

'Off with you,' she says again. 'It's late. Time for me, too.'

So I climb up to the hayloft.

Before I can fall asleep I hear shouts in the yard and someone yelling blue murder, calling people to come. I'm dozy and can't work out who's yelling, or why. Dead scary. Quiet as can be, I peek out the window. Just a small bunch of people in the yard, and the main one's Grandpa Kolka.

I go down. I can see Mum lying on the ground with a scrap of rope round her neck. It was Grandpa Kolka who cut it. Maybe he was sorry he'd given her the hooch and wanted to help her drink it – can't say. Anyway, he came round just in time: she'd only just stuck her head in the noose and kicked away the stool. He cut the rope before she could say knife.

They splashed water on her, brought her round, stood around gasping a while then went their ways. I sat for ages next to her till she suddenly started sobbing and groaning.

'Aaahh, aaahh,' she goes.

Then she gets up and goes off to her room.

'Grandpa, eh, Grandpa?' I ask. 'Why's she like that?'

'Coz this ain't the war,' Grandpa says. 'Or if it is, it ain't that one. What, were you at the forester's?

'Yeah. Did she do right to kill?'

'Yeah,' Grandpa Kolka says. 'Who?'

'But why?' I ask again. 'Why's she like that, eh?'

'Easy to see,' Grandpa says. 'A Russian girl can pity all right, but she's no good at getting her own back. She was sorry for that Lithuanian of hers.'

'Maybe she shouldn't have killed?' I ask.

Grandpa grunts and goes off home. He's always like that.

Nothing doing, back to bed.

In the morning I come into the kitchen and Mum's sitting on the floor, in the corner, and stroking the cat, smiling.

'Pussy, pussy, fluffy little tummy,' she says all tender-like. 'Fluffy little tummy.'

'Mum, Mum,' I cry.

But she just goes on about her pussy-cat.

Two days I stuck around her, trying to make her eat something. Grandpa Kolka came round often enough to grieve for the poor soul. But she was just: puss, puss. Then they took her away and I moved over to Grandpa Kolka's for good. He fed me, put clothes on me, see I was only a kid.

Charlie Chaplin

That steam-engine – stumpy and with a funny pot-bellied funnel – was nicknamed Charlie Chaplin by Battle-Axe. That's also what people started calling its driver, although Pyotr Fyodorovich Isakov didn't look anything like the famous comic and, what's more, was completely indifferent to the cinema. He was tall and bony, with a thick grey moustache. At the end of his run he would always have a thorough scrub in the bathhouse, catch up on his sleep on the top shelf, then change into a stiff black suit and a black hat with a round crown. On his impeccably white shirt he wore a narrow tie held in place by an elastic band. He married late. His bulky, broad-boned wife had the nickname Auntie Horse. She worked at the paper mill, and shift after shift she lugged heavy piles of pulp on her belly and chucked them into the mouth of the hideously whirring mill. After her shifts, Auntie Horse washed the blood off her stockings in the shower-room and grouched: 'This is turning me inside out! Thank God I've had mine already . . .' She'd sigh heavily as she looked at the young girls who worked alongside her. One of them, Lyusya, was going out with her younger son, and Auntie Horse doggedly pestered the foreman to move the girl to a different section: 'She's still got to have kids, man!'

Engine-driver Isakov was a taciturn and calm fellow, with no particular passions or quirks to speak of. Whenever he'd earned a few days off, he liked pottering about in the vegetable patch, pruning the apple trees, chasing moles and listening in spare moments to the bird that had made its home in the long-vacant starling-house. In the evenings he and Auntie Horse dolled themselves up and went off to the cinema, where Charlie Chaplin slept right through the show, scrunched up on a creaking wooden seat. Over dinner he drank a small glass of vodka. On summer evenings he liked lying in the grass at the end of the garden and gazing pointlessly at the stars.

There had only ever been one event in Pyotr Fyodorovich's

whole life which could be called an adventure. Held up for a few days in Vilnius, he was introduced by fellow drivers to a nice lady called Anya and spent two nights at her flat. But since Pyotr Fyodorovich wasn't used to giving himself free rein, the liaison ended there, even though Anya invited him back and Pyotr Fyodorovich felt cosy with her. With a heavy heart, he told her he wouldn't come round anymore: a man shouldn't be happy and live as he pleases. After breaking off with Anya, a little crack seemed to open between his ribs on his right side, and every now and again a faint ache reminded him of it.

The steam-engines on the line were replaced by diesel locomotives. Charlie Chaplin became a shunter, and brought grain and pulp to the mills.

Pyotr Fyodorovich's eldest son had got married long ago and lived in Kazakhstan. Every couple of years he visited his parents with his Korean wife and Korean kids. His youngest son, Misha, was serving in the army – in Afghanistan, people said.

Misha returned home alive, but withered and jittery. Hearing that his girl Lyusya had got married, he went on a riotous bender with his mates and got run over by a train. When he got back from his shift and heard the news, Pyotr Fyodorovich could no longer speak or move his arms, and his left eyelid drooped feebly down.

After losing both legs below the knees, Misha seemed to calm down. He sat out the winter at home, quietly drinking his way through his miserly allowance. At the start of spring he moved over to the booze store. He grew a wild beard and didn't use prostheses, tottering around on his stumps and dragging his dirty trouser legs behind him. In the morning, the pointless folk (that's what alkies were called in the town) would drag him out from the pile of crates by the wall and shove his stumps in an urn to keep him steady, while they went off to look for a stiff cure for all their hangovers. In the evenings Misha Schnapps, as he was now known, crawled into the heap of junk by the shop wall and slept until morning, frightening tardy passers-by with sudden fits of snoring.

After she was pensioned off, Auntie Horse turned up at the square every morning and sat on an overturned bucket which she'd bring along with her. She'd let herself go after her son's accident: in winter and summer she wore a padded jacket and rubber boots, hiding her straggly grey locks under a kid's hat with a shaggy bobble of faded reddish-brown. She'd spend entire days on the square, arguing with the winos and keeping a close eye on her son until Pyotr Fyodorovich took her home. He felt sorry for his wife, whom they now called Auntie Testy: she'd become really quarrelsome. People would say hello to her and she'd swear viciously in reply. The sun would shine and she rubbished scantily dressed women, the heat and thirst. It rained and she slagged off God, who didn't even know how to drench this disgusting world properly with water, shame it wasn't kerosene, to be lit with a match then stamped all over so not the faintest memory of it remained. She'd get up in the middle of the night, open the cupboard and take out her white wedding dress, which was wrapped in yellowed newspapers tied with coarse thread. She wanted to try it on but was afraid to do so, thinking that at her age women only wear dresses like that to hang themselves in . . .

Pyotr Fyodorovich would hear her moving about, and he even spied on his wife once as she took the dress out of the bundle. But he didn't say anything. He'd also taken up his pension. The little steam-engine Charlie Chaplin was driven down an out-of-the-way siding and forgotten.

One day, reluctant to throw out some leftover paint, Pyotr Fyodorovich whitewashed a section – one and a half metres by five – of a wall that had been standing since time immemorial in the disused yard over the road. Naturally, kids scrawled obscenities all over it the next day. Pyotr Fyodorovich painted it again, the kids made a mess again. So it went on. The struggle with the kids absorbed the old man completely, but it didn't make him bitter: catching the filth-mongers on the scene of the crime, Charlie Chaplin would limit himself to a severe ticking-off. The adult population of Seventh Street observed this war first with curiosity, then with compassion, and by the end with real irritation. Tired of punishing the kids, they turned to Pyotr Fyodorovich: isn't that enough fooling around, wasting paint and effort? But

Pyotr Fyodorovich could no longer stop himself. Misha Schnapps's antics caused him terrible anguish, while the rustles on the other side of the wall at night stopped him sleeping: his wife would spend hours ironing the bridal dress that she was afraid of wearing. To escape this life, Pyotr Fyodorovich time and again took up his brush and paint . . .

The women of Seventh Street asked policeman Lyosha Leontyev to shame Charlie Chaplin into stopping. Lyosha had a chat with the old man, but it went no further. When he was asked how much longer this would go on for, Lyosha said pensively:

'While he's on his own two feet, we're on ours. He falls down, we'll be on all fours.'

This tirade, though, merely intensified the irritation of the grown-ups and the frenzy of the kids.

On the morning when the pointless people dragged Misha Schapps out of his den and realized that he was dead, Auntie Testy came trudging onto the square as always with her bucket. For a long time she couldn't work out what the winos were trying to drum into her. Then she loaded her son on her back, but fell over. They helped her.

Pyotr Fyodorovich made the coffin with his own hands.

After the wake, when the guests had left and the eldest son who'd flown in from Kazakhstan was asleep, Auntie Testy finally put on her white dress and walked up to the mirror. She was shaking all over. She felt alone and in pain, and went off to look for Pyotr Fyodorovich. She found him soon enough. Seeing him, the woman slowed down. The old man in a stiff black suit and black hat with a round crown was sitting on a low bench by the wall. He hadn't managed to finish painting the top left corner. Auntie Testy felt cold. It seemed to her that things and people had shrunk so much from the sudden freezing chill that she could gather them in her hand and lift the world to her face. But before calling her son and carrying the old man off home, she took up the brush and finished painting the wall, which shone scarily white in the dark of the night, and this whiteness slashed the eye like a bright light suddenly beamed in one's face . . .

Blue Lips

The way to school led across the German cemetery. You could, of course, choose a different route, along the cobbled road that was separated from the railway track by a low fence welded out of steel girders. Then the cemetery would be to your left, behind a neat line of small two-storey houses, its presence betrayed by the all-pervasive scent of thuja and the dark-green clouds of the chestnut trees, which shut out half the sky. The school workshop was housed in the little church on the other side of the cemetery, and to get there we ran past black and grey tombstones with foreign inscriptions. Part of the cemetery was occupied by the school sports field, for which several dozen marble gravestones had had to be cleared. They were left in a heap by the wall of the brick shooting-gallery until enterprising Lithuanians took them away (these marble blocks with scratched-out inscriptions can be seen to this day in cemeteries from Klaipeda to Mariampol). There were experts in the folklore of resettlement who, fascinated by tales of magnificent subterranean passages stretching right up to Berlin, maintained that the graves and family crypts in which our school steward stored chalk, buckets and brooms, had been used by the Germans for hiding countless treasures – precious Meissen porcelain, gold chains and coins, magic books and maps of their underground world. People who'd grown up using WCs simply had to be rich. Digging in their vegetable patches, the settlers stumbled now and then on a dozen plates or forks, concealed by the Germans before their deportation; when they started levelling the meadow with bulldozers, not far from the old Protestant church on the main square, they turned up copious gold and aluminium coins: there was a bank here once, razed by English bombers flying in from Bornhölm . . .

All this merely strengthened the belief that somewhere, if you only looked hard enough, precious hoards were hidden, for which all these plates, forks and random aluminium trifles served as harbingers. Treasure-seekers picked away at the walls of the crypts, shifted the tombstones and the fat marble crosses. They came at night, since the settlers were already burying their own dead in the German cemetery, and the appearance of a person with a pick-axe was considered a sacrilege. They even tried on several occasions to displace an enormous grey granite slab, two metres by five and overgrown with lichen and moss, but all they managed to do was chip away at the corners. A communal grave was thought to lie beneath. No one, though, had bothered to read the moss-covered inscription; only in one spot did they scrape off enough lichen to make out the date – 1761. In those days people only knew of the existence of East Prussia because lads from Chernigov and Ryazan had fallen to Lewald's infantry on the swampy meadows near Gross-Jägersdorf (where, one hundred and eighty-four years later, my father's tanks would pass through).

That summer my parents had bought me a camera, while a friend of mine had been given all the essential equipment for developing and printing. For several weeks we were in seventh heaven, photographing everything we saw: houses, landscapes, the girls next door, dogs. Developed the films. Printed pictures, hunched up in the small storeroom, scalding ourselves on the red-hot cap of the enlarger. The photos came out pale, but our thrill didn't derive from the similarity of the pictures to the originals, yelling 'Look, it's me!' No, it was the miracle itself that excited us: the capacity of optics, mechanics and chemistry to freeze an instant at our will, to wrest this instant from moving life and transfer it onto a piece of paper. There was something both joyous and frightening about this. The instant, dried up like a butterfly in an album and shrouded in mist, was preserved unchanged, while people grew old, buildings decayed, and dogs got run over . . .

In August my friend's parents took him on holiday to the Crimea, and my passion for photography cooled. Every now and again, though, I'd still sling my camera over my shoulder and head off to the river or the nearest wood. Or to the German cemetery, whose peacefulness, steeped in the smell of resin, was only occasionally broken by the cooing of pigeons. Arranging myself comfortably on a plain stone bench, I spent hours in a half-slumber, surrendering the world to the plundering of my imagination. Rapaciously, it grabbed a chance dog or a chance passer-by and transformed them without their noticing into the detail of a dream or a fantasy, into crystals and monsters – the all-transforming chemistry of dreams . . .

'Where else does a real photographer pass the time, if not in the cemetery?'

I jerked awake and nervously tidied myself up: beside me sat our German teacher, nicknamed Der Tisch ('The Table'). Nikolai Semyonovich Solomin.

'Death and photography are related activities,' he clarified. 'Just like death and art. Art in general is the trade of death.' He smiled. 'The art of capturing the moment is the art of killing.'

I gulped. Looked around. Not a soul in sight. Just a pigeon cooing somewhere high in the branches. Two people sitting on a bench under thickly entwining thuja trees oozing the hot smell of resin. A kid caught unawares by a strange man who'd suddenly started talking about death. In a cemetery.

'Do you often come here?' he asked without looking at me. 'I do.'

I tried to explain that I'd come just to take a peek at the 'communal grave' – the granite slab dated 1761.

'So let's go.'

He swept to his feet and strode off down the path, not even bothering to check if I was following. This gave me some heart. 'Teachers don't murder their pupils,' I thought. 'Specially not right near the school.'

He was on the short side but he still had a stoop. His clothes – a crumpled grey shirt and baggy trousers – hung like a sack off his dry, gaunt body, which was crowned by a head shaped like a chicken's egg, flecked with greying hair. His eyelids were always half-lowered, as if he were embarrassed to turn a full gaze on the world. His chubby lips were the colour of pale lilac. As teachers went, he wasn't a bad sort. Since the death of his wife and the marriage of his only daughter (whose faultlessly sleepy-sweet face no one would be likely to remember even at the third glance), Der Tisch had lived a lonely, reclusive life. Every morning he bought a bag of cheap fish scraps at the shop on Linden Street and fed the stray cats that came running from all over the neighbourhood. Voluntarily, he ran a photography club at the school, and dozens of kids eagerly signed up at the start of the year; but after five or six classes, only two or three would be left.

Lifting his feet up high, Der Tisch crossed the narrow clearing, overgrown with brittle pale grass, and squatted before the grey slab. We started scraping the moss and lichen off the inscriptions with our hands. It soon became clear, though, that there was only one inscription, the date 1761; the rest was all fanciful, criss-crossing lines forming some kind of pattern. Looked like a drawing.

'It's a depiction of a griffin. It lived in these woods from antiquity,' said Der Tisch. 'It filched calves and sheep, then one day it was killed. Inside the bird they found the rusty armour of a horse, and seated upon it the rusty armour of a knight.'

I nodded sleepily. Yeah, sure. A knight's armour, clenching the white standard of the Hospitallers in its rusty hand. Of course. Resourceful people made excellent bows out of the ribs of gigantic griffins. The griffins' straight claws were used for arrowheads that could pierce a steel-plated shield from a hundred paces. The best strings for such bows were woven from witches' hair, which could be procured at great expense from the hangmen.

'These hangmen – there were three of them – lived in the lane behind the church, next to the market square,' Der Tisch continued calmly. 'Their skill was renowned even beyond the German and Polish lands. It's said that the one who was invited to Muscovy to hang the tiny son of the second False Dmitry came from Wehlau. After that, the hangman gave up his trade and entered a monastery. The gallows in Wehlau were on the bank of the Pregolya. Sorcerers came here from the whole of East Prussia with their dogs, so as to dig out the mandrake root that grew on the spot where semen dripped from the hung body. The dog would drag the root out of the earth with its teeth, then die in horrible agony.'

He joined his hands piously and closed his eyelids, as if in sympathy for the dead dogs. Whose horrible death agonies Der Tisch had undoubtedly witnessed.

I was so struck by his tale, and even more so by his terrifyingly lifeless manner of speaking, that I didn't even stop to consider the source from which Der Tisch might have gleaned all this information. Such a source, of course, could only have been his imagination. As it was with me. As it was with the other settlers, who knew nothing about East Prussia and viewed it as an alien land scattered with miracles mutating into monsters. After the last trainload of deported Germans left in the direction of Pasewalk, not a single person had remained who could say of East Prussian time and space: 'That's me'. The settlers were in the grip of myths and legends. When they spoke of the past of this land, they resembled people who, on waking in the morning, try to convey in words those vague or indeed painfully vivid images that have visited them in their dreams. 'Here was the studio of the watchmaker Michael Keller', Der Tisch would say, or, 'Here was the only restaurant in the world that served two hundred dishes with river mussels. The ground floor had light-blue tiles, the first floor had pink ones,' and there was something in his tone of voice that made you believe it: yes, the studio had been here, and the restaurant there. Light-blue and pink. Of course. Like in a fairy tale. Had to be true, then. There had been griffins, who swallowed heavily armed Hospitaller Knights, and excellent bows were made from their ribs. What else could the ribs have been used for?

It was only when we were already outside his house that I snapped out of it. Looking at me with his sad sleepy eyes, he muttered pensively:

'I could teach you photography. If you want, I mean. The art of transforming time into space.'

I nodded. Of course. And why not? As we parted, he warned me that he suffered from 'trite maxim incontinence', and asked me not to pay any heed. I promised instantly: I didn't know what trite maxims were anyway.

School started again. The notice went up for the photography club. Naturally, I was one of the first to sign my name in Der Tisch's exercise book, but I soon realized why kids got fed up so quickly with these after-school sessions, during which Solomin spoke tediously about light, perspective, refraction, composition and subject-matter. In our town people didn't get themselves a camera in order to create works of art. Entire families went to Andrei the Photographer's studio, *The Three Palm Trees*, to have their picture taken; others went on their own for their ID. Andrei was invited to weddings and funerals, but never to take a landscape. The Photographer, who wore a wide-brimmed hat and a long scarf thrown carelessly around his neck, could remember only one extraordinary occurrence during his professional career: the teeny hunchback sisters Sweetie-Pie and Fish-Pie (one was a telephone operator at the post office and had the knack of adding an affectionate suffix to any word you could think of; the other, meanly pursing her tiny, heavily made-up lips, sold flat fish pies from her stand near the Ladies at the bus station) called him over once to record for posterity their inconsolable sorrow over the flower-decked corpse of their beloved dog, Phiz.

The club-goers were bored. The rain, pelting down whenever we went out to take pictures, only made things worse. I soon became Der Tisch's sole audience. This didn't upset the teacher at all. On the contrary, left one on one with me, he was transformed and became once again the daring fantasist who'd won me over with his story about the griffin and the mandrake.

Together – he with his Leica, me with my Smena – we wandered round the town and its outskirts. He talked, I listened. The teacher spoke about luckless St Adalbert, who came to enlighten the Prussians in a country that didn't know what beer was, and died at the hands of a heathen; about the first knights on their way to the desert of terror, dark and cold, that stretched from the Vistula to the Niemen and served for centuries as the site of endless battles in which Germans, Swedes, English and Burgundians fought Poles, Lithuanians, Tatars and Russians; about English children who still sing of the poor knight who set out for wild Prussia; about boastful Ottokar II, who credited himself with the founding and building of the city of kings, Königsberg; about the desperate farmer–colonists who sought refuge behind castle walls from the savage Lithuanians; about the thousands of settlers from German lands who came to East Prussia on the orders of Frederick the Great and found refuge there from the horrors of the religious wars; about Lochstedt Castle and the Order's amber treasure vault; about the trade-flushed crusaders who raped Polish women, flouting the Order's ban on even kissing their own mothers; about the great Hohenzollern, Albert of Brandenburg, who created the duchy that would later became a sanctuary for Lithuanian bearers of the Enlightenment and for the Russian Old Believers who fled Moscow's iron hand for the shores of Lake Dusz and became German soldiers in 1914, crushing Samsonov's forces on the same battlefields where, some five hundred years earlier, Jagiellon, Wytowt and their allies from Smolensk had routed the crusaders of Ulrich von Jungingen . . .

He formed highly elaborate constructions out of complex sentences, making my head spin with participial and gerundive clauses.

Still talking, he would suddenly stop in front of a wall or tree, fix up the tripod which he always dragged around with him and take half a dozen photos. I could never understand what he found so special about this spot, this wall or this tree. A wall like any other, a tree like any other. No two ways about it, a real failure of a picture – bland as anything. Once I timidly hinted as much to Der Tisch. He smiled feebly in reply, muttering something about the expressiveness of the inexpressible . . .

When the apple trees blossomed in spring, I invited my teacher to see our garden, where a view opened out onto the boggy meadow with the stadium in the middle, the dyke on the Pregolya and the park, with its heap of treetops in every shade of green. A path split the garden in two and, swerving just once by the old apple tree with the triple trunk, led right up to the rusty gate by the concrete compost pit surrounded by pines. It was the apple tree that caught Der Tisch's eye. His face suddenly took on an angrily concentrated expression, and his eyes narrowed. He set up his tripod and looked for a good while through the viewfinder, turning the focusing lens. Finally, he pressed the button. Then again. And again. He took thirty-five pictures. Afterwards, without a glance in my direction, he hastily gathered up his equipment and all but ran out of the garden. Annoyed by his strange behaviour, I decided to stop going to the photography club.

My father didn't approve of my friendship with the teacher. Jerking his firm, rounded general's chin (that's what it was called by Name of Lev, who once a week had the honour of shaving my dad. The queue at the barber's – ten or so ageing men sitting on creaking chairs along the wall – would stop chewing over the latest news, and silence reigned in the room as Name of Lev worked the leather-handled Solingen blade at an ever-increasing tempo, sonorously removing the foam from the general's chin and cheeks. The procedure was crowned by a roasting-hot napkin with which Name of Lev dabbed his client, before – *finale* – applying it to his own greasy, sweaty face. Done. The queue, noisily releasing its breath, started creaking away with its backbones and chairs. Father would light up a strong cigarette, wink at himself in the mirror and walk out. He was head of the biggest factory in town and most of the locals depended on him for their well-being), my dad announced in his tough voice:

'Blue lips don't like life. That Solomin watches life pass him by. You don't know how to choose your friends.' Then he concluded bitterly: 'Just like me.'

'Blue lips?' said Mum in surprise. 'He's just got a bad heart, that's all . . .'

Der Tisch didn't come to school the next day: he'd fallen ill. Straight after lessons, I went to visit him. He lived in a small house overlooking the river, on a street sloping down to the watermeadow. If the Pregolya came up too high in spring, the cellars in the street would get flooded. From a distance – from the bridge, say – this mass of tiled roofs, showing scarlet amidst the lime and chestnut trees, might warm the cockles of admirers of Brothers Grimm and Andersen, but life in these damp-infested gingerbread houses that lacked running water wasn't the greatest of joys.

Der Tisch wasn't surprised by my visit, but he was clearly embarrassed. He led me through to the living-room: a sunken green plush sofa, a round table in the middle, a tiled stove in the corner, a dull family photo on the wall – him, his wife and his daughter – and a small, tinkling glass cupboard between the windows. While he was busy in the kitchen, I inspected the spines of his books: Goncharov's *Oblomov*, *For our Soviet Motherland*, with a handsome stamped portrait of the General-issimo, *Twenty-Five Lessons in Photography*, a Tübingen edition of Schiller, a deluxe jubilee Kleist, a gilt-edged Goethe (I found out later that my teacher had got this off his neighbour, who'd made a partition out of German books between the pigsty and the woodshed), *Anna Karenina*, a one-volume Leonid Andreev with a black portrait of the madman on the cover . . .

He brought in some cups on a tray, a jar of gooseberry jam and a big tin kettle, which he banged down on the bare table. He took a dark, paper-stoppered bottle from the cupboard, just behind *Anna Karenina*, and poured a few drops into his tea, releasing the smell of honey and cherry.

The room was dusky from the thickly-growing thuja trees in the front garden.

'Forgive an old fool,' Solomin muttered. 'But it was hard for me to explain the reason to you there and then . . . It still is. You see . . .' He brought his cup to his blue lips and I glimpsed crossed Saxon swords at the bottom. 'The house where you're living now was once mine . . . It belonged to my father-in-law, I mean . . . My wife's father.'

I waited.

He sighed.

'All right, be patient. I'll have to start from the beginning . . .'

He was born in a remote and destitute Belorussian village near Orsha, in a land where people were dying from hunger and disease. After the death of his father, who was heavily wounded near Gumbinnen in '14 and at Perekop in '20, the family – Mother and six children – moved near to Donetsk with the other villagers. They found work restoring the Donbass region, which had been destroyed in the Civil War. The men went down the pits, and the women and children joined the local collective farm. It was easier to survive the great Ukrainian famine in the mining region. Far more terrifying was foot-and-mouth. Every day, vets and police would drive out with another dead cow and bury it in the snow-covered steppe. At night the entire family to which the cow had belonged would set out for the burial site, start a fire and eat all they could. Afterwards, some would die. Mother favoured Nikolai: he learnt to read early and could recite the Old Testament by heart for hours, occasionally garbling unfamiliar words. After school came the animal-research institute, then the army and the war, which Solomin began as a battalion clerk. His regiment was encircled in the Battle of Kharkov and he was taken prisoner. That hot summer of 1941, thousands of POWs went insane from hunger and thirst in bare ravines that stretched for miles. Sugar-beet was sent down to them once a day along wooden chutes and they were given a small amount of warm murky water. From above the guards gazed with horror at the threadbare Russians as they chewed filthy beet or lay silent on the parched earth under the blazing sun. Eventually, they were taken to Germany. Solomin ended up in East Prussia and was assigned to work for Herr Theodor Tietz, who was in the dairy trade. Every morning milk cans arrived on carts and narrow-gauge tracks, and Wehlau cheeses and butter were made from the milk at the Tietz's little factory. In season Herr Tietz used to hire Lithuanians from outside, whom he called by the local term *burasy*, in accordance with an old tradition inherited from his ancestors, settlers from near Salzburg. With the onset of war, it had become much harder for the *burasy* to make it over from the banks of the Niemen to the banks of the Pregel. By then, though, a new unpaid work-force had appeared – Russian POWs, along with activists from the Polish nationalist movement who'd been thrown into the Stalags. Solomin and the other Red Army soldiers were quartered in the long, low tile-roofed house that was usually set aside for the *burasy*. Solomin made quick progress with the language and it wasn't long before Tietz, a thickset, greying, taciturn man with Tatar eyes, put him in charge of the Russians. On Sundays Solomin was invited round to his boss's for lunch with the family. He'd scrub the worn linen suit given to him by the old housekeeper under the tap in the garden (with ashes instead of soap). The Russians ribbed him good-naturedly. It was only Tolya Afroskin, Solomin's room-mate, who whispered to him with loathing, 'You sold out, Nicky, you sonofabitch, just you wait . . .' At table, Solomin always ended up opposite Herr Tietz's green-eyed daughter, Maria, and every time he looked at her sweet little lips or chubby arms he felt a tightening in his throat. Mashenka (that was how he called Maria to himself) would also get embarrassed and turn red. The housekeeper Madame Reboul (her ancestors were French Huguenots who found their promised land in Prussia) would give a disapproving shake of her pointed, capped skull. Only Herr Tietz, carving the meat and sipping red wine, was unperturbed. Nor did he mind his daughter's evening strolls with the Russian in the garden, which sloped gently down to the meadow criss-crossed with draining ditches. When his daughter told him she was pregnant, Herr Tietz retired to his room and, as he put it, had a night-long chat with God. The next morning he went off to see Captain Stribrny, on whom the fate of the POWs depended. Heaven knows how they resolved this knotty problem, but they did. Solomin became Herr Tietz's son-in-law and business partner. Mashenka gave birth to a green-eyed girl and to two more daughters a year and a half later. The young couple lived upstairs. The eldest girl, Katya, loved being given piggyback rides by bony Madame Reboul, who, bursting with emotion, would start chanting austere

Huguenot prayers. Solomin would lie down on the floor, press his cheek to a sun-warmed, painted board and groan softly-softly: at such moments he feared death more than anything. 'That's you done for then,' Tolya Afroskin would snigger. 'Marrying a Nazi, spawning little Nazikins.' 'I love her, Tolya. And the girls too . . .' Tolya would pull a wry face. 'Just try saying that to our lot: I loved them, those Nazis and that country of theirs, while they mutilated my country.' He coughed: a bullet had got him in a lung in the Battle of Kharkov. 'So the way you see it, we're the only ones who are human,' Solomin would try to reason. 'They're not, right?' 'Of course they are. But there's a war on.' At the end of '44, Soviet troops entered East Prussia. By early '45 they were almost in Wehlau. The POWs were cleared off to Pomerania or even further, to Germany. The same fate – no matter what – threatened Solomin too. Could he make it to Magdeburg in one piece? Could the Tietz family escape the inferno of East Prussia (where refugees were perishing in their hundreds on the ice of the Frisches Haff)? At a family meeting they decided to split and entrust their lives to the Lord. The Tietzes set off west with a light load, hoping to cross Pomerania to the River Lahn, where Herr Tietz's brother lived. Solomin and Tolya Afroskin, wearing their Red Army rags, headed off through forests towards the Soviet troops. A few days later they looked like fugitives from hell. The SMERSH officers interrogated them individually. Then they assigned Solomin to a sapper batallion and sent Tolya to Siberia, where he died in the camps without having breathed a word about his turncoat friend. Corporal Solomin reached Prague, was wounded, shell-shocked, decorated, and in '49 returned to East Prussia, which by now had acquired a Russian name. The house on Seventh Street had been occupied by new tenants who'd never heard of any Tietzes. Maybe they'd been deported, if they hadn't got away in time with the retreating German forces. Solomin went upstairs, lay down on the floor and pressed his cheek to a sun-warmed, painted board. The lady of the house began to cry from sheer bewilderment. Somehow he succeeded in calming her down, then left. After all the bombing and shelling, little had remained of the town at the confluence of the Alle and Pregel. Even the rivers now had different names, Pregolya and Lava. But Solomin stayed. While working at the school, he also managed to graduate from the teaching institute. He got married, buried his wife, saw his daughter through her wedding and was left all alone with his memory. He threw himself into photography. He got his Leica for a quart of vodka at a reparations warehouse. An aching had begun to tug at his heart. He made many attempts to track down Mashenka, but in the '40s and '50s, and even in the '60s, there was no way these things could even be hinted at – neither to the authorities nor to acquaintances. He kept trying to tell the story of his life as if it had happened to another person, but each time he was cut short: 'While we were dropping dead at the front and back home, that rat was starting a family and gobbling butter.'

Here Der Tisch broke off. He drained his cold tea and nodded pensively.

'The art of memory boils down to the art of forgetting,' he announced unexpectedly. 'Although the word "art" is superfluous; it assumes the will to forget. But the will doesn't come into it . . .'

His father-in-law Herr Tietz had his quirks, even if he never showed them. But when Solomin admitted to him once his sense of terror – a feeling which intensified the keener his sense of happiness – Herr Tietz said: 'You're scared of what you might lose . . . Do you believe in God, Nikolai?' Solomin felt embarrassed. 'In any case, you'll have heard of the immortality of the soul. Dying, we merely cross into another world. It's just like this one – the same butterfly wings, the same corns, the same sighs. There we live our previous life once more, from its beginning to that instant when, in the eyes of the living, it broke off. We're born. Grow up. Get married. Suffer the same anguish, rejoice at the same joys. Die, are born, and so on *ad infinitum* . . .' 'But that's what hell is!' Solomin exclaimed. 'What could be more terrible?' 'Who told you our life here was paradise? Both realities, this one and that one, are simultaneously real and illusory. Everything merely depends on the place . . . on the point of view . . . It's excruciating. It would be easier to see *that* reality as illusory, as a dream, but alas. If time is infinite, we abide at any point in eternity. If space is boundless, we reside at any point in space . . .' 'But you're a Christian, Herr Tietz! What you're saying is the destruction of God . . .' Herr Tietz grinned. 'You're partly right. But instead of "destruction" I'd use a different word . . . the maturing, say, or the maturity. The maturity of God, why not? This is a wiser God. Made wise by our experience. Maybe also a more tired God. Even, I suspect, a more indifferent one. Though I don't think there's anyone God loves. He can't love anyone or anything. God is the world created by Him. Endless and eternal like God himself. There's no room for another. The appearance of the Other would be a challenge to the very fact of the existence of God. Any Other would be an endless and eternal God, inevitably crowding out the First. So He, in principle, cannot love or hate . . .' 'But if we are eternal,' Solomin interrupted, 'then we have no need for justification or love, and our life, therefore, is senseless!' Theodor Tietz shook his grey head. 'Try not to link the force of love with the force of death. It's hard, but perhaps it's the only solution there is . . .'

On July 27, 1962, Solomin's little daughter caught a mustard white butterfly in the watermeadow by the Pregolya, and brought it to her father in her sweaty hand. They let it go. Solomin pressed his daughter's tiny palm to his lips. It released the faintest scent of lemon, which vanished in a few seconds. The man straightened up with difficulty and looked around. Meadow. River. Tiled roofs over lime trees. The languorous drone of dragon-flies. A girl. Her little palm, smelling faintly of lemon. Him. All this had happened, he suddenly realized. In July 1944. At the end of July. Maybe even the 27th. 'It's baking,' Mashenka had said. Her chubby shoulders were peeling: she'd been in the sun all day. Her eyes had gone dark. With his daughter in his arms (he'd carried her asleep from the meadow), Solomin was standing under the triple-trunked apple tree and gazing entranced at the woman drenched in honey-coloured light, at her shoulders and arms, at the sweat-darkened cotton print on her breast. Laying his daughter on a towel on the grass, he went to fetch some water from the tap and returned to the apple tree. Mashenka took off her frock and started pouring water over herself from the jug, glancing over her shoulder at her husband. 'I can't get dry.' She laughed softly. 'Katya's sleeping.' 'Mashenka,' he whispered, 'God, how I love you. And the girls, and all this . . .' A naked green-eyed woman under an apple tree, a little girl sleeping in the grass, the sun, the languorous droning of the dragonflies, the faint scent of lemon . . . He remembered it all the second he saw the old apple tree in our garden.

'And that's why you took thirty-five photos of this tree,' I murmured. 'That same one . . .'

'It's not about the apple tree.' He sighed. 'It's exactly the same place. Only the time is different, or so it seems to us . . . That's where she was standing.'

I thought I was beginning to understand.

'So you photograph memorable places?'

'Yes. I suppose they are memorable. In the sense that they're part of that life. The true one. Maybe truth and happiness are concealed in the world that we're used to considering illusory, as existing only in our memory, our imagination . . . But memory is real. It's a complex combination of electric signals,' – I winced in surprise – 'that permeate the matter of the brain. Consequently, this illusion is a material one. I am fated to strive towards it, although I am not sure that the aim is attainable . . .'

I nodded. Why not? It's possible. I even forced a polite grin: you need to watch out with nutters. Be on your guard.

After June 27, 1962 (he'd ripped the sheet with the cherished date out of his calendar and pinned it to the head of his bed) his passion for photography acquired a new meaning. From that day on, he'd sought to record all those places where Mashenka Tietz-Solomina had ever been. Remember how she'd sat, in this spot or that. How she'd stood. Lied down. Where she'd looked. Over there. No, must have been over here. Head turned, eyes half-shut, a lilac twig in her right hand. Or in her left? Probably. She'd taken a step. Screwed up her eyes. So the sun must have been over there. He waited by the plain old wall until the sun occupied the position it had occupied then so as to photograph emptiness. Here. And there. Because Mashenka was living that same life, and sooner or later she would appear invisibly by that wall, as she had then, on May 14, 1942. Or that September evening in 1943. He studied the negatives and the finished prints assiduously. At times it almost seemed to him as if there was something on the negative – a shadow? a scratch? – which for whatever reason couldn't be transferred to the positive, so he changed the lighting, lenses, chemicals, film . . . He heaped negatives one on top of the other so as to achieve a thickening of emptiness, so that a barely discernible shadow might become clearly visible, dense, fleshy. An outline. A face. A chubby hand waving. A twig of blooming lilac. A child's lemon-scented palm . . .

'Blue lips don't love life.'

My dad's words came back to me.

Sometimes Solomin would freeze in front of the mirror, anticipating that instant when his reflection would drop its guard and allow itself a gesture or a smile betraying his previous life, *that* life. Sometimes he fancied he'd caught one of those gestures and he was scared: a meeting with oneself doesn't promise happiness. In any case, such happiness was only for the desperately brave, and he wasn't one of them. He'd chosen a different hell.

He showed me pictures in which it was hard to make anything out: piled on top of each other, the negatives had thickened the contours of objects so much that they had been rendered totally indistinct, as though plunged into the ancient chaos of undifferentiated existence. Perhaps this was the image of *that* world, which, splitting into layers, thinning out and disintegrating, enters in fragments our world of mortal forms.

We said goodbye. Just as I imagined, it was for good, although I hadn't expected Der Tisch to die so soon: he wasn't even fifty! He was found on the floor, lying with his cheek pressed to a sun-warmed, painted board, a dead smile on his lilac lips. I didn't go to the funeral. I don't think he'd have held it against me.

To exist means to exist in someone's imagination, outside which there is no life, Bishop Berkeley once observed. Blue lips, green eyes, a child's lemon-scented palm, griffins, rusty knights, love, immortality ... God above, these are just words, linking space and time and forming some semblance of life ...

All Those Sailing Past

Even after twenty years, when her bosom friend was dying in agony from cancer of the stomach, Sonya Polorotova still did not learn from her what it was that she had told Misha, Sonya's husband, on the day of their wedding, and that had worked Misha up into such a terrifying state. Trying not to attract the attention of the guests enjoying their vodka, Misha had run upstairs to the cosy little room with a view of the river through a semicircular window, where his young wife was slipping a stocking off a rosy-pink leg. She realized from Misha's expression that something out of the ordinary had happened, but in her embarrassment she couldn't get a word out: this was the first time in her life that a man had seen her naked hips. Her husband looked at the chubby leg still sheathed in a stocking, then at the other one, and fainted on the spot. Sonya started screaming. Guests ran in. Although he was breathing, Misha just lay there without moving, eyes closed. They tried to bring him round, but to no avail.

After a long examination, Doctor Sheberstov said that Misha had probably sunk into a lethargic sleep, the result of some powerful nervous shock. A sleep like that could last for a week, a month, or ten years.

Sonya took Misha home, put him in the tiny room under the roof and asked his grandma in dismay: 'What do I do now? Leave?' The old woman shrugged her shoulders. 'Up to you. You're his wife – ask him.' She seemed not to have understood what had happened to her grandson.

Sonya stayed.

Misha had been the lock-keeper; his wife replaced him. She worked the gates and the winches, painted and cleaned, and helped the workmen who came over several times a year. With the old woman she looked after the livestock and the vegetable patch.

Feeling dreadfully embarrassed, Sonya washed her husband twice a week with a soapy sponge. Afterwards, crimson all

273

over, she put on a clean blouse embroidered with lace and lay down beside him. Misha's body was barely warm. Before falling asleep, Sonya would fill her husband in on the town gossip, and on Saturdays she read something out loud to him – *The Three Musketeers* or *Eugene Onegin*. Then she'd switch the light off, stare for ages through the semicircular window, and drop off.

Her ex-best friend worked at the baker's shop where Sonya bought bread almost every day. Seeing Sonya, she'd purse her lips in contempt. They'd exchange lethal stares, but one couldn't make her mind up to ask, and the other to answer, what really did happen on the day of her wedding?

Sonya thought about the moment when Misha would finally wake from his lethargic sleep and ask what he needed to ask so badly, and she realized that their conversation would be a difficult one. She prepared for it in front of the mirror, although she couldn't even imagine what Misha might reproach her for. She even bought some lipstick so as to greet Misha with a dazzling scarlet smile, but after making herself up she just felt miserable: her lips looked like moist earthworms.

Every day she diligently tore off a page from the calendar which she'd hung on the wall so that, on awakening, Misha would immediately be able to work out the time in which he was living.

Sonya liked letting the boats through the narrow old lock. Leaning her elbows on the rail of the bridge, she smiled at the skippers of the barges loaded with gravel and sand. The sun-burnt boatmen nodded their heads and smacked their lips as they gazed up at her chubby pink knees. These people were special for Sonya. She didn't know or want to know where they were from or where they were going. The main thing was that they were passing through, sailing past, and not standing in one place, like houses, trees or Sonya. They flowed past, like water and time, while Sonya's time seemed more like eternity. She was waiting for her journey to start, waiting for her husband to wake. Sometimes she asked herself awkward questions: what if she had a calling for a different life and was wasting her time by waiting? What if Misha, in a country of fleshless apparitions, was living another life with some other woman, with children, boneless joys and sorrows about which his earthly, rosy-pink wife knew nothing?

She could look at the flowing water until her head started spinning and the old woman called her in for lunch.

As a young girl, Misha's grandmother had been to Venice with her mistress, the landlord's wife, but her memory of the city was poor. She spoke about San Marco and the thousands of pigeons on the square. The mistress used to throw them crumbs from a white table, crying mournfully: 'Pidgies! Pidgies!' As for granny, she spent most of the time in the kitchen or busy with her mistress's wardrobe. Only once did the mistress take her along on a boat trip down the Grand Canal. It was a fresh sunny April day. The walls of the houses glistened with a golden sheen. It smelled of rot and ladies' perfume, and the sharp sweat of the gondoliers. The ladies in the boat laughed and returned the greetings of the other passengers on the many gondolas heading towards the sea which opened out beyond the Giudecca . . . That's all that had stuck in the old woman's memory: a great deal of light. Radiant air, the iridescent sparkle of the palaces bathed in liquid gold, the lapping of water that burned like mercury and oranges . . . And the cheery, carefree people in white dresses and airy white hats. Hearing the old woman's stories, Sonya would close her eyes, and it seemed to her that the golden sheen, the light-flooded fresh April air, and the mercury and orange of the splashing water were piercing the deepest depths of her poor heart that was all worn out with waiting, and she breathed more easily, and it no longer ached so painfully near her left shoulder-blade.

Eleven years after Misha fell asleep, granny died. She left a large photo album called *Venezia* with captions in Italian, and a flattish round jar that had a French label on the lid and smelled inside of the garden of paradise.

'What are you frittering your life away for?' said Battle-Axe after the funeral. 'All these years and you still haven't decided if you're going to wait for him or live your own life . . .'

'Waiting and living, they're the same thing,' answered Sonya, flushing pink.

She was courted by the head of the river section, a tall man with a moustache who wore an old but painstakingly ironed suit. Once a week without fail, he looked in at the lock. Sonya gave him a meal with wine, after which they listened to records, flicked through the Italian album and chatted about this and that. One day Nikolai Semyonovich stayed longer than usual. When he embraced her, Sonya started shaking and pressed hard against him with all her ripe body. But at the last instant she suddenly burst into tears, embarrassing her guest. Nikolai Semyonovich took it hard but he carried on visiting her for a number of years. She didn't let him embrace her again, though.

Late at night, when the town fell asleep, Sonya would get herself up in her white wedding dress and row upriver along the moonlit Pregolya. The boat beat gently against the mild current. The oarlocks creaked softly. Sonya quickly got tired. She would take her hands off the oars and, leaning back, close her eyes and slide into a reverie. The current took the boat slowly towards the lock. Sonya screwed up her eyes so tightly that she saw sparks, and light began to stream through the cool of the Venetian day, when the walls of the houses glisten with a golden sheen and there's a smell of rot from the river and of ladies' perfume, when carefree people in white are laughing and water burns like mercury and oranges . . . The bow of the boat would bump against the black gates of the lock, and Sonya would take up the oars with a sigh.

Sonya was called to her ex-best friend, and she ran frantically all the way to the hospital, but she didn't make it: the poor woman had died, without revealing what she had said to shake Misha Polorotov up so badly twenty-six years before. Sonya accompanied the deceased on her final journey and cried: she was sorry for her friend, sorry for herself, for granny, for Misha, and last of all for the Venice that she would never see . . .

★

It was gone midnight when Misha Polorotov suddenly woke and sat up in his bed. A light was on in the room. A smell of river sandbanks and night violets wafted through the open window. Misha tried to shout for his wife, but no sound came out. He looked at the calendar and shook his head. Only a tube of lipstick, dried up like a brown date, lay on the dressing-table. Wrapping himself in a grey cloth blanket, Misha went downstairs on trembling legs, struggled into his rubber boots and walked out onto the dyke, alongside which twisted the Pregolya, silver in the moonlight and bordered on both banks by dewy osier thickets. A black boat appeared round the bend. The current was carrying it towards the lock. Her head lowered, a woman in white was sitting in the boat.

Misha stepped into the water and stopped the boat with his hands.

'Sonya', he called softly.

The woman raised her head. She was wearing a white wedding dress and on her a head a wreath of flowers made from tulle. She was smiling vaguely, as if in her sleep. She found it hard to breathe but her heart had suddenly stopped aching, as though before death. Carefree people dressed in white were smiling. The light-soaked air was glittering and quivering over the Grand Canal, over the Pregolya, over all that was sailing past, an immortal assembly with which poor Sonya, too, was now united.

The April Testament

'Whose turn is it to wind up the clock?'

With this thought Ivan Antonovich Volostnov sat up in his bed – slowly, so as not to awaken the ache in his right side – and lowered his feet onto the wooden floor, which had grown chilly overnight. 'Whose turn to wind up the clock? It's already five to.' He frowned: if life didn't get in the way, he always rose at ten to six.

Squatting in front of the glass box in the living-room, he waited for the hour to strike before winding up the clock with the key which usually hung alongside on a brass hook screwed into the wall.

The clock was his pride and joy. A massive dark-cherry case, a big golden dial under thick glass, black Arabic numerals with surprisingly coquettish little tails and crests à la Beardsley. Solid, reliable, strict. Like Ivan Antonovich's very life. The family walked around the clock on tiptoe. Once a year Volostnov summoned the watchmaker nicknamed Achtung, who gave the mechanism a thorough looking-over and greased it when necessary. The inspection took place in Volostnov's presence. Over a number of years he'd acquired a detailed knowledge of the subtleties of his timepiece and could have serviced the clock himself, but he chose not to: every man has his own job to do. At the end of the inspection, Achtung would be brought a shot of vodka and a roll, and, for all the watchmaker's hints that another round and a bit more might be a nice idea, Volostnov observed established procedure here too. Handing Achtung his money, he saw him out the door: till next year.

His wife wound up the clock on Mondays, his eldest son Andrei on Tuesdays, his eldest daughter Sofia on Wednesdays, her sister Katya on Thursdays, while he did it himself on the weekends. Only Fridays broke the routine. This day was allocated to his youngest son Vita, known in town as Vita Pea-Head; he'd been feeble-minded since birth and, despite his father's persistent efforts, had never learned to wind up the clock at the right time. His dad expressly forbade his family to do it for him. On Fridays Ivan Antonovich would get his son up earlier than usual and lead him into the living-room. When Vita saw the dark-cherry box, his head instantly shrank into his shoulders and he started twitching idiotically. His father would direct him with a severe gaze to the brass hook, point to the keyhole and bid him emotionlessly: 'Turn it.' The son would turn the key anti-clockwise with all his might, and Ivan Antonovich would be forced to drive Pea-Head away so as not to damage the machinery. Every Friday was the same.

After a shave and a cup of weak tea, Ivan Antonovich went up to the little room under the roof, sat at the table, dipped his steel nib into the inkwell and in his neat, handsome script wrote the word *Will* on the first page of a school exercise-book. Placing the pen carefully to one side, he leant back in his chair and remained in that pose. He didn't know what to write in the exercise-book. The house was state property: Ivan Antonovich and his family had received it as settlers who'd arrived in East Prussia 'to restore the pulp-and-paper industry'. He couldn't bequeath the house. Nor had he managed to save any money. As for his belongings ... maybe only the clock? He'd got it by slipping a litre of vodka to the guard at the reparations warehouse. But can such a thing be measured in vodka or money?

The pain in his right side made itself felt again. Ivan Antonovich gritted his teeth and screwed up his eyes. No one had ever heard groans or complaints from him. Nor would they. In early 1942 he was operated on without anaesthetic in a field hospital; even then he didn't groan or complain. The doctor had said to him: 'After operations like this, people become different.' For some reason that had cut him to the quick. Different? He didn't want to be different: he didn't know what to expect from another him. This terror – before the 'other' – didn't subside even after he was discharged from the army, or after he married and became a father, or after he was sent, together with other workers and engineers in the pulp-and-paper industrial complex, to this unknown land where he received a house and acquired a clock. It was the clock that rescued him from his terror of the other: no outsider would be able to invade his strictly regulated life, whose every detail was subject to unshakeable rules. Thanks to the clock, Ivan Antonovich had organized his life in such a way that, even with his eyes closed, he merely had to stretch out an arm and he'd immediately find the thing or person he needed. The family obeyed the rules, and only hapless Vita had turned out like a broken tooth in a gearwheel. He hadn't even learned to wind up the clock. Or did he not want to? To spite his father? Ivan Antonovich chased that thought away. He was his son, after all . . .

His daughters, Sofia and Katya, had once lived in this little room under the roof. The eldest, Sofia, had married a barge skipper, despite her father's warning that life wouldn't work out with a man who urinated overboard in the mornings. She hadn't listened and left. Sitting at the head of the table under a portrait of the Generalissimo, depicted wearing a white tunic and gold shoulder-straps, Ivan Antonovich had told his daughter: 'You'll have to answer for all of it. Come back and we'll take you in, and the kids too.' His wife started crying, but that's what a woman is for: a man's left hand and left eye, tempting and swaying him towards bad decisions. So his daughter left. She had a wretched life dragging the kids from hostel to hostel and waiting for her layabout husband to get back from another trip along the murky Prussian rivers. But she didn't return to her mum and dad: character-wise, she'd taken after her father. Bequeath the clock to her? She wouldn't take it – too proud. What did she need a clock like that for anyway in her gypsy existence? Clocks like that should be stood in a proper home, not in a field.

Andrei had vanished soon after. Ivan Antonovich had never concealed from his wife, or from Andrei himself, that he thought his eldest son was a duffer. As a kid, Andrei liked running after the funeral processions and gawping at the cemetery rituals. And the games he got up to . . . He'd lie down in a corner of the yard and ask his sisters to pour sand over him. The girls would make a little mound and decorate it with flowers, shining among which would be the little boy's joyful face. He could lie for hours like that. He had the same expression when he was burrowing among mounds of books, if his dad, known in town as head of the Dump, let him do so. Dump was the name given to the little square by the river, not far from the cardboard-processing plant. Special trains were driven there three times a week with books, magazines and newspapers, all sentenced to recycling as cardboard. A crowd would gather for the train's arrival. People ferreted among the mounds and that was how they filled their bookshelves at home. After gathering an armful, Andrei would find some quiet corner of the Dump and flick through the smelly, mouldering volumes at his leisure. He never talked back to his father, but one day, gazing at the portrait of the Generalissimo, he suddenly blurted: 'We should get rid of him. Others have got family on their walls, we've got this ugly mug . . .' Ivan Antonovich was taken aback. 'Bothers you, does he? He doesn't need feeding.' Then he added seriously: 'Read a few less books. Start thinking for yourself. Life won't change for better or worse just by swapping portraits.' Andrei was sent kicking and screaming by his dad to the factory school. He ran away and disappeared. His mother was on the point of tearing off to look for him, but Ivan Antonovich stopped her: every man chooses his own fate. What will be, will be. But he felt sure: just wait till life took his son by the throat – for what else could it do? – and the boy would get the wind knocked out of him. He'd lie down smiling in the grave and wait for the end . . .

The pain in his side had abated. Volostnov rose gingerly; not so bad, he could cope. He limped over to the low semi-circular window. A cold, chilly April. An icy wind from the sea was bending the black branches of the hornbeams. Only the thujas weren't bothered: they never changed. That was why Ivan Antonovich liked thujas.

From up there he had a good view of Vita pushing his bike up the path. There was only one thing the boy loved doing: haring along the streets on his rusty contraption. A hulking lad with a tiny head on a thin neck. He turned up occasionally at the Dump, where he amused the women by catching rats and throwing them into the raging grinder. The women squealed and laughed until Ivan Antonovich arrived. Then Vita would rush over to his bike (put together by his dad out of rusty old parts) and make a bolt for it, standing up on the pedals. With a twitch of his brow, Volostnov would wipe the smiles from the women's faces: 'Not enough work for you? I can add some.'

Doctor Sheberstov had told him to stop smoking, and at first Ivan Antonovich had obeyed. But, unable to resist, he'd started having the odd one on the sly. He hid his fags – from himself, of course – in this little room under the roof. It had become like a study to him since Katya had left. Before doing so, she'd tried to smash in the clock. She'd only had enough strength for the glass, which had cracked from the blow. He should replace it, but where would you find glass like it . . . She'd fled without even telling her soft old mum. Jumped into the cab of a steam-engine and hadn't looked back till she got to Vilnius, where her good-for-nothing husband was living. A month later she wrote a letter. Her mother was itching to visit, but Ivan Antonovich didn't let her: 'When there's a reason to go, we'll go. There's none now.' Nina had snapped: 'What reason do you need, death? You're so bloody-minded. How long are you planning on living? Forever? People aren't like that clock of yours – they die, you know . . .' He wasn't intending to live forever. And he'd never got to thinking much about death: it would come and that's that. Soon, by the looks of things.

Walking back to the table with a cigarette between his teeth, he lit up and took a blissful drag. The wretched little exercise-book lay in front of him with just one word written out in his painstaking script: *Will*. Ridiculous. Whoever said that man has to bequeath something to someone before he dies? He had nothing to bequeath. And no one to bequeath it to. It wouldn't change anything, anyway, and nor should it. What kind of life was this and what kind of world if they could be changed with the death of a single human being? Zilch, that's what. He hadn't signed up to a world like that. His was a different constitution.

'What constitution?' Doctor Sheberstov had enquired gravely. 'Don't believe anything, don't fear anything, don't beg for anything?'*

Ivan Antonovich had hesitated, then nodded.

'That's the kind criminals have,' the doctor said with a sigh. 'But I don't believe we've had the honour yet . . .'

Volostnov shook his head.

'Criminals is exactly what we are. All of us. Only some don't know it. Maybe because no one has ever laid eyes on the real law. Say they come for you now and take you away to some dark hellhole, who'll you prove it to that you're not a criminal? You'll be a criminal if that's what's needed. Isn't that how it is? Russia, my friend . . . So live while you can. That's the whole constitution.'

'That's not a constitution, Ivan,' Sheberstov had objected. 'That's instructions for the slaughter-house.'

'I don't know any others. You?'

The doctor said nothing.

There was no one Ivan Antonovich could leave the clock to. Not to Sofia, not to Andrei, not to Katya, and certainly not to Vita. Life had played a mean trick on him. He tried to keep well away from his son, and Vita tried to keep away from his dad. As if each had agreed not to test the other. As if there really was no spanner in the works. In the end it was always Ivan Antonovich who would wind the clock up on Fridays anyway. As if his son didn't even exist.

However much Sheberstov had tried to dodge the question, Volostnov eventually got it out of him: 'Yes, Ivan, it's cancer. You'll last a bit longer but not much . . .' So that was why his wife had been on at him recently to visit Sofia, or Katya in Vilnius . . . Cunning of her but not clever. A typical woman's belief: before dying, you should pray for your sins. He had no sins to pray for. And why was he supposed to think that a fatal disease had been sent to him for his sins? He'd got

* A rule for living among inmates of the GULAG.

sick and that was it. Like lots of people. Everyone dies from a disease, even if afterwards those near to them say they died from old age. The main disease is life. So it had all fallen into place: the wheels had turned, the hands had met, his hour had struck, and that's all there was to it. Why make some great drama out of it with blaring brass trumpets and bawling women?

Ivan Antonovich didn't like funerals. If it was left to him, the body would just get taken away, quietly buried and forgotten. He only needed to picture his wife sobbing over his coffin and he felt sick. A senseless ritual. That's why it was decked out with so much pomp, for people to hide the sense-lessness from themselves. And to convince themselves that there was some meaning in life. There wasn't – not in life, not in death.

The clock struck nine.

With some difficulty, Volostnov made it down to the living-room. Took his medicine.

The house was quiet: all that could be heard was the tap-ping of the pendulum in the dark-cherry box behind the cracked glass. Beating time. Driving on eternity, wave upon wave.

He'd let his wife go to see Katya – that had put a smile on her face. He was struck by the thought that it would be good to die while she was gone. Die like intelligent animals die, well out of sight.

Ivan Antonovich looked out of the window. From beyond the trees – soaring over which was the tin cap of the water-tower, crowned by a greenish bronze ball – came a loco-motive's terrifying hiss. Dragging wagons to the Dump. Or grain to the mill. Volostnov lowered himself onto the green plush sofa: he was tired. But he'd be working in the evening; whatever happened, he didn't want anyone feeling sorry for him, no, no way . . .

. . . The first wagon finally appeared round the corner, with the signal-man on the brake platform. The light from the lantern held high by the man in the tarpaulin cloak barely

pierced the veil of the drearily drizzling rain. The short train –
a locomotive pushing the tender and four wagons – was
crawling almost noiselessly along the river, which was faintly
covered in a watery mist. Plywood pipes with bast beards at
the dripping joints extended along tall rusty supports on the
bank. It was through these same pipes that the shredded
paper entered the cardboard-processing machine located in
the massive red-brick building by the river.

With a soft patter over the track joints and a faint screeching of the brakes, the train crept past the crowd that had
gathered under an awning around a legless man on a wooden
board with bearings instead of wheels; it crept past the rain-
sodden, bloated mountains of used paper that crammed the
asphalt triangle between the river and the slope criss-crossed
with vegetable patches. This was the Dump. In a slate-roofed
brick shed in the centre of the triangle, a mill roared away
desolately: it was a well with a wide concrete maw raised a
metre above a permanently drenched floor. Wearing grey
jackets and padded trousers, wellies and dark headscarves
pulled low to reveal only puffy noses and lips, women lifted
the soggy paper with enormous forks and hurled it into the
well, into the water which swirled like a raging funnel, and
there, deep inside, the steel blades turned paper into pulp.

The driver sounded the whistle. The train clanked and
came to a standstill, stretched out along the platform.

The people stirred beneath the awning.

'Let's go, lads,' the manager Vasily Ivanovich commanded
quietly as he pulled his hood over his grey hair.

The loaders calmly drank up the vodka the boss had provided for them (an essential condition of labour, or else no
one would have agreed to slave all night in the icy rain) and,
spitting and blowing their noses, moved off to the first wagon,
dragging wheeled carts welded from steel pipes. Usually, their
first task in the wagon was to clear a space where the carts
could be turned round. Then they'd load them with used
paper and, grimacing and barely managing to keep the carts
from toppling, wheel them out along gangways onto the
platform.

Ivan Kovalajnen hooked his foot on a cramp-iron and noisily rolled the door open. The loaders threw down the gangways, which had been knocked together out of thick, iron-bound oak beams. Volostnov shouted into the darkness sparkling above the searchlight turrets, asking for the beams to be lowered. Two thick yellow columns slid down from the wagon's shining roof and met in the doorway, wresting a wall of book spines from the dark.

'Books again,' the manager sighed. 'I ask you . . .'

Volostnov spat out his fag-end.

'Don't worry, Vasily Ivanovich. They can't swipe all of them.'

The manager glanced at Ilya Dukhonin, who was sitting on his board with his arms folded over his stumps.

'We should get rid of all these people . . .' The manager nodded towards the shed, outside which avid rummagers were already milling. 'You're the guard here . . .'

'Get rid of 'em,' echoed the legless guard. 'Look, there's Vita . . .'

Volostnov frowned. Vita Pea-Head was squatting a little distance away by glossy stacks of sooty pulp.

'Vasily Ivanovich!' shouted the foreman Leon Spadaris, who towered head and shoulders above the crowd of loaders. 'Vasily Ivanovich! Ivan Antonovich! Over here, both of you!'

Thrusting his hands into the pockets of his army cloak, the manager strode off towards the wagon, weaving between the piles of used paper.

The driver gave a long drawn-out cry and the locomotive, clanking away and shrouded in steam, broke off from the train and headed into the dark towards the station. People were walking over from that direction. 'How do they know it's books that have been delivered?' Volostnov wondered. 'Only the tonnage is recorded.' He hurried off after the manager.

Spadaris handed the manager a book. Vasily Ivanovich held it to the light, glanced at the cover and whistled. Flicked back his hood.

'Well?' Spadaris asked.

A crowd of sullen men held an expectant silence.

'Wait here.' Vasily Ivanovich passed his hand over his white head. 'Have a smoke, I need to make a call.'

Volostnov watched as the manager all but ran towards the brick shed.

'What's he up to?'

Ivan Kovalajnen silently passed him the book. Gold letters glimmered dully on the cover: *J. V. Stalin. Works.*

Spadaris whistled.

Gramp Mukhanov, who'd walked up noiselessly from behind, looked over Volostnov's shoulder and choked on his roll-up stuffed with top-quality Georgian tea instead of tobacco. Volostnov looked round. Doctor Sheberstov touched the brim of his hat. With a nod, Volostnov greeted him and the policeman Lyosha Leontyev, who, next to the huge doctor, looked like a teenager kitted out in uniform.

Leontyev switched on his flat pocket torch and turned the book over.

'Registration number eight hundred and forty-four, library of military unit eight seven one zero zero.' He handed the book over to Sheberstov. 'I expect they've disbanded the unit and written off the books . . .'

'This ain't *The Three Musketeers* we're talking about,' said Gramp Mukhanov.

The manager was hurrying over from the shed to the crowd.

'Start unloading!' He waved. 'What are you waiting for?'

The loaders didn't budge.

'So everything's as it should be,' Spadaris said pensively. 'So this is the deal now. I get it.'

Puffing and panting, the manager yelled at the foreman:

'How many times do you need to be told, Spadaris? Look lively!'

Ivan Kovalajnen climbed lazily into the wagon, stuck his short crowbar under a stack, leant into it, and a heap of books fell onto the gangway. Spadaris opened the next wagon: identical gold-lettered tomes were in there, too, and a dull stream of them poured out onto the asphalt, some of them falling down the narrow gap between the wagon and the platform.

Vita Pea-Head suddenly leapt to his feet. Paying no attention to his grim-faced father, he elbowed people aside, jumped into the wagon and began frenziedly hurling books onto the asphalt.

Something had happened. No one understood what, but the crowd surged towards the wagons. People threw themselves furiously on the books, shovelling them out of the wagons, piling them rapidly on carts and wheeling them off to the shed. The frightened women in grey jackets forked up the books and chucked them into the roaring maw of the mill. The steel blades relentlessly ground up the cardboard and paper. The pumps wailed as they forced the paper pulp into pipes that trickled at the joints. 'They're making cardboard out of Stalin,' Volostnov thought dully. 'Then roofing paper. To cover sheds with.' The cardboard-processing machine in the massive building by the bridge over the Lava droned away as it steadily squeezed out a thick ribbon of damp grey cardboard, which was then wound into rolls. By morning an entire warehouse would be filled with identical rolls. From there lorries would take them to the roofing-paper factory belching away on the other side of the railway line parallel to Seventh Street. The rolls would be set on steel spindles and the cardboard would be passed through a bath of molten pitch. Sliced up into little rolls. To cover pigsties with.

Someone brought what was left of the vodka over to the wagons (or perhaps, given the occasion, they'd even run over to the night store for some more and got the shop-girl out of bed). They drank from the bottle and climbed back into the wagons, where a scaly mass of books, like dough left to stand for too long, was still forcing its way out. The excitement had infected everyone. 'Go on! Get mashing!' Ivan Kovalajnen was yelling. 'For the motherland! For Stalin!'* One-eyed Elya caused riotous mirth when she panicked and dropped her glass eye into the raging mill.

Ignoring the rain and the cold, the revellers dragged over books and hurled them into the mill, drank vodka, fell over

* The cry with which Red Army soldiers were supposed to go into battle.

and laughed as they hared around the asphalt triangle flooded in the thick yellow glow of the searchlights . . .

Volostnov observed the night-time pandemonium from a distance. It seemed to him as if his body had been purged of life, as if he was no longer in pain and would never again feel living pain, and if there was to be life and pain, it would be the different life and pain of a different person . . .

He started.

'What?'

'I said are you asleep or what?' repeated the manager.

Volostnov cast his eyes over the Dump, flooded in the glow of the searchlights. People were bustling about as before, dragging books from the wagons to the shed. The rain had ceased. The wind was cleaning out the sky, and here and there stars glimmered between the clouds.

The manager offered him a dry cigarette and struck a match. Ivan Antonovich lit up.

'You OK?'

'I'll be all right,' Volostnov said with an effort. 'It happens. After you've been wounded, you know . . . Can't see a thing, can't hear a thing . . .'

The manager also lit a cigarette.

'What did you finish the war as?'

'Infantry sergeant. '42.'

'Lieutenant-colonel, '45.' The manager grinned. 'For the motherland, for Stalin . . . You can't make a monument out of bronze for anyone in this country. Only plasticine. Don't you think?'

Volostnov nodded.

'Now what's happening?!'

Appearing suddenly in the doorway, Vita Pea-Head had clambered with surprising agility up the cramp-irons and ledges onto the wagon roof and was hollering away, his teeth bared ferociously. 'My son,' thought Ivan Antonovich. 'It's my son . . .' A column of thick yellow light rose slowly to envelop the madman.

'You'll fall, you idiot!' shouted Spadaris. 'Get down!'

Spilling from the wagons, people still wore drunken smiles

on their faces as they watched Vita's acrobatics – he was trying to undo his trousers. At last he managed to untie the rope which he used as a belt, pulled his pants down to his knees and began peeing on the books, shrieking as he did so. The onlookers avoided meeting one another's gaze, holding a stupefied silence. No one stirred when, after shaking out the last drops, Vita pulled up his trousers, bowed his legs ridiculously, leapt screaming onto the mountain of books and slid down to the asphalt on his bum. Still yelling, he flipped over onto his stomach and thrashed about with his legs and arms, trying to climb back up. But he wasn't able to, and so he began crying, flinging his arms out wide, as if he wanted to embrace the avalanche of books.

'It's my son,' Volostnov thought once more. 'And I'm his father . . .'

Doctor Sheberstov turned up the collar of his raincoat, adjusted his hat and, pushing his way sideways out of the crowd, hurried off along the platform into the dark. Lyosha Leontyev rushed after him, his legs comically twisted in his coarse-cloth boots. The rest followed – some with books under their arms, others without – and a quarter of an hour later the only people left at the Dump were the loaders, the manager, Volostnov and Vita. Ivan Antonovich walked drunkenly over to his son and sat next to him. The big lad sat up sharply and stared in terror at his father. 'He's afraid.' Volostnov's thoughts were like cold boiled noodles in fat. 'Who does he see in front of him? Surely not me?'

'All right!' shouted the manager. 'You've had your fun! Now all this has to be cleared up, Spadaris. Maybe you'll have a drink, sergeant?' he said, turning unexpectedly to Volostnov. 'I'm asking you if you want some vodka . . .'

Volostnov shook himself awake. 'No, thanks.'

His son crawled away, jumped to his feet and rushed over to his bike, which was leaning against a pile of pulp.

'Vita!' Volostnov shouted. 'Wait, I'm telling you!'

But Vita had leapt on his bike and raced off into the dark towards the crossing.

Ivan Antonovich couldn't run. The pain had returned in

his side and spread all through his body. Breathing heavily and spitting on the cobbled street leading up from the crossing, he passed a row of yellow two-storey houses, came out on a slabbed pavement and trudged on towards Seventh Street. Past the hulking school building, barely visible in the dark, with a tiled roof and a tower above the clock where the rusty golden cockerel lived. Past the old German cemetery where the monuments to Russian and German victims of the First World War stood face to face. Past the water-tower with its pointed tin cap crowned by a greenish bronze ball. He turned into Seventh Street, laid with red bricks several layers deep (a horizontal one, then a vertical one, a horizontal one, then a vertical one, and a road like that can never get worn down). His eyes went dark. Reeling, he took a few more steps and collapsed on all fours. Threw up. With quivering hands he fumbled for his matches in his pocket and struck one. A bloody-green puddle had spilled over the pavement. Pain shook his body and thudded in his head. Tears welled, and this angered Volostnov: blubbering like a kid would be the last straw. No one had ever seen his tears, nor would they. It was the other man, a different man, who was ready to start bawling, ask for pity, call his children and his wife, repent and pray . . . Or was it him who was ready? Was it him, unnoticed by himself and those around him, who had become different?

Switching on the light in the living-room, he heard a strange sound coming from the kitchen. He was soaked through. His heart was leaping frantically, like in boiling water. Every step cost him a colossal effort. Before heading towards the kitchen, he leaned against the wall. Caught his breath. Everything was fine. He wouldn't give in to life's ruses. Or death's. He was stronger than they thought. Everything was just as it should be. The clock was tapping away. The key was on the brass hook. Volostnov was on his own two feet, he wasn't shouting, he wasn't crying and he didn't need anyone else. They were making cardboard out of Stalin, then roofing-paper, then covering the sheds. So? It meant that's how it was now. It didn't mean he should give up.

Eventually, he took a step towards the door leading into the kitchen. No, he wouldn't start calling Sofia, or Katya, or Andrei, or his wife . . . Nothing had happened. He felt shivery all over. It was dark in the kitchen. Someone was wheezing. Or whimpering? Trying not to make any sudden movements, Ivan Antonovich felt for the switch. It was Vita. His son turned round, shrank into himself, grabbed his own neck with his hands to muffle the sounds bursting from within. Ah, so it was him crying . . .

'Don't cry,' Volostnov whispered. 'Help me along . . .'

The boy jumped up and backed away, knocking over a stool. The sound frightened him.

'Don't leave . . . I'll cope but don't leave . . .' Ivan Antonovich shook his head. 'It's all right . . . just stay here a bit . . . anywhere . . .'

He turned his back to his son, took a large reckless stride, and immediately fell flat on his face. He managed to stick out his elbows at the last instant, but the blow was so powerful that he lost consciousness. Alone. That's good. When he came round, he crawled over to the stairs. Remembered his exercise-book with that one line, that one and only word: *Will*. Must destroy it. The shame of it. Volostnov had really flipped, people would say. He'd even thought of writing a will. Destroy it. He got up on all fours, looked around. Everything began to swim before his eyes. Approaching him soundlessly from behind, Vita made a clumsy attempt to lift his father, wrapping his arms around his body. Volostnov howled with pain. Scared, Vita let his dad go, and Volostnov all but fell on his knees. He motioned to his son, who crawled under his arm and strained to help him. Staggering, they started climbing the stairs, veering between the wall and the banister.

Different, Ivan Antonovich suddenly remembered: had he really become different? Didn't seem like it. In a situation like this, there was nothing else for it. In a situation like this, he was obliged to maintain that same order which he himself had once established. Any other kind of order was false.

No, he wasn't about to start calling his children and his wife, he wasn't the type. And the fact that he had nothing to bequeath was no great tragedy. Life won't change with one death. That's how it had always been in Russia, for a thousand years: the world crumbles but life goes on, and that's the only salvation, and the only people who save themselves are those who've got the hang of living in a permanently crumbling world. Volostnov was no exception. That's why death meant nothing. Not in this world at least.

Vita helped him to his bed. Before lying down, Ivan Antonovich ripped the page with the word *Will* out of the exercise-book and burned it in the ashtray.

A sharp pain woke him in the morning. He managed to slide out of the bed, which had kept the memory of his daughters' smell, and tried to get up. 'I've got to stand up. I can't, but I have to. However hard it is. There's nothing else for it.'

It was still dark outside.

Each step sent pain shooting through his body. It got worse on the staircase. His eyesight gave up: green and red swam before his eyes. Clutching the banister with damp hands, he climbed down. The air seemed icy even though the house was warm. The light was on in the living-room. Ivan Antonovich heard the loud ticking of the clock and moved towards the sound. The red and green veil obscuring his vision dimmed and seemed to fall away. He saw the clock and the sweaty back of his son, who was squatting in front of it. Volostnov wanted to shout to him, but there wasn't enough air, or strength. Shaking all other, he froze on the spot, scared of letting go of the banister. He could see Vita clearly now as his son carefully slid the key into the slot and hesitantly turned it clockwise. That's right. But why was there no air, Ivan Antonovich wondered in astonishment? Where had it suddenly got to? The key turned in the lock, crunching faintly. Once more. And again. Enough. As though hearing his dad's wordless command, Vita yanked out the key and hung it on the brass hook. He turned round and smiled at his father.

'Don't be afraid,' whispered Volostnov. 'Just don't be afraid of me . . . Don't . . .'

The world crumbles, life goes on. The clock struck the hour.

Ivan Antonovich lowered himself onto a step and slumped shoulder-first against the wall. His vision went dark again. He stretched his quivering arm out in front of him, felt for Vita's shaven head, pulled it near, drew it close, touched it with his lips, drew it close again – the only person he had left, this mad backward child, pitiful, deprived of reason, but not of love, no, not of love – and, with a terrifying release of air, stretched out fully sideways on the steps, and when the last chime sounded, his life was already over . . .

Three Cats

Old Three Cats lived in a basement on Seventh Street. She was offered a room lots of times but she'd refuse out of hand. She had no relatives in town and received no letters, although once a year she did send someone a postcard in a well-sealed envelope. She'd wander around town all day long, her hands clasped behind her back, and two shiny cats snaked along after her (the third was the old woman herself). On Saturdays and Sundays she sold vegetables at the market, and wicker baskets that she made herself. She didn't sell many baskets.

In the evenings she spat on her fingers, unscrewed the bulb hanging from the ceiling on a bare cord and lay down on a crackling mattress, thrown onto a board made from off-cuts. A padded winter jacket given to her by Battle-Axe hung on a large nail driven into the wall. In the corner stood a rough-hewn stool which Three Cats had dragged over from a dump. No one ever saw what she ate. At the shop she only bought bread.

Her mattress was rumoured to be stuffed with money. When she was asked about this directly, she'd lift her tiny head, which was graced by a little face the size of a child's palm, and reply defiantly: 'There's treasures all right, but not for your sight.'

The townsfolk learnt of her death from the drawn-out howling of the cats, who darted into the corridor with a wail when people arrived, and vanished for ever into the basement gloom (the residents were disturbed for years to come by their weeping voices, which easily pierced the thick walls and entered straight into human hearts).

Before dying she'd burnt all her papers, including her passport and her pensioner's book: the whim of a batty old woman. A thick piece of paper was clenched in her dead hand, covered in ornate handwriting with old-style letters:

My dear – my very dearest – Katenka! I am in hospital once more, after the battle at Peremyshl. Here I have become close friends with the Austrian lieutenant Klaus Wegener. Any day now he is leaving with a party of POWs for Moscow, and from there, it would appear, to Kostroma. He has promised to pass this note on to you. I fear we shall not meet again, and this feeling merges all my memories into one. The past is the only eternity available to us. I shall never forget that night, the open grand piano that seemed to tremble by the window giving onto the garden, that luxuriant lilac shrub, drenched in rain and burning with the light of the moon. I take with me the memory of your high chest, of your stomach pure as gold, and your somewhat moist, sensitive spine beneath my lips . . . Forgive this last impertinence, but I no longer distinguish truth from invention. Resting my trust in God's grace and your love, I remain − forever now − your devoted servant Nicholas Menshikov, your silly Nicky. 12 April 1915.

In a coffin hastily knocked together from off-cuts, her tiny face the size of a child's palm flickered among a heap of dark rags and was turned to the sky, where her high chest, her stomach pure as gold, and her somewhat moist, sensitive spine were awaited by the eternally devoted Nicky.

Her mattress really did turn out to be stuffed with paper money, mainly crumpled one- and three-rouble notes. There was enough for the funeral and for the wake.

You Only Live Twice

'Excuse me, are you German?'

Andrei the Photographer turned round.

The girl jumped down from the footboard of the railway carriage and adjusted her dark auburn hair, gazing with a smile at the strapping bony man wearing a black broad-rimmed hat, a long black raincoat and a narrow scarf swept foppishly round his neck. She was wearing high-heeled shoes and a print dress trimmed with lace that had yellowed somewhat from lengthy storage in a trunk. She'd thrown her raincoat over her shoulders and was holding a cheap brand-new handbag.

'The last German was deported from East Prussia two years ago,' he said in confusion. 'I could take your photo if you like . . . I'm a photographer . . . Be my guest!'

'The train stops for three minutes.' She smiled and shook her head. 'You're mad. You haven't got a camera, either. Come to that, you don't even look like a German, more like a gypsy.'

'It's close by.' Andrei tried to put on a pleading expression, but even that was beyond his strength.

The girl was still smiling, but her look was a serious one.

'This is madness, don't you see?'

'Madness,' he agreed. 'The train stops for three minutes. It'll leave any second.'

He took a step to the side and bumped into a bookcase which two young men, wearing identical cloth caps with spots and a button, were about to load into the carriage. The bookcase swayed and Andrei steadied it awkwardly with his hand.

The girl burst out laughing.

'Let me try guessing your name,' he suggested. 'A lottery. If I guess right, you . . .'

She shook a silk finger at him.

'Zhenya,' he said in a doomed voice.

She looked at him, no longer smiling.

Departure was about to be announced any second.

'All right,' she said eventually. 'Which way?'

He'd lied, of course: it was about twenty minutes' walk from the station to the studio. They didn't hurry, walking arm in arm and ignoring the passers-by, who were taken aback by such frivolity.

'But you're not listening to me!' she suddenly exclaimed.

'I am listening. Your mother's a lawyer, your father died at the front, you had an almighty row with your fiancé and left Saratov to come here, you've got an aunt in Königsberg, you're bringing her a gift of six silver spoons and you're hoping she'll help find you a job . . . Are you really called Zhenya?'

She roared with laughter.

'Of course!' She had tiny bluish teeth. 'Six spoons – just think!'

White and scarlet roses bloomed in the little garden in front of the grey two-story house under a tiled roof, where the photographer had his studio. They were tended by his ageing cleaner Heffalump, a rude and lonely woman with a moustache and enormous bony fists. She used to say importantly that she'd once been in love, but nothing had come of it. While Andrei served the customers, she read books from his modest library.

'Roses!' Zhenya said in a happy, empty voice. 'Heaps of them!'

In the hallway she casually threw off her light raincoat – Andrei caught it – and walked through to the studio, where a wooden camera rested on a stand shaped like a dragonfly. Andrei kicked away the chair on which his obedient customers usually sat until they were stiff, and pushed an armchair towards her with a tall straight back decorated with carved chimeras, dragons and snakes with entwining scaly tails, gaping mouths and forked tongues. Zhenya leant back in the chair, crossed her legs, let her transparent arms fall on the armrests, and threw a questioning look at the photographer, who had realized only now quite how tall she was.

'Just a sec,' he said, racked by inarticulacy. 'Just one second.'

A few minutes later he returned with an enormous armful of white and scarlet roses.

'This is madness,' she said once more, then suddenly stood up. Keeping her intense dark gaze fixed on him, she untied the belt on her dress. 'Help me then!' She turned her back to him. 'There are hooks there.'

They were woken by Heffalump and her obscene lamentations for the ruined roses. She climbed up to the photographer's flat, stamping her coarse-cloth boots. Andrei had barely come to his senses when the cleaner walked into the room and stared straight at Zhenya, who was sitting up in bed, smiling and holding a sheet with a scarlet stain in front of her.

Heffalump's moustache twitched.

'Well,' she said eventually. 'If that's how it is . . .'

She went away.

After a quick bite to eat, they tore off to the station. Jumping onto the step, Zhenya asked without a trace of shyness whether Andrei would be coming to see her the next day.

'Tomorrow at two I'll be by the Schiller statue,' Andrei said. 'People always meet there. It's a famous spot.'

Two young men in identical spotted cloth caps with a button shoved Andrei to the side and only just had time to heave a bookcase into the carriage. Zhenya waved from behind their backs. The train moved off.

When Andrei got back home, Heffalump was finishing off a second bottle of vodka in the kitchen.

'So you're happy,' she said clearly, without turning towards the photographer. 'And you love her. And you want it to be like this forever . . .'

He stared at her in astonishment.

'Well if you want it forever,' she drawled, 'then never see her again. Never.' She finally looked at the gob-smacked photographer and repeated with a good-natured smile. 'Never. You only live twice.'

'Twice?'

'Everyone asks the Lord for a second life before dying, as if knowing that that'll be the real one and hurrying through it before they die by wheezing, groaning and puking. So do it now, then you won't be sorry later. Really live. Then you won't have anything or anyone, except her. Not up to it? There's not many who are.'

'Three minutes,' Andrei muttered dully.

'What?'

'I was talking about life,' he said, raising the glass Heffalump had filled for him. 'Doesn't matter.'

Andrei the photographer told me this story twenty-six years later, when we were drinking beer in the Red Canteen. He was famous in the town and renowned for his brilliantly laconic and touching inscriptions on gravestones and wedding rings (five roubles for a line of prose, ten for a line of verse). The whole town knew his inscription on the grave of the town's number one layabout and drunkard Kolka, the Camel: 'Wish you were here and I was reading'. All the townsfolk had been recorded in his photos, their lives from cradle to grave. Once or twice a month, after saving up some money, Andrei would vanish out of town for a few days, but every time he'd come back – crumpled and unshaven, with a guilty smile on his flabby face – to resume his duties as the 'master of death' (that's how he called it), seizing and issuing instant after instant . . .

'So you never saw her again?'

He gave me a strange look and said with a smile:

'But then I've never had anything or anyone real in my life, except her. And I had her, I did. Understand?'

'You did?'

'I did,' he nodded drunkenly. 'You only live twice, what's there to say . . .'

The Woman and the River

Ankle-deep in liquid clay, I was squatting with my arms wrapped round my knees and watched, entranced, the flowing substance of the river and my own reflection in the water – a dark figure against a low bank. On the other side children were running and shouting. I seemed to be falling into sleep. On the edge of the bluff behind me, right above me, a girl appeared, reflected in the water. Standing with her legs slightly parted and her head tilted to the side, she was looking at the back of my head. I felt it physically. I strained my eyes. The girl was shortish and, it seemed, pretty, and it seemed, slightly freckled. Sensuous, beautifully cut lips made her look older than her fourteen, well maybe sixteen years. She was wearing a white T-shirt tight on her undeveloped breasts, and a short little skirt. A tiny mole on her right upper eyelid, another, slightly bigger, on her lower lip, and a third . . . But I knew full well where the third was! I stood up sharply and turned around. The girl had vanished. I clambered up rapidly. The surface of the deserted island spread out before me (for what else could it do?) smooth as a table and spotted here and there with low shrubbery; above it the August sky was slowly fading . . . I jumped into the water and swam quickly across the suddenly narrowed river, its yellowish-brown mirror gleaming dully in the rays of the setting sun.

The edge of a dark-blue cloud unexpectedly flashed scarlet. At that very instant a sound rose over the earth: a weak, infinitely sad sound, endlessly fading out. It was a long while before it died.

A woman sitting on a folding chair with a book in her hands told off the kids, glanced at me with an absent-minded smile, and patted her handsome, reddish hair.

I got dressed and climbed up to the dyke: it followed the bends of the river. In the distance, the sluice-gates and the tiled roofs were darkening above the lime trees. The meadow

311

sprawled to the left of the dyke, with the stadium in the middle. A thin mist was rising over the meadow.

There was no girl. There was a girl. Most likely, both statements are equally correct, and this, alas, has to be accepted, even if to do so is impossible. Girl, woman . . . I will never meet her; I will never part with her.

The Rivers, Trees and Stars

'

'Only pigs and snakes don't see the sky,' Misha Lyutovtsev told his wife the morning after their wedding. 'But you and me, we've got to stay human.'

Tonya nodded fearfully, agreeing with her husband. He was a regular sort of bloke on the whole, nothing weird about him.

Misha was a drier at the paper mill, his wife a nurse at the mill's little hospital. They lived in a house by the old park at the end of Seventh Street. With their small pay packets, the townsfolk were forced to keep livestock and poultry and tend vegetable patches. The Lyutovtsevs were no exception, and soon after their wedding they got themselves two dozen hens, a piglet, a cow due its third calf, ten geese, sheep and rabbits. They rose and went to bed in the dark so as to cope with it all: milking the cow and driving it into the street, feeding the piglet and the sheep, cutting fresh grass for the rabbits . . . In summer they had to stock up on hay for the cow and the sheep. When a son came along and then another, they stopped selling milk on the side, but carried on trading in rabbit meat: the little buggers were breeding like crazy. Tonya learned to cure skins and her neighbour Gramophone made hats and kids' coats out of them – they weren't much to look at, but they were warm and cheap.

In a word, the Lyutovtsevs' life was like everyone else's: tough. As if never straightening their backs from morning till evening wasn't bad enough, they'd snatch their holidays in time for haymaking or the autumn harvest.

But, be that as it may, Misha and Tonya kept one hour aside every day for the rivers, trees and stars. 'Just an hour,' Misha had suggested back then when they got married. 'Sixty minutes.'

Tonya had rashly agreed, but a few months later she was already regretting it.

Every day, they dragged themselves out to the park which stretched along the Pregolya. Taking an evening stroll after a hard day is a good thing to do, of course, but what if you've got a household to take care of and pig feed to be cooked by the morning and little ones crying away at home, and if you're so knackered at the end of the day that you can only watch the telly lying down? 'Can't we skip today, just for once?' Tonya protested one day. 'My corn's burning like anything . . .' But Misha threw her such a look that she had no choice but to shove her swollen feet into her galoshes and take her husband by the hand.

They'd walk slowly across the abandoned park under the tall old trees. A little path, half overgrown, brought them out onto the riverbank. Dusk settled. Stars started shining. An hour later, the Lyutovtsevs would return home.

Misha gave short shrift to his wife's attempts to discuss domestic matters during these outings. 'If we've only come here for all this, then this is what we should talk about.' The rivers, trees and stars, he meant. But that's just it: finding themselves face to face with the rivers, trees and starry sky, they became confused and couldn't find any words for a general conversation. After all, what can be said about the river? It flows along between loamy banks, spills over in spring and autumn, flooding the hayfields in the watermeadow, and rumbles quietly under ice in winter. The trees rustle in the wind and shed their leaves to bloom again in spring and turn yellow in autumn. And the stars, well, there's nothing you can say about them at all, they're so far away from people and so impossible to understand. Of course, you sometimes get quiet and warm autumn evenings when you walk out onto the high bank and fill your lungs with air that smells of acrid foliage, and cast your gaze at the Pregolya threading between the osier thickets, and see the smouldering yarn of the Milky Way, and for an instant you feel, to someone, to something, a passionate love which can't be contained in one soul, as if life really is suddenly reduced to this single moment. But how can you express this in words? Which ones? Misha didn't have words like that, nor Tonya either.

Puzzled by this, Misha got himself admitted to the library at the mill and took out various books about rivers, trees and stars. He read them in bed, glancing with disapproval at his wife, who was scared of dropping off but couldn't help herself: tiredness had its way. Little by little, though, they learnt to talk about the particular features of the Pregolya's hydrology, the barks and cores of trees, the size of stars and the distance to Betelgeuse. In fact, they gleaned so much information from the books that an hour wasn't long enough for Misha and Tonya to discuss it all. The words were all new ones, too, learned words that you couldn't get your tongue round.

As the years passed, though, the Lyutovtsevs gradually abandoned reading books, after it dawned on them one day that you can study the geology of river-beds, penetrate the mystery of the blooming of chestnut trees and learn the chemical composition of giant blue stars, but the main thing, the human thing, that remains as elusive, alluring and inexpressible as before: current, growth, light and burning, that's all the flow of eternity, terrifyingly alive and humanly fickle. Before that eternity, thousands of books mean nothing more than the words 'river', 'tree' or 'star', but these words too mean nothing before a river, tree or star.

Yet not even these bitter discoveries changed Misha and Tonya's habit of devoting an hour a day to the rivers, trees and stars. Maybe it's all just a question of habit acquired over long years. Once Tonya admitted that she probably wouldn't feel quite herself if Misha and her didn't get out to the park in the evenings.

The neighbours made harmless jokes at the Lyutovtsevs' expense, but they didn't think they were loopy: just folk out strolling.

As for me, I reckon that if God does exist after all and if the archangel's trumpet gathers together the living and the dead in the Valley of Josaphat on doomsday, and the Judge asks what justifies human life, and the paper-mill drier Misha Lyutovtsev and his wife, nurse Tonya, reply that every day they tried to talk about the rivers, trees and stars, then God will be satisfied with their life and might even call it a happy one, for all Tonya's corns, Misha's ulcers and their endless poor potato harvests . . .

The Tree of Death

Seething stormily in the wind, blazing brightly in the sun, a moist fluffy lilac shrub with blindingly white and pale-violet bubbling ripe clusters scattering sweet drops of light summoning joyful shivers and cheerful exhaustion – a fierily exultant clot of life, lawless as immortality itself . . .

It's a watercolour, all I have left by which to remember Vladimir Nikolayevich Duryagin, our drawing teacher at school. Perhaps it was the best thing he ever did. His present. I've had it for almost thirty years.

My mother used to compare this lumbering, red-faced man to a bear who'd picked a fight with a butterfly: he was useless when it came to 'dealing with children'.

At one time Duryagin had worked as a forklift driver at the paper mill. He was known for his relative sobriety, hot temper and passion for painting. He wasn't alone in his taste for pots and paints: there was also the foreman of the electric section, Viktor Ilyushin, a rosy-cheeked, thin-lipped sceptic, and a reporter for the local paper, Oleg Ptashnikov, a quiet drunkard and father of four feisty young girls. On Sundays, taking easels, snacks and wine, they headed off to the nearest wood or to the islands formed by the loops of the river and the canals cutting across them. They painted in watercolours and in oil: the river, willows, clouds and cows . . . Taking their time, they'd have a drink or two, eat and chat. It was called 'standing on tiptoe'. As Viktor Ilyushin said one day, 'You spend your whole life running by the wall and there's never time to stop, stand on tiptoe and peep over: what's there? Maybe something really disgusting or nothing at all, but you should still have a look.'

They were sometimes joined by Ivan Kozub, who was the drawing teacher then: a scrawny seven-footer who had straight raven hair down to his shoulders and come winter or summer, wore incredibly wide black raincoats that fluttered and swirled about him as he walked. Despite his intimidating appearance – a swarthy hook-nosed face, a protruding pointy chin, shaggy eyebrows from beneath which he shot demonic glances – Kozub was the kindest of fellows and let the kids get up to all sorts of mischief during class. When he decided to move to the South with his wife, who had weak lungs, Kozub recommended that Vladimir Nikolayevich Duryagin should take over his job. So it was that, shortly after his fortieth birthday, the forklift operator with only seven years' schooling to his name became a teacher at the only secondary school in town.

He tried, he really did. He read a lot, did some courses, sat up past midnight writing lesson plans. But all it needed was for someone to snigger when he said 'Let's draw some teddy-bells', and the blood would rush to his head. Pounding a fat tattooed fist on the table, he'd start yelling: 'Outtahere, cretin, immediately and without delay!' Sometimes he'd even get his arms going, and although many in the town thought that education wasn't education without the odd beating, others weren't too happy.

Duryagin was called into the head's office, and no sooner had he crossed the threshold than he was being laid into by the headmaster, Nikolai Ilyich Shchuplov (who famously incurred the wrath of the education authorities for the pictures in his office, where next to a portrait of Vladimir Ilyich Lenin, hung a blown-up picture of Nikolai Ilyich himself from his days as a navigator in the fleet air arm: he was wearing an intercom headset, goggles and a brand-new Order of Lenin on his chest – the composition was called *The Three Ilyich's*) and by the director of studies, Rita Evgenievna. Hulking Duryagin, who'd frozen in the doorway with his fists clenched behind his back, turned purple from shame and fury: he accepted the head's abuse as his due, but as for the snorting of this fine-looking grey cat . . .

'Understood?' The head looked at his watch. Naturally, Duryagin's answer didn't interest him. 'Well, that's agreed then.'

'He hasn't understood a thing!' Rita Evgenievna despaired, clasping her thin freckled hands. 'Vladimir Nikolayevich, you . . . Have you ever loved anyone, for pity's sake?'

'I've got a little girl,' Duryagin finally answered through clenched teeth. 'Natashka.'

'Enough of your philosophizing!' The headmaster frowned. 'Fly away, friends!'

As he was walking out of the head's office, Duryagin suddenly realized quite clearly: one day he'd kill this fine-looking grey cat for sure and feed her corpse to the dogs, after which he'd kill the dogs and feed them to the flies, after which . . . He stopped and gave a deep sigh: what's the use? Flies are immortal.

After school that evening, he took a bottle and went round to see Oleg Ptashnikov, his outdoor companion. A skinny, pointy-bellied woman, worn out by childbirth and her husband's boozing, started screaming at Duryagin hysterically from the doorway. Oleg shoved her aside and dragged his friend off down the street.

'Turned into a real witch, she has,' he muttered on the way. 'Know what her maiden name is? Plump.' He made a wry face. 'Tanya Plump. Hopeless as a bowl of groats. There was a time, though . . . Now all she thinks about is stuffing her mouth and a bit from behind . . .'

Sitting on a bench in the hospital gardens and well hidden by dense lilac thickets, the friends got their worries off their chests, cursing authority and women.

'Know what, Volodya,' Oleg said. 'I was thinking last night: what is it that really makes a woman so different from a man?

'Eh?'

'No, I don't mean hollows and hillocks – that's landscape, geography! This is something else, something important!' Oleg paused and, raising a finger theatrically, announced: 'A woman can't piss into a bonfire!'

He laughed out gloomily.

Duryagin hadn't imagined that the grey cat's question – 'Have you ever loved anyone?' – could sting him so badly. On his way home after his chat with Oleg, he suddenly stopped on the bridge over the Lava. The autumn sun had sunk like a shapeless ball of molten glass behind the osier thickets and chestnut trees. The rolling greyish-green surface of the water, filling with a turbid blue, darkened and dazzled at the same time with the last rays of piercingly orange light. It smelled of rotten leaves, cooling earth and also something sharply fresh, and these smells, merging strangely with the light of the sunset, seemed to cut straight through to the soul . . .

Duryagin shook himself and looked with surprise at his hands resting on the railings of the bridge: no, his fingers weren't trembling, he'd imagined it. What had he got himself, so worked up for? Now that he'd let off some steam, the ticking-off at school no longer seemed quite so hurtful. As for love . . . 'I'm a mad old dog, there's no three ways about it,' he thought with satisfaction, lighting up a cigarette. 'But in all these years – not a finger on my missus or my girl . . .'

His daughter was listlessly eating herring in the dimly-lit kitchen.

Duryagin looked at her straggly grey hair and her glistening gnarled fingers, and said good-naturedly:

'There's enough for three when you're done. When you eat fish only the eyes should be left. Is Mum sleeping?'

'She's lying down.'

The usual thick smell of medicine filled the bedroom.

'What's today Wednesday or Thursday?' Nina Ivanovna asked in a sleepy voice.

With a sigh, Duryagin hung his jacket on the back of the chair.

'I went for a drink with Oleg Ptashnikov. His missus is up the spout again . . .'

'Is he the baldie?'

'Bald? Why bald? Oleg's hairy enough.'

'It's probably Thursday, though.'

Pulling his pants up, Duryagin lay down and, propping his head on his hands, forced his eyes shut.

'Thursday. Tomorrow's Friday, then.'

*

Nina Ivanovna had once been a calenderer at the paper mill. Carefully steering the forklift through the enormous hall, Duryagin would always slow down by the calenders, which rose up almost to the glass ceiling, in order to watch the girl skilfully guiding the paper sheet between the shiny steel rollers. They met at the factory club, were married a year and a half later, and got themselves a house and some animals – chickens, a piglet, rabbits. Shortly after giving birth to their first child, Nina Ivanovna fell ill, so badly that she was registered as an invalid. By the time Duryagin was offered the teaching post, she was struggling to get around the house and spent most of her time in bed: polyarthritis. 'You pulled the short straw with me, Volodyenka,' she said, smiling plaintively at her husband. 'I've dumped everything on you: the house, the animals, Natashka . . .' Duryagin brushed her off: 'I'm strong as a horse.' Then, with a grin: 'And waterproof, like a mushroom.'

That Thursday didn't seem to change a thing either in the life or character of Duryagin. As before, he flared up nearly every lesson, pounded his tattooed fist on the table, turned purple and yelled: 'Hooligan! Get yerself outtahere!' True, he kept his arms in check, remembering his talk with the headmaster. He steered clear of the director of studies, Rita Evgenievna, but not at the risk of offending her: she was still his boss, after all. Once or twice a week he went drinking with Oleg Ptashnikov, who'd finally been thrown out of the newspaper and had got himself a job as the artist at the paper mill. Oleg had gone bald. Two shots of vodka and he was out of it: his conversation became bitty and confused, and Duryagin would head off home, leaving his mate in the hospital gardens, where he carried on talking, talking, talking, now to the glass ('You see, Comrade Glassych'), now to the bottle ('Quite so, Mr Bottlov').

Every autumn a drawing club was set up at school to which about fifty students signed up. Duryagin read us lectures, as monotonous as the criminal code, about composition and perspective (he had a tattered grey copy of *Drawing and Painting* in two outsized volumes, his bible and constitution) and had us drawing cubes and spheres, plaster jugs and cut-glass decanters. Many pupils, unable to bear the hardships of a hike across a grey-white stereometric desert, made a bolt for it. I decided to wait for the end of winter: the teacher had promised a magical adventure outdoors. In spring Duryagin perked up once he was outside, and the club's meetings ceased to resemble a stint in a dentist's waiting room.

But at the start of May the sessions broke off – Nina Ivanovna had died – and never resumed again.

By the time I graduated from university, Duryagin had lost his daughter, too. She'd died from cancer.

I came back home to visit my parents and met Duryagin in the street the next day. Hearing about my brand-new degree, Duryagin invited me over to celebrate. I didn't object. He already smelled of vodka and, even more potently, of mould from his threadbare jacket. He didn't give the impression of a man broken by fate. The tone of his voice was more like self-mockery: 'You see, I never learned how to drink solo. Failed the exams.'

There was a strong wind shaking up the trees and snatching rare drops of rain from the clouds that raced across the dark-blue June sky. Having barely got going, the rain was rushing westwards to the sea.

'Never mind,' Duryagin grinned, catching my gaze. 'I'm waterproof, you know, like a raw fish.'

His flat was clean and tidy but it smelled of mouldy old rags, like his jacket.

'I shave every day,' he suddenly said. 'I got up one morning and realized: if I don't shave, I'll do myself in.' He put a bottle on a table covered with blue oilcloth, got some half-pint glasses down from a shelf and plates with cheese, cucumbers and thick slices of bread. 'I killed off all the animals. Just left the chickens.' He carefully unscrewed the tinfoil stopper. 'Tastes better with a fancy stopper, does it? Seven of 'em.'

'Seven what?'

'Chickens. I just told you: I only left the chickens. Seven. What do I need more for? I'm at school morning till evening. To our meeting.' He downed the vodka and it gurgled resonantly in his shaven throat. 'T'your health. Eat. I like cheese that smells like soldiers' socks.'

Naturally, I thought he'd start talking about his wife or his daughter. He started talking about his daughter.

'I didn't love her.'

He didn't love her.

On leaving school, colourless Natasha had done a few courses somewhere, then got a job as a cashier at the station. She was quiet as a mouse, and sometimes, when he came home late from school and found the television on, Duryagin would switch it off and hear a placid rustle from a dark corner: 'I'm in here, dad . . .'

After Nina Ivanovna's death, Duryagin broached the subject of his daughter's marriage plans, and of his grandchildren, ever more frequently. 'No one wants me, dad,' she'd reply calmly. 'Just have a kid for yourself then, from anyone . . . without getting hitched.' 'I can't, dad. The doctors say I've got a disease.' 'What disease all of a sudden?' 'Everything hurts inside. Has done for ages. And I bleed a lot.' For some reason, her dad didn't dare ask where.

Soon after, she was hospitalized and operated on. Afterwards, Doctor Sheberstov told Duryagin that Natasha had cancer and didn't have long left.

'She can stay with us for the time being. Your place is empty, there's no one to give her a glass of water.'

'So she's in the yellow ward, then?'

'Yes.'

All the townspeople, even those who'd never been in hospital, knew that the narrow, single-bed ward on the ground floor, with walls that had once been painted yellow, used to be set apart for the hopelessly sick. And although it had been repainted several times on the orders of the head physician and was mostly used now for post-op patients, many of whom returned home in better shape afterwards, the 'yellow ward' had remained a synonym of the death sentence.

On his way to school the following morning, Duryagin brought his daughter some apples and chocolates.

'I don't need a thing,' Natasha said. 'I'm not allowed, anyway. Just come and see me, please.'

'I'll come, course I'll come . . .'

He began visiting his daughter twice a day: he dropped in to say hello before school, and sat with her till late in the evenings.

Duryagin hadn't imagined that just sitting for two or three hours with his taciturn daughter could be such an agonizing chore. He didn't know what to say, and even if he did find something to talk about, she'd reply in a monosyllable or just sigh softly. Sundays were hardest of all.

To give himself something to do, Duryagin brought along his album and pencils and started sketching a portrait of his daughter. He drew the high-ceilinged narrow ward, the bed, the bedside table, and only then his daughter covered in a blanket. The sort of things he most liked painting were quirky reliefs of fabrics, the play of light and shade on a crumpled canvas or the splendour of flowing silk; he liked painting women's hair, too, but when he did faces, they came out cold and static. Here, though, he could find neither folds of fabric nor hair: his daughter was so fleshless that the blanket lay flat, as on a table, while her hair was hidden by a white kerchief. The artist had to make do with a small shapeless nose, the corner of a chin, and the shadows of the eye sockets.

'The lilac is such a beautiful tree,' she suddenly whispered. 'The tree of paradise . . .'

Stopping for a smoke on the bridge on the way home had become routine now. Clasping the album tight under his elbow and huddling up against the fresh spring wind, Duryagin would gaze without thinking at the glassy broken-up ripples of the river, glinting under the setting sun. There was a spring smell of thawed earth and also something sharply fresh that seemed to cut straight through to the soul . . . With a sigh, Duryagin chucked his stub over the railings, adjusted the album under his arm, and suddenly froze on the spot. He'd understood: his daughter was dying, and he'd never loved her, and he'd be left with this drawing. This one. He ripped the sheet out of the album, and screwing his eyes up, tore it into shreds. He flung it into the air; the wind caught it.

The next day he came to his daughter with a box of watercolours.

'But I liked the sound of the pencil,' Natasha said. 'Sheerk, sheerk . . . So warm.'

'Never mind,' her dad muttered. 'It's summer soon. I'll do you a lilac.'

And he started drawing a lilac.

Duryagin poured out another vodka. We drank it.

'Now we're going in there.'

He led me into the living-room.

In this spacious room furnished with dismal plywood, a table under a plush cloth and a fringed lampshade, the walls had been hung from floor to ceiling with watercolours depicting a blossoming lilac.

Duryagin switched on the light, although it was already bright in the room, and spread out his arms.

A cigarette between my teeth, I walked slowly alongside one of the walls. The lilac was blossoming luxuriantly, the lilac was raging in the storm, the lilac was drooping in the rain, the lilac was blazing like silver, the lilac was sailing in the bright light of spring, the lilac was showing rabidly white against a violet sky before a storm; it was everywhere, like life; and for an instant I imagined what this man felt, painting a lilac day after day by the bed of his dying daughter as she breathed quietly in the narrow yellow ward, and I suddenly felt terrified and turned my eyes away from the last watercolour, for it really was the last: the date was marked at the bottom, the day of Natasha Duryagina's death.

'The tree of death, that's what,' Duryagin said in a dull voice. 'Horrid, eh? I didn't love her.'

'So what's this?'

'That's not love. That's . . . that's for Chrissake for God's sake forgive me, please, my little girl, my only girl, my dearest, my Natashka! . . .'

I didn't dare comfort him.

We had one for the road.

'Are you leaving for good? Hang on then. Which did you like best?'

'Vladimir Nikolayevich . . .'

'Shush. None of your philosophy.'

He brought a watercolour from the living-room, rolled up in newspaper. I can't say for certain whether it smelled of that same trashy *White Lilac* scent used by nearly all the women in the town.

'Keep it out of the rain.'

'I've got a briefcase.'

We said goodbye. Forever, as it later turned out.

A few days later I left.

The watercolour survived. It's been hanging over my writing desk for nearly thirty years now. Seething stormily in the wind, blazing brightly in the sun, a moist fluffy lilac shrub with blindingly white and pale-violet bubbling ripe clusters scattering sweet drops of light summoning joyful shivers and cheerful exhaustion – a fierily exultant clot of life, lawless as immortality itself . . . the tree of death, the mould of an immortal soul, yes-yes, an immortal soul and loving, loving, loving . . .

Voinovo

'Grandpa painted it,' said the old woman dolefully. 'He was Russian Orthodox and a soldier in the German army. But don't go telling anyone about this icon. It ain't pure.'

'The Virgin?'

'This Virgin found herself a husband.'

'What, Our Lady?'

Euphemia, a nun at the Old Believers convent in the once German, now Polish territory of former East Prussia, told me this story.

In 1832–1834, Russian Old Believers fled tsarist oppression in Latvia for East Prussia. There, on the shore of Lake Dusz, Catholic Poles helped them build the village of Voinovo. Euphemia's granddad was an icon-painter. To this day his icons are kept in the Rogozhsky and Preobrazhensky parishes. He fell in love with a Pole called Maria and met her in secret. She's said to have been a heavenly beauty. When she became pregnant, Johann – that was grandpa's name – got his call-up for the German army. In August 1914 this Russian joined the attack on General Samsonov's soldiers at the Battle of Tannenberg, the same place where, more than five hundred years earlier, the joint forces of the Slavs, Lithuanians and Tatars had annihilated the German crusaders. At the end of 1916 Johann, seriously wounded, was discharged and returned home. Maria's child had died at birth and she'd been waiting in terror for her secret husband: the doctors had said they could never have children. Worn out with sorrow, Johann left Maria for good and vowed that he would paint an icon such that all his sins would be forgiven. He painted Maria, the Catholic beauty whom he had abandoned and who never had become the mother of his child. It took him twenty years, during which he fed himself on bread and water and hardly left the house. Maria died at the beginning of the war, Johann at its end. A heart attack. Three decades later the Polish

government bought the Voinovo icons, and the convent sur-
vives on the proceeds. Polish poets were awestruck by the eyes
of the icons. The only one not to have been sold was the one
looked after by Euphemia. She had covered it with black cloth
and stowed it away in her cell. When she heard about the sale,
she took it from its hiding-place and found to her horror that
the Virgin's arms were holding a baby. A boy. She knew for
certain that it wasn't her granddad who had painted it. She
immediately wrapped it up in the cloth and never uncovered
it again.

'Show it to me!' I begged.

'No.'

She headed off down to the convent cemetery tended by
the nuns. 'I'll show you Maria's grave.' She put a finger to her
lips. 'Not a word to anyone: she was a Roman Catholic. Here
it is.'

A grey tombstone, name, date. Nothing else.

'What'll happen to the icon, if . . .'

I bit my tongue.

Euphemia sighed.

'I don't know. But I'll tell you what Johann called it. *Love's
Hell*. Do you believe me? It's the truth. How can I show it to
anyone who asks?'

My throat tightened.

We left half an hour later. Twelve miles down the road we
stopped, bought vodka in a village store and drank. I lay down
in the grass and began to cry. God, my God, merciful God . . .

A Samurai's Dream

Yukio Tsurukawa was a Russian Japanese from Sakhalin Island. Graduating from a pulp-and-paper training college, he came to our town and became a foreman at the paper mill. His passport said his name was Yukio Toyamovich, but townspeople called him Yuri Tolyanovich. When she first saw him, old Gramophone asked suspiciously, 'You're not a Jew, are you?' He was nicknamed Samurai, though Yukio himself vigorously objected: 'My father's an accountant, mother, a teacher. Samurai, my foot!' The one reminder of his Japanese origin was an ofuda hanging next to the mirror: a sheet of paper folded like a lozenge and covered with hieroglyphics representing the name of the goddess Amaterasu-o-mikami, goddess of heaven.

It was at the paper mill that he met Lida Kortunova, a pretty and rather brazen young lady. They were soon married and received a flat on Seventh Street. As soon as Lida's belly stuck out a little, Yukio set up the swings in the courtyard for their future child. Every day in spring, he dragged his wife outside to gaze at the cherry tree in bloom, and on autumn evenings, seating her carefully in the sidecar, he took her to the Children's Home lakes, where they would sit silently for an hour or two, looking at the moon's reflection in the water. 'What for?' asked Lida. 'My bum's freezing.' 'For the baby to be beautiful and clever,' Yukio would reply. And he recited poetry to her:

> Oh how bright,
> oh, how bright, how bright,
> oh, how bright, how bright, how bright,
> oh, how bright is the moon.

'That's your Japanese moon,' Lida said pensively. 'You can't say the same about ours . . .'

Lida had a miscarriage. She cried day and night, while

Yukio sat on the swings in the falling snow and chain-smoked.

'They're different, your blood and mine,' Lida said. 'Mine's Orthodox Christian, your's alien.'

'I'll get baptized if you want,' her husband said. 'It won't hurt.'

Lida doubtfully shook her head.

'Even your dreams are alien.'

'How do you know?' Yukio asked in astonishment.

'You can't fool God.'

After a second miscarriage Lida started drinking hard and carrying on with men.

Yukio went to Kibartai and got baptized.

Coming back home, he caught Lida in bed with Vanya nicknamed Stink, a crazed alky.

'Go away!' Lida yelled the moment Yukio appeared in the door. 'I fuck who I like! Least our blood's the same!'

Yukio went outside and sat on the swings.

Snow was falling, quiet as dreams.

All sleepers are of the same blood, Yukio thought.

In the morning, when the long-singing bird the cock had crowed, Lida stepped outside and found her husband dead – his heart had stopped.

The swing was swaying to and fro, as if two sets of hands were pushing it, Jesus Christ on one side and Amaterasu-o-mikami, goddess of the Japanese heaven, on the other.

The moon was shining, snow was falling, and it was Russia.

Squeak–squeak–squeak . . .

Merry Gertrude

On March 18, 1916, on the Russo-German front near Stallupönen, only a single artillery shell was fired. It struck the roof of an isolated farmhouse. At that very instant Lieutenant Sergei Ivanovich Lamennais, who'd come by to visit his mate Misha Ragozin, was raising a lighter to his friend's cigarette. Misha was on observation duty and had been kicking his heels for several days now by the telescope in the attic of the abandoned house. The shell seemed to explode right over their heads. The last thing Sergei Ivanovich saw was the cigarette in Misha's hand drawing the lighter's flame; a second later scalding, sticky liquid burst like a fountain from the very spot where Misha's head had just been and blinded the lieutenant.

The man carried into the German field hospital was holding a lighter in his feverishly clenched hand. His mouth was crammed with fragments of crumbled tiles. His face had become a dark red mask; bones and bits of lung poked out from a shattered thorax. He had to be operated on several times. His life was saved, but for a long time he couldn't speak and his hearing and vision were poor. No documents were found on him; his shoulder-straps had been ripped away in the blast. It was only from the shreds of his overcoat and underwear that it could be established that he was an officer. Several months later, when he had learned to move about on his own and to react to the simplest commands, he was moved to the POW camp near the town of Wehlau, at the confluence of the Alle and Pregel rivers.

His countrymen tried to get him talking, but with no success. He didn't answer to any names or ranks, and merely smiled in reply. Those who looked after him said that his underwear, however much it was worn, never got stained. In the minds of the superstitious soldiers, mostly yesterday's peasants, this fact set the mute well apart from the others. Soft-hearted soldiers would take him with them when they went to work on nearby farms to top up their miserly camp rations. But the officer wasn't much good at anything, however much he tried to keep up with his comrades.

The owner of one of the houses on the outskirts of Wehlau would pucker up her face in sympathy when she saw him clumsily digging up the soil.

Frau Gertrude Keller's husband, the watchmaker Hugo Keller, had died the death of the brave in France, leaving his wife a very modest livelihood, a tiny workshop and an unquenched thirst for motherhood. A wide forehead, clever grey eyes, tightly-drawn pockmarked cheeks joined by neatly cut lips that were always ready for a friendly smile – such was Frau Keller, a calm, physically robust woman who wasn't much inclined to view life as a punishment for anyone's sins. After the death of her husband she had stopped having dreams at night; now they visited her in the daytime, clouding her gaze in a kaleidoscope of boneless apparitions. The muti-lated face of the officer who had lost his memory aroused Gertrude's pity, and she looked for ways to ease his burden. She found light work for him to do around the house, gave him ersatz coffee with potato pancakes, and spoke to him about her dead husband. One day Sergei Ivanovich wandered by accident into the little room that had served as the work-shop of the late Hugo Keller, touched the pendulum of the clock standing in the corner, and realized that he didn't want to leave this room, this town, this country. Gertrude found him at the table in the workshop. He turned round, smiled, and said in Russian: 'Clock. Time.'

The war ended. Sergei Ivanovich stayed on at Gertrude Kel-ler's house. The neighbours just shrugged their shoulders and tried not to be too hard on the young widow. With her calm and friendly disposition, she touched even those whose hearts were frosted over with the icy scales of prejudice. She called him Misha. Gradually, he got used to answering to this name. Every morning he found a juicy scarlet apple on a light-blue plate on his bedside table. He would disappear to the work-shop for entire days, pressing a watchmaker's glass to his eye and trying to get to grips with the intricate mechanisms. In time he acquired such a mastery of the trade that the only person whom the respectable burgers learned to trust with their watches was the Russian, Misha. Michael. Gertrude was delighted. She taught her husband German and read Schiller aloud to him. She had the twelve-volume Tübingen edition, which Sergei Ivanovich read in moments of leisure in the workshop, pushing his eyeglass up his forehead and moving his lips.

In early 1925, a daughter was born to them and they called her Louise. Her father made her some little clockwork animals. Michael and little Louise could sit for hours in the workshop, one working, the other watching as her father repaired time. Every now and then he interrupted his work and gazed for a long while at the girl. It was at just these moments that an angel of God rose up soundlessly in the doorway. Louise would see it clearly but she was scared of stirring lest she upset her father.

At the end of the twenties, Sergei Ivanovich was examined by the famous psychiatrist Doctor Eberle-Hoffmann, who described 'the Michael Keller phenomenon' in specialist journals as an interesting example of reverse amnesia. 'The loss of memory is so great that it is astonishing that this man has not forgotten his native tongue, although his speech is said to be highly limited . . . But, of course, what is most amazing is that this man, who was maimed in the war and lost his homeland, has preserved in his heart a certain light, a certain higher joy bestowed by God only on the chosen few . . . His influence on patients who come into contact with him is simply astounding. Those who have spent a couple of days with him in the ward have shown a sharp improvement in their condition . . .' On this question, Prof. Heidegger wrote the following in his intimate journal (from which would grow his famous work, *Time and Essence*): 'The existence of good and evil is inconceivable outside duration, outside time, out-side history, while Joy ("the Michael Keller phenomenon") overcomes this duration and, "absorbing good and evil", acts as a psychological attribute of eternity. Michael K. exists simultaneously in time and in eternity, like every person, but his existence is realized in the form of a dream possessing a self-sufficient content . . .'

On Sundays, Misha went to church with his wife and daughter, and after lunch, if the weather permitted, the three of them would take a boat down the Pregel. Now Gertrude was having dreams that could be touched, and boneless apparitions no longer troubled her.

Probing the subtleties of the watchmaker's craft, Misha acquired an intimate knowledge of winders and gear trains, Graham's deadbeat escapement and the inventions of the Schwarzwald watchmakers; he realized that watches are the children of space, which disguises itself in the eyes of the world as time. For several months he tried to construct a mechanism which would allow him to go back into the past, but his patience finally snapped and he smashed his construction into smithereens with a hammer. He realized that he was lost in time and that going back into the past would mean learning the secret of eternity, a secret alien to mortal man. Yet man still succumbs to the ploys of the future, which tries to convince him that he controls the present. In fact we control only the past, Misha concluded sadly, that past which is our present and our future; the future as such is a fiction, a dream, and only in dreams do we penetrate the timelessness ahead of us, which draws us on like happiness. Dreams and death are related, like miracles and monsters, and the miracle of dreams is the only door leading from time to eternity . . .

Every morning he found a juicy scarlet apple on a light-blue plate on his bedside table. All day long he studied the silver intricacies of clockwork. At night he stretched out with a sigh of relief on starched sheets, relishing the camomile scent of Gertrude's body. This was life, this was happiness.

In March 1945, sitting by the table on which Louise was lying with her arms folded on her chest – she'd been killed by shrapnel in an air-raid – Misha and Gertrude listened to the cannonade approaching the town from all sides. Clocks ticked in the workshop. Gertrude would whisper away. Early one morning, when they were about to leave for the cemetery, a Russian tank stopped outside their house. A thick-set lad with fair hair climbed out of the hatch with his helmet in his hands. He walked up to the porch and knocked at the door, but neither Misha nor Gertrude stirred. Seeing the coffin, the soldier looked embarrassed and asked in a whisper: 'Got a light, granddad?' The watchmaker flicked his lighter and raised the flame to the cigarette. The Russian lit up, coughed and closed the door softly behind him. 'Time to go, Misha . . .' said Gertrude. 'I'm not Misha,' said her husband. 'My name's Sergei. Sergei Ivanovich Lamennais. For Christmas I was given a horse with a flaxen mane, then we went riding in a sleigh.' He thought he was about to start crying, but he didn't.

He left on foot after burying his daughter. The people and monsters who inhabited Gertrude's dreams forced their way out into her daily life, and she didn't even seem to notice her husband's disappearance. Every morning she placed a juicy scarlet apple on a light-blue plate on the bedside table. It began to wrinkle and rot before she could close the door.

Bone-weary and dressed in a threadbare coat, the old man covered hundreds of miles, begging for food with crowds of war invalids and sleeping wherever he happened to find himself. One day at noon, he nudged open the door into the library of the Lamennais estate, which had miraculously survived and even had books on the shelves – albeit completely different ones. There was a clock on the mantelpiece. He pressed a hidden spring, took out the key from inside and wound it up. A fragment of Beethoven's famous Finale rang out. The haggard-looking girl who worked in this village library gazed in amazement at the disfigured old man, blinking his half-blind eyes by the fireplace. Getting mixed up with his words, he asked what had happened to the old landowner's library. The girl shrugged her shoulders and opened a little closet where all the gold and violet-bound tomes had been thrown. Sergei Ivanovich unerringly picked out a large volume from the pile. Opening it, he read:

Freude, Freude treibt die Räder
In der großen Weltenuhr . . .★

Only then did he notice the half-faded cursive note. He fixed his eyeglass and recognized the handwriting of his youngest sister, Vera. She had written into the unknown, addressing her message to him, Sergei Lamennais: *Dearest Seryozha, I just knew that you would open Schiller on this page some day and read my note. They've already shot mummy and daddy in the yard behind the flower-beds. God knows what will happen to me, Katya and Lyuba, but we're hardly likely to escape . . . Do you remember how we cried over these lines? That was an eternity ago. Stupid dreamers, stupid school-kids! And yet I feel a strange joy and belief that He won't abandon us and this country, this people, and that the living and the dead will be united by His joy, the righteous and the guilty, and the world will hold out, it will, Seryozha! Goodbye, Seryozha, goodbye, dear brother, pray for us just as we pray to God for you. It's as if Schiller saw what would happen to us and saved us and our faith for the future. I'm kissing the edge of this page. This is it, I think. Goodbye.*

Sergei Ivanovich suddenly realized that the abyss of time yawning before him was more terrifying than the abyss of eternity. Life, it seemed to him, was as distant and alien to a man as his soul. He wished he could die right now, this minute, and it was torture to know that it was impossible. He kissed the edge of the page, covered in French words etched in pencil aslant the German text.

With the book under his arm and his eyeglass pushed up his forehead, he walked out of the house. A few hours later, he was arrested and shot. The book and his German identity card were filed as material evidence.

Gertrude carried on living among monsters, ticking clocks and plates bearing rotting apples. Her entire life was condensed to a single day, a day that kept waning towards sunset for another thirty years. To the amusement of the new

★ Joy it is that drives the wheelworks / Of the clock that is the world. (Schiller, *Ode to Joy*; translation by Mike Mitchell.)

346

Russian inhabitants of the town, who called her Merry Gertrude, she would dance on the spot for hours, humming in a monotone: '*Seid umschlungen, Millionen.*'* She lived among people and dream monsters, and that was why she didn't notice the arrival of death, which opened a door into the world where Misha was waiting for her, and Hugo was waiting, and Louise, and, at long last, the God of joy, who never had learned the difference between German and Russian dreams . . .

* Be embraced, ye millions. (*Ode to Joy.*)

Max's Apple

The idiot Quiet Kolya died only ten paces away from me. He smiled sadly and, without taking his eyes off me, fell slowly – first on his knees, then on his stomach – into the scarlet dust of Seventh Street, which was lit from the side by the setting sun. A golden apple dropped from his unclenched, rusty hand and rolled to the feet of a boy gripped by terror and frozen in indecision: feverishly I tried to work out whether I should run for my life or pick up the apple, glinting as though it had been bathed in liquid glass . . .

The only thing that linked us was the memory of the beautiful Magdalene. Whoever thought of giving such a name to this girl in a light-blue dress, with light-blue bows in her bright wheaten hair, who was always out playing with her thoroughly scrubbed and blindingly white pup, whose name I have since forgotten? Magdalene. Beautiful Magdalene. There was a medieval tale about a beautiful Princess Magdalene, but naturally, this slip of a girl bore no relation to the heroine of that story. She was three, I mean one hundred years younger than me, we were neighbours and she was Max's granddaughter, or great-granddaughter. Max was the only German male not to have been deported in 1948, because he possessed the secret of cultivating astonishingly beautiful roses. Such was the consensus among the townsfolk. How else could you explain why all the Germans were kicked out of former East Prussia except Max? The roses, of course. And also, perhaps, the apples which he tended in the garden of the mental hospital. Rows of apple trees, countless apples. No one in town had apples like those anymore. They'd run wild. You had to know how to care for them. Only Max knew. The apples that he cultivated at the hospital were known simply as Max's apples.

But it wasn't for the apples that we used to sneak into the garden of the mental hospital. Here there were a fair few secluded corners for a peaceful smoke well away from any grown-ups. And if Max caught us, we knew that he wouldn't tell on us. We lounged in the tall grass, puffed cheap tobacco and waited for Magdalene to come running over to Max. Her blue dress, blue bows, bright wheaten hair, her blindingly white shaggy pup: all this would burst alight behind the trees, gather pace and expand, filling the garden like a comet exploding on its way ... We bandied wisecracks, scared of admitting to ourselves that she was beautiful. Whether or not the apples were tasty, I can't remember, but those sensations of light, brilliance and radiance associated with young Magdalene are alive and strong to this day.

Quiet Kolya was forever tagging after her, smiling his pitiful smile and holding a golden apple at the ready in a hand thickly overgrown with ginger hair. An apple for Magdalene. If she suddenly felt like one. People made fun of him, of course, but he didn't take any notice. When she (we were neighbours) used to tease me, plumping the heavy pulp of her buttocks on my knees and demanding that I hold her tighter, tighter, tighter still, or else she'd fall for goodness' sake, Quiet Kolya would peep at us through a chink in the fence, clutching the golden fruit so firmly that strips of apple peel poked out between his fingers.

She died before she was twelve. Drowned. She was buried in her blue dress, with blue bows in her bright wheaten hair. Sentimental old women never tired of telling the story of the blindingly white dog that kept running away from his masters to howl on beautiful Magdalene's grave. I used to dream of a doll buried instead of the girl: at night it would suddenly rear up in the grave and try to bite me.

Death appeared to me in all its splendour and horror.

I thought a lot about death. At first it seemed to be hiding behind a door painted with breathtaking skill in the corner of my bedroom. Heaven knows why a nameless artist had suddenly thought of painting a fractionally opened door in the corner of the room, a door to which I would press myself almost every night, trying to catch voices, whispers, rustles, sounds. Oh God, that door! I never did manage to open it in my dreams, although now I think I can guess who I'll be meeting there.

When my parents left my childhood home, it suddenly transpired that the porch had three steps, not four, as I'd always thought. Three. But even now, attempting in my dreams to return to the parental home, I trip – on the fourth step.

I think it was Aristotle who introduced the notion *ta genomena* into aesthetics: that's what happened, that's exactly how it was and no other way, a concept which still embarrasses those who, in the search for the harmony of fact and invention, steer a course between the play of the mind and the memory of the heart. At times I understand with disheartening clarity: Max existed, Magdalene existed, Quiet Kolya existed, struck down by love at my feet. But as for the apple, perhaps it didn't. I'm not sure. Or did it? After all, without it, there'd be no story . . .

I've seen plenty of funerals and I've even taken part in the processions. Swaying on the potholes in the red-brick road, its sides lowered, the black-lacquered lorry would come sailing past our house on Seventh Street. A calico-covered coffin would be resting in the loadspace on shining boughs of fir and bundles of fragrant thuja. Friends and relatives shuffled along behind, while half-drunk musicians breathed down their necks, led by Chopin, Wagner and Half Pint, blowing heavenly sad sounds out of his crumpled trumpet . . .

But the first time I really came face to face with death was soon after the funeral of beautiful Magdalene when, smiling sadly, the idiot Quiet Kolya walked up to me out of the blue with a golden apple in his palm, and suddenly fell and died, dropping the apple into the scarlet dust of Seventh Street; it rolled down to the horror-struck boy.

And?

Of course, I trip on the fourth step.

Ta genomena.

Magdalene died. Quiet Kolya died. Max died.

But the apple keeps rolling . . .

Buida

(Instead of an Afterword)

'Who on earth eats herring with white bread?'

The voice belonged to an old man who had a mole resembling a button on his right wrist. It seemed as though you could undo his hand, fold back the bluish-white skin like a cuff, and see the scarlet flesh and yellow bone.

'That's why he's a Buida,' grandma sighed without removing her pipe from her mouth. When she wasn't smoking, a slender dull chain round her scrawny wrinkled neck kept the pipe fastened to a chest saturated in the smell of tobacco. 'It's in the name . . .'

The old man, our neighbour, sometimes dropped in for a cup of tea with my gran. I don't remember his name. All that's stayed in the memory is the question 'Who on earth eats herring with white bread?' and the button-mole on his right wrist. And also: a vague sense of the mysterious but indissoluble link between name and fate.

As a child I suffered in secret on account of my peculiar surname. Our neighbours on Seventh Street had names you could take seriously: Ivanov, Cher Sen, Dangelaitis, Lifshits, but there was me stuck with Buida. At first the teachers compounded my misery by placing the stress on the final syllable. (I got luckier with my first name, at least. After the flight of the first human into space, the cheeky seven-year-old declared to his mates that he'd been named in honour of Yuri Gagarin, of whose mission gran had learned from the Bible on the day of my birth.)

I didn't even have a remotely decent nickname, unlike the many flamboyantly nicknamed townsfolk whose real names sometimes only revealed themselves on their tombstones. Kolka the Camel and Vita Pea-Head, the barber Name of Lev and Mashka Goebbels (she also got called Gob of Shit for swearing like a trooper and, after tanking up on hooch with chicken droppings, demanding the annihilation of 'all the Yids': there were only three or four Jews in the town and she thought they put the evil eye on her chickens and piglets), the twin sisters Sweetie-Pie and Fish-Pie, the chairman of the local soviet Katznelson-Longjohn, and that unsurpassed chatterbox, old Gramophone ... Even Gramp Mukhanov, who smoked venomous cigarettes stuffed with Georgian tea instead of tobacco, seemed to have a moniker for a name: Grampmukhanov.

I'd probably have felt like a pariah had it not been for the story of Motya Ivanova. Everyone knew that Nikolai and Katya Ivanov had once taken in a baby girl, who'd been abandoned at the station by her heartless mother. I sometimes met Motya at the Children's Home lakes, where dreamers came to talk out loud to themselves and where others, crushed by grief, could cry their hearts out. Then, twenty years later, a down-and-out wino suddenly showed up in town claiming to be Motya's mother. She'd have become a laughing-stock straightaway were it not for the sudden transformation of the quiet, dreamy Motya, who rushed to the woman's defence. She was ready to grab anyone by the throat who dared say a bad word about the tramp. Nikolai and Katya gave in and put the woman up in the attic of their little house. The very next day, the whole town watched as Motya carried her sozzled 'mother' home from the Red Canteen. A week later, the woman was arrested trying to steal a piglet from the neighbours. Motya cried and gave her all her money, but defended her as vigorously as before. At the end of summer, the woman was raised from the bottom of the Pregolya with boat-hooks; a dead perch was clenched between her teeth. She'd been underwater so long that corrosion had devoured the metallic parts of her skeleton – one touch and they'd fall apart – so she had to be buried in a coffin sculpted from soft cotton wool by the inconsolable Motya. When her best friend shyly asked her later about the reason for her concern for the tramp, Motya said dreamily: 'She wanted to name me Liza. Elizaveta is my real name.' And she sang: 'E-li-za-ve-ta!'

I was told this story by a schoolmate, the famous gasbag nicknamed Arsy by the kids on our street. The real name of this chubby short-sighted kid didn't interest anyone. The gang put up with him only because of his skill at inventing entertaining tales. Sometimes these were intricate adventure stories with large casts, and stretched over many evenings. Often enough he cheated, retelling 'in his own words' the stories of Boccaccio and Edgar Allan Poe, Shakespeare's plays and Dostoevsky's novels. I never showed him up, though: I felt sorry for Arsy.

What's more, he had mastered to perfection the most attractive of all the arts: the art of lying. Many really were taken in by his story about the cave under the Taplacken Hills, where a marble female figure of amazing beauty had been preserved in pitch darkness. She was destined to save human-kind from descending into savagery and dying out, but she couldn't be carried outside and shown to people because she was sick with cancer and would perish the instant she was touched by the faintest ray of light. Some people really did set off for the Taplacken Hills and even discovered some kind of a pit there. At the bottom, under a layer of rotten leaves and bird droppings, lay the skeleton of a dwarf, with his left leg missing and an amber cigarette-holder trapped between his black teeth. Naturally, though, no statue or amazing goddess was found there. Or how about the tale of the crusading knights? They'd been sleeping for seven hundred years now in the saddles of their warhorses (whose hooves had been gnawed round by mice) in the crypt of the battered Protestant church on the main square, and were waiting for the day when they could vanquish the devil in righteous battle – he was plotting to rob the Holy Virgin of these lands. Did men not climb down into the crypt with spades, pickaxes and lanterns to see for themselves the glorious Grand Master Hermann von Salza and his knights in white cloaks and black crosses, ready to rush at their master's command to the defence of the city and the world from the enemy of the human race? Or, to top it all, what about Arsy's invention of the eighth day of the week, on which – and only on which – occur the truly important events in human life? 'What's it called then, this day of yours?' Gramp Mukhanov cried indignantly. 'And why did no one know about it before?' 'I can't tell you what it's called,' replied Arsy, puffing out his chest. 'No one knows what'll happen if we say this word out loud: happiness or grief. I can only say that it's got six consonants in a row and a sound which doesn't exist in human speech.' 'But I know that word!' guffawed Kolka the Camel. '*Vzbzdnut!*★ Course the sound's not human. It's arsy. Hanging's too good for you!'

When I asked him one day why he lied and at the same time counted on universal love and a glorious future (he himself used to tell me this), Arsy looked at me pityingly and then, after a dramatic pause, replied: 'Because I have a green heart.'

He lived with his mother, whose name had long been dirt in the town. Pretty much everyone gossiped about her boozy escapades and affairs. Sometimes, when her admirers got drunk and beat her up, her son would throw himself at the offender. Small and short-sighted, he'd shout in helpless despair that he'd kill the scoundrel, but it all ended in a clip round the head or a kick: 'Shut your face, you little git, or you'll be sorry too.' In the end, what probably had to happen, happened: a sober guy with a black slit for a mouth and pinkish stubble on sunken cheeks stuck a knife into the whore. Everyone knew about it, including the policeman Lyosha Leontyev, but there wasn't a scrap of evidence or convincing proof. The murderer carried on as always: every morning he showed up at the sawmill where he made frames and every evening he drank beer in the Red Canteen, wearily brushing all the questions aside: 'It's all crap. As if I needed to kill her . . .' His words carried conviction firstly because he was sober, and secondly because the neighbours had seen Arsy's mother with a knife on more than one occasion: she was always on the point of topping herself on the porch, to finish this God-awful life once and for all. Maybe she really had done herself in?

That was when, for the very first time, the kid turned for help to the king of the Seventh, ginger-haired Irus. As a rule, any prepubescent living on Seventh Street could count on

★ Low Russian: 'to start farting vigorously'.

Irus' protection: it was an unwritten law. For some reason, though, the kids thought there was no point defending Arsy. No point, simple as that. This time, after brief consideration, Irus agreed, but only after demanding a fee: a bottle of beer. 'Just the beer, not the bottle!' he added with a laugh. The next day a fist-fight was held between the king of the Seventh and the presupposed killer, who, alas, came out best in the duel. But the fight made quite an impression on the town and the police went after the frame-maker in earnest. He was arrested and taken away. Arsy went to see Irus, who was all black and blue. 'All right,' the king said gloomily. 'You can call me Igor.' (Only Irus' very closest henchmen merited this honour.) He tossed the copper which Arsy had brought him, and asked testily: 'Now what?' 'The change. Just the beer, not the bottle,' the kid replied without batting an eyelid. 'You can also call me by my real name: Gleb.'

Grandma used to tell me about the custom in her village of shouting names over the stomach of a pregnant woman until the child stirred in the womb. The name to which the foetus responded was its genuine name. My father responded to the name Adam, but his parents didn't like it for some reason and they called their first-born Vasily (pronounced Basil in Belorussian), in the secret hope, I expect, of uniting the boy with the assembly of Byzantine emperors and saints. Father was born on a hot July night in 1919 in a destitute Belorussian hamlet, where the tears of the women were older than them by a thousand years. This possessor of a tsar's name had the great famine, war and Stalin's camps ahead of him. When I spoke up one day about the hidden irony of history and the word-games it plays with us, my father retorted: 'This country is so vast that neither words nor thoughts have any meaning in it. Nor its history, either.'

Poets erect monuments to themselves not made by hands and more solid than bronze, but time, with its inscrutably cruel mercy, may on occasion bring us only a name or a fragment of a verse: not the words, but the fame. We know nothing of Sappho's lover, the poetess Erinna, renowned among her contemporaries for her epic poem, *The Distaff*. We know nothing about Homer, and very little about Shakespeare. Yet we do know of the madness of Swift and Garshin, of the baseness of Heidegger and the collaborationism of Hamsun ... Sometimes such knowledge exerts a certain influence on our understanding of the sources or particularities of a writer's work, but essentially it's useless. Homer's real name is *The Iliad*. Shakespeare's called *King Lear*, Dostoevsky – *Crime and Punishment*.

In his essay 'Nominalist and Realist', Emerson wrote: 'I am very struck by the appearance that one person wrote all the books [. . .] It is plainly the work of one all-seeing, all-hearing gentleman.'

Is he really so wrong? Gogol's true name is *nihil*. He's more than a human being; he's literature.

Gesang ist Dasein, as Rilke believed. 'The song is existence.'

His tombstone is engraved with the words:

> Rose, o pure contradiction, joy
> to be no one's sleep under so many lids.*

For many commentators, these lines are almost the very voice of that non-being, that No, whose spirit has permeated the culture of the twentieth century. But for Rilke, absolute No never existed (true being is *frei vom Tod*, free from death; in the Seventh Elegy: *Hiersein ist herrlich!*, Being-here is wonderful!). For him the poet is Yes, he is Always, it is indeed 'joy to be no one's sleep'. Mine. Ours. Human. Divine. Eternal, like life.

When I published my first short article under my full name in a Polish newspaper – it must have been in '89 or '90 – the night editor called his boss very late in a panic: 'Czeslaw, the text is decent enough, but it's got an April Fool's byline! Maybe we should change it?' 'But that's his real name.' 'God!

---

* *Rose, oh reiner Widerspruch, Lust, Niemandes Schlaf zu sein unter soviel Lidern.*
(Translation by Mike Mitchell.)

How does he live with it?' My name might not mean much to someone from Warsaw, but in the north and north-east of Poland most people were settlers from the western lands of Belorussia and Ukraine, and knew full well that *buida* means 'lie, fantasy, fairy tale' and at the same time 'story-teller, liar, dreamer'.

Well, I suppose there's nothing for it: *Gesang ist Dasein*, Buida is *buida*. The story-teller is the story and that's no merit of mine. Just as there's no merit in a person having a heart, even if it's green. I am what I am: *nihil*. I hope I won't be accused of pretentiousness and arrogance: I didn't choose my name, maybe only my fate. But the name is all that's left, while the fate is all that matters.